"God's blood! Your shot grazed my leg!"

"Damn!" Amanda swore, stuffing the purse in her pocket and the spent pistol in her boot as she transferred the still-loaded weapon to her right hand. It had been an accident. She hadn't intended to shoot anybody.

Amanda backed away. If the driver hadn't alerted the party guests, her shot certainly would. She had to get away.

"I don't intend to kill you," she snarled. "I shall keep you alive so that I can steal you both blind."

"If this is a challenge, my Jasmine Bandit," Rush said, low and laughing, "I accept."

Amanda backed out of reach, gave a whistle and heard her horse moving toward her. "Good. I only hope you have coin enough to finish out the game."

"Oh, I can play your game," he chuckled as he watched her climb into the saddle. "Once I know the rules...."

Dear Reader,

Welcome to Harlequin Historicals, where the new year could be any year—from the turn of the twentieth century to one as far back as our talented authors can take us. From medieval castles to the wide-open prairies, come join our brave heroines and dashing heroes as they battle the odds and discover romance.

In Barbara Faith's first historical, *Gamblin' Man*, Carrie McClennon's simple life is turned upside down by a notorious saloon owner.

Jasmine and Silk, from Sandra Chastain, is set on a Georgian plantation soon after the American Revolution.

Louisa Rawlings's *Wicked Stranger* is the sequel to her *Stranger in My Arms,* and tells the story of the second Bouchard brother.

A luckless Southern belle finds herself stranded in Panama in Kristie Knight's *No Man's Fortune*.

Four new adventures from Harlequin Historicals. We hope you enjoy them all.

Sincerely,

Tracy Farrell
Senior Editor

Jasmine and Silk

Sandra Chastain

Harlequin Books

TORONTO • NEW YORK • LONDON
AMSTERDAM • PARIS • SYDNEY • HAMBURG
STOCKHOLM • ATHENS • TOKYO • MILAN
MADRID • WARSAW • BUDAPEST • AUCKLAND

Harlequin Historicals first edition January 1993

ISBN 0-373-28756-9

JASMINE AND SILK

SANDRA CHASTAIN

started out to be an actress but failed miserably at losing her Southern accent. She switched to journalism where she failed again because, according to the editor of her college newspaper, she could never tell what, when and why without embellishing the story. In the meantime, she got married, raised three daughters and worked full-time alongside her veterinarian husband in their animal medical clinic in Smyrna, Georgia. Now a devoted historical romance writer, she's happy as a pig in a puddle of Georgia mud, doing what she loves best—spinning tales of passion and adventure for all the perennially young who believe in the magic of love.

Special thanks to Felton and Marsha Bohannon
of Bohannon's Books, without whose help
this book might never have happened.

And to Ellis Merton Coulter,
for his love of history and the recording of it.

Chapter One

Broad River Valley, Georgia
Late November 1790

The scream of a horse woke her.

Amanda Caden sat up, her heart racing. There it was again, a shrill unfamiliar whinny in the night. Fear swept through her room like a blast of cold air. But the air wasn't cold. It was warm. Too warm for November. Something was wrong. Then she smelled it—smoke.

"Oh, no...fire!"

Amanda slung her feet over the side of her rope bed and thrust them into the men's trousers she wore to the fields, pulling on a loose shirt as she hurried out into the hallway and began to pound on doors.

"Mother! Catherine! Get up! Fire!"

Her breath came quick and shallow. She didn't want to think what a fire would mean to Cadenhill Plantation's already precarious situation.

"Please," Amanda whispered, "we've already lost Father, we can't lose anything more." She ran down the plantation house steps into the yard and heard the excited voices of the slaves and the dreaded crackle of flames.

As she rounded the kitchen she caught a glimpse of movement, a horse, whinnying as it disappeared into the woods. But as her eyes swept the scene, the horses were no longer her greatest fear. Her prayer would go unanswered. Tonight, in the Broad River Valley, the worst had happened.

The tobacco barn was on fire, the barn filled to the ceiling with the remainder of this year's drying tobacco crop. The empty building that had housed the finest early leaves, the crop already claimed by Franklin, was untouched.

The scene was a nightmare. Flames danced from the roofs into the sky. Great puffs of black smoke poured from the cracks and belched upward.

"Quick!" Amanda yelled. "Settie, form a bucket brigade. Roman, man the pump. Keep the trough full."

Roman nodded, taking his place while Settie directed the slaves already funneling buckets of water down a line that quickly snaked from the horse trough to the tobacco barn. Iris Caden and sixteen-year-old Catherine began filling buckets directly from the house cistern, passing them to Lovie and the other servants who formed a second line. The two youngest Caden girls watched fearfully from the porch, under the care of Orphe, the cook.

Terrible heat singed the air. Smoke swirled. The pungent smell of tobacco burned their eyes and scorched their lungs while bucket handles cut into their hands. The fire never seemed to spread, rather it appeared to flame everywhere at once, eating up the night sky like some hellish monster.

What seemed like hours passed as the sky turned light, both from the fire and from the sun beginning to rise beyond the woods. But there weren't enough slaves and they couldn't get the water to the top where the flames were the worst. Soon the roofs were gone. The walls began to collapse.

Sick at heart, Amanda looked up and saw her mother and Catherine, still in their nightgowns, valiantly moving buckets down the line. Long after they'd lost the fight, they continued to throw water on the fire. Until at last, Roman touched Amanda on the shoulder and shook his head. She stopped and stared at the charred buildings and faced the truth.

The barn was gone. They'd lost their tobacco, the portion of their crop that was to have freed Cadenhill from debt by paying Houston Caden's notes in Augusta and settling the accounts held by Father's stepbrother, Franklin.

As if thinking of her uncle conjured him up, Franklin Caden galloped his horse into the yard and dismounted, dropping the reins into Settie's gnarled hands. "Iris," Franklin said, taking his stepbrother's wife's bleeding palms into his own, "are you all right?"

"We're not harmed, Franklin. But as you can see, the crop has been destroyed. I don't know how we'll manage now."

"Don't worry, Iris. I'll take care of you, just as I always have. Houston expected me to."

"Thank you, Uncle Franklin," Amanda said in clipped tones, "but the Caden women will manage without your help. You aren't responsible for us."

Franklin studied Amanda for a long moment before he answered. "Amanda, you don't seem to understand. I am responsible for this plantation. And I have the legal power, given to me by your father's will, to do whatever is necessary to carry out that responsibility."

Choking back rare tears of frustration, Amanda lifted her head and straightened her shoulders. Houston Caden wouldn't have wanted tears. *Just put me in the ground, girl, and get on with the business of living. Someone will be there to help you,* her father had whispered little more than three months ago.

Then she recalled something else—Houston Caden had warned her not to trust Franklin. He'd made her promise she'd look after Cadenhill, for her mother's sake.

And she had, without Franklin's help, until now.

As if the powers of nature were determined to mock her, the wind rose. In the distance Amanda heard the sound of thunder. "Now it's going to rain," she said wearily, "after we've lost the barn."

"Bad spirits in the air tonight, Miss Amanda." Roman had come to stand beside her. "First the Lord send the fire to burn us up. Now a flood to wash away the land."

"No!" Amanda protested in a hoarse voice as she watched the wind pick up the dirt and swirl it around, re-kindling the coals and sweeping the sparks toward the horse barn in a sheet of fiery rain.

"No!" she screamed, realizing what was about to happen. "Settie! Roman! The horses!" Amanda dashed across the muddy yard toward the horse barn.

"Amanda!" Iris Caden called out. "Let Roman do it."

But Amanda didn't heed her mother's cry. They'd already lost too much this night. She didn't intend to take a chance with Thor, the chestnut stallion her father had given her. Reaching the barn she lifted the heavy bar, pulled open the door and ran inside. Flames were already licking the back wall, filling the barn with smoke as orange fire raced for the loft where the hay was stored. The horses were snorting in panic.

From somewhere behind, Amanda heard stall doors be-ing opened. Out of the darkness the slim black boy who helped in the barn dashed past. "Miss Manda, I'll get Thor!"

"Joeboy, no! It isn't safe." But he wasn't listening. He didn't understand that these horses were frightened and dangerous. Amanda heard the boy begin to cough. If she didn't move quickly they'd all be burned; she plunged into the smoke. Together, they opened the first stall easily. Her father's best gray, sensing freedom, dashed away from the fire and out into the spark-filled night. The second horse was less cooperative. Amanda looped a strap around his neck and pulled. He backed into the corner, rearing in fear, his hooves coming down too close to allow her to direct him. Finally she pulled off her shirt and flung it over his head, covering his eyes so that she could get him moving. At the door she met Roman, who took the strap and led the horse to freedom.

"Joeboy! Where are you?"

Coughing, nearly blinded by the fumes, Amanda whirled and plunged back into the inferno. She could still hear Thor's hooves thundering against the front of his stall. The smoke was so thick now that she couldn't see the stalls. "Joeboy?" There was no answer. Struggling to reach the back of the barn she caught her foot on something and stumbled to the barn floor, her hand touching another human hand. Joeboy. The boy was lying in the open doorway of a stall, gasping for breath.

Amanda glanced frantically toward Thor's stall. She had to get Joeboy outside; she wasn't certain that she had time to free Thor, too. Burning shingles were already falling to the floor, catching in her hair and blistering her bare skin. Lifting the boy's shoulders in her arms she began to back toward the door. Desperately she took in a breath of billowing smoke and began to choke.

At that moment Thor broke through his stall door, rearing on his back legs and screaming wildly to the black horse dancing about in the stall Joeboy had opened.

"Go, Thor! Go!" Amanda shouted at the animal, then gave up and hugging the stalls along the side of the corridor, stumbled backward dragging Joeboy toward safety. Amanda was halfway to the door when Thor came charging by, followed by the young black. One of the horses clipped Amanda's shoulder and swung her around, flinging her into the post at the end of the first stall.

A nail dug into her shoulder. She winced, blinked her eyes and tried to pull herself upright. She couldn't die. She had to look after her mother and her sisters. She'd promised her father. Then someone was there, someone who took the boy out of her arms and disappeared into the blackness.

There was only the roar of the flames. Amanda felt as if she were the only one left in the world. She couldn't seem to move. Somewhere above her there was a cracking sound and burning timbers crashed to the floor. She'd lost the horse barn, too.

Then, too late, the heavens opened and rain fell in torrents, dousing the smoldering coals. Amanda began to laugh. She had the wild thought that the sizzle of the rain hitting the coals sounded like screams.

Not the Lord, Roman, she tried to whisper. What happened tonight was the work of the devil. Cadenhill was in flames and their world was burning with it.

After what seemed like hours, but was in fact only minutes, the rain stopped. The wind gave a last low moan as it ruffled the treetops and died. The fire and destruction had ended as quickly as it had begun.

Amanda heard a loud crack and felt an intense pain. Her vision blurred for a minute, then the world went dark.

Settie carried the unconscious Amanda in his big strong arms, making a path through the slaves standing silent and afraid. For the past eight years, ever since Houston Caden had become involved in the Colonies' fight for independence, they'd looked not to Mrs. Caden, but to Amanda. Now their young mistress was hurt.

By the time Settie stepped into the wide hallway that ran the length of the big house, Catherine was running ahead, lighting the lamps on the second floor.

Iris recovered from her half swoon, quickly shored up her resolve and followed, brushing aside Franklin's offers to help with terse directions for him to wait on the porch.

"Is she dead, like Papa, and Joeboy?" Ten-year-old Cecilia, her nightclothes trailing the floor, stood in the doorway watching, wide-eyed and afraid.

"Of course not," Catherine scolded, calling over her shoulder as she led the way. "Joeboy is all right. He was just scared. Go tell Orphe to heat some water."

At the top of the stairs Catherine opened the door to her older sister's room. Settie laid Amanda gently on her bed and stepped back, worry lining his face like the rows in the field.

Catherine was removing Amanda's shoes when she heard her mother's step on the polished wooden floor.

"Catherine? Settie?" Iris Caden came quickly into the room, caught sight of the blood on Amanda's face. "Dear Lord! Is she . . . ?"

"She just knocked out, Miz Caden," Settie said. "That's all. That wild horse knocked Miss Amanda up against the post and 'cross the back of her head and cut it."

Iris drew in a deep breath and began to examine her eldest daughter. Her fingertips ranged through the mass of fiery red hair now matted with ash and mud. She gasped when she located the broken skin, then Iris collected herself and began to peel away the matted strands of hair from the wound. There was a bruise beneath Amanda's eye and several blisters on her bare arms.

"Go downstairs and stay with your sisters, Catherine. I'll look after Amanda. Settie, send one of the slaves for the doctor, then check the others and make sure nobody else is hurt." Iris Caden stood and waited for the room to clear.

"Oh, Settie," she called after them, forcing herself into the rare position of assuming authority, "you'd better make certain that the fire is watched. And tell Roman to send somebody to look for the horses."

As Settie and Catherine trailed down the stairs, Lovie was coming up, carrying a pan of steaming water in her hands and linen towels slung over her arm. Together, Iris and Lovie managed to undress Amanda and wash the dirt from her face and arms.

"Oh, Lovie, I know that she's twenty-two years old now, but she's still my child," Iris said nervously. "What will we do if...if—"

"You just hush up, Miz Caden. Ain't no bump on the head gonna take Miss Amanda. She's strong, like her papa. You remember when Mr. Houston first brought that wild stallion home? Miss Amanda was determined that nobody would break him but herself. And the first time she got on she got throwed?"

"Yes, I guess I do. She was knocked unconscious then too, wasn't she?"

"Yes'um. And all she needed was to get warm and rested. When she woke up, she gentled that horse just like she'd said she would. Don't nothing stop Miss Amanda."

"I know," Iris agreed, "just like her father."

"Like *you*," Lovie corrected. "You just let everybody else run things 'cause it pleases them to do it. Nothing Miss Amanda needs now but a little rest," Lovie went on. "If she wakes up and sees you all worried she'll be worse off. You go see about the babies. I'll sit here."

Iris nodded and backed reluctantly away. Lovie was right. Early on Iris learned that her strength *was* in allowing others to do what they did best. When Houston came back with that wound in his chest from fighting the British, it was Lovie who took over the nursing. Lovie would heal Amanda, dear Amanda who had never been a child. Now Amanda might never be a woman either.

Iris felt her lungs contract in the sharp pain of grief that seemed always to be with her now. She had never approved of her daughter's passion for growing tobacco, for working in the fields, the barns, even the slave quarters. Instead of lessons, or learning to sew fine seams, Amanda had followed the plantation bosses, Settie and Roman, listening, asking questions and learning.

Finally, it had been Amanda who made the decisions and the two men who followed. That very directness had kept

Cadenhill going, but it also established Amanda's reputation as a sharp-tongued shrew and scared away any mar-
riage-minded men in the valley.

Iris knew that Houston hadn't intended Amanda to
shoulder all the burden of Cadenhill. His will had stipu-
lated that Franklin, his stepbrother, was responsible for
Cadenhill until either Iris remarried or one of the four girls
found a husband. Iris understood why Amanda refused to
ask for Franklin's help, even if others didn't. Franklin had
always supported his stepbrother, but there was something
vaguely unnerving about the man that even Iris recognized.
Still, Houston had seemed to trust Franklin, and because of
that, so had Iris.

"Is Manda all right, Mother?" Sixteen-year-old Catherine and the two younger girls were sitting quietly in the front
parlor, the room reserved for solemn occasions, the room
where Houston Caden's body had been laid out such a short
time ago.

"I don't know yet," Iris admitted, kneeling so that she
could put her arms around and comfort the stoic, ten-year-
old Cecilia and the sniffling, six-year-old Jamie. "She was
hit on the head. Sometimes that makes you sleep for a time.
My darlings, we must be as quiet as little mice so that your
sister can rest."

"We'll be quiet," Cecilia promised, her face stiff in solemn control. The younger Jamie pressed her lips together in
trembling acceptance and nodded her head.

"Good. Now I'd like you three to go out to the kitchen
and help Orphe prepare breakfast. Later we will wash the
jugs. Amanda is going to cut the sugarcane next week, and
we'll start making the syrup."

"But, Mother," Catherine began, "we can't make syrup
now, not with Manda hurt. We don't know anything about
that. Besides, how do we know the cane isn't burned, too?"

Iris started to reprimand her second daughter, then held
her reply. Catherine was just worried. "You're right, Cath-

erine. Worrying about making syrup now sounds frivolous. I'll speak to Franklin. Where is he?"

"He left."

"He left before he knew about Amanda?"

"Said he had to get the tobacco in the warehouse downriver to Augusta before something happened to it. But I wouldn't talk to him about the syrup, Mother," Catherine said as she began to herd her sisters down the hall.

"Why not? I'm only doing what your father would expect me to do, Catherine."

"Maybe, but you know how much Amanda despises Franklin."

"But suppose she's..."

"No!" Catherine said firmly, sounding more like her older sister than herself. "Amanda's going to be fine."

Iris forced herself to be brave until the slave returned with the news that the doctor was delivering a baby and couldn't come until later.

By midmorning, when Amanda still hadn't awakened, and the doctor hadn't come, Iris gave in to her fear and sent one of the stable hands into Petersburg to fetch Houston's old friend, Judge Taliaferro. The judge would know what to do.

Dinnertime came and went. After several more trips to Amanda's room, where she was more hindrance than help, Iris wrapped herself in her shawl and sat on the front porch to wait. Oblivious to the slaves who'd gathered silently at the edge of the yard, Iris Caden stared off into the distance trying to make sense out of what had happened.

Catherine was right about Amanda's feelings for Franklin. But Franklin had always handled Houston's legal matters and acted as Cadenhill's agent in selling the crops. Still, toward the end, Houston had seemed to take Amanda's side in her differences with Franklin. More than once there'd been sharp words between Houston and Franklin.

And now Amanda was hurt. Houston was gone and the future of Cadenhill was being threatened.

"Miz Caden?" Lovie's alarmed voice suddenly called from the top of the stairs. "Better come up here. Miss Amanda's waking up and she's talking crazy."

Chapter Two

"I have to find Joeboy, Lovie," Amanda insisted.

"You don't have to do nuthin' 'cept get back in this bed, Miss Amanda. Joeboy is fine and Roman already lookin' for them horses. I's satisfied that they halfway to Augusta by now."

"Augusta? Yes, that's what I must do, too—get down-river to Augusta." Amanda clung stubbornly to the bed-post. "We have to borrow money to rebuild the barns and buy seed."

Iris rushed into the bedroom and took her daughter's arm. "Amanda Caden. You get back into that bed this instant. You aren't going anywhere."

"But I must, Mother. The barns are gone, the tobacco, the seed for next year's crop. Ohhhh!" She groaned and swayed.

"Just be calm, Amanda. I've sent for Judge Taliaferro. He'll know what to do."

"Carriage coming, Miz Caden," Lovie announced from where she was standing near the window. "It's the judge."

"Thank goodness. Amanda, I insist that you get back in bed while I go and talk to him."

"No! Bring me some clothes, Lovie. I just need to get my balance. I'll be down in a moment. I want to talk to the judge about Papa's will."

"I ain't bringing you no clothes, Missy. And you ain't going prancing down them stairs 'fore God and everybody in your shift.''

"No? Just watch me!" Amanda took a step, teetered back and forth, gritted her teeth and took another step.

"You might as well help her dress, Lovie," Iris said with an anxious sigh of resignation. "She's going to come down the stairs whether we want her to or not. At least she'll be dressed.''

Iris hurried to greet the judge and show him into the parlor. By the time Amanda came down Iris had already explained about the fire and Amanda's injury.

"I didn't know what else to do, Lewis. I hope it was all right for me to call you."

"Of course, Iris."

Amanda cleared her throat. The judge was holding her mother's hand as Amanda entered the parlor.

"Well, Amanda. From what your mother is telling me, you're a lucky young woman."

"Well, I'm not dead, but that's a minor point. I'm glad you're here, Judge. I was about to ride over and ask you to examine Papa's will again. I am certain that it is a forgery.''

Amanda worked her way around the desk, squinting her eyes because of the pain racking her head. She removed the document Franklin had produced just after the funeral and gave it to the judge. "I believe that Franklin in some way altered Father's will to give himself legal control of Caden-hill. My father never meant that to happen."

The judge studied the document for a moment before answering. "The will's authentic, Amanda. Franklin prepared it according to Houston's wishes, and Houston signed it in my presence. There is no doubt that this is his signature.''

"But," Amanda protested, fighting waves of pain that clouded her vision and made her clutch at the desk, "according to Franklin's records, even before the fire, we were nearly bankrupt. Did you know that Franklin had concealed that from Papa?"

Iris gasped. "Bankrupt? That can't be."

"It's true, Mother. Not only do we suddenly owe Franklin a fortune, but we have loans that must be paid by the first week in June. And now that the tobacco is gone, we can't meet those notes."

Iris reached for her handkerchief. "Amanda, we can't be penniless. I'm certain that your father would have told me."

"Oh, dear." Judge Taliaferro placed the document in Iris's hands and said in dismay, "I'm so sorry, Iris. It's true. Franklin told me that he tried to explain to Houston that money was tight, but he wouldn't listen. The plantation profits began to slide some time ago. Toward the end, Franklin simply concealed the truth. He didn't want to worry Houston."

"I don't care what Uncle Franklin's records show, Judge Taliaferro, Cadenhill was doing fine and my father knew it," Amanda said, forcing herself not to reveal her weakness. "My father's strength was gone, but his mind was still good."

The judge cleared his throat. "I don't know what to say, Iris. Cadenhill's situation was already serious, and now your crop and your barns are gone. With these new losses, I'm afraid that you may face difficult times."

"What I want to know, Judge—" Amanda managed a forceful voice in spite of the pain behind her eyelids "—is why? This plantation is self-supporting. I may not know about finances, but I know about planting."

Judge Taliaferro patted Iris's hand, continuing to address her as if it were she, not Amanda, who made the decisions. "If Houston had lived, he would have been able to pacify his creditors, but the truth is, they will refuse to grant an extension to a woman, certainly now when they learn the extent of the damage you suffered from the fire. It will take an act of God, or Franklin's help, to save you. Otherwise, a portion of Cadenhill will have to be sold."

Amanda was shocked into temporary silence.

She hadn't wanted to believe Franklin. She'd been certain that the judge would confirm the forgery of the document, or perhaps agree to act as her mother's agent in having Franklin's control set aside. What she was learning was that traditions were stronger than legalities. Women were not expected to operate plantations. What the judge was saying was that she wouldn't be able to continue to do what she'd been doing for seven years.

"Nonsense!" she retorted. "I'm no addlepated, beetle-headed cat's paw, Judge. Even if this is my father's signature, I don't believe that he knew what he was signing. My father wasn't blind to Franklin's faults. He undersold our crops and overcharged us at every turn. And in the end, Papa knew it, too."

The judge dropped Iris's hand and turned the full censure of his frown on Amanda. "The document seems reasonable, not only to me, Amanda, but to the others Franklin consulted. I can understand your distress, but the courts will be disposed to follow your father's wishes. Cadenhill is technically your mother's, but Franklin, as the administrator, is charged with overseeing the operation of Cadenhill, and that includes satisfying your father's creditors—until either you, your mother, or one of your sisters marries."

Amanda had forced herself to stand quietly behind her father's desk as the judge verified the terms of the will. She'd learned that letting her temper fly would accomplish nothing. The fact that she was helpless was one she wouldn't accept. There had to be an answer.

But she could tell from his expression that the judge wasn't going to listen. To him it was reasonable that Houston would leave Franklin in charge of the women. No matter what Amanda believed, Franklin was a powerful man who'd always been well thought of in Petersburg.

"Now, now, Amanda, Iris," the judge said in a placating voice. "I'll admit that I was surprised at the amount of Houston's debts, but I'm sure Franklin will be able to work out an extension on the loans. As for your debts to Franklin, well, family matters can be kept in the family. After all, Franklin was Houston's brother."

"Stepbrother," Amanda corrected. "They were not related at all. My father was an honorable man. Franklin is a crook!" Amanda was past caring what the judge thought.

"Amanda, dear," Iris Caden said, playing her usual role of peacemaker, "try not to upset yourself. I'm sure that Franklin will find a way around selling our land. We still have some tobacco in Franklin's warehouse, don't we?"

Amanda laughed. "You mean we have Franklin's half of the tobacco crop, Mother, which he claimed first so that he'd get the best prices. Our half conveniently burned in the fire."

The judge pulled out his pocket watch, snapping open the case as he checked the time. "Try not to worry just yet, Iris. Franklin will be back tomorrow night with answers. He's returning on the new stagecoach."

"What stagecoach, Judge?" Catherine spoke up from the doorway, her eyes filled with excitement now that her sister appeared to have recovered from her injury. "We have a stagecoach in Petersburg now?"

"We do, indeed," the judge announced proudly. "Franklin has taken in a new partner, a North Carolinian by the name of Rushton Randolph. He's set up offices right here in Petersburg. Soon we can travel safely from Philadelphia to Savannah on a real road instead of a wagon trail."

"My, my!" Iris shook her head in wonder.

Amanda sighed. They were in danger of losing Cadenhill and her mother and sister were awed by a stagecoach. "Oh yes, won't that be grand," she muttered under her breath.

Franklin had left early this morning. He couldn't wait to get his half of the Cadenhill tobacco safely to Augusta.

Amanda wanted to cry out at the unfairness of it all. Franklin Caden was a thief, even if nobody believed it but her. He deserved to be robbed. If there was a way, Amanda would turn highwayman and hold up the stage herself.

The judge took Iris's hand once more. "Call on me again if you need me." He turned to Amanda with a frown. "Amanda, selling part of the land won't be too bad. Your father had better than eight hundred acres of the most valuable in the Broad River Valley. It will bring a good price."

"Of course it's good land," Amanda agreed. "That's why I have no intention of allowing one inch of it to be sold—to anybody. And I have until June to stop it."

Heartsick over her mother's easy acceptance of Franklin's control, Amanda excused herself and strode unsteadily out the parlor door. She had to find Settie. Franklin might be in charge, but Cadenhill and its people were her responsibility. They'd just survived a fire, and she had to find out for herself that the plantation was safe.

"You know, Amanda," the judge called out as she left, "marriage could solve your problems. As I think about it, Franklin himself might make an acceptable husband for you."

Amanda stopped, her back stiff as she fought to respond with a proper reply, gave up and continued to walk away. "That's exactly what he planned," was her terse answer.

Marriage? Amanda had no intention of ever marrying. Though she'd loved her father dearly, she'd seen her mother's loneliness and grief when he was away. Houston had meant well, but he'd put his dreams first. And Iris had suffered. Amanda wouldn't settle for second place in any man's life.

Catherine was still a bit young to marry, and Amanda had made a life for herself that didn't include marriage to Franklin or anybody else. Her mother wouldn't fight the

man. Their survival was up to Amanda. She had to find a
way to pay off their debts, or Franklin would sell the land,
the land she'd promised to look after. If she was going to
save Cadenhill she had to outsmart, outthink, outsteal a
thief, and she had to do it quickly.

Amanda walked down the hallway and out the door,
finding herself in her mother's garden without having realized where she was heading. She sank down on a wooden
bench and surveyed the light damage to the area.

The ground was dotted with spots of burnt grass, and a
dappled white film of ash had coated the trees and shrubs
like dirty snow. She could still smell the acrid odor of
smoke. Come spring, her mother's flowers would reseed
themselves and spill across the emerald-green carpet of grass
like bright colored snips of ribbon. Too bad Cadenhill
couldn't grow flowers as a crop instead of tobacco.

The pounding in her head slowed to a dull roar. She
hadn't realized how much she'd counted on Judge Taliaferro's support in her plan to find a way to run Cadenhill
without Franklin's interference.

Franklin. Everyone, even her mother, approved of his
being left in charge. Amanda winced, thinking of her
mother's matter-of-fact acceptance of her life.

Iris Caden approached the problem of Cadenhill's sur-
vival just as she did any other disturbance. Accept it and
forget it. Trust in the Lord and take care of her family. To
Iris, it was time to make syrup and that was what she'd do.
Always before, that philosophy had been enough; there had
always been someone to take care of the problems. But
Houston Caden was gone and now there was nobody but
Amanda.

"Amanda?" Iris stepped off the veranda and came to
stand beside her daughter, laying her hand on Amanda's
shoulder comfortingly. "Orphe is preparing supper. Do you
feel like eating something?"

"I'm not hungry just now, Mother. I'll eat later, when my head stops aching." Amanda gave her mother a smile and stood, willing her body to overcome the wave of weakness that swept over her.

Staunchly she made her way to the end of the garden toward the burnt-out barns. Whatever happened life went on. Cutting the sugarcane couldn't be delayed.

Soon the first hard frost would come and the remaining hogs would be butchered and salted down to cure over the winter in the smokehouse. There was less than a month until Christmas. Afterward it would be time to prepare the beds and plant again. But there were no seeds to plant.

If only the hogsheads containing the prime first leaves from this year's crop hadn't already been rolled into Petersburg. She could take them downriver all the way to Savannah herself, and sell them direct to the factor from England. That would save the five percent that Franklin got as the first factor, and another five percent to the factor in Augusta who resold them to the English agent. And with the money she could buy seed.

Immediately after the reading of the will, Franklin had carefully explained to Iris that the crop was to be divided, one half to him, the other half to pay the interest on the outstanding loans. He'd claimed his half as soon as the crop was harvested. Iris hadn't argued. Now Cadenhill's half had burnt.

Amanda still didn't understand how that could have happened. Fires were commonplace on plantations. But the tobacco barns had been located far away from any other building in order to safeguard against such an occurrence. Cadenhill slaves would never have done anything to endanger the crop. And there was no reason for anyone else . . .

Then Amanda remembered the strange whinny that had awakened her. She'd caught a flash of the horse fleeing into the woods, and in that moment she'd wondered what might have spooked the animal. But all the Cadenhill horses had been inside the barn.

Then she knew. Franklin! He'd ridden up from nowhere. Not because he'd seen the flames from town—he hadn't had time to do that—but because he'd set the fire and waited to watch the barns burn. Nothing else made sense.

The thief! The crook! If he hadn't already left with the tobacco she'd go into town and take it back. *Take it back.* That thought kept running around and around in her mind. If she were a man she'd rob him, just the way he'd managed to rob her father all the time he was pretending to act in their best interest.

She could still hear his solicitous tone. "Don't worry about the seed and supplies, Houston, you can pay me later. Don't worry, I've already arranged an extension on your loans. What is family for?"

Then when the crop was sold, the price was always down from what they'd expected. So, year by year, the debt increased, with Franklin always reassuring her father. "Your father took my mother and me in, and cared for us. Giving you credit now that you need it is only fair."

In private, he had approached Amanda with the same kindly solicitude, becoming more and more bold as the years passed.

She still shuddered when she thought about his show of grief at the funeral. After the reading of the will, when everyone was consoling Iris, Franklin had followed Amanda onto the veranda and delivered his ultimatum.

"I'm going to make Cadenhill the biggest plantation in the south, Amanda, and I expect your cooperation. And your gratitude."

"Then you'll be disappointed. You will never get your hands on Cadenhill."

Franklin looked at her for a long time, barely contained anger etched across his face. "I have waited too long for this, my dear Amanda. It's time you understand the truth.

I have no intention of forgiving Cadenhill's debts, or making good the outstanding loans in Augusta, until you accept my proposal, and you will if you want to prevent Cadenhill land from being sold.''

"No!" she'd whispered angrily, trying to pull away from his grip, mindful of the judge and her mother inside the parlor. "Don't try to fool me, Franklin. You've cheated my father for years, and I know it."

"Of course I have," he admitted, pushing her against the hidden side wall of the house. "Now Cadenhill is in my debt and the time has come to collect." He glared at her, daring her to scream as his fingertips played up her arm, slid across her breast and pinched her nipple painfully. "The truth is, Amanda, I can be very nice if you give me what I want."

"You despicable pig!" she'd exclaimed shoving him away. "I wouldn't have you if you were the last man in this valley. We have until June to pay those notes, and I'm going to find a way to do it. If it means marrying, that's what I'll do. But it won't be you!"

"I think not. None of the other men have the money or the patience to tolerate you. You're too shrewish, too set in your ways. And before you go looking for a…patron, I can promise you that you won't find one. Everybody in the valley owes me money, my dear niece, and they can't afford to lose my goodwill."

"Why? Why are you doing this?"

"Why? Because of what I saw in my stepfather's eyes every time he looked at me, regret that I'd been born, shame over his wife's illegitimate child. Oh, he allowed me to take his name, but he never gave it to me legally. Houston was his only son. Now I'm the only Caden left."

"Shame? What do you mean? I never knew Grandfather, but Father always treated you like a brother."

"Oh, he tried to pretend we were equals. But that was just for show. He was the true Caden, the one with the respect, the fine plantation, one of the landed gentry. I was only the by-blow, forced to go into trade."

"At which you've done very well. Do you cheat the other people in Petersburg, Franklin?"

"Of course, when necessary. But I'm also their friend. I look after them, sell to them on credit, buy their goods. I'm their savior, just as I'm yours."

"I'll say this once more, Uncle Franklin. My father asked me to look after Cadenhill, and I will, without you."

"Oh, but you're wrong, Amanda. I see that I will have to prove it to you. Come June, we will be married, Amanda, because you'll do whatever is necessary to save your family and this precious land. I know it and you know it."

But she hadn't believed Franklin—until now.

And he'd shown her how far he would go. She'd tell Judge Taliaferro that Franklin was responsible for the fire. But she'd already tried unsuccessfully to convince the judge of Franklin's thievery; he hadn't believed her then and he wouldn't now. She had no proof that the horse she'd seen vanishing into the woods belonged to Franklin. It would be her word against his that Franklin's horse had not been lathered, had obviously not been run hard when he arrived at Cadenhill. Franklin. Not only did she have to save her land, but now she had to find a way to punish Franklin for what he'd done.

But how? Her barns were gone. Her seed had been burned. And Franklin had not only sealed off any other offers of help, he'd also managed to find a way to get all the money from the sale of their tobacco crop. At least he would have when he returned from Augusta on the new stagecoach. Franklin had worked out his plans very well.

Unless . . .

Chapter Three

The forest was silent ahead of the small black horse that picked its way down the wagon trail. The horse's rider had chosen the perfect spot beneath an oak tree: a black void in an already dark, moonless night. The going was uneasy, even for one who knew well every inch of the woods between Petersburg and the Broad River.

The stagecoach would round the curve, hidden by shrubs and the low-hanging limbs of the oak until the last minute when it could be boarded quickly, surprising Franklin Caden before he knew what was happening. The young horse trembled, then quieted in response to the light touch of the rider's hand. The deed about to be done had been born of desperation, not desire. Now, tonight, in the Broad River Valley of Georgia, in the year 1790, a highwayman was about to right a wrong.

Night sounds came alive again in the stillness. A light cold rain began to splatter a forest so thick that in summer little moisture reached the ground. The highwayman waited in the darkness, listening, loosely holding the reins of the stallion in one hand, and in the other hand a pistol, primed and ready for firing.

Franklin Caden had to be stopped before he destroyed Cadenhill.

He thought he'd given her a warning, issued an ultimatum. He'd thought that by burning her crop he'd force her to accept his control. Tonight, he would learn different. She would take back what he'd stolen.

Long minutes passed. Then—the sound of approaching horses.

Up the trail, the stagecoach lumbered across small bushes, sagging into holes and climbing mounds of rubble. The driver swore and flicked his whip lightly across the backs of the laboring team of horses.

Inside the coach, Thomas Rushton Randolph wished he'd returned from Augusta by horseback instead of taking his own public coach. At least he wouldn't have bounced around the saddle. He'd been assured that the road to Augusta was clear, but he had learned that passable was far from open. His stagecoaches might get through, but comfort for the passengers was still a long way from reality.

The stage sank into still another hole, wobbled and came to a lurching stop, tumbling one of the two satchels Rush carried to the floor. "What's wrong now, driver?"

"A tree limb, governor. Just stay put, it's beginning to rain out here. I'll have it out of the way in a minute."

Rush leaned wearily against the back of the hard board seat. He'd taken the trip with Franklin to check out the facilities for the stage line office in Augusta, traveling downriver with the tobacco on a barge known as a Petersburg boat. As Franklin's partner, Rush needed to learn every phase of the warehouse business, including the movement of their goods.

While Franklin arranged the sale of the tobacco, Rush had contracted with the operator of a livery stable to act as agent for the stagecoach, afterward acquainting himself with the local buyers and agents. Later that day, Franklin learned that a renegade band of Creek Indians had gotten liquored up and boarded one of his barges the night before, wrecking it and leaving it abandoned above Augusta. Franklin left immediately to assess the situation.

Uncertain of what he would find, Franklin entrusted the gold from the tobacco sale to Rush, who would return by stagecoach. Anybody on the dock would expect the gold to go with Franklin, and giving Rush the gold would protect Franklin's profits from the Caden tobacco crop.

Outside the coach Rush heard the rustle of a limb as the driver gave a loud grunt of exertion. Rush decided he'd better give his driver a hand. Because of a broken wheel he was already returning later than he'd planned. If Franklin had arrived in Petersburg, he'd be sending out a posse.

Stowing the valise of money beneath the seat as a precaution, Rush reached for the door handle.

At that moment the door opened silently. Before Rush knew what was happening, a shadowy figure wearing a tricorne hat slipped into the carriage beside him and shoved a pistol against his rib cage.

"The money," a gruff, muffled voice demanded urgently. "Give it to me—quick!"

Rush was astonished, but not afraid. He'd faced consequences worse than physical death during the fight for independence of the Thirteen Colonies. He'd fought hostile Indians in the West, and been jostled by the pickpockets of the worst London streets, and found each a risk easily dealt with.

He had no intention of being robbed in his own stagecoach. With a quick feigned motion, Rush dodged away from the pistol and reached forward to knock it from the bandit's grip. What his hand touched in the melee that followed wasn't a gun but a body, a body with the kind of curves not completely concealed by the frock coat the bandit was wearing. Rush jerked his hand away.

"Get back!" The intruder, seizing on the opportunity afforded by Rush's shock, slid across the coach to the opposite seat and lowered the pistol.

Rush complied. The danger posed by a slim, masked highwayman in northwestern Georgia was more intriguing than threatening, especially when the bandit smelled of flowers and moved through the night with silky grace.

"Well now," he said in a voice laced with amusement, "what have we here, a highwayman wearing a silk mask and the scent of... what is it? Jasmine? A Jasmine Bandit."

"Who are you?" The low voice rose in surprise.

"Not the person you were expecting? Sorry to disappoint you. Thomas Rushton Randolph, ma'am. How may I be of service?"

Franklin's partner? For a moment she was confused. According to the judge, Franklin was supposed to be returning by stage with the gold from the tobacco sale. Could she have misunderstood? It was too late to worry. She'd committed herself and she had to go forward. At least this man wouldn't recognize her.

"It matters little to me who you are," she lied. "Give me your gold or I'll kill you and take it."

The gun wavered, then jabbed into his stomach, forcing Rush to regret his attempt at levity. Lady bandit or not, this woman was deadly serious about her task, and he had no wish to give substance to her threat.

"Certainly, ma'am. I never argue with a gun pressed against my body, especially when the money isn't mine. The gold is in my satchel."

"Put it on the seat beside me."

Her voice was husky and strong. He wondered how it would sound in a different situation. Would she apply the same passion in pleasing a man as in robbing him? In the darkness he narrowed his eyes, trying unsuccessfully to see more clearly in the darkness. She was tall, and agile. Her unexpected entrance proved that she could move through the night with grace.

Bold of purpose himself, Rush admired anybody who went after what they wanted. Even more he admired that she was a woman. A woman who, under other circumstances, he might want to know better—if he could keep her from killing him long enough to get acquainted.

Rush reached down, slowly lifted the valise from the seat beside him and followed the directions issued by his night visitor. Taking the handle, the bandit began to slide toward the still-open door, all the while continuing to press the gun against his body.

The carriage suddenly lurched as the horse stepped forward. The motion rocked both Rush and the highwayman. With little effort Rush slid his knife from his boot with one hand and grabbed the slender wrist holding the gun with the other.

The bandit let out an involuntary cry.

"You say something, governor?" the driver called out.

"No, just talking to myself."

"I'm going to pull this branch up the road and we'll be on our way."

The rustle of tree limbs being dragged drowned out Rush's terse "Maybe we will, and maybe we won't."

"Let me go," the bandit directed in a low voice. "I can still kill you before you can move away, and I will. I intend to have this money."

"And I don't intend to argue—about that," Rush said. "But I never pay a woman unless I receive service in return. I consider this transaction business, ma'am, and sooner or later, I always collect my debts."

The man was big, powerful. Even in the darkness there was a danger about him that seemed to sizzle across the carriage. She hadn't counted on the hammer of her heartbeat or the flush of her skin beneath his gaze. Something about his voice and the firm grip of his hand stretched the tension to a tight thread, making his promise even more menacing.

A business transaction, a debt to be paid. She concentrated her thoughts on the words instead of the man. An exchange she could understand. An exchange was a method of payment with which she could deal. His offer assuaged any guilt she might have felt. She tested the weight of the bag. It was heavy. She would take the gold. She had no choice, but she could give payment in exchange.

"Very well, sir. I, too, believe in the trade of services as payment of debt."

"A lady after my own heart." He gave a low, seductive laugh. "Just what kind of trade did you have in mind?"

Amanda Caden knew that the man holding her wrist could likely overpower her at any minute, probably without the gun being fired. He could likely even... Her thought process leapt ahead to the possibility of what might happen if the situation were reversed. Behind her mask she felt her face flame even more. The heat ran down her arm in a ripple of fire and she knew that the man felt it, too.

For a moment they were motionless. Even as she trembled she realized that he'd chosen not to confront her directly. Why? The danger of his unexpected challenge caught Amanda Caden in its intensity, and she felt her own wicked response of appreciation at a match well made. Fine, she'd boasted about bartering for payment, she'd pay him.

"The only trade I'm prepared to offer, merchant, is this."

Shoring up her courage, Amanda leaned swiftly forward and touched her lips to those of the man she'd just robbed. She meant it to be a quick teasing kiss, a saucy payment of settled debt to save her conscience.

But the danger turned into something volatile, and shock parted the firm lips she was touching. A quiver of heat swept through her and she trembled at the unexpected thrust of the man's tongue into her mouth. Gasping, she drew back, feeling a sharp tug of her hair as the mask came away, uncovering her face in the darkness. With a quick motion she gave a twist to her arm, dropped the pistol to the coach floor and, holding the valise tightly, backed out the door of the coach into the night. As soon as she was mounted, she looped the handle of the satchel over her saddle horn, turned her horse and disappeared into the darkness.

The low, wicked laugh that followed stayed with her all the way back to the plantation. The racing of her pulse continued as she rode into the barn, unsaddled Shadow, gave him a quick rubdown and turned him into the stall she'd filled with hay before she left.

Thor, the big chestnut stallion in the adjacent stall, neighed softly, as if voicing his puzzlement over being rejected. "I'm sorry, Thor, old friend," Amanda said. "I know you're the fastest horse in the valley, but if I'd taken you, we could have been recognized."

Amanda gave her old friend one last pat and left the barn. She'd done it. She didn't know why Franklin's partner had been in the coach instead of Franklin, but she'd succeeded in taking the money that Franklin had tried to steal from her family. If the purse contained money that rightfully belonged to any of the other plantation owners, she told herself that Franklin and his wicked partner were responsible, not her. At least now she could make a token-of-good-faith payment on her father's debt. She'd worry tomorrow about explaining where the money came from.

Unbelievably tired, she started toward the big house. The rain had stopped and a ray of moonlight slipped out from behind a cloud, casting a silvery glow over the two-story whitewashed clapboard house.

Cadenhill, the house, like a shining jewel in the moonlight, never failed to fill Amanda with pride. Because of her father's friendship with the Indians, Cadenhill had been built long before the influx of new settlers who came after the revolution, long before the Creek lands were parceled out by lotteries.

The town proper had been laid out and called Petersburg after its namesake in the Virginia colony. The new residents were not only wealthy, but the cream of Williamsburg society as well, who brought their social customs and manners with them. Still, she thought with satisfaction, none of the newcomers had yet managed to reach the splendor and success of Cadenhill plantation.

Amanda took a deep breath and shifted the satchel to her other hand. Its weight gave her comfort as she crept across the veranda and opened the study door. Only when she was inside did she allow herself to relax. She'd done it—robbed the stage and reclaimed Caden money. The amount would be only a drop in the bucket, but it was a start. And if her plan for the next tobacco crop was successful, she was certain that the men who held Cadenhill loans would reconsider.

She hadn't worked her plan out entirely yet, but she'd use some of the money to buy seed. She was sure that under the right conditions, transplanting the young tobacco plants to the field could begin earlier. If she could move up the harvest, her crop would be marketed before any others. That would bring a higher price. It would be a risk, but the end result would be worth it.

Tiptoeing to the door, she peered into the hallway. A fat candle stood in a large pan of water on a table in the hall, casting a faint glow of light in the darkness.

Satisfied that her mother and her three younger sisters were sleeping, she closed the study door and lit the candle on her father's desk. Releasing a ragged breath, she removed the black tricorne from her head, allowing the mass of auburn hair to cascade across her flushed cheeks, her shoulders and down her back. Her pleasure at her success was diminished only because the man she'd robbed hadn't been Franklin.

Still, she pushed the memory of the man in the carriage from her mind as she told herself that she'd done what was necessary to save her home, just as she always had. She didn't need a husband.

Amanda still remembered the sadness in her father's eyes during one of their last conversations. He'd been writing a letter which he'd given to Settie to post.

"When—if a strong man comes along to help you, Amanda," he'd said, "marry him."

At the time she'd laughed and told him that he was the only man in her life. But Houston was gone now, and no strong helpful stranger had appeared, unless she could count Mr. Rushton Randolph, who'd given her his gold in exchange for a kiss. He hadn't offered marriage.

But he hadn't even appeared to be alarmed, either. In spite of allowing a woman to get the best of him, he'd seemed almost intrigued by the holdup! Robbing the man in the carriage had been curiously exciting, but Amanda had been cheated of the satisfaction of seeing Franklin's face and hearing him beg for mercy.

Rushton Randolph. Any associate of Franklin's was bound to be a dishonest, cheating ruffian, too. She'd never met a man she had much respect for, except her father.

Amanda shivered, telling herself that the trembling weakness that had overcome her was caused by her damp clothing. Still, she couldn't shake the uneasy feeling that had followed her from the stage. Instead, the uneasiness seemed to intensify. Something was wrong, and the sensation was tied in some way to the man in the coach.

Amanda shook her head in denial. Seeing the money, the money for the Cadenhill tobacco, would calm her nerves. Turning her attention to the satchel, she forced open the catch and peered inside.

Her first reaction was shock; her second, pure anger. The blood seemed to drain from her body. The satchel wasn't filled with money, it was filled with clothes—men's clothes—a big man's clothes. The weight in the bag that kept her from realizing her mistake came from a pair of matched pistols in a leather case. No wonder the stranger hadn't put up more of a fight. She'd been hoodwinked.

Devil take it! She'd kissed him in payment for a debt she didn't owe, kissed a man whose touch still made her nerve endings quiver and her heart beat erratically. That rogue, that bold, laughing devil! He'd kissed her and stolen her money a second time.

Thomas Rushton Randolph, her uncle's new partner, was a blackguard and a thief, and from this moment forward her sworn enemy. Amanda Rebecca Caden was acknowledged by all to be a better planter, a better rider, a better shot and better with the lance than any man in the Broad River Valley. First Franklin, now this man had challenged her and won. She'd get even. They both owed her now, and she intended to collect. One way or another.

"Mother, I think we should ask Uncle Franklin for new dresses." Catherine Caden drummed her fingertips on the table and straightened her back as she made her point.

"There will be no new dresses, Catherine," Amanda answered for her mother. "I'm surprised that you would ask."

"But, Manda, I'm not being selfish. I'm trying to help. And attending Charity Taliaferro's Christmas ball is a good place to start. Besides, it isn't up to you."

Iris poured milk into her glass and regarded her daughters. Catherine was growing up and she deserved to be considered. "And how will your attending Charity's ball help, Catherine?"

"Well, if Amanda doesn't intend to marry, it seems only fair that I'm the one to find a husband."

"Catherine, you're too young even to think about such a thing," Iris protested.

"I am not. Truly, I'm not. Oh, Mother, I'm almost seventeen. Most of the girls in Petersburg already have chosen their future husbands and I don't even have a beau. If I have to wait for Amanda to marry first I'll turn into a sour old maid and die of loneliness."

Amanda bit back a smile. Catherine's rationalizing her desire to attend the ball as helping the family wasn't unexpected. Catherine has always been bright and quick. But when Amanda caught sight of the set of her mother's lips, she sighed. How unfair it all was. Catherine was right; she did deserve a new dress, and more. But they needed every penny of the money they had left. There was none to spare for dresses or parties. If they had money, buying supplies could be justified. Buying luxuries could not.

Amanda pushed aside her misgivings and softened her voice. "Because we need the money to plant tobacco in little more than a month, Cat. We ... can't afford new clothes," she added with a catch in her throat. "I won't allow us to ask Franklin for more credit this year."

"Are you sure, Amanda?" Iris questioned as she looked closely at her oldest daughter. "Houston always managed to see that we each got a new gown when the crops were sold. It's been so long since any of us have been into Petersburg. The Christmas ball is important to Catherine. In fact, I'd like both of you to attend."

The shock on Amanda's face was obvious, even to her.

"Attend a ball, when Papa has been buried scarce two months? Mama, that would be scandalous."

"But, Manda, Papa said that we weren't to go on mourning," Catherine argued. "He made us promise. By Christmas it will be three months. Besides, I'm tired of wearing black."

Dear Catherine—young and discontented; Amanda could certainly empathize with her. Both their lives had been rocked by the war and their family's hardships. It wasn't fair to expect Catherine to live differently from the life for which she'd been raised. But that had changed, even before Houston Caden's death, and there was nothing Amanda could do about it.

"No," Amanda said sharply, rising from the table with her cornmeal mush half-eaten. She had to be strong. "I'm sorry. Maybe Papa did buy dresses, but he shouldn't have. There can't be any parties or dresses until we find a way to save Cadenhill.'' Softening her words, Amanda added, ''Perhaps we can manage a dress for the new year. There's all I can promise.''

Amanda strode from the dining room, leaving both Cat and her mother openmouthed at her high-handed way. The sound of Catherine's tight little sniffle followed Amanda.

Her failure to recover Franklin's gold had reached disastrous proportions in the light of day. Since dawn Amanda had been going over the books again. There was no answer that she could see in the offing. Even if she could make an early crop, the sale wouldn't come in time to meet the creditors' deadline. She couldn't sell any of the livestock. The cows had to be kept to provide milk for the children, the hogs as food for the household and the slaves.

Still, Amanda couldn't help feeling like a miserly villain. What difference did one dress make anyway? The judge was right. Amanda had to find a lot of money—or a rich husband—quick.

Iris Caden was ill equipped to do more than follow directions. Not only that, but Amanda couldn't be certain that she wouldn't cave in to Franklin's demands. Everything was up to Amanda. Unless she found another answer, she'd be forced to agree to Franklin's proposal. Thus far, she had come up with only one rather dubious alternative.

But Cadenhill had to be saved.

And the Jasmine Bandit had to ride again.

Chapter Four

Rush walked through the warehouse, stacked high with hogsheads of tobacco, and felt a thrill of pride shoot through him. His partnership with Franklin Caden was still new, less than two months old, but he'd taken the first step toward making a place for himself.

Petersburg hadn't always been a part of Rush's plan for the future. He'd expected to return to Albemarle and grow tobacco, just like his father and his brother. But that was not to be, and seven years later, because of his old friend and mentor, Houston Caden, he'd come to Georgia and the Broad River Valley.

Rush should have come sooner. He'd known Houston wasn't well when he'd received his last confused letter imploring him to come to Petersburg as soon as he received President Washington's commission to build the stage line.

"If anything should happen to me, Rush," he'd implored, "promise me that you'll help Amanda." Rush owed the stagecoach commission to Houston, and he'd sent a letter that he'd come as quickly as possible to help Houston's family in any way he could. But a flood washed away a vital stretch of the stagecoach road and he'd been delayed.

Then before Rush ever reached the settlement, he learned that Houston Caden was dead. He might have turned back, had it not been for his promise, but the farmer who told

Rush of Houston's death advised him to first see Franklin, Houston's stepbrother. Franklin either owned or controlled most of the Broad River Valley. To Rush, in his grief, if Franklin was Houston Caden's brother, that was all he had to know.

On arrival, Rush introduced himself as a friend of Houston. He explained his commission to operate the stage line and that he had gold to invest. Franklin welcomed any friend of his brother's and immediately suggested a limited partnership in the warehouse. Almost before he accepted, Rush had begun to suspect that Franklin wasn't the man his brother was. A stagecoach line was competition that wouldn't be welcomed, if Franklin hadn't needed Rush's gold.

In the beginning Rush had been busy setting up the stage office and he'd delayed calling on Houston's family. But Houston's unfulfilled request gnawed at him. Rush should have gone to Mrs. Caden right away; Houston had asked him to help her. But when Rush mentioned a visit, Franklin had bristled and suggested that he wait. The family wasn't yet receiving outsiders.

Rush learned that Franklin was very protective of his family and for Rush to intrude would go against the wishes of his new partner. Rush didn't insist. He would give the widow and her children another week, then he'd call.

Rush glanced around the warehouse again. By his family's standards, a grading and storage warehouse wasn't much, but it was the first thing he'd ever owned for himself. At least he owned half. And the warehouse was just the beginning. Soon he'd begin looking for land.

He liked what he'd seen of Petersburg. After months of forging a stagecoach road through forests thick with trees, crossing swollen streams swift enough to wash a small house away and hiking through mountains inhabited by hostile Indians, bears, and other surprises, his destination, Petersburg, was like a mirage in the wilderness.

With streets laid out like the squares on a game board, the town was almost as sophisticated as the cities of his beloved North Carolina.

A man could buy a barrel of Philadelphia ale or a bottle of London port or a fur-skin jacket, play a game of billiards or examine the latest London fashions being worn by a display doll. The only problem the residents encountered was also their greatest asset. They were surrounded by water; the Broad River on one side and the Savannah on the other. Other than traveling by tobacco boats or on horseback, once a person arrived in Petersburg he couldn't go any farther. But Rush was changing that. In another three months his stagecoach line would run clear from Philadelphia to Savannah.

Now, as he walked through the open tobacco storage building, Rush breathed deeply, relishing the earthy, sweet smell of the tobacco leaves. He'd grown up with that smell. The Randolphs of Carolina had always raised tobacco, though Rush's plans were to buy land and grow cotton.

After spending time with President Washington at his plantation on the Potomac, Rush had learned how to increase the crop yield through the use of fertilizer. Convincing his brother to use this method had been as futile as making him believe that Rush hadn't shirked his duty during the revolution. Even when George Washington explained otherwise, his family was slow to believe that Rush had acted under orders.

Rush's pleasure turned into a bitter sigh of resignation as he recalled the arguments that had taken place between him and his older brother, Richard. There would always be a barrier there, lowered perhaps, but not totally surmounted. Even Rush's sporadic presence in Albemarle was enough to stir up things, until on his father's death, he'd finally taken his second-son inheritance and set out to make his own way. His leaving had brought a genuine, if unspoken, relief to the Randolphs of North Carolina. For his family had never been able to live down the rumor that Thomas Rushton Randolph had been a Tory spy.

Proud and hurting, Rush had first gone west with the explorers and mapmakers after the war, then back to England, hoping that time would allay the gossip and dim their suspicions. But in the end it had been Houston Caden who, in spite of their separation, became Rush's surrogate family. In return Rush had promised to settle in Petersburg, and help the Caden family.

Now Rush paused at the base of the balcony steps, watching the pickers whose job it was to open the hogsheads and separate the good tobacco from the bad. In the corner of the room stood a pile of ruined leaves, rotten from having been packed damp. To protect the quality of the tobacco sold under the Caden name, these leaves would be rejected and burned. As far as Rush could tell, Caden Tobacco didn't follow the practice of hiding the wet tobacco in the center; he approved of that. His future was tied to the Caden name now, and he intended it to stand for integrity.

Transferring the valise he was carrying from one hand to the other, Rush mounted the stairs. He fingered the satchel and allowed a rare smile to wash across his lips, wondering what his lady bandit thought when she opened her bag and found his dirty linens instead of the gold she'd demanded. His only regret was the loss of his French pistols. He'd bought them in England and they were of the finest workmanship. The weapon his bandit had dropped was distinctive and probably one of a matched pair, but it didn't compare with the ones he'd lost. Still, he'd tucked her pistol into his belt and put the mask into his pocket. The strand of red hair caught in its tie was an intriguing element he'd already decided to keep to himself.

The Jasmine Bandit.

As Rush reached the mezzanine that circled and overlooked the warehouse floor below, he heard the argument. A woman's low voice was spitting with fury.

"You low-down cockroach! I know what you did. I can't prove it, but I saw you. We may have lost the whole crop, but I'll see you in hell before I marry you, Franklin Caden!"

"Perhaps," came Franklin's measured reply, "but meanwhile, you'll do whatever you must to save your precious land, just like your respected father."

"I will never allow—"

"You will do whatever I say."

"But, Franklin..."

The voice softened and Rush could no longer hear what was being said. The woman had obviously changed her tactics. Her threats hadn't fazed Franklin and she'd reverted to using her womanly wiles.

Women! Rush had little use for their machinations. He much preferred the boldness of the midnight bandit. She wanted something and she went after it, ready to face the consequences.

Too bad it had been dark. He'd have liked to see the woman who matched the scent that still lingered suggestively in his memory. He almost wished he had overpowered her and taken her back to his room in the tavern. He would have meted his own form of punishment to the wench....

He pushed that thought from his head reluctantly. Too many months had passed without the company of a woman, but he wasn't interested in tavern lightskirts now. A plantation demanded a mistress and that meant a proper wife. Rush intended to begin his search for both as soon as he was certain that he would be accepted on his own merits without being tainted by his lingering reputation.

Rush moved around the balcony, past Franklin's door and into his new office. It was smaller, less well-furnished than his partner's, but Rush preferred the corner location overlooking the street. There were glass panes in the windows and a desk and chair. He placed the satchel on his desk and walked toward the window, closing it to keep out the damp air blowing in from the river.

Closing the windows magnified the sound of the seductively low feminine voice next door, the voice that played insistently across his mind like a haunting melody.

For a long reflective moment he watched several women shopping along the street below, their servants walking behind, carrying baskets over their arms. In spite of what Houston had promised, Petersburg had been a surprise to Rush. He should have known that the Virginians would take their wealth and culture with them wherever they settled.

According to Franklin, there were formal balls, picnics, theatrical presentations by traveling troupes and excursions downriver to Augusta and Savannah for social occasions. Franklin intended to host a New Year's Day horse race at the newly built Jockey Club. But Rush had been too busy to mix with the townspeople up to now. Being wary of his countrymen had become a way of life in the last years, a habit he found hard to break.

Though Rush could no longer distinguish the words, from the steady drone of the voices next door, he decided that the woman trading insults with Franklin was not giving up. Rush feared, however, that she was destined to lose her argument. He listened intently, curious about the woman Franklin was determined to marry.

Beyond the wall separating the two offices, Amanda Caden lifted her chin and bit back the words she wanted to say. Threatening Franklin was accomplishing nothing. He was right. For the benefit of her family and Cadenhill she would do almost anything. She took a deep breath and offered one last plea, "Franklin, don't force me to marry you. I don't love you. I'll never make a good wife."

"On that we agree, Amanda. But I don't care if you're good, bad or indifferent. I've waited long enough and I mean to have you. Don't force me to prove it again."

Amanda swallowed the anger she felt. Franklin would never give in. His voice was cold and tempered with the cruelty she'd always known was there. He concealed that trait from the world, but since childhood she had been subjected to his vindictiveness. Burning her tobacco was a low to which she had never thought even Franklin would sink. Provoking him further could be costly.

"How did you manage it, Franklin?" she asked softly. "I know you burned our barns and you tricked my father into signing a new will."

"Of course I did, you foolish little chit!" Franklin snapped, allowing his anger to explode for a moment. Then he smiled and smoothed his voice into a syrupy sneer. "I warned you, Amanda, dear. Houston trusted me to keep his best interests at heart. As his agent and lawyer, it was simple enough to add a few extra paragraphs to the will to ensure that the Caden women would be looked after properly—by me."

Amanda felt a wave of revulsion ripple through her as his eyes bored into her. Angrily she tucked an errant strand of fiery red hair beneath the black straw hat she'd worn as her concession to mourning, and smoothed the folds of her threadbare muslin dress. She had paid little attention to the faded color, or the way the garment hugged her body without the corsets and panniers still favored by some of the women in town.

Propriety had mattered little, until now, when Amanda felt Franklin's eyes openly measuring her body in the limp clinging gown. Much to her chagrin she realized belatedly that there was something to be said for the concealment offered by the more fashionable garments.

"It wouldn't be proper for us to marry, *Uncle* Franklin. People would talk."

"That's never before bothered you. Besides, I'm not your uncle, Amanda. Everybody knows that we're not blood relatives. At twenty-two you are already past marriageable age. A union between us would be accepted as not only a charitable act on my part, considering the reputation you have as a hoyden, but also very proper.''

Desperately she continued to argue, knowing even as she spoke that her words fell on deaf ears. ''My father trusted me to run the plantation, Franklin.''

''I have no intention of trying to run the plantation. I only plan to oversee the financial matters. You may continue to root about in the dirt like some field hand, so long as you bathe before I take you to my bed.''

''Bed?'' Amanda drew in a quick, startled breath. Somehow that part of his marriage plan hadn't occurred to her. ''You wouldn't dare!''

''Of course, I dare. When we marry you will become my wife in every sense of the word.'' He stepped toward Amanda, clasping her hand and pulling her forward with an impatient jerk. ''And you will marry me, Amanda. I'll see to that.''

This time her voice rose. What she said wasn't a scream or a hysterical protest. Neither were her words uttered from desperation. Rather they were delivered firmly with such strength and calm that her threat carried even beyond the wall into the warehouse.

''I'll scream your ears deaf if you touch me, just like I threatened to do the last time you put your hands on me, you lying thief. You may call yourself Caden, but you'll never own Cadenhill Plantation.''

''No? You're wrong, my high and mighty little stepniece.'' Franklin allowed his voice to rise in anger. ''Very soon you'll stop looking down your arrogant, aristocratic nose and welcome me, or you'll lose everything.''

Amanda stared at him in fury, squaring her shoulders in acceptance of what must be done. ''All right, Franklin Caden. Hear me, and hear me well. When I choose to welcome a man to my bed, it will never be you. Manage the financial matters of Cadenhill all you like—there's little enough there to worry about—so long as you do it from town. If you set one foot on my land, I'll shoot you and swear it was an accident."

"I think not, Amanda. Our wedding will be the first Sunday in June," Franklin said with cool authority in his voice. "Meanwhile, if you want to prevent further tragedy, you will do as I say. I think we will begin our official courtship by attending Judge Taliaferro's Christmas ball."

Amanda opened the door, turned slowly around and announced quietly, "The judge might not believe you burned our barns, but another incident too soon might make him wonder. As for the Christmas ball, I shall certainly attend, alone."

With her head held high, Amanda Caden swept out of Franklin's office and moved regally down the steps through the warehouse and out the door.

On the balcony above both office doors were standing open. The two partners were watching Amanda's proud exit, around the circle and down the steps.

In the first doorway Franklin Caden smiled maliciously as he watched his future bride depart. Any disturbances at the plantation were due to his niece's poor management. He'd made certain that anybody inclined to assist her knew that she couldn't be depended on. She would come crawling to him, this arrogant woman who refused him.

In the second doorway, Rush Randolph, too, was watching Amanda, but the expression on his face was one of shock. He'd heard Franklin call the woman by name, "Amanda."

Franklin caught sight of Rush. "Where have you been, Randolph?" Franklin moved into his office. "You're late."

After a moment Rush followed, dropped the valise on Franklin's desk and moved to the window. He never got a good look at the woman's face, and her hair had been covered by a bonnet. Yet every worker in the warehouse had stopped for a second and stared at her as she walked through. There was a power about her that a man could almost feel. It wasn't until he took a deep breath that he knew.

Jasmine. The scent of the spring flower still lingered in Franklin's office. It hadn't been Rush's imagination, though the sensual reminder of the woman had plagued his mind for most of the night. The woman who had been arguing with Franklin was the Jasmine Bandit.

And Franklin Caden planned to marry her.

"Well?" Franklin spoke again, more insistently this time. "I trust your return trip was uneventful."

"Ah, yes. Who was the lady?"

"Lady? That's a kindness I would hardly apply. The girl is Amanda Caden, my ward."

"Your niece?"

The Amanda he was supposed to look after was Houston's daughter, not his wife.

"My step-niece. Why?"

"Ah, no reason. Your ward seemed a bit piqued." Rush tried to control his surprise. It wasn't that Franklin was too old for Amanda. Older men often took young brides. But for Amanda, Franklin was—was—wrong was the only word he could find to describe his reaction to the woman he was watching through the window.

"She's being stubborn about setting a date for our wedding. It was . . ." Franklin added a slightly pious tone to his voice. "It was my brother's wish that I assume responsibility for his family and the estate."

"Of course," Rush agreed, "and marrying his daughter is the generous thing for you to do. I quite understand. But . . ." He paused as Amanda lifted her skirts, stepped up into her cart and drove the horse smartly down the rough street.

"But what, man?" Franklin asked, impatient now to direct Rush's mind back to the gold.

"From the sound of the lady's voice, I'd say she isn't in complete agreement with your plan."

"What she thinks is unimportant. She will do what she must. Now, why are you late? After you had me announce that you'd be returning by stage to demonstrate its dependability I'd think that you would make certain that you were on time. Was there trouble?"

Look after Amanda. Help Amanda. Those words echoed uncomfortably in Rush's mind. "Not exactly," Rush answered as the cart passed out of sight. "The trip was...acceptable, though I found the return by coach potentially more dangerous than I'd envisioned. Have you been threatened by highwaymen?"

"Highwaymen? In the Broad River Valley?" Franklin Caden smacked his thin lips and leaned forward in anticipation of inspecting the contents of the satchel. "An occasional boarding of a tobacco boat by some drunken settler, a bit of rustling now and then by a tribe of liquored-up redskins, but a highwayman? Never, in my recollection. Why?"

"Well," Rush said casually, wondering how wise his revelation about the highwayman was, "the stage was robbed last night, by a masked bandit carrying a pistol."

"Robbed? We've lost the gold?" Franklin groaned.

"No. All the highwayman got was a satchel of soiled linens."

Franklin let out a sigh of relief. "A highwayman? Well, the stagecoach line is your problem, Randolph. Our partnership is limited to the warehouse. In the future I'll take my chances on the Petersburg boats."

"Maybe I'll look into hiring some guards, until the criminal element learns that we protect our passengers. I wouldn't want my own partner to refuse to travel by stage."

"Fine," Franklin said sharply. "Now, let's have a look at my gold."

"It's in the satchel, all four hundred twenty dollars of it. I didn't say anything when you were making the sale, Franklin, but isn't that a bit low?"

Franklin looked startled for a moment. "Seven cents a pound. Six thousand pounds at seven cents a pound. That's four hundred twenty dollars in gold, a good price. Let's see it, Randolph."

Rush opened the case, exposing the gold. "I just thought that if you'd held out for more you might have done better. You're the factor, Franklin," he said.

The floral scent left behind by Franklin's future bride was fading away. But Rush's interest in the woman was even stronger. He didn't want to think it was because he'd heard Franklin's plan to marry her. Rush couldn't be certain, but his instinct was that Houston would never have agreed to that marriage. Otherwise why should he have specifically asked Rush to look after Amanda, not Franklin?

Perhaps he wouldn't mention Houston's odd request, Rush decided. But he'd follow through on it. The time had come for Rush to present himself to Petersburg society. And his partner was the one to introduce him.

"By the way, Franklin," he said casually, "I believe I'm ready to meet our customers. Do you think you could arrange a social event?"

"Well, let me think. Perhaps dinner this evening at the Hillyers, followed by the Taliaferro annual Christmas ball in two weeks. Do you have the proper attire to attend a dance, Randolph? We do try to act like gentlemen here."

"I won't embarrass you, Franklin." Rush smothered a smile.

"Will you be attending the ball with your niece?"

"It isn't likely that my niece will attend this ball, Randolph. My brother's family is still in mourning."

"I suppose mourning customs here are different," Rush said, adding to himself, *where I come from they don't wear masks.*

Rush remembered, not for the first time, the bold kiss the bandit had bestowed in payment for the goods she'd stolen. The hat she'd been wearing in Franklin's office this morning had almost covered her hair, but hidden in Rush's pocket was a black silk mask with a knot that had caught a strand of hair the color of banked coals in a winter fire.

Franklin believed that his niece wouldn't be attending. But that wasn't what she'd said. And Rush decided quickly from what he knew of his Jasmine Bandit, that if Amanda said she would go alone, the chances were that she'd do just that. A Christmas ball would be a fine opportunity to confront the saucy wench.

Rush had never cared much for the holidays, but this season was going to be interesting. So far Petersburg had lived up to all Houston's promises: a central location from which he could direct the stagecoach route, an opportunity to buy fertile farmland, and Amanda, the daughter who was even more intriguing than Rush could have imagined. For the first time in a long time, a Christmas ball sounded grand.

Later that same evening, Amanda's thoughts were moving in the same direction. She, too, welcomed the holiday season, the season for entertaining, for visiting, for settling debts and for starting anew. She'd attend the Christmas ball without an escort. A taste of intrigue would only make her plans more enticing to the unsuspecting single gentlemen in attendance.

An exchange of debt for service was what Franklin's new partner had said. She agreed. Once she chose the man she would marry, she'd make him an offer, one that he couldn't refuse. Planting tobacco required care, coddling and constant attention to make it flourish and produce. Finding a man shouldn't be so very different.

But just as planting tobacco called for supplies, so did the planting of an idea. Amanda needed a new gown, something spectacular, something that would bring top price if she, like Cadenhill tobacco, were being offered to the highest bidder. Franklin had cut off their credit, but one way or another, he'd pay.

Reluctantly, Amanda Caden began to dress herself in her father's frock coat and rough breeches. With a casual question at the supper table she'd confirmed that there was a dinner party tonight at the Hillyers, a party that would certainly draw Franklin. Franklin thought he'd found a way to bring her to her knees. Amanda felt no remorse at revenge, not when she could reclaim money that should have been hers. She had only to remember the barn in flames.

The moon was rising. It was almost time to go. Amanda's first attempt at robbery could have been a disaster. It was only luck that she'd escaped. With some time to think about it she realized there were several things she had to consider. First among them was that she couldn't be caught. Second, she'd have to come up with a way to account for her newfound funds. Not getting caught was simple. Nobody expected a highwayman. She had the element of surprise. Explaining where she got the money wasn't so easy.

Amanda sighed. She'd lost one of her father's pistols on her first run. She'd take no chances on losing the other. Instead, she loaded and familiarized herself with the pair she'd taken from Franklin's partner, tucked one in her boot and carried the other in her hand.

Becoming a bandit wasn't the solution she would have chosen, but she intended to enjoy stealing from Franklin Caden, deliberately and with purpose, just as he'd stolen from her father. She would be waiting outside the Hillyer house when he made his departure. She only regretted that Franklin couldn't know that it was she who was robbing him. There'd be no mistake about the occupant of the coach she robbed this time.

The survival of Cadenhill depended on her.

The Jasmine Bandit would ride tonight.

Chapter Five

The night sky was ominous, an eerie mist pierced here and there by a beam of light slipping through the boiling clouds that obscured the moon.

From the house on the hill came the sound of music, a fiddle and a harpsichord playing merrily in the distance. Though less impressive than either Cadenhill or the Taliaferro plantation, the Hillyer place was the largest house in Petersburg. Tonight it was lit up like a Yule log blazing in the night.

Amanda, perched on the low-hanging limb of an oak tree near the gate, pulled the point of her tricorne lower over her face in readiness. She fastened the buttons on her frock coat and shivered slightly, not from the cold but from a strange quiver of anticipation that had begun the moment she slipped the newly sewn silk mask over her face.

Tonight she would have Franklin's purse, fat with gold coins enough to buy both fabric for ball gowns and seeds for the tobacco she meant to plant. Controlling her nervousness she watched two carriages pass down the road, waiting for Franklin's coach, the Caden coach that demonstrated his position in the community. This time she meant to make no mistake about her victim.

Glancing about furtively she turned up the collar of her frock coat. There was no reason to believe that Franklin would recognize her, but she couldn't allow herself to be caught now. Her capture would end any hope she might have of saving her family's future.

Amanda juggled the pistol she was holding and smiled. There was some justice in using Mr. Thomas Rushton Randolph's gun to rob his partner. She touched the second pistol, wedged inside her boot. The thought of revenge soothed her nagging doubt. A Caden had never stolen. She'd be the first. Franklin, of course, had always been a cheat, but he wasn't a Caden.

Inside the manor house on the hill, Rush excused himself from his latest dance partner and slipped into the men's study where a game of billiards was in progress. After an hour of cautious circulating he began to relax. If there was anybody there who knew about his past they hadn't mentioned it. Perhaps he was finally safe from having to defend his actions. Having his fellow plantation owners trust him was important to his plan to settle in the Broad River Valley.

The evening was as dull as he'd supposed it would be, though his acceptance had gone smoothly enough. It didn't take a learned man to understand that his single status, coupled with the suggestion of breeding and wealth, made his presence desirable. Unfortunately, the women were neither desirable, nor did they smell of jasmine.

The billiard players he was watching were arguing about the coming legislative session, as they had been all evening.

"I tell you, Hillyer," Leroy Pope was saying, "the little farmers have the advantage over the big plantation owners now. They can combine their crops and get the same fees we do. They're bringing down the price of tobacco."

"As long as we sell directly to Franklin he'll be the one to control the prices," another planter offered.

"We could take it downriver ourselves," Leroy said.

Another plantation owner spoke up. "You're all wrong. It isn't the amount of tobacco that's hurting us, it's the quality. Letting it lie there in the warehouse open to the weather rots it. Then when it gets to England they throw it out. They aren't going to pay us for bad Georgia tobacco."

"And we'll stay in debt forever," Leroy commiserated. "Even Franklin's highwayman will learn. One holdup and I'll bet he moves on to better pickings."

The argument drifted into the major reason for selling to Franklin. How else could they get credit for the supplies they needed? It was agreed that keeping Franklin's goodwill was the final determinant.

Rush didn't join into the debate. The planters might appear to be successful, but one way or another, Franklin controlled all of them. While they might talk about bypassing him, Rush could see that they couldn't afford to do so. Franklin was in firm control. Rush's thoughts wandered until he heard a familiar name—Cadenhill.

"Even with all its debts Cadenhill is the plum of the valley all right, Leroy," one of the players was saying.

"And the largest," Leroy Pope agreed, "but with Houston gone, Cadenhill will belong to Franklin now."

"Too bad about the fire. Amanda needed that crop," Hillyer said as he tapped his ball sharply into the pocket. "But according to the judge, Franklin only has control until one of the women marries."

"Yes," Leroy agreed, "but Mrs. Caden isn't likely to remarry and Amanda . . . I can't think who'd want to take her on."

"Well . . ." There was a long, reluctant pause from a raw-boned man standing in the shadows. "I don't know as I'd be interested in that wildcat, even if Cadenhill was the prize. I'll admit that she's a comely enough wench, but that stubborn streak of hers—I don't know."

"Wench? Not to my way of thinking," Hillyer disagreed. "Amanda Caden may be a woman, but the truth is, she's a better man than most of us here."

"Yeah," Taylor Pinyon offered. "Me and Jed Willis happened on her once in the woods while we were hunting. Jed just tried to steal a kiss and she pulled a knife on him. Before he knew what was happening she'd cut his ties, and his drawers were hugging his boot tops. The woman just stood there laughing and dared him to set foot on her land again."

"What'd she do to you?"

"Nothing. I didn't stick around long enough."

"The slaves respect her," another voice said. "You couldn't pay one of them to run away. She treats them well, I've heard. Don't know that I approve of her methods, but she grows some fine tobacco."

"Amanda has a mind of her own, all right," Hillyer agreed. "She's smart, but if she got mad enough, your ties might not be the only thing she'd cut off."

"I hear that Franklin's going to marry her," Jed ventured.

Opinions varied among the men present, as one after another expressed his views.

"But he's her uncle," commented one.

"No, they aren't related," came the answer. "When old man Caden married Franklin's mama he took Franklin in and gave him his name, but he never officially adopted him. I'll bet Amanda didn't expect Houston to hand control of Cadenhill over to Franklin."

"Maybe not, but a plantation like Cadenhill being run by a mere girl just ain't proper, even if Houston did let her do it. Franklin's the only man in the family. Amanda'll do well to marry him."

At that moment Franklin Caden walked into the circle of light cast by the rack of candles over the game table and laid his hand on Hillyer's cue. "Gentlemen, I think you'd better concentrate on your game and forget any further discussion of my ward, Miss Amanda Caden. What you heard is right. I expect to marry her come June, when her mourning period is over."

"You're going to marry Amanda?" Shaler Hillyer laid down his billiard cue and extended his hand to his friend and business rival. "Sorry, Franklin, we didn't know."

"Well, it isn't official yet. But it was Houston's wish that I watch over the estate and look after the family. Though my ward is somewhat less than desirable as a wife, I have decided that our marriage is the most practical answer to my overseeing Cadenhill. I hope you understand that, gentlemen."

Hillyer nodded his head in agreement. "Of course, Franklin, that's certainly the Christian thing to do."

"That's what Houston wanted, old friend," Franklin announced, after letting them have their say. He added with just the right touch of drama, "A plantation needs a man's firm hand."

Rush listened. He had to hand it to Franklin. He knew how to play the martyr. Rush was content to stand by, on the fringe of the discussion, studying the men who would be his fellow planters once he found the land he wanted to buy.

Still, Franklin's open declaration of his intentions to wed his ward bothered Rush. He'd heard firsthand the lady's reaction to Franklin's plans. Amanda Caden wasn't a woman who was likely to allow herself to be run over. The picture of her encounter with the hunters in the woods was that of a woman who made her own decisions, just as had been her attempt to rob his coach. From what they were saying, Amanda had little experience with or interest in men. Rush didn't know how to explain the kiss she'd given him.

Neither did he know how to explain the memory of jasmine that seemed to be permanently etched in his mind.

He hadn't expected to find Amanda at the dinner party, but he admitted that he'd held out some secret hope that she'd be there. The time had come for him to call on Houston's family. He wouldn't delay any longer. He'd go tomorrow.

Now too much talk and too much port were making him weary. After Franklin announced his marriage plans, he suggested that they depart. Rush was more than ready. When their hostess voiced her regret, Rush read more than a personal invitation in the intimate squeeze of her hand and the inflection of her voice. So much for fidelity to marriage in Petersburg.

Perched on the low-hanging limb of the oak tree that reached across the entrance gate at the foot of the Hillyer drive, Amanda was growing restless. Her backside itched and the mask interfered with her breathing. She was about to decide that her plans had failed when she saw it, the distinctive black carriage with the gold crest on the door—the Caden coach, the first thing Franklin had confiscated after her father's funeral. She waited impatiently for the carriage to reach the gate and slow to clear the narrow opening.

Holding her breath, Amanda dropped lightly to the seat beside the startled driver as the coach passed beneath her. With a jab of the gun into his ribs and her low threat, the man swallowed his shocked oath and followed her instructions, leaping to the ground and disappearing into the darkness, without the occupants of the carriage being aware of the change of drivers.

Amanda took the reins and directed the horses down the road to a fork leading away from town. When she reached the spot where she'd tied her horse, she brought the team to a stop.

Taking up her pistol, she slid to the ground and jerked open the carriage door, relying on the element of surprise to prevent any resistance from the man she meant to rob.

Amanda pointed her pistol and opened the carriage door. "Good evening, sir..." she began, adopting a muffled growl, then amended her greeting to "gentlemen" as she realized that there were two in the carriage, not one.

"What's the meaning of this?" Franklin leaned forward, ready to reprimand the intruder.

"The meaning should be quite obvious, Franklin," the second man said in a droll voice. "We're about to be robbed. I'd like you to meet the highwayman I told you about."

Amanda bit back a cry of surprise. It was he, her tormentor, the man who'd tricked her into kissing him. She felt like clawing his eyes out. But tonight she had a more important quest. Still, she couldn't hold back a secret grin in the darkness. A bit of sport wouldn't be out of order. He needed a set-down, after what he'd done to her.

Amanda waved her pistol around so that the men would understand that she was serious, then leveled it at a spot midway between the two. The pistol was loaded, though she had no intention of using it, except as a threat. She hadn't expected two passengers, but she could still administer revenge and, as well, the extra booty would be useful. Leaning down, she pulled the second gun from her boot. Her threat had to be authentic or she was lost.

"I don't believe it—a highwayman?" Franklin's voice was racked with incredulity.

"Believe it," Amanda said stiffly, glad that the mask distorted her voice. Why was Franklin's partner joining in her charade? He knew well enough that she was a woman. "Your jewels and your gold, both of you."

"Perhaps we'd better follow the bandit's orders, Franklin. I don't think I want to test—his—aim. At least not in the dark. He just might hit one of us. And I for one would like to keep all my body parts. One never knows when, or by whom, some part might be in demand.''

"Smart move, governor," Amanda quipped, planning her revenge. She already had firsthand knowledge of two of his parts, his lips. That was an acquaintance she had no intention of renewing. However, he had given her an idea. "Perhaps I will make use of two of your parts at that."

Rush was more and more intrigued by the woman standing steady in the darkness. "Which parts of my body do you covet, sir?"

"Your hands, you devil. Franklin, was it? Stuff your jewels into your purse, throw it to the ground and hold out your wrists. And you, you smooth-talking rogue, use your cravat and tie him up!"

"You wouldn't dare!" Franklin protested feebly.

"Shall I demonstrate my determination?" She drew back the hammer on first one gun, then the other, the clicks sounding ominous in the silence.

"No, no! Do it, Rush. Here, use my linen."

Amanda stood away, listening for the jingle of coins as his money pouch hit the ground, followed by the shadow of Franklin's partner, who was following her directions.

"Is he tied up, Randolph?" she mumbled.

"You remembered my name. How nice." Rush smiled. Oh, yes, she knew him. She knew exactly whom she was robbing. What she wasn't aware of was that he was just as knowledgeable about the identity of his Jasmine Bandit.

"As tight as a Christmas goose. What about me?"

"You? You step outside, where I can see you."

"Of course. I don't suppose you'd allow me the same pleasure—seeing you, I mean."

"Not likely."

She had to hurry. The driver might double back and report the robbery to the dinner guests. At any minute they could be after her. This was taking too long.

Franklin's partner, the man who had cheated her out of the gold from the tobacco sale leaned forward, climbed out of the coach and stood up.

Under her watchful eye, Rush reached inside his jacket pocket and removed his purse. Meeting the lady bandit was almost worth losing his money.

Oh, Lordy. Amanda took a quick hurried breath. He was even bigger than she'd thought. She could feel the power of his restraint. There was a deceptive laziness about him, like a panther curiously watching his prey before he sprang into attack.

"Now, pick up the other purse and add your own money and jewels to it," she growled menacingly.

"You won't shoot me, will you? That's a fierce-looking weapon you have there." It ought to be, he thought. It was his. He recognized it when an errant beam of moonlight hit the silver falcon on the barrel. He'd positioned himself between Amanda and the coach, moving instinctively to protect her from Franklin's view. Amanda was safe, but he wasn't as certain about himself. For a moment Rush debated about overpowering her, but decided that for now he was bound to protect her identity.

Houston's request continued to burn in his mind. *Help Amanda.* And after what he'd heard in Franklin's office and what the man had done at the party to thwart Amanda's chances at a husband, Franklin deserved to lose his gold. Still, Rush was certain that this wasn't the kind of help Houston had envisioned that he would provide.

Rush reached down and found Franklin's purse. "Sorry to disappoint you, sir, but I wear no jewels. The only thing I have to offer is my money, and—" his voice dropped to a suggestive whisper "—me."

"You're the last thing I want." Amanda took a step to the side. "Hand over my prize and stand back." Amanda hadn't planned to exchange conversation with her victim, but he had an infuriating way of goading her into saying more than she'd planned. At least she had no fear of his recognizing her. They'd never met. And she was confident that Franklin was too scared and too far away to hear her clearly.

"I believe, my lady bandit," Rush said softly, "that this exchange puts you in my debt again, does it not?"

"Not this time, you thief. When last we met you collected a debt in exchange for a pouch of gold, a pouch that turned out to be your dirty—"

"Undergarments," he finished smoothly. "So I did. Ungentlemanly of me. And now you are here to collect."

"So I am. Hand over the purse."

"Of course." With his eyes now as accustomed to the darkness as hers, Rush could see her lush shape in the trousers and frock coat. She was wearing a black tricorne, cocked at a jaunty angle, and a new mask, rendering her face indistinguishable in the darkness. As the faint scent of jasmine wafted through the night air, Rush felt a tingle of excitement arch between them. He extended his hand.

Forcing Rush to move forward, Amanda waited, intent on retrieving the money while staying as far from Franklin as possible.

"You're right. You paid a debt before," he said in a low, daring voice, "in exchange for services you did not receive."

"Yes. You cheated me, you knave, and you know it."

"So I did." He held on to the purse and gave a slight bow. "And I give you my apologies. That was most unfair. I should return your payment. Of course, that's the right thing to do."

The moon went completely behind a cloud. Before Amanda knew what was happening Rush stepped forward, sliding his strong hand over her wrist, jerking her into his huge body and kissing her.

Whether from the intense excitement of her deed, or whether it was from anger over her stupidity in letting the man get too close, Amanda felt a surge of emotion sweep over her. His lips were rough, demanding, his tongue invading her mouth. He was pressing himself against her like the rutting stallion they used for breeding her papa's fine racehorses. Fire shot through her, feeding her senses and rocking her down to her toes. She could feel his body; the light fabric of her trousers offered no protection from the corded strength of his legs, from the burgeoning part of him already springing to life and throbbing between them.

She hadn't known she was curling her fingertips until she heard the shot and felt the man fall back in surprise. She hadn't even realized that one of the pistols had been caught between them, certainly not that it was being fired.

"God's blood! Your shot grazed my leg!"

"Damn!" she swore, stuffing the purse in her pocket and the spent pistol in her boot as she transferred the still-loaded weapon to her right hand. It had been an accident. She hadn't intended to shoot anybody.

"Rush! Rush! Don't provoke him!" Franklin called out. "I don't want to die over a few pieces of gold."

Amanda backed away, still trying desperately to gather her senses. If the driver hadn't already alerted the party guests, her shot certainly had. She had to get away. Her regret over the gunshot was centered on the risk of her possible discovery rather than on the discomfort of the rogue who had bested her once more.

"I don't intend to kill either of you," she snarled, her throat becoming sore from the affected deep tone she'd adopted to conceal her identity. "I shall keep you alive so that I can steal you both blind."

"If this is a challenge, my Jasmine Bandit," Rush said in a low laughing voice, "I accept."

Amanda backed out of reach, gave a whistle and heard her horse moving toward her. "Good. I only hope you have coin enough to finish out the game."

"Oh, I can play your game." He chuckled as he watched her climb into the saddle. "Once I know the rules."

In a voice barely above a whisper, which only Randolph could hear, she gave one last threat. "Get back inside, you devil, and heed my word of warning. Replenish your purse, and I'll teach you the rules, gambling man." Then, "My thanks to you, gentlemen. You've financed a most worthy cause this night."

Amanda waited until he was inside, gave a jaunty salute and slapped the haunch of the coach horses, sending them in the opposite direction as she galloped away.

She reined in her horse, feeling only a small regret when she saw with what pain her tormentor was struggling to get out of the carriage and into the driver's seat. But he managed and began to slow the horses. No matter. He couldn't catch her.

Amanda turned into the night and rode like the wind. This time, the jingle of the coins in her coat told her that her night's work was a success. The first part of her mission was complete, the easy part. The second part, finding a husband, wouldn't be so simple.

By the time Rush had brought the horses to a stop they were halfway back to town. Though his thigh pained him as if he'd been branded, he knew the leg had only been seared. His Jasmine Bandit had merely ruined a new pair of trousers. He was smiling as he opened the coach door and untied his partner.

"Did you have to bind me so tight?" Franklin rubbed his wrists.

"No. I could have let you be shot instead."

"Why didn't you tell me the highwayman was little more than a boy?"

"Would you admit to the world that a child held us up, Franklin?"

"No, I suppose that would make us look foolish," Franklin admitted. "Perhaps, in the interest of protecting our credibility, we should just keep quiet about this."

Rush climbed inside the carriage. "If your driver hasn't already spread the word, I'm willing to say no more."

"Did you recognize him, Franklin?"

"No. Why would you think I'm on speaking terms with a bandit? Probably one of the new immigrants. Nobody from around here would dare try to rob me."

Rush didn't know why he was so relieved. But he was. Houston's daughter or not, the woman was a thief. She'd already robbed him twice. He wondered for a moment if Houston had known his daughter was this diabolical. If so, it would certainly explain his old friend's request. Rush stretched out his leg and groaned. "You'll have to drive, Caden. The ball took a slice off the side of my leg."

"God's teeth, man, are you mortally wounded?"

"Well, I don't think I'll dance a jig any time soon, but my vital parts are still functional."

"But we have to go after the thief, man. He's got our gold."

"Oh, I intend to," Rush answered with a curiously deceptive air. "That highwayman is in debt to me and I always collect what I'm owed."

Chapter Six

A week later Amanda rode Thor across the field of sugarcane and reined in the chestnut stallion to watch the slaves chopping the cane with machetes. The big purple-green stalks dripped with the pungent-smelling juice.

Settie was directing the loading of the cane onto a wagon, which then hauled it to the grinder. There was a rhythm to the cutting and Amanda felt a great satisfaction watching the harvesting. She wheeled Thor around and followed the wagon back to the mill beyond the barn.

A large mule tethered to the grinding wheel was standing by, ready to lumber around in a circle, forcing the stone wheel to turn. Slaves would feed the stalks of cane between the turning wheel on the top and the stationary one on the bottom. Soon a thin stream of brown-green liquid would begin to run into a trough below.

Roman had the fire burning in the pit beneath the boiling box where the juice would be cooked into thick, sweet syrup. Her mother and sisters were in the house readying the jugs and corks for storage.

From where Amanda was waiting she could see across the north field where the stubble from last year's tobacco crop lay brown and brittle from the first cold snap of the winter. This acreage would be allowed to lie fallow. The last planting had been scarcely worth the effort. It seemed the more she needed a good harvest, the less she had to show for their efforts. The only gamble that had paid off was planting early. Her crop had been the first to market. But it had been Franklin who benefited, not her. Now she had devised a way to bring it in even earlier.

"Miss Amanda?"

Lovie had come up behind Amanda on foot. "Miz Caden says for you to come to the house. The dressmaker is here."

"Hell's doorknobs! She wasn't supposed to be here until after lunch!" Amanda reined Thor around and rode off toward the house at a clip, trying to decide how best to inform her mother and Catherine of what she planned to do. She should have told them at breakfast, but she couldn't, deciding instead to delay the news as long as possible.

Amanda slid off Thor at the back door and draped his reins over the rail. She strode inside and down the center hall to the parlor, where Catherine was plundering through the dress samples in frantic excitement.

"Oh, Amanda, I knew that you'd understand. Don't you just love this shade of blue?" She held the bolt of fabric against her, beneath her chin, and whirled around the floor.

"And I think this nice mauve color might be acceptable, don't you, Miss Gordon?" Iris was studying the dressmaker anxiously. "I mean, I know that the shade is a bit light, but Houston would have loved it."

"Mother—Cat..." Amanda began, wondering how she was going to explain that the dress wasn't for them, but for her. She couldn't. More than ever she understood her father's weakness where his girls were concerned. He couldn't refuse them and neither could Amanda. She'd have to find the money somewhere. She wouldn't ask Franklin.

Then Iris turned to face Amanda. The expression on her face changed from exhilaration to dismay. "What's wrong, Amanda?"

"Nothing, Mother."

"Yes, there is. Tell me the truth. Were we wrong to assume that you'd changed your mind about the dresses?"

"I—no, of course not, Mother. There will be dresses for all of you, Jamie and Cecilia, too, for the new year. But—for now there's only enough money for one dress—mine. I'm sorry." She turned to the dressmaker. "Can you have my gown finished by the weekend?"

For a moment Catherine looked as if she was about to cry. "Yours? You're going to Charity's Christmas ball—without us?"

Another time Iris might have comforted Catherine in her disappointment over Amanda's announcement that it was she who would go to the ball, not her sister. But this time it was Amanda whose hand she took.

"Why, Amanda? I don't understand."

"Quite simply, I'm putting myself on the auction block. I have to find a husband before June. I don't have time to shilly-shally around. The only way to save Cadenhill is for me to marry. Marriage nullifies Franklin's control."

"But Amanda, you can't attend unescorted! There will be gossip. The men won't understand what you're doing and the women will be horrified."

Amanda kissed her mother's forehead and slipped her hand from her mother's grasp. "I promise, I won't do anything foolish. I just don't have any time to waste."

"I never thought that you would, Amanda. Would that I had your restraint and determination. I might see a solution to the problems you've taken on. I don't think Houston knew what he was doing when he told you to look after Cadenhill. But you mustn't go to the ball alone. I'll come with you."

"No, Mother. If I make a fool of myself, I'd rather not do it in front of you." Amanda hugged her mother, then gathered herself to face the ordeal to come. "For heaven's sake, Cat, you know I don't have any idea what I'm doing. You'd better come advise Miss Gordon."

For a moment Catherine hung back, then after a nudge from her mother she swallowed her disappointment and complied. In a moment she was caught up in the excitement of the occasion and began to make suggestions. As quickly as possible Amanda got through the torture of being measured by the dressmaker, and excused herself with the plea of having work to do.

Amanda stood outside the door and leaned against it, listening to her family laughing and talking. It was a long time since she'd heard that kind of joviality in the house. She'd missed it and she hadn't even realized it was gone.

By the next day the dressmaker would have spread the gossip all over Petersburg that Amanda Caden would be attending the Taliaferro Christmas ball in search of a husband. It couldn't be helped. Establishing a social calendar where there had been none was proving more taxing than planting tobacco.

Amanda strode from the house, remounted her horse and rode away, taking her favorite path to the river. As she rode she let her mind skip randomly about, finally allowing it to settle with vengeance on the man she held responsible for the urgency of her quest—Franklin Caden—and his greed.

If it weren't for Franklin, Catherine wouldn't have to wait for her gown and Amanda wouldn't have had to promise something that she couldn't provide. But she had, and she wasn't sure where she'd get funds to spend on new dresses for the new year. One gown was a necessity, but more had been a foolish promise. The gold she'd taken from Franklin and his partner might not be enough to hold off disaster.

There wasn't enough time for the highwayman to ride again before the ball. Catherine would have to wait until New Year's Day. The future of Cadenhill had to come first.

Rushton Randolph arrived at the Taliaferro plantation just after dusk. He studied the mansion and nodded his ap-

proval. It was as elegant as any of those he'd left behind in
North Carolina, though not as large as Randolph Hall, and,
according to the locals, not nearly as fine as Cadenhill.

For Christmas the Taliaferro house was decorated with
pine boughs and holly berries. Nandinas and magnolia
leaves were tied with red ribbons in a garland down the long
white banister. Most of the furniture downstairs had been
removed, leaving only the chairs lining the rooms, which
opened one into the next, making one great hall. Hordes of
guests were chatting and sipping punch around the refreshment table. Hundreds of candles were lit along the walls like
sentries standing at attention. And a combination of in-
struments were tuning up to play.

As was the custom, all the guests who wished to dance had
placed their names in bowls, men's in one receptacle and
women's in another. Rush, intent on observing, declined, to
the disappointment of the women present. Drawing a name
for each dance scheduled before supper elicited excited
voices that rose and joined with the sound of the musicians
tuning their fiddles and limbering their fingers. The dance
cards were filled in and the dancing had begun when the
crowd suddenly hushed.

Rush heard the gasp of the gentleman standing beside him
and followed his gaze toward the woman in the doorway.

Like some titian-haired princess, Amanda Caden stood
regally in the doorway, framed like a painting by a carved
swirl of cupids overhead and a trail of roses down the adjoining posts. Her hair, fastened with lace and ribbons, was
pulled up and allowed to cascade down her back in a blaze
of glorious color. Her emerald-green dress, trimmed with
gold lace, hung in soft folds, her breasts barely covered with
fabric that shimmered in the candlelight like a river in the
sun. And she waited, as if her very presence was a dare, a
gauntlet thrown before the enemy to be challenged.

The red-haired woman in green—his Jasmine Bandit—
had bared her face and left her glorious hair uncovered this

night, but she was a more accomplished thief in the open than she'd ever been in the darkness. She was magnificent. As he caught her eye across the mass of upturned faces, he sensed her uncertainty. Yet he felt the overriding determination that subdued her fear. She was her father's daughter, all right. And he'd been entrusted with helping her.

She was tall and slender with skin brushed by the elements to a rich honey color that spoke of the sun and the outdoors. Her features were not small or delicate; rather they were open and honest. Her mouth, a little too wide, was set in a warning line of authority. Her eyes, shielded by the darkness on his previous encounters with her, were a shade somewhere between the green of an English countryside in spring and the opaque emerald stone just pulled from the earth. Amanda Caden was like that emerald, newly polished and exposed to the world in a moment of majesty, but not yet fashioned into what it could become.

For long moments the revelers simply stared. Then the music began again and those already dancing continued, moving past the doorway without a word to the woman now standing alone. Rush glanced around, waiting for someone to come forward to claim or welcome her. Franklin hadn't arrived yet. The judge was nowhere to be seen and his daughter, Charity, was ignoring Amanda Caden pointedly.

"Well now, would you look at that! It's Amanda Caden. First time I've ever seen her at one of these affairs," commented Pierce Jolley, a local merchant, with amusement. He was standing next to Rush. "I'd heard Franklin's ward was planning to come to the ball. I wonder if he knew."

"Yeah, heard she was hunting a husband," said a man Rush didn't recognize. He swallowed any further comment as he caught the censure in Rush's expression.

"Looks like she's been left at the starting gate, don't it?" a third man commented. "And I thought she was Franklin's intended. Think maybe we ought to welcome her?"

Rush didn't know what that remark was meant to imply, but he couldn't allow Amanda to stand there alone. He started around the edge of the room, fighting off the welcoming comments of the women who thought he might be about to claim them for a dance. His leg still twinged, but the wound had only been a graze. His explanation that he'd taken a spill from a horse had been accepted and, after a few snickers, forgotten.

"Mr. Randolph, good evening," a woman called out as he moved past.

Another tried to intercept him by standing as he passed. "You aren't dancing, Mr. Randolph. Did you put your name in the hat? My Louise is looking forward to dancing with you."

"Mr. Randolph, my husband says that your stage line is coming along."

One after the other tried to engage Rush in conversation. He had purposefully avoided dropping his name in the bowl for the first half of the evening. The last thing he wanted to do was get himself into a situation not of his own choosing with some matchmaking mother, for he knew the scarcity of available men since the revolution.

Proudly, but with a hint of uncertainty flickering in her eyes, Amanda continued to stand in the doorway. Rush didn't understand why the men hadn't descended on her like bees flocking to a honey tree. She was the most beautiful woman he'd ever seen, and they weren't blind.

But they hadn't and, somewhere inside his mind, Rush cringed because he understood. Franklin! The women were jealous and the men had been warned off.

In the doorway, Amanda wished fervently that she'd never commissioned the dress, never allowed Settie to hitch up the wagon and drive her to this plantation, and never thought that she could openly offer herself up for bid. Her father had been fond of saying that there wasn't a man in the house who had sense enough to know what she was worth.

Tonight she intended to look them over, see if he'd been wrong. It looked as if he hadn't been.

Just as she was about to wheel around and leave, she saw him, working his way around the room toward her, the one man she didn't want to meet—Franklin's partner—Thomas Rushton Randolph. Rushton Randolph was a danger to her. He was the only one who might recognize her as the Jasmine Bandit. And he was heading straight toward her.

Damn! The man was not just handsome, he was extraordinary. She'd never thought much about heaven and hell, but she suspected that Rushton Randolph would make a perfect Lucifer, particularly tonight. There was a hint of amusement laced with power in his face, bolstered by the careless way he moved, and the knowledge that she'd been staring at him. He towered above the other men. His black velvet coat spanned broad shoulders; his dark wine breeches hugged muscular thighs and buttoned just below the knees. Black stockings and plain shoes with silver buckles completed his dress. Severe, plain even, yet his garments fit his large body as though both clothes and man were sculptured from some great piece of the gray marble that sliced through the hills in the valley.

He was intensely masculine, yet his features were classic and pure. An unwelcome rush of fear raced through her as their gazes met and held. But it was the face, the laughing black eyes and the thick hair that made him so dangerous. He was no angel. Amanda knew that well. Rushton Randolph was the same black-hearted devil who had kissed her, not once, but twice. Her heart began to feel as if it were strangled by the tight bindings beneath her gown.

Trying not to panic, Amanda glanced around for a friendly face. There was none. The only face, now scowling, was the one heading toward her. Rush Randolph. The only consolation she had was that he didn't know who she was.

"Good evening, Miss Caden. I'm sorry I didn't see you arrive or I would never have let you stand here alone. You should have allowed me to call for you."

Rush took her gloved hand, touched it to his lips and tucked it beneath his arm, drawing her into the room as if he'd been expecting her.

"Smile, darling. Let them think this was planned." Rush tightened his fingertips on her hand and inclined his head as though they'd just shared a special secret.

"What?"

"You are about to be burned at the stake for making all these other women look like melting icicles in your presence. Hold up your head and show them who you are."

Amanda forced her lips into a smile. "Let me go. I don't know you, sir."

"I think you do, my Jasmine Bandit."

Amanda felt the air whoosh out of her lungs.

"You're out of your mind, sir." Amanda tried to think of what to do. She'd never expected to be instantly recognized, not by this—man. The worst had happened. What would he do?

"Don't worry, my lady. Your secret is safe with me. I'm not about to give you away. I'm about to save your beautiful neck." He gave her a smile that dared her protest. "At least I'm trying to, if you'll cooperate."

Amanda couldn't move. She couldn't speak. Everyone in the ballroom was staring at them. Even the music seemed to stop. All Amanda could hear was the pounding of her heart. She'd known the evening would be bad, but she had never expected to lose all control. Then suddenly she looked into his eyes and saw the hint of conspiracy and glee.

He was a daredevil, this newcomer. He knew the risk he was taking in defying those who had so pointedly ignored her. She felt the beginning of a smile tug at the corners of her lips. He was offering his help—again. She disliked the man heartily, but she'd accept his offer.

"Good evening, Mr. Randolph," she said stiffly, dropping her eyes as she consciously softened her tone. "I'm sorry that I'm late."

He looked puzzled for a moment, then laughed as he tucked her arm beneath his and directed her farther into the room, as if their meeting were prearranged.

"You are a rare treat, Miss Amanda Caden," Rush said, stopping this time and acknowledging with slight bows the same women he'd ignored a moment ago.

"And what are you, Mr. Randolph?"

"I'm either a fool, or a very wise man. I haven't decided yet. The only thing I'm certain of is that I'm the only one here who isn't too timid to claim you. What exactly are you doing here—checking out your future victims?"

"Victims? You're a fine one to talk of victims—you who've thrown in with a crook. Where is your partner, by the way?"

"If you're looking for your fiancé, I don't believe that he's joined the ladies yet."

"He's not my fiancé. And if I were looking for a man, it wouldn't be him."

"Then it must be me. Here I am. Do with me what you will. Good evening, Mr. Jolley. I believe you know Miss Caden?" Rush stopped opposite the man, waiting for the merchant to acknowledge Amanda's presence. "I understand that you're into horse racing, Mr. Jolley. Miss Caden is a good judge of horseflesh, too."

"Eh, yes, certainly. Everybody knows she has the fastest horse in the valley. Good evening, Miss Caden." Pierce Jolley gave a half bow, his face flaming as he realized that Rush had overheard the earlier comments.

Amanda nodded and turned quickly away, anxious to find a spot where she could quietly die. "What are you doing, Rushton? I'm not looking for a horse."

"No, I'm thinking that you're the one that's being marketed this evening. I saw you standing there surveying the ballroom. You may have these people fooled, but I know who you really are, and you're after something."

Amanda said nothing, wishing that she'd never, ever decided to come here. Her plan was disintegrating into a failure more devastating than she'd envisioned. Not only was she being shunned, but her means to finance Cadenhill's future was in danger of being exposed.

What did the man want? She ought to jerk herself away from him and go home. There had to be another way to find a husband. Then she caught sight of the envy on the faces of the women watching frostily from across the room.

"I'm not after anything, Mr. Randolph, except some punch. Do you think you could get me some?"

"And let you dash out the door the minute my back is turned. No, darling. You came here to be seen, I'm thinking. So let the men look and the women die of jealousy."

"I would if I thought it would do any good."

Rush heard the faint quiver in her voice. She truly was scared, though he'd never have known it. For a moment he was angry at the men in Petersburg. What fools they were. "At least you're honest, Miss Caden. You're just inexperienced. Look, haven't you ever heard that all you have to do to sell a racehorse is to have somebody bid on him?"

"I'm not a racehorse, Mr. Randolph. And I'll thank you to let me go."

"No, you aren't. But so far, it looks as if I'm the only bidder you have. Uh-oh, she's not a bidder, but she's a force to be reckoned with. Be nice, bandit."

"Good evening, Amanda." Charity Taliaferro danced by, pausing for a moment as she stared furiously at the man escorting her surprise guest with such ease. "We're so pleased to see you. We really didn't expect you out yet, with your father's being put away such a short time ago. Is Catherine here?"

"Catherine isn't feeling well," Amanda said softly. "As you know, my father didn't believe in lengthy mourning. He would have wanted us to accept your invitation. I hope you don't mind that it is I."

"Of course not." Charity frowned slightly as she examined the dress Amanda was wearing. It was clear from her expression that she did mind. Very much. "Where is your fiancé this evening?"

"I have no fiancé, Charity. I'm here alo—"

"She's here this evening with me," Rush broke in. "I'm escorting Miss Caden in Franklin's place."

"Oh, I see." The dance ended and a new partner stepped up to claim Charity for the waltz that was beginning, drawing her away from Amanda and Rush. Reluctantly Charity allowed herself to be whirled away and into the crowd.

"Why'd you say that?" Amanda tried to pull her hand away from Rush's grip. "You're not my escort. I'll not have it. You'll ruin everything I want to accomplish. Go away!"

"Amanda Caden! You're a single woman, and single women in Petersburg may dash about the countryside under the cover of darkness, wearing a mask, but they don't attend a ball without family or a proper escort. Though I'm afraid you've already created a scandal, so you might as well pretend that you're enjoying yourself and dance with me."

"Dance? I don't know how to dance. I never had time to learn." What she should have said was that she never took the time. Only a few lessons from her mother had gone a long way. And the only steps she'd ever learned were those of the minuet. This was not a minuet. This was a waltz.

"I'll teach you and you can tell me what this is all about. What did you plan to accomplish by coming here this evening in a dress that practically says 'take me'?"

Before she could protest, Amanda felt herself being turned in Rush's arms so that she had no choice but to look up at him. Up. That was a luxury she didn't often have. Most of the men in the valley were only slightly taller than she, if that. She tried to jerk away, a flash of anger coloring her eyes when she could not. With his right hand firmly holding her waist and his left hand holding her hand he forced her to follow his movements.

"Just let yourself feel the rhythm, Amanda. This is a waltz, not a fencing match. It's all right to touch now and then."

It wasn't all right. It was all wrong. The evening wasn't going the way she'd planned. From the time she'd slipped the green dress over her body she'd felt the excitement begin. Like seeing the first green shoots of tobacco poke through the soil each spring. Like waiting in the darkness for the carriage to appear the first night she'd gone out to steal. Like the moment Thomas Rushton Randolph had touched his lips to hers.

Now her heart was beating wildly, a rapid persistent hammering that thundered so loud she feared its sound would carry over the level of the music and the merry laughter of the dancers. She tried in vain to push away the feeling of danger that seemed to intensify with every touch of Rushton Randolph's hand against her back. The wild quivery feeling had pulsed unbidden into life and she couldn't call it back.

She couldn't stop it, either. She couldn't take the chance of offending the man who'd become her champion; he could just as easily become her persecutor. Amanda tilted back her head and smiled. She was dancing with the only other man in Petersburg whom she wouldn't consider for a husband. Still, she was forced to admit, as she began to follow the pattern of dance Rush was leading, that the men whirling by were watching more boldly. Maybe there was something to be said for having a bid.

"A racehorse, hmm?" Suddenly she felt a lilt of excitement, which was also an apt description of her first venture into society. Besides, she couldn't stop Rushton Randolph if he chose to give her away. She might as well accept his vow of silence and try not to antagonize the man—at least until she'd accomplished her purpose.

"A fine chestnut filly, prancing at the starting gate," Rush said, pulling her close for a quick second as they whirled around the room. "Just go on pretending that you're interested in me, and I'll do the same."

But he found to his surprise he wasn't pretending. The woman was enchanting, and he was enjoying himself in a way he hadn't expected.

"Tell me about your horse. I'm told he's the fastest one in the valley."

"Thor is magnificent. Father brought him back from Charleston when he was only a colt. He's the offspring of a champion."

"As is his mistress," Rush said. "All she needs is someone who recognizes a winner."

Amanda threw her head back, allowing a peal of laughter to escape her lips. "Maybe you're right, Mr. Randolph. Maybe this is a horse race. I like contests and I intend to win my prize. Even if it means pretending to be interested in a rogue like you."

"Fine. And I intend to collect the debt you owe me, too," he answered just as lightly, pulling her a bit closer under the pretense of twirling her around.

"What debt, Mr. Randolph?"

"I believe there is the matter of a purse of gold, taken from my person. I think that means I'm due another kiss."

"Over my dead body," she snapped.

"That wouldn't be much fun. I prefer the woman beneath me to be alive—very much alive."

"Is this called flirting, Mr. Randolph?"

"I believe it is, Miss Caden."

"Then I'd prefer that you stop flirting. It isn't necessary at all, Mr. Randolph."

"Oh, but that's what is expected of a gentleman who intends to win a kiss from his lady, Miss Caden."

"You've already kissed me, twice. I won't let it happen again."

"But you've already announced to the gentry of Petersburg that you're available. They'll never believe that you're some shrinking violet. They're going to expect you to be a bit more outrageous. And you aren't, not yet."

"And what makes you think I'm not?" she asked seriously, then remembered that they were being watched and gave him a wide smile.

"Very good. You're learning. The dress is a good start. You look like—" he gave her a rakish grin as he slid his gaze across the low-cut dress and back again "—I won't say an angel because I know that you would never try to fool anybody with such a pose."

"Then what, Mr. Randolph? You seem to be rather well acquainted with women. What kind of woman am I?"

Rush hadn't intended to flirt with Amanda Caden. Standing in the doorway she'd seemed so alone; he understood being shunned. His impulsive offer to be her escort was prompted by a rare twinge of compassion rather than the kind of stubbornness that often placed him in tricky situations.

It was clear that Amanda cared little for what society thought. Her courage stoked his own. Perhaps if she'd been in Albemarle he might not have been so quick to leave home. She'd have understood his love for his family home and his great pain at being ostracized.

He abhorred the custom where local planters increased their land holdings and passed on the entire estate to the oldest son, whether or not that son cared about planting. The Randolph estate belonged to Richard, Richard the first son, Richard the image of his father. Richard who never had the imagination to try new crops and new methods, but only followed in his father's footsteps, planting the land over and over, year after year, until it was used up.

All Rush's suggestions had been laughed off as being foolish ideas. Finally he'd given up and gone to England, where he'd stayed until the revolution broke out. Then, because of Houston Caden, he'd taken on the role of British sympathizer. Rush had never believed that his family would turn their back on him. He'd expected them to understand and believe that he was simply following orders. They hadn't. He'd become an outcast.

Just like Amanda.

He could understand what she was doing and why. And he could help her, just as her father had helped him. He *would* help her, damn it, he was obligated. But more than that, the past was the past, and he refused to let it temper his actions anymore. If Petersburg townfolk learned that he'd once been accused of being a traitor to the patriot cause, he'd deal with the backlash—just as Amanda was dealing with her past.

Her flashing green eyes, the scent of jasmine, the bold dare in her expression all tantalized him. But this woman was his partner's intended fiancée. He acknowledged the risk he was taking—acknowledged it and tossed it aside.

"What kind of woman do I think you are?" He repeated her question. "The kind of woman who needs a man like me."

Amanda gasped. The waltz ended, and a voice cut short the reply she tried to articulate.

"Excuse me, Miss Caden," the voice ventured, "but I wonder if I might claim you for the next dance?"

Jamerson Kitchens was standing at Amanda's shoulder, waiting hesitantly. Behind him Amanda could see Franklin enter the room, cast his eyes around the dance floor and see her. He blanched and headed in their direction.

The music started again.

"Why not, Mr. Kitchens? I think that would be lovely." Amanda moved from Rush's arms into those of the startled Jamerson Kitchens and together they joined other couples in a minuet. Thank heavens Jamerson had stepped forward before Franklin reached her, she thought.

Amanda took a deep breath and tried not to think about how near to disaster she'd come. Mr. Randolph could have given her away. He still could. She didn't know what to do or how to stop him. Her fate was in the hands of a bold outspoken blackguard. But he hadn't exposed her. She didn't know why. She couldn't let her fear of him thwart her plan. Either he was telling the truth about concealing her secret, or he wasn't. She had to take the chance.

Amanda gave her partner a bright smile, pushing aside Rush's outrageous statements. Three dances later, she was forced to admit that she was out of breath and that Rush had been right. The only thing necessary to market a good horse was one high bid. If the right person thought the horse was valuable, every other bidder reconsidered.

Now she was having a glass of punch with Shaler Hillyer, watching the envious looks of the other women, who were forced to dance with the men whose names they'd drawn, whereas Amanda, who'd arrived late and had no dance card, was able to pick and choose. If the truth were known, Amanda had yet to see a man who interested her, but at least the bidding was proving more interesting than she'd expected, until she heard a dreaded voice speak her name.

"Amanda, my dear, I'm so glad that you changed your mind and decided to attend the ball."

Franklin Caden stood beside Amanda. His sticky gaze seemed not only ready, but designed to devour her with its intensity. "I believe they're about to serve supper. Shall we adjourn to the dining hall?"

Amanda found herself being led into the dining area, her arm held tightly in Franklin's grip. She frowned at her father's stepbrother, clenching her teeth in silent fury. He was announcing his claim and if she allowed him to, she'd never accomplish her goal.

"Turn me loose, Franklin," she whispered, "or I shall smack you!"

"Not tonight." Franklin laughed. "There are too many people watching. You wouldn't dare. Did I tell you that you look lovely this evening, my dear."

Franklin's smile was entirely too close to a leer and the old familiar revulsion quickly swept over Amanda. He was right. Once again she couldn't protest.

"I fear I'm about to faint, Franklin. Suddenly I feel very light-headed." Amanda closed her eyes and fanned herself with the lace handkerchief she was holding.

"Fine. Faint if you like. I'll be glad to see you home. No one will be surprised at your collapse. After all, you're here attending a Christmas ball when your father is scarce in the ground. You're wearing a gown that most women here would say came right off a London doxy. Such action will make them consider my marriage offer a kindly act. Let me help."

Franklin took her feigned attack as an excuse to slide his arm around her waist and assist her away from the dancing area. In the crowd his fingers brushed boldly against her breast even as he nodded graciously to passersby.

"You snake," Amanda hissed under her breath, widening her smile at Jed Willis and Taylor Pinyon and the young woman following them, whom she recognized as Taylor's sister.

Amanda remembered their encounter in the woods that day, and she could tell from Jed's expression that he remembered as well. Tonight she didn't have her knife, but her eyes cut to his suspenders and both of them recalled his standing there with his breeches hugging his ankles.

"Aren't you going to ask her to dance, Jed?" Taylor asked, with a snicker.

"I don't think so. You go ahead. I seen you drooling over her. I don't have to be scratched by a bear but once to be scared of its claws."

"What did she do to you?" the young woman asked, eyes wide as she leaned coyly against Jed's arm.

"It doesn't signify," Jed answered in a growl. "Tell your sister to behave herself," he said to Taylor, "or I'll let her find another partner for supper."

"Behave yourself, Sissy," Taylor snapped, his eyes still focused on Amanda. "It don't seem to bother Franklin none that she's so bold. And she is a sight prettier than I remembered."

Taylor's sister went on in a voice just loud enough to carry. "Now, Taylor, it might pay you to make up to her some. It's obvious what the woman's doing. She's an old maid, and she knows it. This is her last chance to catch herself a man."

"Not me, but I'll bet there are some who'd take the dare."

"Well," Sissy said, "she was too good for us when her papa was alive. The rest of us have already decided that she won't be invited to any decent woman's house in the valley."

"Still, she's got all that good farmland . . ." Jed argued.

"So's her sister," Taylor observed. "If you want a woman, Jed, I'd think about her sister, Catherine. At least she's a lady."

"Well, Amanda." Franklin's voice was obscenely smug. He'd heard the conversation, too, and he was ready to use it to his advantage. "You must see how hopeless all this is. Whatever your plans were for this evening, I don't think they're going to work out."

Across the room Rush Randolph leaned against the veranda door and watched. His leg throbbed from both the dancing and his recent wound. Watching his Jasmine Bandit in the company of his partner bothered him—more than he cared to acknowledge. Rush felt a fierce stab of unexpected jealousy.

And then Amanda turned, catching his gaze with eyes filled with desperation.

Before Rush realized what he was doing he was halfway across the room. "Amanda, forgive me for leaving you alone for so long. Are you ready for supper? Good evening, Franklin. Lovely party, isn't it?"

Adroitly, Rush managed to transfer Amanda from Franklin's side to his own, gave a quick bow to the Willises and threaded Amanda between them and then away from the startled Franklin Caden toward the other side of the room.

"You've saved me again, Mr. Randolph." Amanda breathed a sigh of relief. "Thank you." She added, "I think."

"You're welcome, I think."

"I don't seem to be handling my auction very well. I can't get away from Franklin without finding myself caught by another rogue. I suppose this means you expect further compensation?"

"Compensation? Yes—repayment is exactly what I had in mind, my little bandit." Suddenly the veranda door was open and they were standing outside in the cool night air.

Too late she remembered Rush's threat. She was already in debt to him, and he was a man who always collected. She tried to turn away, colliding with him in the turning. Her knee caught his leg and he groaned, buckling slightly before he found his footing.

"God's blood, woman! First you shoot me, now you're trying to wound my—other parts."

"Oh...your wound." Amanda caught herself. She'd shot him, all right, and she hadn't even inquired about his leg. Of course asking would have given credence to his charge. But there was no point in pretending that she wasn't guilty. She was. He knew it and she knew that he knew.

"I'm very sorry about that," she said contritely. "But you shouldn't have kissed—startled me."

"And I suppose you expect an apology?"

Light from the ballroom spilled across the balcony. The whirling dancers inside cast shadows across the floor, like silhouettes dancing in the moonlight. Amanda walked away from the light where she couldn't see the amusement in Rushton Randolph's eyes.

Being alone with a man was new to her. Being held in his arms, smelling his masculine scent resulted in an unsettling quivering in her stomach. He made her uncertain and she didn't like that. But the uncertainty was more than indecision. Her stomach was tied in knots, and instead of cooling, her breathing seemed to fan the tiny flame of heat inside her, coaxing it into a roaring fire. She felt as if she were burning from the inside out.

What happened between a man and a woman was no mystery to Amanda. She'd run the plantation too long to be ignorant of reproduction. But suggestive conversation and flirting was something she wasn't prepared for.

"You'd better kiss me quickly, Amanda. We'll be missed, and that will further soil your reputation." He walked over to where she was standing.

"You're joking."

"I never joke about kissing a beautiful woman." This time Rush didn't hurry her. He simply took her face in his hands and touched his lips to her startled ones, parting them with warm, gentle pressure.

Adding to the fire skimming along beneath her skin, a curious weakness invaded her body as his hand curved her shoulder. His mouth was warm, tinged with the fruity taste of the punch he'd been drinking. His lips played across her mouth, never invading, yet never releasing so that she couldn't claim satisfaction of the debt and pull away.

Against her will she relaxed and swayed closer.

"Amanda," he whispered as his hand crept across her shoulder and settled on the back of her neck.

She heard the swift intake of his breath and felt the brittle tension in the air between them, the same kind of thick, hot pressure that seared her lungs in the fire.

"No," she protested in sudden doubt, "you shouldn't."

"That's only one little kiss. I figure that I'm due at least one more real kiss in payment for my silence. You remember, an even exchange?"

She remembered. What she didn't remember was sliding her arms around his neck, or turning her face so that he could claim her lips with ease. But she had, and she did, and this time the kiss was neither gentle, nor slow.

Unbidden excitement crackled as she felt his hard length against her. His taut muscles rippled beneath her fingertips as his hand slid around her ear and paused beneath her chin. His thumb traced the hollow in her throat and moved lightly across the bare tops of her breasts as he reclaimed her lips with urgency. This time he plundered her mouth, tugging at her with his tongue like the current of the Broad River tearing at the bank. She was being swept helplessly along, and suddenly, feeling trapped, she jerked away.

"Please stop—"

Rush leaned back against the veranda rail and took in a deep breath, forcing himself to relax. He hadn't intended to lose control, merely to teach the wench a badly needed lesson. But the moment their lips touched that had changed. Now it was he who needed to regain the upper hand.

"I'd better tell you that I have no gold in my pockets tonight. So you might as well not don your mask and gun."

Mask and gun? Amanda forced herself to remember why she was here. The remembering brought a flush of anger at her weakness. "What I need tonight isn't dress money, Mr. Randolph. Tonight I'm looking for a husband with a safe filled with gold."

"Then I'm afraid that you're going to be disappointed. Other than Franklin, there probably isn't a man here tonight with enough gold to buy a chamber pot."

Amanda gave out a chortle of disbelief. "There's you, Mr. Randolph. Do you have a safe filled with gold?"

There was something serious about her question, about the way she held so still in the darkness, waiting for his answer. He could have lied, but he didn't. He simply told the truth, "Not full, not yet, but I intend to."

"Then if you have no gold, Mr. Randolph, you're of no use to me. I'd better go back inside."

She started back toward the French doors, paused and looked back at the man who, only moments before, stopped her heartbeat. "I can't afford to waste my time on a man who can't give me what I need."

"You're wrong," Rush said softly. "I may not be able to give you what you want, but I'm the only man here who can give you what you need."

Chapter Seven

Rush Randolph was at the warehouse early the next morning. He intended to study the problem of protecting the tobacco from the elements.

Stepping inside the warehouse, Rush took in a deep earthy tobacco breath and glanced at the crude calendar hanging beside the door. The stage had been due yesterday. It was a week since the last coach had come through. The mail, carried by horseback, was more reliable so far than his stages.

Now that he'd reached the area where he wanted to settle, he was anxious to get the stagecoach line operational. He hadn't set a timetable—until now. Until he'd met Amanda Caden and learned that Franklin Caden was determined to marry her in June.

"Randolph, I'd like to see you in my office."

Franklin Caden was standing on the balcony overlooking the warehouse below. From the look on Franklin's face, Rush knew that he was displeased. He'd expected that. Claiming to be Amanda's escort at the Taliaferros' ball had bordered on a public insult to Franklin, though he'd quickly fallen in with Rush's explanation that he was only escorting Amanda at Franklin's request. Franklin had insisted on following Amanda home, and Rush had expected to hear about it today.

"Certainly, Franklin," he agreed, and followed his partner up the stairs and into his office.

Franklin closed the door and walked slowly around his desk, pulling a cigar from his pocket and taking a long time to prepare and light it. He didn't invite Rush to be seated and Rush didn't speak.

"I'm generally regarded as a fair man," Franklin began, "and there are few citizens in Petersburg who would take issue with me or my decisions."

Rush continued to wait. Franklin wanted to be in charge. Rush had learned a long time ago that there were times when it paid to let people think they had the upper hand.

"You came here at my brother's request, therefore I feel responsibility for your acceptance. You're new in our community and can't be expected to understand our traditions. So I am willing to give you the benefit of the doubt. Do you understand what I'm saying?"

"No, I can't say that I do. Go on, Franklin, explain."

"Last night I was made to look like a fool in front of the citizenry. I will not have that."

"I'm not sure what you mean, Franklin. Perhaps you'd care to be more specific."

"Amanda Caden," Franklin said, his lips narrowing into a thin line of challenge. "I told you that I intend to marry her and then you claimed to be her escort. I won't be made to look a fool. Do you understand?"

"I think so, Franklin. But I believe we have a problem here."

"Yes, and I'm taking care of it—now. You will have nothing further to do with my fiancée."

Rush concluded that any disagreement he voiced would be tantamount to holding a red flag in front of a bull. But even if he could forget Houston's odd request that Rush help Amanda if anything ever happened to him, he couldn't justify letting Franklin claim Amanda by forfeit. Though Franklin was his partner, Rush's loyalty still belonged to

Houston. Boldly he allowed himself to speak the truth as he saw it.

"The lady tells me that she is not your fiancée and that, in fact, she is looking for a husband. I hadn't intended to offer myself as a candidate—until last evening. But I have changed my mind."

This time Franklin could barely contain his fury. He held his breath until his cheeks were red and his eyes began to bulge. "You are my partner, Randolph, in a business venture that benefits us both. But that could change."

"Agreed. Would you care to buy back my half of the warehouse?"

"That is impossible at the moment, Randolph. I have to be concerned with the plantation debts. But Amanda Caden will be my wife, or she will lose Cadenhill. If you think that you, or any other man in the valley, is more important to her than her land, you're dead wrong. I warn you, stay away from her."

Rush turned toward the door, stopped and looked back at Franklin Caden. "You're right. Our partnership is business. I can separate that if you can. And Cadenhill is more important to Amanda than a husband. Land, family, I can understand that. And I understand Amanda. Pity you don't. That's why you're going to lose both."

The door closed behind Rush, but not before he heard Franklin's parting words. "You don't know it, Randolph, but if you don't conform you're on shaky ground here, just like Amanda. I've sponsored you and I can ruin your reputation just as easily."

Rush didn't answer. Franklin was right. Though their business dealings were secure, Petersburg was like Albemarle, measuring a man by his reputation. And that had always been his Achilles' heel. No matter how often his past actions had been explained, the shadow of doubt remained.

Just like Amanda. Franklin's words were more true than he knew. And this wasn't the first time this thought had occurred to Rush. Amanda was attempting to conform. He could tell her that it was no use. He'd tried and failed, and so would she.

After Rush left, Franklin narrowed his eyes and sat behind his desk. Perhaps in his greed he'd made a mistake. Perhaps Randolph's usefulness had ended. Franklin had Rush's gold and there was no reason to cater to the man further.

In fact, it was to Franklin's benefit that the stagecoach line not prove to be profitable. After all, people had been using his Petersburg barges for transportation up to now. There was no reason for them to change, and there was certainly no reason for Franklin to share his profits with the stagecoach line. The less profit Rush showed, the more likely he was to move on, after he was forced to sell out—cheap.

Franklin thought about the night he and Rush had been robbed and he began to smile. Why not encourage the bandit? In fact, why not give him a helping hand?

The public knew about the robberies. They didn't know that he was a lone bandit, and Franklin saw even less reason to share that knowledge. In fact, it was to his advantage to enhance the reputation of their thief.

Rush was on his way to Augusta tomorrow, where he'd spend Christmas, returning in time to wager a large share of his remaining gold on the horse race that Franklin was holding on New Year's Day. Franklin decided that after he'd taken Randolph's gold, he'd make certain that the highwayman made Rush very unhappy in Petersburg. He'd show Mr. Randolph that he'd been a bit too clever this time.

Franklin had a plan.

Meanwhile, Franklin would have a little talk with his sister-in-law, Iris. Too bad Iris wasn't a few years younger. She was much more malleable than her daughter. He could have married her and gained control of Cadenhill. None of this would then be happening. But it was Amanda whom he wanted, whom he'd always wanted, whom he intended to have. Cadenhill was simply a bonus.

Amanda was the prize.

Amanda gave Thor his head. The trees, mostly evergreens, shielded the sunlight from the forest floor as the horse crashed through the pine straw on sure hooves, dodging rocks and jumping gnarled roots and brambles. These wild rides had set Thor's reputation as the fastest horse in the valley and had provided her with salvation during the long weeks and months when her father had been involved in the struggle for independence. This time the ride brought no solace.

The day was warm. She pulled off the battered felt hat she habitually wore and let her hair fly free. She rode past the spot where she'd met Jed Willis and Taylor Pinyon in the woods last year and grinned as she remembered slicing Jed's suspenders. He'd been embarrassed, but even in his undergarments, with his trousers hugging his ankles, he'd been unable to conceal his interest in her.

Neither had Mr. Thomas Rushton Randolph, she thought. Her face flamed as she remembered his kiss on the patio, changing to a frown of displeasure as she recalled the disapproving looks of the guests who'd seen her return to the ballroom. She hadn't known what to expect from her foray into society, but she hadn't expected her uncle's partner to ruin it for her.

She wondered what the Petersburg community thought about her now, after the Christmas ball, then decided she didn't really care. If a man wasn't strong enough to speak out for her, she wasn't interested. She had no use for a man who didn't know his own mind or have the strength to stand by his principles.

But now her principles put her and her family at risk. Cat was too young to marry, and she couldn't imagine her mother taking another husband. Everything was up to Amanda. Attending the Christmas ball had been the first step in her desperate effort to join the society that she'd always rejected. And had it not been for Mr. Randolph's rescuing her, her public attempt would have been a failure.

Her private ventures as a highwayman had been more successful. Still, she had to find a better long-term solution. Robbing crooks like Franklin and the bold, kissing devil who was his partner was one thing, but she couldn't justify robbing her father's old friends. She nudged Thor, urging him to go faster.

Bursting out of the woods onto the riverbank, Amanda moved so quickly that the mounted man in the path watching her race across the field had no chance to move out of the way. Both horses reared, snorted and fought for the path.

"Hell's doorknobs," she swore and slid from the horse's back. She stepped into the woods in a motion so fluid that the trespasser was able to move past without being pushed into the water. "What are you doing on my land?"

"Your land?"

Amanda slapped her crop across her knee and whirled around ready to use it for a weapon if necessary. "You!" It wasn't being angry that made her voice so sharp when she recognized the intruder. It was surprise.

Rush Randolph sat astride his horse as if he owned the forest. His dark wine-colored riding coat was buttoned snugly over his broad chest, falling across well-corded thighs and muscled legs encased by highly polished black Hessian boots. A fall of dark hair ruffled his forehead, framing laughing eyes and an amused smile.

"My land, sir. This is Cadenhill and you're trespassing. I'll thank you to leave."

"Suppose I tell you that I'm here on business."

Amanda didn't answer for a moment. "Business? I can't imagine what kind of business we could have." She didn't know what she'd expected him to say, but that wasn't it.

Oh, but I can imagine, Rush wanted to say. Standing there, eyes flashing, flaming hair caught by the rays of the sun, Amanda Caden couldn't begin to understand what he could envision between the two of them. She was wearing a pair of men's trousers, a white shirt laced at the neck and a kind of vest. There was a sprig of pine straw caught in her hair, and he almost reached out to remove it when he realized that she would likely use that crop on him. He'd better state his business.

"That your mill downriver?"

"Yes. Did you come to buy meal?"

"No. I came to buy land to plant cotton. This ground looks fertile and it's close to the water. Would you consider selling this strip of land?"

"Sell Cadenhill? Never! Besides, this land is too close to the water for planting. Most years it floods."

"But this land wouldn't be used for planting. I'd want the strip north of here for that. Here I'm interested in the fish."

"The fish? You're going to become a fishmonger?"

"No, I'm going to use the fish to grow cotton." Rush nudged his horse forward. He had caught her attention. She'd forgotten about throwing him off her land.

"Cotton? I don't understand. What do fish have to do with cotton?"

"Fertilizer." He slid from his horse and tied him to a tree. "The Indians learned about fertilizer long before we ran them off their farmlands, but it was General Washington who put the practice into use."

"What? Running Indians off their land?"

"No, fishing the Potomac and burying the fish in the fields he intended to plant. The crop yield is much improved."

"Oh? And do you know this to be true?"

"I saw it with my own eyes."

"You know the President?"

"I know him, as did your father."

Amanda felt a quickening of her pulse that she tried to push away. She didn't like the strange feelings that persisted in bubbling forth when he was near. He made her think of him, and not the more important issues that needed her attention. Yet, talking with Mr. Randolph was almost like having a discussion with her father. He was willing to consider her questions and few men did that.

She turned away from the big man who'd caught her attention with his knowledge and walked closer to the water. "Did you know my father?"

"Only indirectly," Rush lied, holding back the truth. Explaining that he'd worked for Amanda's father, that he'd allowed himself to be branded as a spy at Houston's urging, would likely come as a shock to Amanda. If Houston had wished his daughter to know, he would have told her. It would be a violation of Houston's trust for Rush to tell her now. Though Houston had never asked it, protecting his part in the false treachery had become more important now that Rush had learned of his death.

There was no need to force Houston's family to live with the suspicion that Rush had to live with, even if Rush's name had been officially cleared. The matter of his pretending to be a British sympathizer was something that he'd hidden for so long that he did so now out of habit.

Rush let her wait, content to enjoy the quiet moment in the woods with this woman who'd so captured his thoughts and protective nature. "How goes the auction? Have you had many bidders for your company since the ball?"

"Bidders? No, I haven't. You were wrong about creating interest. I put myself on the auction block, and nobody offered a serious bid."

"And they won't," Rush said, wondering how much he should tell her, then decided that the truth was kinder than having her believe that she'd been spurned. "Your uncle put out the word to every man in the valley, including me, that as his fiancée you aren't to be trifled with."

"I am not his fiancée!" Amanda said in a slow rage. "Franklin is a thief. He is the last man in the valley I'd marry."

"Good, I wanted to hear you say it. I don't think we'll tell him yet. Just let him go on believing that he has everything under control. That's the way we'll handle it."

"We? Handle what?" she asked curiously, turning back to face the man who seemed to forever be involving himself in her problems.

"Keeping him from doing something stupid, like convincing your mother to sell part of Cadenhill just to show you that he can."

"He wouldn't dare!"

"Yes, I think he would—particularly if he knew what was really going to happen." Rush moved nearer, until he was standing so close that he could see the little tremor of motion in the nerve at the corner of her lip.

"What's that?"

"That you're going to marry me."

He hadn't known he was going to say that. He hadn't even given voice to the thought. But it made sense. He wanted a home, a plantation to raise tobacco and cotton, and a family. Marriage to Amanda Caden seemed a reasonable solution to both their problems.

"Marry you?" This time her lips were already parted in a gasp when he kissed her. This time he didn't stop with a gentle kiss, nor with a rough quick one. This time he assaulted first her lips with his lips, then her body with his hands. The sound of the river, the cool crisp air all disappeared in a second as Amanda felt the swift response of her body. Like a leaf caught in the Broad River she felt herself being twisted, swirling around in an emotional eddy of touch that closed out everything but the man holding her.

When at last he pulled back, leaving her lips swollen and her eyes stormy with desire, he said, more seriously than he'd meant to, "I certainly didn't plan it, Amanda Caden, but you and I belong together. You may not know it, but your body does, and somewhere in the back of that devious mind, you recognize that we have common goals that makes this even more right."

"What I recognize is that you're a devil, a man without scruples. Kissing me senseless. Sweet-talking me with fertilizer and tobacco. You're no better than Franklin. All you want is my land and you'll marry me to get it."

"My darling Amanda, please believe me. Cadenhill is only an added attraction to an arrangement that seems more interesting with every kiss."

"Stop kissing me. I know that you're an extraordinarily handsome man, and that the ladies fall all over themselves to attract you, but I'm not one of them. I'm no common doxy, ready to lie down for you, ready to—"

But she was.

And that was what frightened her. Always she'd been in control. Even as a child the slaves had come to her for direction. Her father had consulted her on day-to-day matters. Her world had been secure with parameters she understood.

Until Thomas Rushton Randolph pushed through those boundaries and teased her with feelings she couldn't control.

Marriage to Rush?

No! That was too great a risk. He was too powerful. Her life would never be her own again, and she was afraid of how much she was tempted by his suggestion.

Rush's eyes flashed as he slid his fingertips beneath her shirt and laid his hand across her breast, holding it for a long moment while he gazed into her eyes. He didn't speak. He simply waited for the telltale tremors to race through her body, for the flush of pink to steal across her face, giving substance to the claim he'd just made.

"What are you doing?" Her attempt at consternation was lost in the breathlessness of her voice. "Stop—"

He continued to look at her as he lifted the breast beneath the shirt so that he could take it, shirt and all into his wet, hot mouth. He brought her tirade to an abrupt stop, working the rough fabric of the shirt across the nipple, he brought it to a hard, throbbing peak before he reluctantly pulled away.

"Why are you doing this?" she asked. "What kind of woman do you think I am?"

"I think you're a real woman who's never known the wild, fierce need of a man. But you will, my Jasmine Bandit. You will. You and I are both misfits and we need each other." He groaned, feeling the painful response of his body. He forced himself to still the urge to press himself against her as he remembered his promise to Houston Caden.

"I'm going to Augusta tomorrow, to meet with some of the city fathers. I've promised to stay through Christmas. Until I return you are to forget husband hunting."

"Who will you meet in Augusta?" The question jumped out before she thought. What she ought to be doing was screaming for Settie, she thought, or jerking herself from his grasp and running away into the woods.

"Various merchants and government officials. Why?"

"Because they're the men I need to speak with," she said, "the men who hold the loans on Cadenhill, Franklin's cronies. Franklin says they will not deal with a woman, but I have to try. I think I'll accompany you."

Rush was stunned at the thought of taking Amanda. Stunned and dismayed. While he could understand her desire, it wasn't possible. He'd promised Houston to help her. Taking Amanda downriver would get him strung up to the nearest tree, not to mention what it would do to what remained of her reputation. And it wouldn't help Amanda's cause. He might as well tell her what he'd learned.

"I'm sorry, Amanda. I'm afraid that Franklin has already made it known that you're the one who's run the plantation into the ground. I don't think they'd receive you, nor will they think kindly of helping you."

"Of course you'd say that. You're his partner. Birds of a feather flock together. And you want Cadenhill, too."

One look at the desperation on her face and Rush wished he'd agreed. "Maybe there's another way. I'm to do two things. Buy tobacco seed and fertilizer to be brought back by barge, and take invitations to some of his business associates to attend a horse race on New Year's Day. I suspect Franklin's cronies are the men to whom you owe money. He mentioned that he intends to show them Cadenhill."

"He wouldn't!" Amanda was stricken.

"Don't worry. I doubt he intends to sell any of your land. This is just his way of pressuring you."

"Well, it won't work. I won't sell."

"Perhaps you can use this to your advantage. I'll escort you to the race and see that you have an opportunity to meet with them. They won't refuse me."

Amanda thought quickly. Talking with them was what she'd hoped for. She'd attend the race. But more than that, the information Rush had just given her provided other answers as well. She'd managed to get the tobacco beds ready for planting. All she needed now was seed. And her prayers were being answered. Supplies from Franklin. Monied guests being delivered by Rush, and a horse race to boot.

She knew that she'd sworn to rob only Franklin and his partner, but taking gold from his friends, the men who'd refused to grant her an extension on her loans, seemed sweet revenge. Besides, she rationalized, indirectly she would still be stealing from Franklin. She'd steal the money that he planned to take in wagers and pay off her debts with their money.

* * *

The birds were suddenly singing.

Her lower body, still touching Rushton Randolph's, felt as if it had been wrapped in a spiral of heat. She was trembling, and it came to her as she arched away from him that he wasn't having any easier time understanding this strange energy between them than she.

Amanda began to smile. Rush had given her solutions to problems that seemed hopeless only minutes ago. Each time they met, he helped her. Suddenly she felt very good. "I'll miss you, Rushton Randolph, but I think you owe me now. What can you give me that might pay for two kisses?" She pulled herself out of his arms, glancing down at the wet spot on her shirt.

Beneath the damp spot was the outline of her nipple, a small chinaberry pushing saucily against the fabric of her shirt. It tingled.

Rush felt an answering rhythmic surge in his body. He knew what he wanted to give her, but taking her would incur a debt that was beyond anything he could justify. It was a matter of honor; he couldn't seduce his mentor's daughter. He'd offered himself as a husband as a practical matter, but it was beginning to seem more and more like a good idea.

"I don't know, Amanda, darling, what are you asking?"

"I'll think about it while you're away, Rush. When will you return?"

"I'll be leaving tomorrow. I'll buy Franklin's supplies and send them along by return barge and I'll be returning by stage on New Year's Eve in time to escort you to the race and to the ball," he explained, slightly suspicious about her sudden coquettish behavior.

"Fine, I shall attend Franklin's race. But I don't need an escort, Mr. Randolph. I expect to take my mother and my sister, Catherine. I'll set my price for the kisses then."

"I'll look forward to an exchange of services," he said in a low voice. "Now I'll take my leave, Miss Caden. Don't go on any more auction blocks while I'm away."

"Oh, I shan't, Mr. Randolph," she said stepping away. "I have other things to occupy my time."

"And what would that be?"

Her green eyes shimmered with vitality. He could feel the energy of her presence, feel it spiral between them like some invisible cloud of hot air.

He reached out and pulled her back into his arms. Being close to her without kissing her was impossible. This time she didn't even try to pretend that she was avoiding his lips. This time she slid her leg between his and pressed herself against him as she parted her lips. This time she allowed her hand to play seductively up and down his spine as she returned his kiss.

Then, just as suddenly, she pulled away.

"I think, Mr. Randolph, that you are truly a devil. You bemuse a woman, cast a spell on her, then make her behave in a most unladylike manner. I may not be wise in the ways of courtship, but as you said, a man never wants a horse until someone else has bid on it. I make you no promises, except that I shall continue to seek a husband. Whether or not it is you depends on who makes himself available. As you said, I'm a good judge of horseflesh. Thanks for the kissing lessons. Can you swim, Mr. Randolph?"

He stared at her in confusion. She'd been as moved by their kisses as he. She'd even responded by touching him. What was she asking now, for swimming lessons?

"Yes, but it's a bit cold for swimming yet."

"You don't feel cold to me."

"I'm not cold, you wench, I'm burning up."

"I know." She gave him a broad smile and a swift shove.

As he tumbled backward into the river he heard her laugh.

"You owe me, Amanda!" he called out angrily as he began to make his way to shore. "And the next time I see you, I intend to present my bill."

"I don't think so," she said and climbed on her horse. "The next time we meet, rogue, I'll be the one doing the collecting."

Chapter Eight

Cadenhill smelled like Christmas: pies baking, a turkey roasting on the spit, pine boughs and holly berries hanging from the banisters and doorways. Iris Caden had done all she could to carry on for the little ones, even if their usual celebration had been cut to the bare essentials.

"Orphe, have you seen Catherine?"

"No, ma'am. She probably out walking in the woods. Seems like she can't set still lately. I ain't never seen her so restless."

"I know," Iris agreed, glancing at the little girls chasing each other around the base of the large chinaberry tree outside the kitchen door. At least they'd enjoy Father Christmas, thanks to Houston and his last trip to Carolina, when he'd brought back dolls, straight off the boat from England. They'd been packed away, saved for the holiday. For Catherine and Amanda, there were no gifts.

Iris sighed. She'd been brave, for the children's sake, but inside she was angry, angry that Houston had seemed to find the liberation of the Colonies more important than his family. He hadn't been forced to go. And she'd needed him, by her side, in her bed, in her arms. For a moment, she leaned against the column on the porch, looking out over the plantation.

It wasn't fair. She shouldn't have to be strong. She was only a mother, a wife, without a husband to keep her safe. She didn't know what to do about the crops, or debts or Franklin. "Damn you, Houston Caden. I loved you," she said, allowing herself for a long moment to admit the loneliness that kept her company every moment of the day. Women weren't meant to be alone. Amanda didn't understand that yet. But someday she'd feel differently.

Amanda didn't talk about it, but it looked more and more as if she would have to marry. Her eldest daughter was determined to preserve Cadenhill, and Franklin seemed to be the only man in the valley who had the means to do so. Iris felt a great sadness. Her marriage to Houston had been for love. She'd wanted the same for her daughters. But Amanda had come into the world as an adult. And a responsible adult put personal feelings last.

Certainly Amanda always had, until the Christmas ball. Afterward she'd become more angry, more emotional, more desperate. Iris could only guess that something had happened that night. She could only wait until Amanda was ready to tell her what.

Iris shivered and pulled her shawl closer. Down the road she could see a rider approaching. Company. Maybe Lewis Taliaferro had come to call. He stopped by from time to time, just to check on the Caden family. Lewis understood loneliness, for he'd been widowed nearly two years. Lewis could tell her about the ball.

But it wasn't Lewis who pulled up and let the horse's reins fall carelessly into the hands of the small brown boy who was standing by.

It was Franklin.

"I'm sorry, Franklin. Amanda isn't here. Shall I send for her?"

Franklin shook his head. "No, it's you I've come to talk to anyway. May I come in?"

"Of course, come into Houston's study. I have a fire going. Can I get you something? Coffee? Chocolate?"

"No, I'll have a brandy, if there is any."

"Yes, I think Houston had a bottle on the sideboard." Franklin followed Iris inside and poked the fire, adding a log while Iris poured dark liquid into a small glass.

"What I want to talk about, Iris, is a bit touchy, but I think you'll appreciate what I'm going to say."

"Yes, Franklin?"

"Amanda disappointed me greatly at the Taliaferros'. I don't think she quite realizes the situation in which Houston left Cadenhill, Iris, but I expect you to make her realize that she must not continue to carry on in such a brazen manner. I really cannot allow it."

"I'm sure I don't know what you mean, Franklin. I've never known Amanda to do anything dishonorable."

"It isn't that, Iris. I realize that she lacks experience in polite society, but I would have thought that you'd taught her not to associate with—with a traitor to the revolution."

"Traitor? What are you saying?"

"You know, of course, that she went to the ball alone, after refusing my invitation?"

"Yes, I tried to talk her into letting me accompany her. She...she refused. But a traitor? Whatever do you mean? The Cadens were as loyal as any man in town, more so than most. Who? With whom did she associate?"

"My partner, Thomas Rushton Randolph, a man who worked with and for the British during the revolution. A man who very possibly conspired against Houston in his work for the cause."

Iris clutched her throat, her face turning white. "I can't believe that—"

"Believe it," he snapped. "Amanda let everyone think that man was her escort, and then, as if that wasn't enough, she allowed him to take her in to supper."

"But Franklin, I don't understand. The revolution was over long ago. Many people here in the valley were British sympathizers. If Mr. Randolph was a traitor, that's past, too."

"Perhaps in some cities. But here? No."

"If that's true, why did you allow him to become your partner?"

"Because he had gold, Iris. And I needed gold to save Cadenhill. But I expect Amanda to marry me, and I won't be shamed by her association with some Englishman who ran off to British territory with Benedict Arnold. You are to put a stop to any further relationship between Amanda and Randolph immediately."

"Of course, I'll talk to Amanda," Iris said, studying Franklin with shrewd insight. It was all right for him to take the Englishman's gold, but it wasn't all right for Amanda to claim the same thing. There was something wrong here, but she couldn't quite figure out what it was. Still, instructing her daughter was her responsibility, and Houston would never have approved of a Cadenhill woman associating with a man who betrayed Houston's own beliefs.

"I expect you to do more than talk, Iris. Any further contact between Amanda and Rushton Randolph is to be stopped immediately." Franklin swallowed the last of the brandy in one gulp and left the room, colliding with and jostling Lovie aside without a thought.

"I heard what he said. That man is up to no good, Miz Caden," Lovie observed softly.

"Perhaps not, but I have to believe that Houston knew what he was doing when he left Franklin in charge. I will talk to Amanda. She wouldn't take up with a spy, even to save our land."

"I don't know anything about no spy, but I know Miss Manda, Miz Caden, and she ain't nobody's fool. She know what she's doing."

"I hope so, Lovie. For all our sakes."

* * *

Christmas Eve came and went. There were no gifts for the slaves this year. Only a Christmas Eve bonfire outside the big house where the workers gathered, singing songs, eating roasted pork and drinking the special cider that Iris Caden broke open for the celebration.

Father Christmas brought the little girls dolls and the Caden women finally got their new dresses. Amanda had solved the problem of paying for the dresses by selling the fake emerald necklace that had been her mother's birthday gift. The money could better have bought supplies, but after Cat's disappointment over not attending Charity's Christmas ball, Amanda couldn't refuse her a bit of joy.

Still, without Papa, Christmas wasn't the same. Instead of the goose they usually had, Amanda and Settie had gone into the woods and killed a wild turkey. That, and food from their pantry, was enough. Afterward Amanda mounted Thor and rode away into the forest.

She passed the slave quarters and noted the faded whitewash. Once the quarters had been as sparkling white as the big house. No more. Amanda caught sight of a man and woman disappearing into the woods. She'd noticed them before. On Cadenhill neither she nor her father had ever arranged marriages between their people, letting them make their own choices. Come spring, the couple she saw would probably be jumping over the broom—if not before.

At least these two had found each other. Her marriage plans were no further along than they'd been a week ago. Not one man had come to call. Franklin had seen to that.

Except Rushton Randolph.

Again Amanda was drawn to the spot by the river, her anguish spot, she decided. She'd told herself that she was riding here to think, to remember, to bring into the open the feelings that she'd so carefully hidden from herself. It was obvious that her plans weren't working.

It was obvious, too, that Rushton Randolph had given her a way to help herself—not through his open pursuit of her at the ball, or his proposal that she should marry him. No, he'd given her a way through the information he'd so carelessly imparted on their last meeting. He'd thought that she meant to meet with Franklin's associates and plead her case. She would. But before that, she intended to meet them in secret for another purpose.

Franklin's friends. Crooks. Birds of a feather. And Rushton Randolph was to protect them from the highwayman on their trip from Augusta to Petersburg on the new stage. Near the river, Amanda dismounted and walked. Her mind kept wandering from the barns and her problems. It should be focused on finding answers instead of thinking of the man who wanted to use fish for fertilizer to make his crops grow.

She couldn't marry him, of course. If she'd ever thought about marriage, she would have said she wanted a bold, outspoken man—until she'd met Rushton Randolph, who'd likely have her planting rutabagas and turnips instead of tobacco. He'd kissed her and she'd melted. Clearly, if she were going to maintain control of Cadenhill she had to find another candidate, quick. She'd choose a man less flamboyant, less powerful, less heart-stopping. Mr. Randolph might be the only man in the valley bold enough to pursue her, but he was ambitious, just like Franklin, and he didn't even try to hide it. That was reason enough to decline.

If Rush Randolph and Franklin Caden were the only men in Petersburg, she'd be forced to go to Augusta, or Savannah. But time was her enemy. She'd already laid out the special new seed beds, to be covered with muslin tents. She was ready to plant. She just had to have the seeds.

In six months it would be June.

In one week Rush would return.

The Jasmine Bandit would ride again.

Chapter Nine

Roman found an open warehouse doorway, slipped inside and ducked behind the barrels of molasses. He didn't like being in Augusta. He didn't like what he was doing this night. He'd never refused to follow Miss Amanda's orders and he wouldn't now. But tonight he was afraid.

Then he heard it, the name Caden.

"This salt, molasses and seed goes to Petersburg, too. Load it on the barge. Don't you leave none here. You know Franklin Caden. He'll count every seed. If there's one thing missing we'll catch the devil."

"Yes, suh. Dat Mr. Caden, folks say he so stingy he squeaks."

Roman listened. Mr. Franklin's Petersburg boat was picking up supplies. Roman knew about this captain, that he'd be off checking out the nearest Augusta tavern while the supplies were being loaded.

When the rain began Roman cursed silently, then realized that it was a blessing in disguise. If the supplies had to be covered to protect them from the storm, he'd be hidden, too. Cautiously, he ventured from his hiding place and glanced around. Already the workers were bringing canvas out to cover the goods. Franklin Caden might be many things, but his goods were of the best quality and commanded the highest prices. He protected them.

Ducking his head to blend in with the hired hands, Roman took the corner of a piece of canvas and began to cover the end of the crates. Once the hiding place was secure, he melted into the darkness beneath the shelter.

Soon the captain returned and the boat began to move. Knowing the river's ability to change from its normal course into a raging torrent, he'd decided to get beyond the shoals before the current became too swift to navigate. Roman leaned back, allowing the tension to ease. He still couldn't believe what Miss Amanda planned to do, but he couldn't let her do it alone.

Roman sat, holding his eyes stubbornly awake. Just as he'd been told, when Franklin wasn't on board, once the barge reached the quiet water beyond the shoals the captain always pulled into Kelly's Cove for a little rest. The crew never rushed their return to Petersburg.

Roman was probably the only one who felt the subtle shift of weight on the boat. Someone had boarded. Someone was moving stealthily alongside the crates where they were hidden.

Miss Amanda?

Roman rose slowly, peering out from the edge of the covering. A figure dressed in black was moving quietly along the side of the barge. The lantern hanging from the captain's lean-to outlined the silhouette of the figure, throwing just enough light to reveal the mask and the gun.

It was she.

Miss Amanda was about to become a thief and rob Mr. Franklin's barge. Roman shook his head. What he was seeing didn't make no sense. It would have been a lot easier, if she had to turn thief, to break into the store, but no. She had to dress up like her daddy and rob Mr. Franklin's barge. And he was helping her.

Then it happened. The figure tripped in the darkness, dislodging a barrel that rolled across the bottom of the barge. The deckhands came to life. Roman dashed out of his hiding place, trying desperately to figure out a way to keep her from being discovered.

"Halt!" The captain stepped out on deck.

One of the deckhands made a grab for the bandit. "I've got him, Captain."

The gun she was holding clattered to the floor and landed at Roman's feet.

"Look out, there's two of them!" another hand shouted.

Before Roman stopped to think, he picked up the gun and fired it. The deckhand quickly let go of the bandit and stepped back.

"Why'd you turn him lose, you idiot." The captain swore.

"Hold it, Captain!" the bandit said in an odd, raspy voice. "I have two other weapons. I don't want to hurt you. I just want some of your supplies."

Roman hadn't believed it. But the husky-voiced bandit was truly Miss Manda. And Roman was ready to protect her with his life, even if what she was doing was against the law. Miss Manda really was robbing Mr. Franklin. Roman liked that. He liked that a lot. Roman began to grin.

"You—" Amanda moved toward Roman and took the gun "—I want tobacco seed, fertilizer and two bolts of muslin. If you value your life, you'll unload them on the bank—quick."

Roman quickly followed her orders.

"You won't get away with this," the captain said belligerently. "There are four of us and only two of you, and one of your guns has already been fired."

"There's only one of me," she corrected in an attempt to protect Roman. "But my guns are pointed directly at you, Captain. If I were you, I'd order my crew to be very still."

The captain took only a second to comply, ordering his hands to line up at the opposite end of the barge. "This boat belongs to Mr. Franklin Caden, of Cadenhill plantation, and he won't take kindly to being robbed."

"I know to whom it belongs," the bandit answered in the same gruff voice she'd adopted. "Mr. Franklin Caden is the man I intended to rob."

She backed away, then leaped lightly to the bank. "You there," she growled at Roman, "take their poles and push the barge out into the water."

Roman quickly complied, standing beside her in the darkness as the barge, without poles to direct it, was caught by the downstream current and carried away.

Forgetting that she was dressed as a highwayman, Amanda turned to her old friend, hugging him joyously once they were out of sight. "Roman, we did it. We've got the seeds and fertilizer to plant our spring crop."

Roman shook his head vigorously. "Yes'um, but I still don't know why you want to take such a chance. Suppose we'd got caught. What your mama gonna say 'bout this?"

"Roman, Mama must never know. Nobody knows about this but you, and you must swear that you'll never tell anybody."

Again he nodded. "No, ma'am. Roman ain't going to tell nobody. Now, let's us get home, Miss Amanda, before that captain figures a way to turn round and come back." Roman secured the supplies on one of Mr. Caden's grays, then mounted the second one as Miss Amanda climbed on the black. They rode into the woods.

The moon skimmed the edge of the trees, climbing higher and higher in the sky as they rode. A new moon. Roman couldn't be certain, but he thought the new year was close at hand. Somehow that seemed appropriate.

Miss Manda, turning river pirate. Miss Manda, who'd just robbed Franklin Caden.

Roman grinned. They had seed for planting.

Cadenhill would be all right.

"Mama, why is Manda still in bed?" Catherine Caden followed her mother into the parlor. "Is she sick?"

Iris Caden fidgeted with the lace doily on the back of the chair and considered her answer. "No, I don't think so, Catherine. I believe she's just very tired. I don't think she's been sleeping very well."

"She might sleep better," Cat observed more shrewdly than Iris expected, "if she went to bed at night instead of tearing around the plantation at all hours like some hooligan. What does she do, anyway?"

"I'm not sure, Catherine," Iris admitted. "But I'm certain that it's for our benefit. Let's just let her sleep for a while."

"All right, Mother, but when she wakes I want to talk to her. Charity Taliaferro sent me a note. Uncle Franklin is sponsoring a horse race on New Year's Day at the Petersburg Racetrack, with a barbecue afterward at the Jockey Club. She's asked me to accompany her. May I?"

"Franklin is giving a barbecue?"

"That's what Charity says. He's invited a bunch of men from Augusta to come up for the race. It's going to be the most exciting event of the year."

"I'm sure it is." Iris felt a stirring of resentment. She was beginning to have strong second thoughts about Franklin. For all the years that she'd been married to Houston he'd been loyal to his stepmother's son, but more and more, Iris was beginning to wonder if Franklin deserved that trust. It seemed out of place for Franklin to entertain at a social event at the same time they were having difficulty paying their bills. Though, Iris admitted, this event could be a business venture that she didn't understand. Franklin could have their best interests at heart.

"Then may I send word that I will accept? Her father and her aunt will be there, Mother. I'll be properly chaperoned."

"I think we should all go." Amanda Caden had walked into the parlor. "I'm sorry that you didn't get to attend the

Christmas ball, Cat. So maybe this will make it up to you. In fact, I'm considering entering Thor in the race."

"Amanda! You're going to race Thor? I can't believe you're serious. Who'd ride him?"

"Me," Amanda answered her mother, and waited for the explosion she knew would come.

Catherine's "Whoopee!" preceded her mother's shocked response. "Amanda. I've not said anything up to now about your unladylike behavior, but I think it's time that you and I have a serious talk. Catherine, go and find your sisters. Make certain that they're doing their lessons."

"Oh, Mother," Catherine protested, "I'm sixteen years old, practically old enough to be married, certainly old enough not to have to leave the room when something important is being discussed."

"Then you're old enough to follow instructions as well," Iris snapped and waited for her second daughter to leave the room.

"Mother," Amanda began, "there is a two-hundred-and-fifty-dollar prize for the winner of the one-mile run. That money could be applied to our debts. Heaven knows there are few ways available to me to make money. I don't see how you can ask me to turn it down."

"You will not ride that horse, Amanda, and that is final. It was bad enough when you discouraged every young man in the valley from coming to call, but when you finally decided to join polite society you went alone. Not only did you present yourself in a most unacceptable manner, but you allowed your name to be linked with that of a man who has been accused of being a traitor to the very cause your father died for."

Amanda's protest died in her throat.

"Traitor? What are you talking about?"

"I'm referring to Franklin's partner, Mr. Rushton Randolph. He was known to be a British sympathizer."

"So were many other people. Who told you such a thing?"

"Franklin told me, Amanda. Apparently Mr. Randolph did more than sympathize. Franklin has it on good authority that Mr. Randolph deserted with Benedict Arnold to British territory. Franklin says that you are forbidden to associate with the man any further, and I agree."

"I'm forbidden? Franklin forbids me to associate with Rushton Randolph? How dare he? I don't for one minute believe that Randolph's a spy, if for no other reason than Franklin said it. Besides, why would Franklin take a spy in as a partner?"

"Because he had gold and Franklin needed it, for the family."

"And you believed Franklin?"

Iris looked at Amanda, the tight, hurt tone of her voice saying clearly what her bland expression didn't. There was something between Amanda and Mr. Randolph. Iris didn't know what, or how, but in spite of Amanda's attempt to conceal her feelings, this man had touched her in a way that nobody else in the valley had done.

"I don't know, Amanda. Perhaps I was wrong," Iris amended her words softly. She might not approve of Rushton Randolph, but she cared about Amanda and wouldn't tread upon her feelings. "But we don't know much about the man, do we?"

"We know enough." Amanda turned away from her mother toward the veranda door. Normally, she'd never defend Rushton Randolph, but she refused to believe anything Franklin said. He'd never done anything in his life if it wasn't to his advantage, and eliminating Rush from her list of possible suitors was reason enough for the weasel to lie. Besides, if Franklin felt so strongly about this position, then maybe she would consider Rush as a suitor.

The sun was already high in the morning sky. There were chores to be done, decisions to be made. She'd consider her mother's concerns, for Amanda loved her mother. But first, there was Roman and the planting to be dealt with.

Amanda leaned over, feeding her mane of red hair into the crown of her old felt hat, then pulled it down on her head.

"Mother, if I am to win, I must ride Thor, but I'll try not to embarrass you. With that in mind, will you please look at my wardrobe? I'd rather not look as if I've borrowed my gowns from someone at the Old Dragon Inn."

Amanda, concerned about her clothes? She'd even looked a bit girlish as she'd asked about the clothes. Perhaps there was hope yet. As Iris watched Amanda stride across the garden she was glad of her daughter's lift of spirits, even if it was because of a horse race. Amanda deserved some pleasure in life.

Iris began to plan. But now it was nearly nine o'clock and time for the children's geography lesson. She lifted her skirt and stared with dismay at the worn condition of the parlor rug. Cadenhill needed so much, and those needs lay heavily on Amanda's head. Iris wasn't sure what Amanda needed. She hoped it wasn't this British spy.

Amanda abhorred Franklin. But Iris clung to the thought that Franklin was safe. He was familiar. Still, if he was the wrong choice for Amanda, Iris would accept that. Iris could make up her own mind, after she'd seen the man Amanda was accused of being interested in. Houston was gone now. For Iris, her children were her life, and she would protect Amanda, if she had to.

Against Franklin or the British spy.

Chapter Ten

Amanda knew that the news of the barge robbery must be all over the valley, but nobody had mentioned it at Caden-hill.

Under her direction the slaves had built small brick hearths in the middle of the tobacco beds beneath the new tentlike structures she'd fashioned from the stolen muslin. For two days she'd kept herself busy, too busy to think about her troubles. She had her supplies, though she was no nearer finding the money to pay off the note than she'd been at the beginning.

But slowly a plan had begun to emerge, starting with to-night, when Rushton Randolph was to return on the stage-coach from Augusta with Franklin's guests.

Now, it was nearly midnight. With her blood strumming in her veins, the highwayman soothed the black horse as they waited just off the stagecoach road south of Peters-burg. Tonight was her fourth outing as the Jasmine Bandit, but it wasn't becoming any easier. Making Roman a part of her plan was risky, but since the night of the barge he had appointed himself her guardian. To Roman, robbing a stagecoach was too dangerous for the Jasmine Bandit.

Dear Roman. She regretted what she was doing. It was one thing for her to be caught, but involving Roman could be more serious. The slaves were her responsibility, and she was taking a chance on endangering Roman's life.

Earlier, she and Shadow dragged the fallen tree limb across the road, hiding the rain-swollen ditch that had washed out the road. If the ditch didn't do damage to the wheel, the limb ought to stop the carriage.

The air was crisp and cold tonight. The last of the unusually mild weather was gone. At the edge of the forest Amanda positioned Roman and the extra horse she'd brought, close enough to create confusion if she ran into trouble, but far enough away to remain out of danger. Roman was not to interfere unless Amanda commanded him too.

Amanda pulled her coat collar higher at the neck and leaned against the black horse she called Shadow, to absorb his body heat. Since the night of the barge holdup, she'd been planning the robbery of Franklin's friends. Though Rush had said he'd return in two weeks she knew that, unlike the Petersburg boats, the stagecoach schedule was not yet that well established. At the noon rest stop Roman had arranged a small accident to a wheel in order to delay the coach's arrival in Petersburg until night. Now it was late, and cold, and Amanda tried not to think of what lay ahead.

Rushton Randolph. Even his name set off tremors of unwanted anticipation in her traitorous body. She'd promised to let him know what she expected in return for the bonus kisses he'd claimed. Her jest had been uncharacteristically merry for her. Polite conversation and flirting had been just as foreign to Amanda. Yet every time the man touched her she seemed to respond in a way that was both new to her and incredibly exciting.

Tonight she would collect her fee and she didn't know how he'd react. Besides his pistol she'd hung Settie's musket from the saddle horn. Amanda didn't intend to allow herself to be overpowered by Franklin's guests.

As the moon moved higher in the sky she began to worry. The first time she'd held up Franklin's coach, she'd been too angry to be scared. The second time she'd expected only Franklin and had been surprised to find Mr. Randolph inside as well. Tonight the number of victims would make her venture risky.

But success would fill her empty pockets, and give her the satisfaction of knowing that she could find a way to save her land without either Franklin's or Rush's help. And she was determined to succeed.

Still, she was tense. The tension transcended her attempt at control and nudged Shadow into an unusual dance of movement. She'd been incredibly lucky so far. Nobody yet had made a serious attempt to thwart her demands, and she well knew that Rush could have stopped her at any time.

Tonight would be her most serious undertaking. It would have been easier for her to ply her trade among the people she knew. But robbing her father's old friends was something she couldn't do. Times had been just as hard for them as for the Cadens. But these men, Franklin's cronies, were the same men who held the loans on Cadenhill. That made them fair game. Anybody who did business with Franklin was tarred with the same brush, including, she admitted reluctantly, his partner.

She didn't understand why the men were coming to Petersburg for a horse race, but the new stage line offered travel opportunities their neighbors had not enjoyed before. And everybody along the Savannah River knew that Petersburg's social life was lively.

Times had been difficult for the colonists during the revolution, followed by years of establishing a new government and finding a direction for the individual states. And the founders of Petersburg had been very much involved in those political issues. But Amanda had paid little attention to that.

Cadenhill, not politics, had been the focus of Amanda's life. She'd tried to fight the plantation's slide into financial disaster as her father's health had deteriorated, and he'd seemed to rely more and more heavily on Franklin's help.

To Amanda, the scheduling of a horse race seemed a foolish undertaking when the beds were being made ready for planting the tobacco. But the plantation owners rarely concerned themselves with the actual work, so absenting themselves from their estates for a few hours of merrymaking was of no great concern.

Deep in thought, Amanda almost didn't see the glimmer of the coach's lantern flickering through the trees until she heard the approach of the carriage. The coach jostled along, bouncing from one pothole to the next until it came to a crashing halt against the tree limb barrier that she and Shadow had set up.

Before the driver had a chance to dismount, the coach door opened and she recognized the large figure of Rush Randolph. "What now, George? I thought this stretch of road was clear."

The voice of Rush Randolph was weary and a bit anxious. Amanda waited. She knew the journey had been long, else they'd have arrived before the midnight hour. She choked back her last-minute reservations. What she had to do couldn't be helped. Too much depended on her success.

"Wait," Rush told the driver, "they'll have to get out to get the carriage across the ditch."

A second man climbed out. "God's teeth, Randolph, I thought this was to be a pleasant journey. So far we'd have done better to take our chances on our own mounts."

Rush and the driver began to tug on the tree, but it was obvious that two men wouldn't be able to move it.

"I'm sorry to inconvenience you, gentlemen," Rush was finally reduced to saying, "but if we expect to reach Petersburg tonight, you're going to have to lend a hand."

Grumbling, the men piled out of the carriage and took hold of the tree, tugging as it halfheartedly and with little success.

"Look here, Randolph. This is your coach and your team. I think you're going to have to unhitch them and drag this thing away. I'm getting back inside."

"Not just yet, gentlemen." Amanda urged Shadow into the road. She positioned herself so that both her pistol and the musket hanging from the saddle horn were visible in the light of the carriage lamp.

"Good Lord, a highwayman!" one man exclaimed.

"So, we meet again," Rush said, abandoning his hold on the tree and approaching the horse, which neighed nervously at the man's bold approach.

"You know this bandit?"

"I do. When last we met I carried away a bullet wound in the leg." He recognized her all right. He recognized his pistol, too. She probably had the second one primed and ready.

"Where's the safe journey we were promised?"

"No more conversation, gentlemen," Amanda commanded gruffly, throwing down a satchel at Rush's feet. "I'll have all your wallets and your jewels. In the bag—quick!"

In the silence the loud click of her pistol hammer underscored her seriousness.

"I believe we'd better comply," Rush agreed, his voice laced with the suggestion of amusement. "You never know what a bandit will do when—he's excited."

Rush picked up the purse and passed it among the angry passengers, who tossed their valuables into the bag with disbelief.

"Franklin promised us safe passage, Randolph."

"What do you plan to do about this?"

"Don't worry, gentlemen. I'll make certain that my partner makes good on all your losses. I always find a way to recoup lost funds, one way or another. I'm a man who believes in an even exchange of services."

Rush held the bag. With his back to the passengers he allowed himself a hint of a smile. She was cool in the face of disaster. But she couldn't see the driver, who'd made his way through the shadows and was coming quietly up behind her. He had no weapon, but the limb he was carrying was enough to dismount the woman who was focused so intently on the men she was facing.

For a moment Rush considered allowing her to be captured. She deserved it. This holdup would do the reputation of his stage line irreparable damage. Yet, in a way, he was responsible. He'd told her about Franklin's guests and their fat purses. He'd even told her the exact date of his return.

Truth was, he admired her courage and determination. Ever the champion of the underdog, Rush found still another reason to rationalize marrying Amanda, though carrying out that offer was beginning to seem less likely.

Still, Rush couldn't allow physical harm to come to the woman he was sworn to protect. Nor would he be responsible for her ruined reputation if the blue bloods of Petersburg learned that Amanda Caden had turned into a highwayman.

It was at that point that Roman's horse neighed.

One passenger swore. "Careful, men. This one's not alone. There's a whole gang of them waiting in the woods."

Rush couldn't see Amanda traveling with a gang. But he, too, had heard the horse. The sound didn't stop George's steady advance. Amanda was likely to be hurt, even if she wasn't alone.

Quickly, without any of the onlookers being aware of what was happening, Rush stepped forward, looped the handle of the satchel over her horse's saddle horn, while at the same time he grabbed it and pulled himself up behind

Amanda. "I've got him!" Rush yelled. "Drop your pistol, thief."

There was a sound of movement in the woods as whoever was there rode away at a fast pace.

Shadow reared up and, following the orders issued by Rush's heels digging into his haunches, broke into a run and disappeared into the darkness. "Whoa! Whoa, you crazy horse!" Rush yelled, all the while urging him forward.

But Shadow didn't stop. Rush didn't want him to. Continuing to yell disparagingly at the horse, Rush gave Shadow his head, allowing him to plunge through the woods. Limbs and bare vines caught at the riders, tearing Amanda's hat from her head, catching at her hair until it was knotted and flying wildly across her face.

Amanda struggled to hold on to her pistol as she tried to escape Rush's death grip. Both his arms encircled her waist, and his chin was digging into her shoulder as he pressed his cheek against hers. Like demons from hell they charged through the woods until at last Shadow began to slow his mad pace.

"Let me go! You black-hearted devil. Let me go!"

Rush seemed to ignore her. He certainly didn't loosen his grip, tightening even as she struggled. Giving one final twist she tried valiantly to dislodge him. Instead, as Shadow jostled their movements, Rush's hands were suddenly holding her breasts.

Amanda caught her breath and froze. What she felt was a slash of sensation that started somewhere beneath Rush's hands and swept up her throat to paralyze her voice.

"Be quiet, darling," Rush said sharply. "I think we're far enough away so that your victims won't hear. But my driver won't give up so quickly. Who was in the woods?"

"One of my hands. But he's—gone. He won't interfere unless I command it." Amanda emphasized the *won't*, hoping that if Roman were nearby listening he'd follow her instructions.

Shadow was heaving, his great chest moving in and out with his breathing. Every intake of air seemed to push Amanda's legs closer to Rush's. Every heartbeat of the horse seemed to match the thunder of her own. She stopped fighting her captor. He had her trussed and spitted. All he needed was a roaring fire and she'd be ready for roasting on a stake.

Adding to the aggravation was the feel of his rough face against her cheek, and the hot breath that touched her neck where her frock coat had been opened by his hands, hands that were making light, teasing movements against her breasts. She gasped, catching her breath and holding it so that he couldn't know what havoc his touch was creating.

"Let me go!" she managed to whisper.

"I can't, not yet." Rush was surprised at his relief. He hadn't allowed himself to acknowledge how concerned he'd been that the Jasmine Bandit would be caught. And he would have been responsible. Knowing how desperate she was, he'd told her that the men on board would be carrying large purses and when they'd arrive. The danger tonight had been real. Now that it was over, the tension that had stilled his heart drained away, leaving fear where mere concern had been. He took a deep breath, taking the elusive scent of her into his lungs. "I believe there is the matter of exchange of services."

One hand left her breast and moved up her body, caressing her neck, catching in the tangles of her hair. His anger was tinged with passion that slowly began to build. "What do you intend to offer, my Jasmine Bandit?"

"A wound in the other leg, if you don't unhand my—my person!"

A small laugh of disbelief escaped Rush. "Don't even think about it, vixen. All I have to do is tell the world and you'll be hauled off to jail."

"But you won't, will you?"

Amanda knew that she was short-tempered and stubborn, but even she understood that goading this man would be unwise. Still, she was having trouble finding a course of action that would free her from the rogue's embrace without her also losing the purse she'd risked capture to take.

Then, in the silence where the only sounds were those of quick breaths and erratic heartbeats, she understood. He was as caught up in the moment as she. His fingertips were no longer holding. They were painting her body with heat, turning her anger into a different kind of energy, more powerful, less manageable. She let out a long ragged sigh and let herself go limp against him. If she could distract him she'd find a way to escape.

"That's better," Rush whispered, planting his lips against her cheek, gently at first, then more urgently as he forced her to tilt her head. "Just move your leg across the horn so that I can turn you to face me."

"Why?" She hadn't meant to sound so breathless. She hadn't meant her heart to thunder against the fingertips that were ranging lower and lower. The gun was still heavy in her hand, the hammer cocked, ready for firing. But taking a shot at the man from their present position might mean wounding Shadow. She couldn't take a chance on that. But if she followed his directions she could confront him head on—or gun to chest—or gun to his other parts.

She didn't have to be reminded of that part of Rush that was pressing itself against her rear. She'd been aware of the growing announcement of his interest and her mad acknowledgment of its demand. They were so close that every move he made branded her skin.

Now he was touching her, bare fingertips to bare skin, and kissing her. Before she was swept away she had to stop him. Quickly, before he could adjust to her actions, she turned her face to his, catching his lips with her own.

A deep throaty sound filled her ears as Rush plundered her mouth. So caught up in the unexpected fever of her offering, Rush almost didn't hear the soft wonder in her voice as she whispered his name, "Rush—"

Then just as suddenly, Amanda pulled back, gave Rush a shove and dug her knees into Shadow's sides. As Rush tumbled off, Amanda drew in the reins and let out a triumphant laugh.

"Debt paid, Mr. Randolph."

"Not yet, Miss Caden. Take care. After this, Franklin will be after you. The next time, I might not be able to save you. I'm not sure that I can afford to."

"Ah, but you've done very well, Mr. Randolph. I now have seed, supplies and the start of a fund to repay Cadenhill's debts."

"Fine. And while you're counting your riches I hope that you've figured out how you're going to explain your new wealth. Sooner or later somebody might begin to ask questions. Three robberies and Miss Amanda Caden has money when nobody else in the valley does."

"No, Mr. Randolph," Amanda corrected as she whirled around and rode off in the night, "not three holdups, four."

The travelers grumbled as they heaved at the tree trunk. Rush's explanation of his failure to retrieve their purses because the horse reared fell on deaf ears. The holdup put the final cap on the men's dissatisfaction with the Randolph Transportation Company and with their host, Franklin Caden.

Tired, disheveled and hungry, they were a surly lot when they finally got under way again. The new sound of approaching horses and the command "Hold up and throw down your gold," came as an unpleasant surprise. This time it wasn't a single bandit, but a band of robbers who brought the stage to a halt.

It took a great deal of explanation before the latest cut-throats accepted that they were too late. There were no purses, no money, no prize. Finally, rather than return empty-handed, the new bandits settled for one valise and the driver's musket, which had lain unused earlier.

"What next, Randolph," Martin Overstreet asked, "a flood, or perhaps an Indian raid?"

Rush was having trouble understanding what had just happened. "Forgive me, gentlemen," he answered distractedly, "this is obviously not what I'd planned."

"Franklin will hear about this," another promised. "His may be the best offering of horseflesh in the state, but any travel I undertake in the future will be to Savannah or Charleston, where people are civilized."

Rush didn't bother to defend his position any further. He was tired and more than a little confused. Amanda's daring holdup was a nuisance, but he understood her motives, and in some private way, respected her action. But this second group was clearly another matter. Something about their actions seemed directed. They knew what they were doing, and they didn't seem terribly concerned that they were unsuccessful, suggesting that the purses were not the motivating reason for their holdup.

According to Franklin there had been no problems in the past with bandits, other than an occasional raid by marauding Indians. Why now?

Franklin. Rush knew that Franklin was having second thoughts about having taken Rush in as a partner. Would he stoop to such lengths?

No, it would do Franklin no good to have his guests outraged. He'd already paved the way to relieve them of their funds through bets on the race. He would have had no way of knowing that Rush would say that Franklin would stand behind the losses.

When the coach finally reached Petersburg the moon was low in the sky and the pale lavender fingers of dawn were slipping over the trees. The innkeeper, hastily covered by a voluminous robe, ignored his bare feet and yawned widely as the passengers claimed their rooms for the remainder of the night.

Rush guaranteed their bills, directing their host to send the charges to his office for payment. By the time he went to his room he was tired, and he was beginning to have a bad feeling about the night's activities.

Tomorrow he'd call on Miss Amanda Caden.

Tomorrow came earlier than Rush expected. He'd barely closed his eyes when the pounding began on his door. Forcing his eyes to open, he made his way to the door.

"Randolph! Open this door!"

"Franklin? What's wrong?"

"What's wrong?" Franklin Caden stormed into the room. "We've been robbed. That's what's wrong!"

Rush lit a candle and threaded his hands through his hair. Though he'd removed his coat, he was still wearing his traveling clothes. "I know. Our highwayman is becoming more bold. Your guests may be concerned, but at least they're not out of pocket."

Franklin jerked around. "What do you mean, my guests? I'm talking about the thief who robbed my barge three days ago. He stole my seeds and fertilizer and yard goods. The only thing the thief didn't take was the salt and the furniture we were carrying."

"We?" Rush was stalling. Franklin wasn't talking about the stagecoach. He was talking about one of his barges being robbed. Surely Amanda hadn't taken up river robbery. That was a real danger.

"Technically, of course, the barges belong to me, and any profit or loss doesn't affect your portion of the warehouse. But this bandit had a gang. He has to be stopped before he becomes any more brazen."

"Surely you aren't saying that our stagecoach bandit held up a Petersburg barge."

"I can't be certain that it was the same thief. But the boat captain said the thief was young and slim, and wearing a mask. That sounds like the same person to me. And I intend to stop him."

"Oh? How?"

"I've already taken steps," Franklin said quietly. "I shall be prepared in the future and catch him before he costs me any more money."

"And how do you plan to do that, Franklin?"

"I don't think I'll tell you, Randolph. How do I know that you're not involved in this? After all, the holdups didn't start until you arrived. For all I know you're in cahoots with him."

Rush groaned. "Franklin, surely you can't mean that you suspect me. I've been a victim of your highwayman three times. I've probably lost as much money as you."

"Not if you're in on the thefts."

"And I suppose I gave instructions to have myself shot?"

Franklin frowned, wheeled around and started out the door. "Maybe not, but the wound was superficial. I warn you, Randolph, there isn't much that goes on in this valley that I don't know about. I'll find the culprit and stop him— sooner or later."

Rush sat on the bed and tried to clear his muddled thoughts. If Franklin was angry now, he'd be furious when he learned that his guests had been robbed. Tomorrow was here. He thought he'd just keep quiet about what happened. His plan to call on Amanda Caden took on new urgency. His need to see her again was as great as his fear for her safety.

Franklin was right. There was little that happened that he wasn't aware of, and sooner or later he'd wonder where Amanda's windfall had come from.

Sighing, Rush pulled fresh clothes from his valise and began to dress. He didn't know what Amanda intended to do, but it looked as if his coffers would be further emptied. The only plan he could come up with to explain her new-found funds was that they came from him.

Amanda might have been up half the night, but he'd bet his life that she was already dressed and giving orders to her hands. When he'd promised his old friend Houston Caden that he'd help Amanda he hadn't known what that would mean. But Rush was beginning to understand that when Houston asked President Washington to give Rush the assignment to build a stagecoach line to Savannah, he'd had ulterior motives. The Broad River Valley was a fine place for a man to buy land and grow cotton. But Rush couldn't get on with that part of his life until he fulfilled his promise to look after Amanda.

Cadenhill was the driving force in Amanda's life.

Amanda Caden was rapidly becoming the driving force in his.

The inn was still quiet when Rush left. Franklin's guests were unlikely to stir before noon. By that time Rush intended to have visited Cadenhill and be back. The race wasn't scheduled for three days and he had much work to do if he intended to be free to take part.

He'd invited Amanda to attend, but she'd refused. Still, he hoped that she might change her mind. At the stage-coach office he checked to make certain that George, his driver, had made it back, and that the horses and coach were being readied for the next leg of the journey. After being stopped several times by early-morning shoppers, Rush made his way out of town toward Cadenhill.

The morning air was cool, invigorating but not cold. The mild winter was a surprise to Rush. He was enjoying it. North Carolina was a bit colder, but nothing compared to the winter he'd spent in Canada with Benedict Arnold before General Washington had called him home.

During the years afterward, when he'd fought the stigma of being called a turncoat, he'd explored the west, tromping through drifts of snow that reached his waist. Time hadn't helped. No matter that President Washington had proclaimed his innocence, there were still those who believed Rush had actually run off to Canada and deserted the cause.

Rush's greatest regret was that his family had suffered. His father became ill. Relations already strained were pushed to the breaking point. When overzealous citizens had tried to confiscate his family estate, it had taken direct intercession by Houston Caden to prevent its takeover and eventually clear Rush's name.

Now it was up to Rush to return the favor. Rush couldn't fault Houston for leaving Franklin in charge, for Houston couldn't be certain that Rush would follow through on his promise. But he had, and he'd already seen and heard enough to understand that Amanda needed her own champion now. Rush intended to intercede for her.

But how?

He'd already announced that he intended to marry her. But she seemed intent on rejecting him. Perhaps he was going about his courtship the wrong way. For now, the stagecoach line had to command most of his attention. But Amanda was on the way to getting in over her head if he didn't step in. He didn't have time for playing games. He'd have a serious talk with his future bride. Today.

The Jasmine Bandit had to disappear.

Chapter Eleven

Amanda saddled Thor and began to make her morning rounds. Settie seemed pleased when she showed him the new seed. He'd get started sowing in the beds immediately.

It was close to lunchtime when Amanda left the running of the plantation behind and rode into the woods. Resolutely she had refused to consider her mother's startling revelation about Rushton Randolph being a traitor. Distracted by her thoughts, she rode upriver, past the mill to the spot where she'd encountered Mr. Randolph before.

The woods were quiet. The loblolly pines had strewn the ground with a fresh carpet of brown straw that crackled under the horse's hooves. Here in the stillness she could give free rein to her thoughts, her confusion. Sliding down from Thor's back, she let go of his reins and began to walk.

Thomas Rushton Randolph a traitor? A British sympathizer? She couldn't believe such a charge. He was outrageous, a wild rogue who'd kiss a lady before she knew what he was about, but a spy?

She gave no credence to such a charge. Hadn't he helped her? First by telling her of the prize to be had if a bandit were to hold up the stage, then by pretending to seize her when her capture seemed imminent.

Why was he constantly rescuing her?

She had to wonder at his reasoning. After all, he was allowing her to rob him. What could he hope to gain? He
seemed to like kissing her. And he had offered to marry her.
Amanda bemoaned her lack of experience with men. All she
knew was that Rush wasn't afraid of her. She thought that
he might even admire her as a bandit. But marriage? No,
there were too many suitable, proper women in the valley
who would fill that bill far better than she.

What did he really want?

Slowly she began to reason it out. Bit by bit his interest
came clear to her until she thought she understood. Rush
was no fool. He'd made it plain that he wanted to buy land
and grow cotton. Why buy land if he had the means to get
it without spending any money at all? Why not marry it?
Even paying off the notes would be a bargain.

She'd told him that she was looking for a husband, any
husband except Franklin—and him. And he'd kissed her
every time they were together, as if he'd enjoyed it, and
she'd allowed it and she'd kissed him back.

Amanda had never thought about marriage. She'd never
envisioned a life for herself other than Cadenhill and its
care. Taking a husband was to be endured as a means of
keeping the land. Her thoughts of marriage had gone no
further than that. Now this black-eyed man had come vio-
lently into her world, bringing new feelings about marriage, about being with a man. Sweet, foreign urgings swept
over her and she could almost see Rush, feel his lips touching hers, hear his flirtatious talking.

"He's trying to get around me, sweet-talking," she
mumbled to herself. "No—he's sweet-loving me, that's it.
Well, I won't play along with his game. The knave, the
blackguard, kissing me so that I'll never—I'll never—"

"You'll never what?"

As if she'd wished him there, Rush Randolph was standing in the path just ahead of where she was walking. Dressed
in a rough green shirt and the long brown work breeches of

the working class, he had one foot propped carelessly against the trunk of a huge live oak tree as if he were waiting for her.

"I won't marry you, Mr. Randolph, so you might as well save yourself the effort."

"It won't be effort I'll be saving once we're married, Amanda, it'll be money. That's why I came to talk to you. I can't afford any more robberies by the Jasmine Bandit."

He didn't give up. Marry Rushton Randolph? The very thought turned her mind into clabber as she searched for some way to stop his words. She seized on a charge that she didn't believe even as she made it. "Why can't you afford it? Have you spent all your English money?"

English money? Rush didn't answer. His expression didn't change. Only the rippling of a nerve in his neck revealed how disturbing her statement had been. It was happening once more. He'd be forced to fight the stigma of being called a spy all over again. Would it never end? Rush let out a long uneven breath.

"So the story has caught up with me again. And you believe that I was a traitor?"

No, I don't believe that you were a traitor. I just need to stop you from getting any closer. "Weren't you?"

"What shall I say? Yes? No? Which will you believe and which will you not?"

"The truth, Mr. Randolph. I'll believe the truth."

"The truth can sometimes mean one thing to one person and something entirely different to another. I gave up on the truth, long ago. I thought you were different, Amanda, that you judged a person for who he is, not what he's accused of being. I guess I was wrong."

Rush continued to stare at her for a long moment. Sadness tinged his eyes and a hint of moisture gathered there. "One thing I'd like to know, and I think you owe me this for my keeping silent about your midnight marauding. Who accused me?"

She wanted to say she was sorry, that her accusation was an instinctive protective mechanism to keep him from intruding further into her life, but the intensity of his gaze confused her. "Franklin told my mother. He's forbidden me to see you again."

"Ah, Franklin. I should have known."

In the end Amanda put her doubts behind her and tried to be as honest as she could be with the man still lazing against the tree. "Perhaps you should know, Mr. Randolph, the people in the Broad River Valley were loyal patriots. I doubt they'd accept a traitor. But I make up my own mind about who I trust. Why did you come here this morning?"

"I came here to warn you, Amanda."

"Warn me about what?"

"Being too free with the use of the monies you've collected. Franklin knows that you're broke. He also knows that there is a highwayman on the prowl. It won't take him long to put the two things together. I came to tell you that the Jasmine Bandit has made her last ride."

"You came to tell me?" She couldn't keep the incredulity from her voice. The very idea of this man attempting to run her life as though he had the right! She'd throw him off Cadenhill and dare him to set his foot on her property again. If he could give orders, so could she.

"Mr. Randolph, I think you should know that I would never marry, if I had a choice. But if I do, it will be to a man who respects my authority. If you don't stop...stop accosting me, I'll be forced to take action against you."

"For what?"

"For—" she stumbled. How could she say for kissing her every time they were alone? "For..." she said again, searching for something to give substance to her threat. "For being a traitor. No—for intruding in my life, for confusing me by your kisses."

"I see." And he did. Amanda had held herself in check for so long that his very presence threatened her tenuous control. He didn't like making her feel fear, but short of leaving her to Franklin's devices, he didn't know what he could do to give her back her confidence.

Amanda, feeling a wave of fresh emotion sweep over her, was sorry she'd threatened him. She didn't believe Franklin's charge. She'd just grabbed the first thought that came to mind as a barrier to hide behind. Rush had already shown a certain kind of loyalty to her. He hadn't turned her in. And she instinctively knew that he was the kind of man her father would have liked. But he'd backed her into a corner and she'd responded with the only weapon she had.

She hesitated a long moment, then said the only thing she could. "Just leave me alone, Mr. Randolph, or I'll have to find a way to stop you."

"May I suggest an even exchange of confidentiality. If you won't spread the spy story, I won't tell the valley what Miss Amanda Caden does at night."

"You wouldn't tell!"

"I would if I had to."

"You're no gentleman."

"I never said I was."

Garbed in men's breeches, Amanda stood defiantly before him, her legs spread slightly, like the captain of a sailing schooner leaning into the wind. Rush felt his admiration grow.

She looked like some unsophisticated pioneer woman, all innocence and fire. A tendril of flame-colored hair had escaped from beneath that ridiculous man's hat, and it shimmered in the sunlight, demanding to be touched. Even from where he stood he could smell the delicate jasmine scent so at odds with her manly exterior. Jasmine—so uniquely Amanda.

He wanted her to trust him. He wanted her to throw caution to the winds and say, "Yes, we're both misfits. Let's take them on together." But it was obvious that she wasn't going to take that position.

But damn it, Amanda was a woman who ought to have understood. He felt the pain slice through him as he accepted the finality of her answer.

His disappointment wasn't the issue here; his commitment was. Houston had been Rush's advocate in the face of public opinion. Rush could do no less.

Taking a breath of air, Rush grimaced and returned to the issue at hand. "I know you have little use for me, Amanda, but I'm sworn to offer you my help. Whether you use it is your choice."

Raising her green eyes suspiciously, Amanda asked, "What does that mean, you're sworn to offer your help? Who asked you to?"

"I wasn't supposed to tell you this, but it was your father's wish. We . . . we worked together."

"My father?" She let out a long breath. "My father asked you to help me?"

"Yes. Amanda, you do whatever you think best about me, but what I'm about to tell must never be revealed. Your father is dead now, and there is no reason to sully his reputation. Yes, I was a spy and I worked directly for the spy master, Houston Caden, during the war. He's the man who recruited and trained me."

"I don't believe you. How?"

"I was at university in England. After that, I stayed on for a time. When the revolution started I came home and joined the cause. I was assigned to Benedict Arnold's staff. You know that Benedict Arnold betrayed the Colonists and defected to British-held territory. Houston thought I could convince Arnold that I was a British sympathizer. I was assigned to accompany another officer, who'd served under Arnold, and follow the general."

"Why?"

"There was reason to believe that Arnold wasn't the only high-ranking officer who supported the English. My job was to find out who and to secretly funnel information back to General Washington through your father."

"And did you succeed?"

"Too well, I'm afraid. There were many, including my own family, who never believed that my defection was simply an order to be followed."

His own family? Amanda heard the pain in his voice. She'd heard that same disappointment in her mother's voice when she'd despaired of Amanda's activities. But her mother would never have believed that she was a spy.

"Afterward, when people refused to believe in my loyalty I went west with the explorers, then back to England for a while. Finally when it seemed that nothing was going to erase the taint of traitor from my name, Houston Caden wrote to President Washington on my behalf.

"President Washington came to my defense, explained my actions to my family, then arranged for me to get the stagecoach line. I was only too pleased to consider your father's request that I settle in Petersburg. By that time he was ill. In his last letter he seemed very confused, very worried. He asked me to keep an eye on you and I agreed. I think he hoped you'd like me."

"I don't believe you," she said, too quickly. But maybe she did. Or maybe it was the faint hope that her father had never meant for her to belong to Franklin as everybody believed.

"You don't have to believe me. The issue of my credibility isn't important here. Saving your land is. Toward that purpose you have decided to take a husband. Obviously you intend to reject me as a suitor, but as you've already learned, I'm as stubborn and as determined as you. I owe it to your father to help you find an answer."

"I don't need your help. I'm making my own plans. I'm going to the race with dual purposes in mind, an extension of our loans and a wager of my own."

"You're going to need a lot more money than a wager on a horse race."

"I'll get more."

"How are you going to explain where it came from?"

"I've been thinking about that. I'll say I got a loan."

"Where? From whom?" Rush hated himself for being hard on her, but Amanda had to be forced to see what she was doing.

"From an old family friend."

"Amanda, I don't think a man in Petersburg has that much money to lend you. Franklin knows that."

"Then I'll tell him that it came from someone in Augusta."

"But you haven't left Petersburg. How did you manage to convince someone to lend money to a woman already in debt, who doesn't hold clear title to the land? Besides, these men are the ones to whom your father owed money. After Franklin gets done with them they aren't going to extend the loans to you, and if they're riled up they might demand payment immediately."

She stared at him, frustration etching her face into a frown. "They can't do that. The notes aren't due until June."

"Houston's debts aren't due until June. But Houston's dead. They can, by rights, demand payment now."

"I can make a partial payment, in good faith."

"And we're back to where we started. Where'd you get the money?"

"Hell's doorknobs! I don't know. There has to be a way."

"As I see it, Amanda, you only have one way out and that's marriage. The question is, do you want to rely on Franklin, or on me?"

Amanda pulled off her hat and stood slapping it against her thigh. He was right. She hadn't accomplished anything. She was back where she'd started. The only solution was marriage. She could pick a thief or she could choose a man Franklin called a traitor.

Both men wanted Cadenhill.

Amanda blinked back unbidden tears of frustration. She wouldn't cry. She hadn't cried in public since she was twelve years old and her dog died.

Within arms' length, Rush waited, feeling her pain as if it were his. Amanda couldn't know how lovely she looked in her misery. Her hair tumbled across her shoulders, free and wild, and he wanted to catch it in his hands and pull her into his arms. His need became so strong that he took an involuntary step toward her.

Frightened by the look in his eyes, Amanda let out a soft cry of denial, "No. I don't want you to touch me."

"I think you do, Amanda. I think you've chosen, whether you intended to or not." This time he reached out and pulled her close.

There was a strength, a confidence about his authority that Amanda found herself accepting. But this time she didn't close her eyes to what was happening. This time she felt the intensity of her defeat, her confusion and fear crystallize into one powerful emotion—need, and she lifted her head.

His kiss wasn't gentle. It was hot and rough, his tongue forcing open her mouth and exploring the wet softness of her, sending a shocking trail of fire that danced along her nerve endings and stoked a fire in her stomach. Feeling him press against her, she groaned as he cupped her bottom with his big hands, lifting her into the hardness that rested against the throbbing part of her. She felt the fire move lower, settle in that place and begin to flame.

Amanda was quickly losing touch with all sense of place and time. She couldn't remember why she'd fought against this wonderfully compelling feeling, or why she'd thought that Mr. Thomas Rushton Randolph was such an evil man. The hot aching coil in her lower body seemed in cadence with the pulsating rhythm of her heartbeat, and she pressed herself shamelessly against him.

Delicious new sensations assaulted every part of Amanda, and she felt her knees quiver with weakness.

Gloriously he took her lips and wondrously she responded, until she felt him kneeling, pulling her down to the path with him, pushing her back against the pine straw as he covered her body with his own.

"Don't," she said, pulling her mouth away so that she could breathe. "Don't—"

"Don't what, my darling? Don't stop?"

"No, don't do this. I can't seem to think when you touch me, Mr. Randolph. I don't know what I'm doing but I—please!"

Her wild plea cut through the haze of sensation that had closed out Rush's every rational thought. Then she was lying on top of his body and he didn't remember moving. Her face was flushed and her hair was tousled wildly. Her shirt had been pulled open, or maybe he'd opened it, and the pale top of one breast was exposed.

Their eyes met and awareness slammed into Rush like an icy wind. Rush knew that Amanda had tried to bring their loving to a halt. A proper woman would have screamed and run away. But Amanda wasn't a proper woman. In spite of her forward manner, Rush knew that she'd never been with a man like him, a man she responded to with such honesty. Rush inhaled roughly, drawing cool air into lungs heated with desire as he pulled back and slowly, with trembling fingers, retied the strings on her shirt.

Gone was her fear, replaced by the heavy glazed look of passion, passion tinged with awe. "I'm sorry," he said, pushing her head to his chest as he began stroking the crown of magnificent hair. He tried desperately to still his breathing.

"Amanda, darling Amanda," he said finally. "I'm sorry. I'm at fault. You haven't had enough experience with men to know how explosive we are together. Sometimes it's that way. Sometimes..." He didn't know how to justify what he was feeling, nor did he want to make her uncomfortable because she returned these feelings.

She'd become as still as the silent green water flowing beside the path where they were lying. Rush groaned.

He was a man, a man who'd made a promise to himself that he'd take care of Amanda. Then the first time he was tested he went past the bounds of propriety, bounds he knew well. He had no right to bring her to this state.

Still reeling from his own near loss of control, he went on, "I want you and I could take you, here and now, in this forest, but that wouldn't be right. That wouldn't be fair. Ah, but, darling, it would be so grand."

Rush caressed her shoulder, sliding his fingertips through her hair, spreading it gently across her body as he would that of a child who needed comforting. Gradually his breathing slowed. He'd never before come so near to losing control with a woman. All reason left him every time they were together.

What had started as a game of flirtation with a saucy bandit had rapidly become an obsession that transcended any concern over his reputation or his future. He hadn't expected such response. He hadn't expected to feel so responsible. But he did, and the woman who elicited this possessiveness had to be as shaken as he.

"You're right, Mr. Randolph," she said unsteadily. "There's something about your kisses that makes me lose my senses. I can't hold you responsible for that. And I don't. I'll have to learn about men and how to control myself. Apparently I'm not to be trusted."

She rolled off him and came gracefully to her knees, trying to find a way out of a situation so completely foreign to her that she felt as if she'd lost her way in a fog of heat.

"You're also right about accounting for the money. But I don't have to do anything about it immediately. Franklin has told me that I have until June to find an answer, and I have to believe him. Perhaps I'll think about this for a time. But I won't rob your coaches anymore, I promise."

"And I'll see to it that you're protected. Nobody will learn the identity of the Jasmine Bandit from me. I can't promise you that I won't kiss you, Amanda, but I won't let it go this far again."

She gave a soft cluck to which her horse responded by trotting to her side. Rush watched her set her foot into the stirrup and climb on the big chestnut stallion. From where Rush stood he could still feel the connection between them, and he shifted his stance to relieve the pressure of his trousers on the swollen part of his body that was protesting her departure.

I promise not to rob you. He let her words reassure him as he rode back to town. The scent of jasmine from her hair went with him as he rode. He'd absorbed the touch and taste of her. They'd shared a mutual desire that had been thwarted.

The frustration relaxed, leaving an ache inside him where there ought to have been satisfaction over convincing her to agree to bring her midnight activities to an end. But in spite of that small degree of success, he knew, as he neared the outer edge of Petersburg, that without understanding when or how it had happened, he'd left something of himself back there in the woods.

But Amanda was right about one thing. She had until June. So did he. Perhaps he'd handled the situation badly. He'd overwhelmed her, yes. But the thought of another man sharing what he'd just experienced troubled him. Rush understood now what Houston had done and why. He'd hoped that Rush and Amanda would find in each other what they both needed—a place in the heart.

He needed a wife. Amanda wouldn't be the kind of woman an ordinary man could mold, and Rush wouldn't want to. If he intended to convince her they belonged together, he'd have to mount a very different courtship. He'd never courted a woman before. But a courtship would be nice.

A June wedding would be nice. Cadenhill would be beautiful in June.

And so would Amanda.

Chapter Twelve

Franklin Caden's face turned bloodred. "What do you mean, Donovan? Somebody else got there first?"

It wasn't enough that his barge had been pilfered; now he learned that his guests had been robbed of the money he'd intended to take from them in wagers on the race—by the same bandit if he was any judge of it. Rush hadn't even mentioned it. Franklin sat behind his desk, staring at his henchman, his face livid with anger.

"Just what I said, bossman. When we stopped the stagecoach they didn't even have a stickpin left between them. Another gang had already waylaid them."

"A gang?"

Donovan licked the tobacco stain from the corner of his mouth and shuffled his feet as he tried to avoid Franklin's wrath. "The one doing the talking wore a mask. Your partner, Mr. Randolph, almost stopped him before he run into the woods where the rest of 'em was waiting."

Donovan had heard the driver say that he only saw a single bandit, but somehow explaining to Franklin that his gang had been beaten out by rival thugs didn't seem as bad as one lone bandit. And if Franklin's guests wanted to claim that four grown men had been overcome by a gang instead of one, who was he to argue?

"All right," Franklin said with authority. "From now on I want a guard to make every trip with goods leaving Petersburg, and on every stagecoach. I want this gang captured and brought to me. Don't fail me, Donovan."

"Sure, Mr. Caden. We'll get him. Don't worry."

Franklin came to his feet and began to pace. His plans hadn't gone as he expected. In fact nothing had gone the way he expected since he'd taken Rushton Randolph in as a partner. Rush had been honest with Franklin about his past and Franklin hadn't cared. Truth was, he'd made a little money on the revolution himself, courtesy of the British, and in the beginning he hadn't been certain that Randolph hadn't known. Taking Randolph in as a partner had served two purposes—keeping him quiet and relieving him of his gold. But Randolph had never mentioned knowing about Franklin's illicit activities and Franklin decided that it was because he hadn't known.

Franklin glanced at his pocket watch. It was time for him to face his guests. They would be rising by now, and if he intended to do any profitable wagering on the upcoming race he'd better begin pacifying the men who'd been robbed on the stagecoach.

Rushton Randolph's coach. Randolph was bound to protect his passengers. He'd made that fact public information. He'd be forced to replace their lost funds. Fine, in the future Franklin would have easy pickings, courtesy of his partner.

Maybe he'd assign Donovan a few more night raids. There was more than one way to get rid of a nuisance.

The day was bright and sunny. The Old Dragon Inn was filled with smoke from the fire, where a roast of beef was turning on the spit. But there was also a leftover smell of stale ale that mingled with the odor of unwashed bodies. Franklin wrinkled his nose. He'd speak with the proprietor. Petersburg was as fine a city as Charleston or Savan-

nah. It was time that the inns were equally as pleasant.
Maybe what Petersburg needed was a public bathhouse.

After their night's ordeal, Franklin's guests were unusually jovial in their greetings. He was a bit surprised as he joined them at the table where they'd just finished a meal of meat and bread. He was pleased that they weren't angry until he learned that Randolph had given them Franklin's guarantee that their losses would be made good.

"Folks in Augusta have always known that the Cadens stood behind their word," Wilkins Mason was quick to say, washing down his food with a pint of ale.

"Sure. Just like your brother, Houston," Clyde Bolling agreed. "If he'd invited us to be his guests, he'd have done the same."

"The Cadens have been around since the beginning. Good reputation, good people. A pleasure to do business with you, Franklin," the third man agreed.

The fourth man, Patrick McLendon, leaned back in his chair and let his gaze play across the table. He didn't miss the surprise in their host's face, nor the discomfort. Clearly, Franklin Caden hadn't planned to make good on their losses at all. But the mention of his brother and the gentle reminder that these men did business with him downriver had put him in the position of having to agree.

Patrick McLendon was a bold, fun-loving Irishman with a great shock of thick brown hair that seemed permanently lightened by the sun. His blue eyes could be filled with mischief one minute and churning with dark anger the next, but always he prided himself on his control.

Sailing to the Colonies on a trading ship before the revolution, Patrick had liked the looks of the raw new country. Ireland was worn-out, overcrowded and overcontrolled. He'd immediately recognized the similarity between the new country and himself. From the decks of a pirate ship he'd risen to a position of some wealth. based on honesty and the kind of wild instinct that told him how far to go and when to pull back.

Cotton, not tobacco, would be the way of the future. Cotton and trade. And he'd decided quickly enough that the only man who had the means to accomplish what Patrick wanted was Rushton Randolph. He'd been in the warehouse when Rush bought Franklin's supplies, watched him scout out the local businessmen and talk with the plantation owners who always stayed at the Planters' Hotel. There'd been plenty of conversation about cotton, but only the Sea Island brand was worth the trouble. Patrick already knew that. He knew, too, that the green seed variety would grow well in the interior, but removing the seed was so time-consuming that it wasn't profitable.

Patrick had even managed an introduction to Randolph so that he could size up the man better. It was while he was sharing a meal in the hotel dining room that Rush had brought up his plan to grow cotton.

Downing his tea, Patrick wiped his mouth on the back of his hand. He knew full well that he didn't belong with these men. He'd recently come from Charleston to Savannah as a broker, yes, but more than that he was a gambler who backed men and ideas, who had accumulated enough money to play with whatever interested him. He'd come for the race, ostensibly, but what he'd really come for was to investigate the rumor that there was a man in Petersburg who claimed to have developed a new machine to remove the seeds from cotton—that and to meet Rush Randolph.

Impatient to get on with his mission, Patrick stood up. "Think I'll walk about for a while, Franklin, check out Petersburg, if you don't mind."

Clearly startled, Franklin checked his watch again. "But I thought we would head over to the Jockey Club and I'd introduce you to some of our fine citizens. I want you to see my horses."

"Jockey Club?" Patrick couldn't conceal his disbelief.

"Certainly. Petersburg is every bit as advanced as Charleston. I'm hosting a barbecue before the race, and a ball afterward at the club."

"And your partner, Mr. Randolph," Patrick went on, "will he be at the club? Or was his ordeal with the bandit more debilitating than he let on."

"Ordeal?" Franklin sensed something not quite right about McLendon's question. "What ordeal?"

"He almost caught the bounder. Actually mounted the horse behind him before the bandit knew what had happened. If the horse hadn't reared and run, I don't think Randolph would have fallen off. Too bad, he had the bandit in his grasp."

"I hadn't heard about that. In fact, I don't know where Randolph is. I've been looking for him myself. He's probably out trying to convince the farmers to assign their slaves to maintain the section of road that goes through their land. Keeping the road clear is a problem for his transportation company."

"As well we can testify," Clyde Bolling offered. "It was a tree across the road that led to the robbery."

"But since Franklin is going to replace our funds I think we ought to forget about that unpleasantness and buy him a real drink," Mason added and stood.

McLendon watched the others leave the inn and walk toward the livery stable. Randolph might be off dealing with farmers, he thought, but he'd give a pretty penny to find out what really happened the night before with the bandit. The others might not have realized what was occurring, but it had been clear to Patrick that it was at Randolph's urging the horse bolted into the woods. And if he'd ever heard any playacting, that yelling at the horse had all the markings of a stage actor in one of those traveling melodramas.

Patrick smiled. He had two days before the race. He'd find out what he needed to know.

The noonday activity on the streets of Petersburg was surprising. Housewives and their slaves were in and out of the stores, bartering goods for supplies and gossiping with the friends they met. Franklin had been right about one thing, Patrick acknowledged: Petersburg was surprisingly sophisticated. It was rare in 1790 for a community to have a racetrack and club, not to mention a billiard parlor.

Patrick sauntered down the wooden sidewalk, ignoring the curious glances from the women he passed. To him, women were simply women—pleasant pastimes, but not to be taken seriously unless they were a necessary part of whatever project he was involved in. Across the muddy street he saw the sign, Randolph Transportation Company. It was freshly painted and had been fastened below the older sign identifying Caden Warehouse.

He stepped onto the street, his mind intent on Rushton Randolph. Ordinarily he would have heard the approach of the horse, but at that moment a herd of loudly protesting pigs spilled into the street just beyond where Patrick was crossing. Somehow the pigs and the horse hit the street at the same moment. It was hard to tell which spooked which, but suddenly the street was turned into a muddy melee.

Between the oinks of the pigs and the neighing of the horse Patrick heard the woman scream. No, he decided as the horse charged straight for him, not a woman, a girl. Until she reached him, she managed to hold on. Then the horse stumbled and she was falling from the animal's back. Quickly Patrick hurdled the pigs in time to catch her as the melee moved past them.

Catherine Caden slid from the horse, and closing her eyes, she landed with a thump. The blow made her feel as if she'd swallowed her heart. She'd never breathe again. She'd expected to die by being trampled by pigs' feet. Instead, she'd been saved. All she was conscious of was the feel of a strong body and the clean smell of a man. Struggling to still her whirling head, she opened her eyes, intent on thanking whoever had saved her from a most unladylike dismounting.

"Thank—" Her words died as she looked up into a pair of laughing blue eyes, the most beautiful blue eyes she'd ever seen. The man holding her was surely a god from the books of myths and legends in Papa's library. His sun-streaked hair was a mass of curls held back with a leather thong that allowed tendrils to escape and frame his face in the midday light. He was strong and big and he was smiling in amusement.

"Oh, I'm sorry," she managed to say. "I truly do thank you for saving me. If you'll just put me down, I have to find Uncle Franklin and then I have to—"

"Begorra, lass, I don't think you want me to put you down right here," Patrick said. "No bigger than you are, little darling, the mud would likely cover you and not even the little people would find you in that muck."

"You're Irish?"

"Yes, ma'am. It's Irish I am, and you're…?" He glanced around and realized that all eyes were focused on them standing in the street alone, no pigs, no horse, no longer a distraction at hand. Patrick walked toward the Caden Warehouse, which had been his destination before this enchanting child had dropped into his arms.

"I'm Catherine Caden," she answered, with no attempt to keep the bemusement from her voice. "What's your name, Irishman?"

"Patrick McLendon, darling. Do you always travel with such an unusual entourage?"

"Entourage? Oh, the pigs. Certainly not. I don't know where those dreadful things came from. I was riding my horse. I would have taken the carriage, but Uncle Franklin has brought it into town and the only other thing is the farm cart. You can see why I wouldn't want to come into town in a cart, don't you?"

Patrick was having trouble seeing anything except the lovely creature he'd captured. She was small and pert, with impish eyes that were neither green nor brown, but somewhere between. Her hair had been braided, but along the way—either during her wild ride or perhaps before—her ribbon had been lost, and now her strawberry blond hair shone like a halo of silk in the sun.

"Certainly. A cart could never create such a dramatic entrance as a runaway horse. You're Franklin Caden's niece?"

"Well, not really. I mean he's my father's stepbrother and we were taught to call him Uncle Franklin, but we're not related by blood."

"I see." Patrick continued to hold her long after he reached the sidewalk. He passed the apothecary shop and entered the open doorway to Caden Warehouse. Inside he stopped and looked around, finding the steps that led up to the balcony where the offices were located.

"I think that you can put me down now, Mr. McLendon," Catherine said shyly.

"Yes." But he didn't.

At the top of the stairs he pushed open Franklin's door and stepped inside the empty office, standing for a moment before he reluctantly lowered his captive to the floor.

"Your uncle isn't here, Miss Caden," he said. "I believe he might be with his guests at the Jockey Club. I would be happy to assist you in reaching the racetrack but I don't think they allow children there."

"Children?" Catherine's apathy vanished. "Children? I would have you understand that I am sixteen years old. I am not a child. That's what I want to talk to Uncle Franklin about. I have decided that I don't intend to wait for Amanda to marry. Uncle Franklin thinks he's going to marry her. But she's going to be an old maid. It's me who is looking for a husband."

"You intend to marry Franklin Caden?" Patrick couldn't conceal his surprise. Granted she was older than he'd first thought, her small round breasts heaving now as she practically spit fire at him.

"Of course not. But it's obvious that Amanda isn't going to, and I have no intention of being a spinster like her. My mother was with child when she was seventeen and I intend to be the same. Are you married, Mr. McLendon?"

"Me? Certainly not."

Catherine took a step back and studied the big, light brown-haired man. She walked around him, viewing him from all angles before she spoke again. "You're dressed like you have money. Do you?"

"I have enough," Patrick replied, beginning to enjoy the young woman's determination.

"Do you know the Caden family? I mean, do you know that my father is recently deceased and that my sisters, my mother and I inherited Cadenhill?"

"I've heard."

"Then you know how valuable the plantation is so you will appreciate what I have to offer a husband."

"Now, wait just a minute, Miss Caden. I never said I was interested in marrying, and if I were, you're much too young for me."

"I don't think so, Patrick," Catherine said smugly. "I shall attend the races on New Year's with my family, and I expect you to come and walk about with me."

"Why would I do that?" Patrick asked, genuinely stunned at the plans the little flirt was making.

"Because," Catherine said, with a sudden smile, "because you'll do very nicely as a husband."

Quickly, before Patrick knew what she was doing, the girl stood on her tiptoes, closed her eyes and pursed her lips.

"I'd like you to kiss me, please, Patrick," she said and waited.

"Kiss you? What you need is a spanking," Patrick said. Or a good scaring, and he could do that. He lowered his head and brushed her lips lightly. "You wish to be kissed?

Never let it be said that an Irishman refused to kiss a beautiful—woman."

Catherine drew back and studied him as seriously as before. "I liked it, but I think, if you set your mind to it, you could do it better."

Patrick didn't mean to roar, but he did. And he might have given her a demonstration had she not dashed around him and run out the door. Instead he followed her to the balcony and watched her dance down the steps, stopping in the doorway to give him a quick wave before she disappeared into the street, leaving him openmouthed and stunned at what had happened.

Patrick decided that he'd better get to the track. He was afraid of taking a chance on what might happen next. Rarely did he find his self-confidence ruffled, but Miss Catherine Caden, who was sixteen and looking for a husband, had just shattered his usual aplomb.

Patrick McLendon wasn't a farmer. He was an adventurer, in search of a cottonseed-removal machine.

And Petersburg was turning into an adventure he hadn't expected. First he'd had his money stolen by a bandit who seemed suspiciously female. Now he'd just crossed swords with a child-woman who wanted a more personal prize—a husband.

And she'd set her sights on him.

On the morning of the race, Amanda was pacing the bank of the broad river, wrestling with the problem of what to do about Rushton Randolph. He'd saved her from certain capture after the holdup, by pretending that Shadow had run away.

Amanda did her best to erase the picture of the man from her mind. She concentrated on the problems to be solved on Cadenhill. They'd butchered the hogs, cut them into hams and salted them down for curing in the smokehouse. Lovie and Jelene made sausage and boiled down the fat into lard for candles and cooking. The tobacco beds were covered with tents of muslin under which fires were being maintained to protect the tender young plants from the cold.

For now that was all she could do to protect the land.

Except find a husband.

A husband. All Amanda's thoughts came back to that. Rushton Randolph pushed his way inside her thoughts like a swarm of pesky gnats in summer. The man seemed to know what she was thinking and what she planned to do. More, he even suggested her next move at the same time that he was warning her to stop her midnight activities.

He was truly an irritating contradiction. Yet he seemed determined to help her.

Could his claim of knowing her father be true? She knew that her father had done little actual fighting, serving instead in the central war office as a planner. That he had been wounded at all was a freak occurrence; he was simply caught traveling between General Washington's army camp and the central headquarters.

Houston Caden had never talked about his war activities, choosing instead to discuss the uniting of colonies into one nation. He'd thought that by joining together they could survive and grow. A dreamer and a planner, that was her father.

But had he brought Rushton Randolph here for a reason? Perhaps, but as a candidate in her husband search? No. Rushton said he came in search of land to plant cotton. Once she regained control of Cadenhill she'd never willingly give over its control to a man again.

One last time she'd try to scout out local prospects. There had to be at least one pliable man in the valley. She'd attend Franklin's horse race and ball. But this time she wouldn't allow either Franklin or Rushton Randolph to interfere. This time she'd take her mother and Catherine.

This time she'd be safe.

Chapter Thirteen

When Amanda returned to the house Catherine was already dressed for the race and waiting on the porch.

The little girls were sitting on the bottom steps, trying desperately to keep quiet, hoping against hope that if they were very good they might be taken along.

"Do hurry up, Manda," Catherine scolded, following Amanda into the house and up the stairs. "I don't want to be late. There's the race, then the ball. Isn't it exciting?"

"Catherine's right," Iris Caden said as she exited her bedroom, pulling on a white linen mobcap with a full crown. "If we're going, we should be on time."

The ribbon trimming Iris's cap matched the jacket of her dress and the frill on the sleeves. She knew their walking dresses were a bit out of date, but she and Lovie had managed to update one gown by using parts of a second one.

Amanda's dress had been the most difficult to fashion because she was taller and more developed than her mother and Catherine. The French-style chemise had lent itself nicely to lengthening the dress by adding a rose-colored border that picked up the color of the flower embroidered on the fabric. The mushroom-shaped hat of white muslin that matched the dress was excessive, in Amanda's opinion; she refused to go out looking as though she was wear-

ing a toadstool on her head. As a last resort she'd finally
agreed to carry the hat.

Settie had already transported the ball gowns to Franklin's house in town, and had returned to pick up the ladies.

While Amanda dressed, Catherine fidgeted, and Iris gave
last-minute instructions to Lovie and Jelene about caring for
Jamie and Cecilia.

Scant moments later when Amanda appeared, fully
dressed, both Cat and Iris Caden gasped, consternation
marking their faces. "You're ready?" Cat asked.

Amanda stopped and leaned over, allowing her hair to
pool in the crown of the hat, then cramming the offending
object on her head.

"I decided to wear it," she said. "It covers my hair."

"It also makes you look like you're wearing a muffin on
your head," Cat said with a giggle.

"No worse than that yellow hatbox you're wearing,"
Amanda retorted and glared at her younger sister, who was
dressed in a soft blue muslin patterned with tiny flowers of
palest yellow. Her frown softened as she realized how
grown-up Catherine had suddenly become. Gone was the
long-legged, excitable girl. In her place was a young woman
with shining eyes and a take-on-the-world air. Amanda
wasn't sure when the change had begun, but Cat seemed to
have blossomed almost overnight.

Amanda sighed. She knew she was behaving badly, but
she was unsettled over the coming event. Rushton Randolph would be there, and in spite of her firm decisions
about her future plans, she didn't know how she could face
him after the liberties she'd allowed him to take in the woods
yesterday. Perhaps, she thought, looking as if she were
wearing a toadstool on her head might enable her to avoid
his attention.

Of course, it might also cost her the attention of any of
Franklin's guests. Gaining that attention was—since her
mother had forbidden her racing Thor—the purpose of this

outing. Helplessly she raised her gaze to face her mother. "I don't know what to do with my hair, Mother."

"I'll help you," Iris said, cautioning the girls not to speak by a frown and shake of her head. "Catherine, see if Settie's brought up the wagon."

"Wagon, Mother?" Catherine said crossly. "Why did Uncle Franklin take Papa's carriage anyway? What will people think when we arrive in the same wagon we use to haul manure?"

"You don't have to go," Amanda said, more sharply than she intended. But the closer the time came to leave the more unsettled she became.

Catherine took one look at Amanda's expression and fled. The last thing she wanted was to be left behind.

Amanda whirled around and returned to her room, sitting down at the dressing table she rarely used. She pulled the hat from her head, allowing her hair to fall down her back.

"I think I ought to braid it like Lovie's. I don't know why women think they have to have curls and gewgaws in their hair anyway."

"Let me, Amanda." In mere minutes Iris had fashioned a fringe in front and loose ringlets around the sides and down Amanda's back. "You have such beautiful hair, just like your father."

"I do?"

"When he was young. He was the most handsome man in Savannah. All the women were after him."

"How did you know you were in love, Mother? How in the name of heaven will I—does a woman ever know?"

"I wouldn't worry, Amanda. You'll figure it out. Sometimes the Lord puts us where He wants us and holds us there till we understand what He expects us to do."

Amanda stood, tugging at her neckline, trying to raise it without having it seem obvious. "Well, I wish He wouldn't be quite so subtle. I'm good with horses and tobacco. Men don't make any sense at all."

"They don't have to," Iris said softly. "They're just men. I don't know about others, but the women in my family know when they find the right men. Their hearts care."

Amanda left the room, puzzling over her mother's revealing words.

For Amanda the drive to the track was not a comfortable trip. Catherine was right; Franklin had to be persuaded to return the carriage. It was New Year's Day and though the sun was shining, the wind was cold and brisk. Amanda's hair was flying about her face when they reached the wooden structure with glass windows that Franklin called a club.

Settie drove the wagon into the area reserved for carriages. Amanda waited for her mother and sister to be assisted from the rear. She watched Settie handing the reins to the small brown boy who was in charge, dreading what was to come. The dress she was wearing seemed to constrict her, sliding too low here and riding up there. As for the hat, she'd agreed to carry it for fashion's sake, but now she wished she was wearing it and that it had a veil behind which she could hide.

"Manda, get down. It's cold here in the shade." Cat was stamping her feet impatiently.

The little girls would have been a welcome diversion. And Cat was wrong. It wasn't cold here. At least Amanda wasn't cold. It didn't come as a surprise when she heard the voice that ignited the warmth in her body.

"Good morning, Miss Caden. I'm delighted to see you, again."

"Amanda, who is this gentleman?" Iris asked.

Amanda swallowed hard and lifted her eyes to meet the man standing beside the wagon, ready to assist her to the ground.

Gone were the rough worsted trousers of the back country. This morning Thomas Rushton Randolph was wearing a light blue frock coat with tails over a yellow vest and a pair of tightly fitting dark blue breeches fastened just below the knees with silver buttons; his stockings were a shade of blue somewhere between. His leather shoes were unadorned. He carried a leather riding crop, which he placed under his arm as he held out his hands.

"Please, allow me to assist you down so that you can introduce me to your family."

Amanda would have said no. She would have said that she could dismount by herself. She would have, but she couldn't. Her dress had become wound about her legs and she seemed to be standing on the hem. Before she realized what was happening, Rushton Randolph had lifted her and was swinging her easily to the ground.

For just a second he held her, focusing a dizzying conspiratorial smile of delight on her before stepping back and turning to meet her mother. "Permit me, Mrs. Caden. I'm Rushton Randolph, Franklin's partner. I can see where Miss Amanda gets her beauty."

Iris fought herself for a moment, caught between the natural good manners she'd been taught to use and her shock at learning that this handsome man was the one Franklin had accused of being a spy. It was clear that Amanda was unsettled, and clear that Mr. Randolph was determined to ignore her daughter's lack of etiquette.

"I am Iris Caden, Mr. Randolph. And this is my younger daughter, Catherine, who seems to have momentarily lost her tongue. Catherine!"

Catherine curtsied. "I'm sorry, Mother. I was just so surprised. Amanda, you never told me about Mr. Randolph. I mean that you knew him, or that he would attend the race." Catherine addressed Rush, "Are you here with— someone?"

Amanda caught her sister's casual question as well as the quick look she took around the area. Cat was up to something. She'd had that feeling ever since they'd decided to attend the race. It wasn't just the ball gown, though that had been reason enough for her sister to act like a silly goose. But Catherine hadn't been silly at all. And that was what bothered Amanda.

Now, Rushton Randolph was openly sliding his arm beneath hers, staking his claim even before they entered the clubhouse. Then he placed his other arm beneath Iris's, and started toward the door.

"Come along, Catherine," Iris instructed, suddenly grateful for a man's support, even if it was a man she wasn't at all sure Houston would have approved of.

"I've heard so much about you, Mrs. Caden. Houston considered himself a lucky man to have such a family."

"You knew Houston?"

"Yes, ma'am. I knew him in Philadelphia. He was a very fine man. In fact, he'd asked me to call on him when I arrived in Petersburg. He was responsible for President Washington giving me the appointment to open up the stage line. I was very sorry to learn of his passing. My condolences."

"Thank you, Mr. Randolph."

Amanda didn't respond. Her heart was thudding so hard that she was afraid to open her mouth for fear that it would jump right out of her chest.

The Jockey Club was constructed of whitewashed pine with a roofed veranda overlooking the field below, which had been turned into a racetrack. Around the outer edges of the dirt track was a split rail fence that separated the spectators from the horses.

At the clubhouse, Rush stepped back, allowing first Catherine, then Iris and finally Amanda to precede him into the building.

"Amanda, my dear." Franklin hurried across the lounge with his hands outstretched. "Iris, Catherine. I'm delighted that you decided to accept my invitation."

As he reached Amanda she turned away, giving him barely a nod. "Are the horses on display, Franklin?"

Rush took a step to follow her, then stopped, torn between following Amanda and his obligation to Iris.

Iris, sizing up the situation, adroitly transferred her arm to Franklin's. "Please go with her, Mr. Randolph. She's liable to decide to send for Thor and ride him herself."

"Ride Thor?" Franklin's voice was filled with dismay.

"Don't worry," Iris reassured Franklin with a laugh. "I was only teasing. Now do escort me inside."

"Do come on, Uncle Franklin!" Catherine said impatiently. "I want to see everything and—everybody."

Swept along, Franklin had little choice but to escort his sister-in-law and his niece. His partner had outwitted him again and he was beginning to find that very irritating.

Beyond the lounge, a noisy crowd was gathered, ready for the first race to begin. Amanda brushed past the crowd, avoiding the men she recognized as Franklin's friends from Augusta. She was too unsettled to present herself to anybody just yet. She needed a moment to gather her poise. As she reached the stable area Rush caught up to her.

"Wait, Amanda."

"Go away, Mr. Randolph!" Amanda tried not to see Rushton Randolph crook his lips into that devastating smile of amusement. She pretended an extraordinary interest in the paddock ahead.

"Now, now. Don't be cross, Amanda. You'll never catch a husband like that. You didn't even stop and say hello when you passed all those bachelors back there."

"I don't want—" She cut off her retort. She didn't want a husband, but she was bound to find one.

"You don't want any of them," he finished for her.
"Fine. Because you're going to marry me and the sooner
they know it the better."

When she turned to complain, he caught her elbow and
gave her a kind, gentle smile that melted the irritation. His
smile was so much like the one her father used to wear when
he teased her that she couldn't hold back a smile in return.

And there it was again, that hot feeling that swept over
her. They simply stood, staring at each other, oblivious to
the fact that all those standing on the veranda were watching in surprise.

Amanda suddenly took in a quick breath of air. Her
movement broke the moment and she glanced around,
catching sight of Franklin staring down at them with pure
malice.

Rush, too, saw Franklin, and felt Amanda flinch. He
turned away, catching Amanda's elbow and nudging her
toward the stable.

Woodenly, Amanda moved forward. She didn't want to
walk with Rushton Randolph. But she wanted even less to
have to smile and make small talk with any of the men
watching.

As they moved across the grass, her body felt like a field
of grain caught by a summer breeze. Merely being touched
by Rush gave her a quivery sensation. She felt herself wanting, responding in ways she'd never imagined. She felt anger, too, and uncertainty and anticipation and so much more
that her nerve endings tingled everywhere she and Rush
touched.

The horses were being held in a small corral by their riders, awaiting the signal to walk to the starting line. The
jockeys, though lacking the fancy uniforms of the race-
tracks in Virginia, each wore some distinctive color, either
on their hats or around their necks.

Amanda was grateful for the nervous motions and sounds
of the horses. She was both sorry and grateful when she and

Rush arrived at the fence. Amanda propped one foot on the rail and stared at the entrants. Thor was equal to any one of them. She was sorry she hadn't overruled her mother and entered him. Winning the purse could have gone a long way toward explaining her newfound wealth.

"Look at the bay," Rush said. "He's a beauty."

"Yes, but he doesn't compare with Thor."

"Thor. That's the big chestnut you were riding in the woods, not the black horse the highwayman rides?"

"Yes, the chestnut. I raised him from a colt. He's very special."

"And you wanted to enter him in the race?"

"Oh, yes! More than anything. But Mother thought it was improper."

"You didn't intend to ride him?"

"I did. Thor doesn't normally take to strangers."

"Like his mistress, no doubt. Shall we walk down nearer the track?" Rush asked.

Amanda glanced around. The track was to her right, beyond the stable. Behind her was the clubhouse, built on top of the hill. The only way to get closer to the track without returning to the clubhouse was by a path that led behind the stable and past a small stand of birch trees.

"I don't think that would be acceptable," Amanda said. "My mother wouldn't approve of our disappearing from sight."

"You're right, but it's the only way I can kiss you without an audience."

"I told you. You are not to kiss me again," Amanda directed. "It isn't proper. You're to stop—at once."

"I'm sorry, my dear. I'm afraid I can't do that."

Rush took a step closer, propping one foot on the rail surrounding the corral. He didn't look at her, but she was so conscious of his nearness that she couldn't marshal her thoughts.

"So this is what we've come to bet on."

Amanda turned at the sound of the man's voice. It was a lilting voice, filled with laughter. The stranger, wearing a russet-colored coat and carrying a beaver hat, joined them, studying the horses briefly before turning his attention to Amanda. "Hello, Randolph. And this is . . . ?"

Rush frowned at the intruder. "Miss Amanda Caden, this is Patrick McLendon, one of Franklin's guests from Augusta."

One of Franklin's guests? Amanda hadn't seen this man before. He was not the kind of pliable man she was searching for, but she couldn't deny that he was appealing.

"Are you a gambler, Mr. McLendon?" Amanda asked brightly, pleased that he had interrupted the intensity of the moment.

"In a manner of speaking. I take a wager now and then."

Amanda, conscious of Rush's displeasure, smiled broadly. "And do you always win?"

"Not always, but often enough."

"Beware, Patrick, Miss Caden is quite the eligible young lady," Rush said smoothly, ignoring Amanda's glare.

Patrick was quick to catch the undercurrents between Rushton Randolph and Amanda Caden. Amanda seemed to be welcoming him more warmly than her eyes bespoke. And Rush was practically boring holes in his jacket.

"Are all the Caden women looking for husbands?"

Amanda straightened up. "What do you mean, all the Caden women?"

"Well, earlier I was propositioned in the middle of Petersburg, by a child with strawberry blond hair and hazel eyes who said her name was Catherine Caden."

"Catherine?" This time Amanda's surprise wasn't feigned.

"Don't worry, Miss Caden. I didn't accept. I must have been waiting for you."

"Catherine?" she asked again. Catherine's recent disappearances and subsequent happy mood were beginning to make more sense; she'd been daydreaming about this man—though Amanda couldn't imagine how Catherine had managed to get away and ride into Petersburg without anyone knowing. Amanda turned to search the veranda for her sister. She didn't have far to look.

Catherine was running down the path toward them, her bonnet bouncing dangerously on her head, her hair coming loose from its ribbons and flying in the crisp air.

"Manda, Mr. Randolph! Mother is looking for you. Hello, Patrick McLendon. Are you glad to see me?"

"Catherine! Behave yourself!" Amanda cautioned sharply. "A proper young lady doesn't ask for compliments."

"Why not? How else will I know?"

"A man always lets a woman know when he's glad to see her," Rush said. He captured Amanda's arm and turned her back toward the clubhouse, whispering softly, "Of course, chances are, she already knows. Will you have supper with me this evening?"

"I will not!"

"Then a dance, a waltz perhaps."

Amanda felt her pulse shudder. She remembered too well the last time she'd danced with Rushton Randolph. She remembered the veranda and the kiss he'd taken, too. The tightness in her throat prevented an answer. Instead she managed to nod. A dance would be safe. A dance would allow her to feel his arms around her where it would be safe.

Without being quite sure how it had happened, Patrick found himself following Rush and Amanda, Catherine firmly attached to his arm.

Catherine chattered brightly about the coming race and the other social activities in Petersburg. Patrick, after an attempt to disengage himself, found himself caught up in her enjoyment of the day. The girl was like a sunbeam dancing across a bright blue sky.

Amanda, holding herself so stiff that a strong wind would likely have broken her in half, hardly knew what to say. She already wished that she hadn't agreed to the dance. How was she to seek other prospective suitors when Franklin's partner kept interfering? Not only had Rushton Randolph boldly claimed her attention before all of Petersburg, he'd managed to drive a wedge between her and the only other man who might have interested her—Patrick McLendon.

Cat's casting her aspirations on Mr. McLendon was girlish foolishness. Amanda knew that Iris would never allow her sister to remain with Mr. McLendon. Once they reached the veranda, her expectations were realized. Iris summoned both girls over to sit on the benches beside her as the first race was called.

"How well do you know these men, Amanda?"

"Not well, Mother. The black-eyed one is Thomas Rushton Randolph, of the North Carolina Randolphs. He's Franklin's partner, the man who is supposed to be the spy."

"I didn't now that you were so well acquainted."

"I . . . well, I met him at the Taliaferros' ball. He's interested in buying land to raise cotton."

"I see." And Iris was beginning to see that Mr. Randolph might be the reason for Amanda's restlessness. Iris smiled. She hadn't believed that a man would ever come along who would be able to reach Amanda. She was willing to admit that she'd been wrong. But pressing Amanda would be a mistake. She suspected her daughter's newfound interest in the opposite sex was fragile and that it wouldn't take much to destroy it. Wisely, she changed the subject. "And the other man?"

"Patrick McLendon, an Irishman who's full of blarney. He claims that Catherine proposed to him in the middle of Petersburg."

"Catherine! That can't be true."

"Oh, but I did," Catherine interrupted. "I think he'll do splendidly. Unfortunately, he doesn't know it yet. But that's all right. I'll teach him."

"You'll do no such thing, Catherine Elizabeth Caden. I forbid you to chase after a man who is twice your age!"

"He's only thirty, Mother. And I'll be seventeen on my next birthday, old enough to accept a gentleman's attentions."

"Perhaps," Iris agreed reluctantly. "But I'd have to know a great deal more about any suitor. And you're not seventeen yet. In the meantime, you'll sit beside me and behave yourself."

Catherine only smiled and caught first her upper lip, then her lower one between her teeth. Charity Taliaferro claimed that she had her own pot of lip rouge, but until Catherine could buy one, she'd color her lips naturally.

The other members of the Petersburg community soon intervened, and much to Amanda's and Catherine's relief, they were caught up in a renewal of old acquaintances and Iris was unable to question either of them further.

Across the porch, Patrick and Rush lit cigars and enjoyed them for a moment before they talked.

"You intend to marry Amanda Caden?" Patrick's voice was a bit tighter than he'd expected.

"I intend to, yes."

"She doesn't seem particularly interested."

"About as much as you're interested in her sister Catherine."

"Catherine is too young to know what she wants."

"I think not, my friend. And I'm of the opinion that the Caden women make up their own minds and go after what they want."

"Well, they're impulsive and outspoken. On that I agree."

Rush was standing with a clear view of the Caden women. Catherine had moved her chair so that she could frequently turn her face in their direction. Amanda was avoiding any movement that might allow her to catch sight of the men.

Across the way, Catherine openly examined the Irishman, who'd appeared as if in answer to her prayers. He might not see her, but he wasn't totally impervious to her attention, and oh Lordy, was he a handsome man!

"As far as Catherine's age is concerned," Rush observed, "at sixteen my mother was already married. My brother was born before she turned eighteen."

"My mother was forty when she died giving birth to her tenth child," Patrick said in a low voice. "I'm not interested in marrying Miss Catherine Caden. I'd feel like I was taking a babe to raise. I know how it feels."

"To be forty?"

"No, to be the babe. I was that tenth child. So far I've managed to avoid any possibilities of fatherhood. But young Miss Catherine Caden is trying my fortitude."

"You wouldn't be the first man to take a younger bride. I've been told they keep a man on his toes. Though for myself, I prefer them a bit older."

Franklin Caden disentangled himself from his guests and walked across the open space between the women and the rail. "Gentlemen, you don't seem to be enjoying yourself."

"You mean we aren't betting, don't you?" Patrick McLendon shaded his eyes with his hands and turned his gaze in the direction of the starting gate. That Catherine Caden was between him and that point was not completely beyond his attention.

At that point Catherine turned slightly and caught his gaze. She tried to still the ripple of joy that washed across her face, tried and failed miserably. Having done so she openly faced him for a moment before being forced to respond to a remark made by a woman sitting in front of her.

Patrick was startled. The horses were halfway around the track and his attention was still fastened on the starting gate. It mattered little. Franklin's horses had won every event so far, which was what Patrick had expected, and they hadn't even seen his champion yet.

Franklin didn't miss the exchange between Catherine and Patrick McLendon. He cursed silently. Now he not only had to worry about Amanda and Rushton Randolph, he also had to make certain that Catherine's obvious infatuation with Patrick McLendon didn't interfere with his plans for Cadenhill. Perhaps inviting McLendon had been a mistake. But McLendon was rumored to have money and to be willing to take a gamble with it. So far that had not proved to be the case. Franklin knew he had to do something to entice the man, or he would miss the opportunity. Well, Franklin mused, he wasn't above taking a risk. All he had to do was think of a means.

"Care to make a wager, Franklin?" Rush said quietly, turning Franklin away from the other men by taking a step to the side.

Franklin followed. "What kind of wager, Randolph?"

"Your best horse against a horse of my choosing?"

"A horse of your choosing? What a strange way to put it. But, why not? My horse's sire was a Derby champion from England. Imported him myself. There isn't a horse in the valley who can outrun my King Arthur in the mile."

Except for Amanda's horse, Rush thought.

"You have a racehorse, Randolph?" Franklin asked curiously, moving even farther away from the other bettors. This suggestion offered definite possibilities.

"Not my horse yet," Rush said, thinking of Amanda's wish to enter Thor, "but a horse I'm thinking of buying. This will be a test of his skill."

A method of further shrinking Rush's cache of funds was presenting itself to Franklin. Now all he had to do was set the stakes to his advantage. "Of course, Randolph, providing the pot is rich enough." Franklin could barely control his glee.

"You name the purse."

"Gold, I should think, or—" Franklin was struck with sudden inspiration. "Your interest in the warehouse."

"My interest in the warehouse?" Rush considered the suggestion for a moment. He hadn't thought that far ahead. He'd just wanted to give Amanda something. But perhaps this might be a means of reclaiming his investment. It was common knowledge that Thor was the fastest horse in the valley. With more funds, he could invest in more land. With the return of his gold, he could buy Cadenhill land.

Or save Cadenhill for Amanda.

Across the veranda he caught sight of Amanda, sitting erect and trying heroically to take part in the inane conversation that race goers indulged in. He saw the quiet desperation in her face and he wanted to pull her away, walk with her in the woods where they could talk about farming, and gristmills, and fish. But more than that he wanted to protect her.

"Why not?" Franklin asked. "You could move on farther south, perhaps to Augusta where there must be more opportunity for a man like you. Make your bet, Randolph. I'll take it, whatever it might be."

"Trying to get rid of me?"

"Oh, I shall do that. And I'll marry Amanda, Randolph. It's just a matter of time. She lacks funds and she has no opportunity to find them. I've seen to that."

Amanda and Franklin? The thought of that made Rush ball his fists. There was no way in hell that he'd ever let Franklin have her. "Here's my bet, Franklin," Rush said in a voice that could be heard by all. "My half of the warehouse against full payment of all Cadenhill debts owed to you."

"What?" Franklin had counted on a large wager, but reclaiming his warehouse?

Patrick, who'd been observing quietly, let out a low laugh. "You asked for it, Caden. Take the bet."

Franklin swallowed hard. He looked around. McLendon wasn't the only one to hear Randolph's offer. Of course he'd win. Still, a deep-seated fury filled him. He'd regretted taking Rushton Randolph as a partner almost from the moment he'd accepted his gold. But he'd thought to find a way out, just as he always had when a person had outworn his usefulness. Now he was having his own hand forced, and it made him reckless.

"Agreed. When?"

"Tomorrow. One o'clock."

"And the horse?"

"Amanda Caden's horse, Thor."

"Thor?" Franklin felt suddenly weak. He'd been tricked. "What makes you think my fiancée's animal is a racehorse?"

"Fiancée?" Patrick McLendon questioned.

Amanda had heard Thor's name in the murmur of voices behind her, and stood.

"Amanda, where are you going?" Iris Caden started out of her chair in alarm.

"To find out why those men are discussing Thor. Thor is mine, not part of the estate, and I don't trust Franklin. Please, stay here, Mother," Amanda said, as she headed toward the cluster of men. "I'll be back soon."

"Miss Caden?" Patrick acknowledged Amanda's approach with a slight bow. "I had no idea that you owned a racehorse."

"I don't. Why would you think that?"

"Mr. Randolph and your uncle have just wagered on the outcome of a race between your horse, Thor, and your uncle's champion. The bet is Randolph's half of the warehouse against payment in full on all Cadenhill's debts held by Franklin."

Amanda turned a stricken look toward Rush. "You did what?"

"You wanted to race him. It's done."

Amanda was stunned. The man was not only a devil, finding another way to torment her, but a fool as well. He thought he was David come to save her from Goliath. She'd wanted to race Thor, and he'd arranged it. But at what risk!

"When?"

"Tomorrow." Franklin could barely control his glee.

"I thank you, Mr. Randolph, but I can't allow it," Amanda said quietly. "You could lose everything."

"Or win—everything."

"Amanda, what's happening?" Catherine had broken away from Iris's restraint and come to her sister's side.

"Thor's going to race Uncle Franklin's horse."

"Manda, what will Mother say?"

But the terms of the bet were already making the rounds. For a moment, the event on the track was ignored. For a moment there was nobody on the platform but Amanda and Rush. For a moment she understood what it meant for a heart to care.

Then, slowly and openly, the man who'd put his worth on the line for Cadenhill allowed his lips to spread in a daring smile. At the same time one rakish eyelid lowered in a deliberate wink.

"What about it, Miss Caden?" Rush asked. "I really think that we ought to talk strategy, perhaps over supper?"

"No, I—I can't."

"What do you have to lose, Manda?"

Only my heart.

Rush tapped his ashes over the rail and took a long drag on the half-burned cigar. "The time comes when everyone must choose sides, Miss Caden, and take a stand. Where do you stand?"

"Choose?" Like you did. Like my father did. As infuriating as he was, he was right. He was offering her a solution at no apparent cost to herself. Generous? No, the offer wasn't made from generosity. She wasn't fool enough to believe that. He'd already announced his plan to buy land.

If he won the bet he still owned half of the warehouse. And in addition, he'd won the right to claim her and Cadenhill.

Why must choices be so hard? Marriage vs. control. She'd lose herself, but she'd save Cadenhill—as she'd promised her father.

Cadenhill. The catalyst for such greed. Rush Randolph had found something he wanted and he was going after it. She could understand that, and in some way she could even silently admire his courage. After all, hadn't she done the same? She gave him a lost look, half of fear and half of resignation, giving him the only answer she could have.

"I accept."

"What do you mean you're going home?" Iris Caden, eyeing her eldest daughter in dismay, was standing in the middle of the large bedroom Franklin had provided, where they could rest and change clothes for the evening supper and ball.

But Catherine, not Amanda, answered. "Manda can go home if she wants. But I'm not. You already made me miss the barbecue. Tonight at the ball I shall have supper at midnight with Mr. McLendon."

"You'll do no such thing, Catherine Caden," Iris announced firmly. "And you won't go home either, Amanda. Settie can fetch the horse if you insist on allowing him to be raced."

"But I can't stay here, Mother. I have to..." Amanda walked across the room in her petticoat, her heart heavy and her mind clouded with conflicting emotions.

As if she understood, Iris crossed the room and put her arm around Amanda's waist. "You can't do anything to stop this, Amanda. Mr. Randolph has made a very generous attempt to save our land. I think that we must accept his kindness in the spirit with which it is offered."

"But, Mother, he wants more."

"What does he want, Amanda?"

"He wants Cadenhill. He wants to marry me to get it."

"I didn't hear any mention of marriage in the wager."

"No, but that's what he wants."

"And you, Amanda? What do you want?"

"I want... I want things to be as they were before Papa died. I want to grow tobacco and ride through the woods on Thor. I don't want to feel things I don't understand."

"I know, my darling. But life doesn't let us stay the same. We have to grow and change and make new places for ourselves. That's the way it has always been for a woman. Accept it, Amanda. And once you stop fighting it, you'll learn what great joy there is waiting for you."

"I'm not fighting, Mother," Catherine said seriously. "I intend to marry Mr. Patrick McLendon and teach him what kind of joy there is waiting for him."

"Nonsense, Catherine. You don't have any idea what you're talking about!"

"Then tell me, Mother, why does my heart squeeze itself into an hourglass every time I look at him? Why do I want to sing and dance? Why does my skin feel like a hundred red ants are scurrying underneath it every time we touch?"

Iris turned to her younger child in amazement. "Has that man taken liberties with you?"

"No, Mother. I don't even know what men—Patrick—is supposed to do, except kiss me, and I'll have to say that he doesn't appear to know much about that."

"Catherine, what have you done?"

"Nothing yet, Mother. But I intend to, and with Mr. Patrick McLendon from Ireland. Mother, who are 'the little people'?"

"They're imaginary folk who are supposed to either bring great luck or wreak great havoc. I'm sure Mr. McLendon must have brought a tribe of them with him, for 1791 is starting off as a very confusing year."

Amanda swung around, walked toward the window and glanced down into Franklin's yard. She'd always avoided Franklin's house. It was like him, small but pretentious, with real glass panes and little flourishes of wooden trim around the edges of the porch. She turned again and paced back toward the bed now piled high with their ball gowns and petticoats. What would she do if Thor won?

The debts owed Franklin would be cleared. But there were still the outstanding loans due in June. Worse, if Thor won, she'd be obligated to Mr. Randolph.

If Thor lost, the consequences would be disastrous for her champion. He'd lose a large portion of his investment, his partnership in the tobacco warehouse. And she'd be responsible, all because she wanted to race her horse.

Such a muddle. In long strides, Amanda moved back toward the window, ignoring her mother's worried look as she tried unsuccessfully to close out Catherine's continuous humming of the popular song, "A Frog Went A-Courting."

"You're right, Mother." Amanda finally stopped and sat down on the window ledge. "The bet has been made. I can't stop it. Whatever happens will happen. I owe Mr. Randolph my appreciation and my apology."

"Seems to me," Catherine observed shrewdly, "that you owe him a bit more than that."

An even exchange of services. That was what he'd ask. That was what she'd owe him, what she'd be forced to give. But she had only one thing that belonged to her. She only hoped that it would be enough.

Chapter Fourteen

"So, McLendon, how'd you get tied up with Franklin and his cronies?"

Rushton Randolph stood in the bar, staring out into the reception area of the Jockey Club as the guests began to arrive. Tonight, he was dressed all in black, except for a white lawn shirt and stockings. Only the red heels of his shoes gave a hint of color.

His companion wore a gold embroidered vest and matching hose, over which he wore a blue frock coat with double lapels. Under his light brown hair and lashes, Patrick's sky-blue eyes sparkled. He would never admit to anyone, least of all himself, but he'd dressed carefully, thinking of a small hazel-eyed girl with sun in her soul.

"I met him at the Planters' Hotel. He heard I had money and thought he'd relieve me of some of it."

"What brought you to Augusta?"

"Cotton."

"You don't look like a planter."

"I'm not. I'm interested in buying and selling. What do you know about a man named Joseph Watkins?"

"Watkins? There are several Watkinses who live on the Savannah River just above Petersburg. I've had some dealings with a Joseph Watkins on Thornhill Plantation. Why?"

Patrick studied Rush, as if trying to decide how much to reveal. Finally he decided that it would take a man like Rush to make the arrangements. "I don't know how much you know about cotton, Randolph, but suppose there was a way to remove seed from the kind of cotton you could grow here..." Patrick paused and let his words sink in. "You begin to see what I have in mind."

"I can see the profits that could be made, but what does Mr. Watkins have to do with your plan?"

"Rumor has it that he's built a machine that will do it. That's what I'm here for, Randolph, to buy his idea."

Rush laughed. "Why are you telling me? Why wouldn't I outbid you and buy it myself?"

"Because you won't. And because I'm going to let you in on the deal."

"Why? What makes you think he'll sell it?"

"He might not. But I need someone to introduce me, stand good for me, so to speak. I'd thought to offer Franklin the opportunity, but on closer examination I've decided that would be asking for trouble. I think I'd rather take a chance on you."

Rush didn't answer immediately. The thought was staggering. Not the machine, but the possibilities. Acre after acre of cotton growing, being harvested and turned into salable products that would compete with the cotton from the islands off Georgia and South Carolina. Dared he hope that his dream was about to come true?

Maybe. If he won the race. Provided that McLendon wasn't another Franklin. Provided that Amanda and Cadenhill became his. If he lost, his planting would be limited to what he could grow in a wooden barrel, until his stage line began to show a profit.

"I'll introduce you, McLendon. But it's my thinking that we'd do well to keep quiet about what you're doing."

"Agreed. Now if you want to claim your lady, we'd better step into the other room. Otherwise she's going to be spirited away by your partner."

Rush emptied his glass and turned toward the entrance. He caught sight of Amanda at the same time the whiskey hit his stomach. The resounding jolt that followed felt as if someone had pierced his body with a spear.

Amanda stood, defiance evident in her proud bearing and stern expression. She seemed to glow, wearing a dress the russet color of coals banked on a winter's night. Light from the candles glimmering along the walls and hanging from the ceiling caught in her hair like stars.

"She's beautiful," Patrick said as he took a step forward. "But I don't believe for a minute that she's as innocent as she looks, the little flirt."

"Innocent?" Patrick's statement puzzled Rush.

"Well, perhaps the little darling is just teasing me. It's the devil in her that's testing me and she's looking like an angel."

"Amanda may be a lot of things, but an angel isn't one of them, Patrick."

"It's Catherine I'm referring to, Randolph."

Across the room, Catherine had already seen Patrick McLendon, but tonight she'd decided to let him do the asking. She handed the servant her cape and adjusted the folds of her dress. Blue wouldn't have been her choice, but it was what her mother had decreed and it was new.

Tonight, Catherine planned to dance with every young man there. No point in making it so easy for her future husband. Charity had told her that. Charity knew about men and how to attract them. Catherine had decided, after watching Mr. Randolph's attempts to attract Amanda's attention, that perhaps a little disinterest might be indicated. When the dancing stopped for a midnight supper, Mr. McLendon was certain to ask to share it with her.

Over the crowd of guests, Amanda, standing quietly beside her mother, caught sight of Rushton Randolph. She knew that sooner or later she'd have to talk with him. She'd sent Settie for Thor. There was the race to discuss and how it would be run. But it was too soon. She was wound tighter than the pulley on the mill. Another turn of the band inside her stomach and she'd snap into a hundred pieces.

Taking a deep breath, she did the unthinkable. "Mother, would you accompany me in taking a seat with the ladies? I think I'd like to discuss something other than crops and races. Will you join us, Cat?"

Iris gasped. Was this her daughter? Did she really want to talk about recipes and dress patterns? Something was badly askew here. Then she saw Rushton Randolph and Patrick McLendon almost upon them, and knew. Amanda was running for her life. And, to Iris's surprise, Catherine was agreeing.

Just as the two men reached the Caden women, Amanda and Catherine, arm in arm, turned away, leaving the newcomers surprised and irritated.

Iris smiled. Her girls were learning. She nodded at the two would-be intruders and smiled before turning to follow her daughters. Iris had spent most of the afternoon trying to decide how she should handle the two suitors for her daughters' hands. In the end she'd decided that she'd do what Houston would have done—let them make their own decisions.

The evening should be interesting.

Tomorrow might be more so.

Donovan's mouth was too dry to spit.

He didn't like what he was doing. But Franklin Caden paid well. And Franklin did like fire. Donovan struck his sulfur match against the stone and caught the spark with a handful of dried grass. A brisk wind fanned the fire and in minutes the shed blazed up as fast as the tobacco barns had.

184 Jasmine and Silk

Quickly he mounted his horse and rode away, leaving the Randolph Stagecoach office in flames.

This was the third station along the route that he'd torched tonight. With any luck Mr. Randolph wouldn't learn about his losses for several days. Donovan finished the jug of ale he'd brought to keep himself warm, and dropped it along the road. Franklin Caden would be pleased. Donovan was already mentally spending the money he expected to receive.

Rush and Patrick found an occasional dance partner, but for the most part, they watched Amanda and Catherine being whirled about the floor by others. When the dance master announced the last waltz before supper, as if on pre-arranged signal, both men left their resting places at the bar and moved across the room.

"Miss Amanda," Rush said in a low voice that defied argument, "I believe this is my dance?"

"Why, Mr. McLendon," Catherine was saying to Rush's companion, "I don't recall promising you a dance."

"You don't?" Patrick's eyebrow lifted as he waited, hand extended.

Amanda and Catherine glanced at each other for a long moment, then allowed themselves to be claimed.

Rush's hand tightened on Amanda's as he positioned his other hand on the lower part of her back. He pulled her to him and swept her off across the floor.

"You've been quite busy tonight, Miss Caden," Rush said. "Did you find many bidders for your hand?"

"None I'd have."

"Good."

That was all that was said, but Rush closed the distance between them appreciably and the tenseness became something more exciting than anticipation. A guilty flush stole over Amanda's face as she caught sight of her mother's thoughtful expression across the room.

Rushton Randolph was still an impossible rogue, and her enemy. But he was her rogue. She boldly raised her gaze to take in his dark eyes and wicked smile.

Her hand rested on his shoulder as she felt the subtle motion of his body keeping perfect time with the music and the movements of her body as well. She heard the whispers as they swirled around, the soft swishing of her skirt against his trousers, and smelled the dizzying male scent of him.

This was what she'd been waiting for all evening. Her lips curved into a smile and she flung back her head and gave herself over to the intoxication of the moment.

"Yes indeed, Miss Caden, you're very beautiful. You know that, don't you?"

"Only because of you," she whispered daringly, throwing caution to the winds. He was so willing to sacrifice everything for her, why shouldn't she show him her appreciation?

His middle finger slipped from their hand clasp and began drawing slow, sensual little circles against her palm. Amanda drew in a quick breath as she missed a step in the dance. She moistened her lips and felt his heated gaze follow the little licking motions of her tongue.

Rush unexpectedly leaned forward, whispering in her ear, "Do you know how much I want to kiss you?"

She didn't answer, but thought, Yes, I know, because my heart is galloping a thousand miles an hour and my body feels as if I've swallowed one of those candles and it's melting my insides.

The music was ending. Across the room Amanda saw Catherine make a misstep and stumble into Patrick McLendon, who held her for a long moment before blushing and stepping away. Catherine tucked her hand beneath Patrick's arm and started toward the room where the supper buffet had been laid out, ignoring the request of at least three young men who'd obviously become enchanted with her.

Her mother was wrong, Amanda thought. Sixteen was old enough to turn a man's head, and sometimes old enough to choose which man's head a girl wanted to turn. Poor Patrick, he was lost; he just didn't know it yet.

"Ah, Amanda, here you are." Franklin Caden appeared at Amanda's side, eyes narrowed almost into a dare. "I shall take you in to supper now."

"Oh, no, Franklin," Amanda quickly refuted. "I've promised Mr. Randolph that I will take supper with him. I'm sure Mother will be glad of your company."

But Amanda was wrong, for Iris was walking with Judge Taliaferro. She didn't even notice Franklin as she listened intently to whatever the judge was saying.

Franklin glanced around. Catherine was with Patrick. Iris was with the judge, and he'd just been rejected by the woman he'd claimed he was going to marry. He felt the eyes of everyone in the clubhouse staring at him with a certain glee.

She'd gone too far. With no further thought of propriety or good manners, Franklin lashed out at the woman who had turned her back on him. "Amanda, as your fiancé I demand respect, and as your guardian I expect you to obey me."

Amanda stopped short, her heart suddenly slipping into her throat before she choked it back. "I am not your fiancée, and I will not be answerable to you for my actions."

"And I shall refuse to stand good for new dresses that I have not authorized. Are there Caden funds of which I'm not aware?"

A sudden silence swept over the room.

Amanda knew that she was lost. Whatever her answer was would be her undoing. If she admitted to having funds, the creditors present would demand payment on their loans. If she said the bill had already been paid, Franklin would demand an explanation.

She could only meet his challenge with one of her own. "Why, I'm the highwayman, Franklin," Amanda said with a laugh. "Didn't you know that I've taken up a new profession?"

Rush blanched. She was really taking a chance. But perhaps that was the wise course of action. The real bandit would never be expected to point suspicion toward himself.

"Now, now, Amanda, darling," Iris said with a laugh. "Don't tease Franklin." She turned to her husband's stepbrother in an attempt to soothe the harsh words. "She sold the last piece of my jewelry to pay for our new gowns. That and—"

"And of course, there's the deposit I made on the horse," Rush finished. "You recall that I said I was contemplating buying the animal, don't you?"

Iris gasped. "You're going to sell Thor, Amanda? I don't believe it."

Amanda turned her eyes to Rush, the man who was rescuing her again. "Yes. I'm considering selling Thor, Mother. If he wins tomorrow, I'll be selling him to Mr. Randolph."

"Oh, Amanda, I'm sorry. I'm not sure your father would approve."

It was clear that Franklin didn't like the new turn of events. From the quizzical expression on his face, Rush wasn't even certain that Franklin believed Amanda's story. Rush wasn't certain that he believed it, either, but he had to admire Amanda's courage and determination.

"If you wish to sell Thor," Franklin snapped, "I'll buy him and apply his price to your debts."

"Sorry, Franklin, but Amanda's already made a deal with me—unless of course you'd like to refund my deposit?"

Amanda pressed her hand to her left temple. The situation was becoming much too tangled, events moving beyond her control. She had to put a stop to any further exchange.

"Please excuse me, Mr. Randolph. I've suddenly developed a headache. I think I'll retire for the evening, after I've checked to make certain that Thor has been bedded down for the night." Amanda turned and looked toward Iris. "Mother?"

Iris took her daughter's hand, but flashed a reluctant look at Lewis as she did so. "Of course, darling. Just let me get my shawl and I'll return with you."

Rush stepped forward. "No, Mrs. Caden, you don't want to take a chance on soiling your new dress by going down to the stable. I'll escort Amanda there. Then, when she's satisfied that the horse is all right, I'll ask one of the club maids to accompany us back to Franklin's house. Amanda will be fine, I promise you."

"Patrick and I could accompany you, Amanda," Catherine offered.

"No," Amanda said. "You stay, both of you stay. There is no reason for you to miss the buffet. Please, Mother. I'll be all right."

Iris looked from Rush to Amanda and back again before answering. "All right. If you can borrow one of the ladies' maids in the cloakroom."

In no time Rush made satisfactory arrangements and, having retrieved Amanda's cloak, found himself hurrying to keep up with her fast pace toward the barn.

"Why are you in such a hurry, Amanda?"

"I'm not."

The stable loomed up before them. Amanda fumbled with the door and stepped inside. "Settie?"

"Miss Amanda? What are you doing out here?"

"I just wanted to check on Thor. Is he all right?"

"Yes'm. He be fine. You get back to your party."

"All right, thank you, Settie."

The maid was waiting beside the Caden carriage as instructed. Rush couldn't help but chuckle at the thought of

Franklin's surprise if he discovered his carriage was missing. Rush assisted the maid and Amanda inside, then mounted his horse and followed them back to Franklin's house in town.

Once Amanda was on the porch, Rush gave the driver leave to return the carriage and the maid to the clubhouse.

Amanda stood watching the carriage disappear. She knew she shouldn't stay outside in the dark, waiting for Rush to join her. But she did.

"Why are you really doing this, Mr. Randolph?"

"Doing what?"

"Risking your interest in the warehouse for me?"

"I told you the truth, Amanda. Your father helped both my family and me. I promised him that I'd help you, and that's what I'm doing."

"But suppose Thor loses?"

"Then I'm no longer Franklin's partner. I will have lost a part of my inheritance, but that's a gamble I'm willing to take."

"Why?"

"Because of this."

He lowered his head, at the same time catching her in his arms and pulling her to him. She ducked her head, avoiding his kiss, burying her face in the hollow of his throat. That was a mistake. She could feel the warmth of his skin beneath her cheek, the thudding of his heart and the strength of his body against hers.

"Kiss me, Amanda."

"No. I don't want you to kiss me. It does things to me, makes me feel odd." Already the closeness of their contact was sending little tingles along her arms and down her body toward her legs. "I want—"

"You don't know what you want, Amanda, but I do. For I want the same thing. When we're married I'll show you.

I'll teach you everything there is to know about needing and
wanting and feeling.''

"No, Rush, no. I won't. I can't."

"Yes, you can. Stop fighting me, Amanda. Once Thor
wins the race tomorrow you'll be out from under Franklin's control, and so will I. We'll figure out a way to pay off
the loan holders from Augusta and then—"

"If only I could believe you."

"Believe me, Amanda."

Even as their mouths touched, Amanda knew that she
trusted this man. This time her response was instant and
freely given. With a quick cry of passion she opened her lips
and took his tongue inside, shivering as his fingertips spread
through her hair, loosening it from its pins and allowing it
to fall across her shoulders.

"Your hair is so beautiful," he said, between kisses. "I
want to see it spread across your body." His fingertips
slipped inside the bodice of her gown, touching, kneading.
Pulling her against him, Rush pressed his lips against hers.

Amanda moaned. Excitement raced through her and she
felt the tight bunching of muscles between her legs. One
breast was uncovered and Rush pulled away long enough to
capture the nipple with his mouth. She'd turned to mush.
Her legs had no substance and if Rush had not been holding her she would have collapsed outside Franklin's front
door.

She must be mad, she thought, to allow him such freedom of her person. Then she heard the opening of the door.

"Is there someone here?" Franklin's housekeeper was
standing in the doorway.

"Yes," Rush answered, stepping in front of Amanda
while she straightened her clothing. "I've brought Miss
Caden home. Will you see that she gets to her room?"

"Yes, sir. Come in, Miss Caden."

"Thank you, Mr. Randolph," Amanda managed to say. "I'll see you at the track tomorrow."

"Indeed you will, and afterward, too. I expect us to have some celebrating to do."

"I hope so. I certainly hope so."

For if Thor loses, so do we—everything.

Chapter Fifteen

Word spread across the Broad River Valley about the race between Amanda Caden's horse, Thor, and Franklin's English champion, King Arthur. By one o'clock the track was lined with spectators, and the veranda was packed with invited guests.

Franklin was pacing from the tension. Last night the bet had seemed an unexpected opportunity to reclaim his warehouse and bind Amanda to him permanently. Now, as the hours passed and the betting grew heavier, he was beginning to have second thoughts. Suppose that wild stallion of Amanda's won?

As his doubts grew, so did his anger, and it settled on his partner, Rushton Randolph. The man had interfered with his plans at every turn, first by catching Amanda's eye, then by forcing Franklin to make good on his guests' losses to the bandit, then by advancing funds to Amanda through his offer to buy the only thing on Cadenhill over which Franklin lacked control—her horse. Now, this race. Franklin paced back and forth, oblivious to the curious glances of his guests who, after starting out backing Franklin's horse, were now betting heavily on Thor.

By one o'clock, Amanda was inside the stable soothing Thor's nervous stamping and talking to Joeboy, the slave boy who was to ride the horse. "Don't worry. Just ride him as if you were taking him for a run by the river." Lovie had managed to find a bright red shirt and a floppy hat with a red feather for the boy to wear. Not a jockey's colorful costume like those of Franklin's riders, but Joeboy was excited nonetheless.

Catherine, who'd been the first one dressed and ready, offered Amanda a bright red silk scarf. "Tie this on Thor's halter for luck, Amanda," she said, giving her sister a quick squeeze. "Oh, look, there's Patrick. Isn't he the most handsome man you've ever seen?"

Amanda raised her eyes. Patrick and Rush were looking down toward the stable. Patrick was like a prize rooster, colorful and proud. But it was the other man who drew her attention. He was standing where the rays from the sun caught his face and gave it a golden glow. She'd thought of him as a dark man, but today when he smiled, his face seemed to light up. Or was it just that she was seeing him from a different perspective?

Catherine was halfway up the path when Amanda felt the wind pick up and rustle her cape. She pulled it closer and turned back to face Thor. A stiff wind could affect the race. Even as she stood there, the trees began to bend and sway.

Amanda was tired and a little cold. Whether because of tension over the outcome of the race, or the maddening twitching of her body that had continued long after Rush had gone, she'd slept little the night before. She'd found she couldn't sit, or stand, or be still; every inch of her body seemed to be moving, and there was nothing she could do to quiet it. Finally, just before dawn she'd fallen into a light, restless sleep. Now she felt sluggish and uncertain.

Having Rush lose his money because of her was a burden Amanda didn't want. Cadenhill was the only weight she could carry. Yet it was more than the bet that had nagged at her peace of mind. Her life was changing and she couldn't seem to stop it. Only a few months ago, Cat had still been a girl, their father had been alive, and Amanda had been free

to do the things she loved best—work with the land and ride
Thor across its expanse. Now she was dressed up in one of
her mother's altered gowns, attending a horse race as a
spectator.

Amanda sighed.

"Don't worry, Amanda. He'll win." Rush was standing
behind her, quietly reassuring, lending her badly needed
support. For one moment she almost turned and buried her
face against his chest. She was worried. And she wanted to
feel his arms around her. She needed his comfort and concern. Instead she raised her eyes and asked the question
she'd been afraid to ask. "What if he doesn't?"

"Then we're really no worse off than we were to begin
with, are we? You still have Cadenhill and I still have my
stage line."

"But you will have lost the warehouse, and I will still have
to worry about the debts due in June."

"So? We'll find another answer."

But Amanda wouldn't be reassured. Woodenly she allowed Rush to take her arm and together they walked back
to the clubhouse. They found seats in the front row beside
Iris and Catherine. Amanda sat stiffly, neither seeing nor
hearing the current of excitement around them.

The starter blew the trumpet, calling the horses to the
starting line. Amanda sprang to her feet. She couldn't sit
there and watch someone else ride Thor. Too much depended on the race. "I'll be right back," she said and ran
down the path to the stable. "Settie! Bring him back."

The servant turned and led Thor and Joeboy back to the
corral, meeting Amanda in the barn. Moments later Thor
danced out of the dark building and up to the starting gate
where Franklin's horse was pawing the ground. Rather than
have them run the more popular quarter mile, straight
ahead, Franklin had set the length of this event as one turn
around the mile track; he wanted to show off his new oval
racetrack.

Rush watched as King Arthur danced about while Thor simply raised and lowered his big head, shaking it and making a sound that was half whinny and half sneeze. He gave the absurd impression that he was embarrassed about the fuss being made over the event.

Rush gripped the rail and leaned forward. Where was Amanda? It was time for the race to start. Then Rush took a good look at Thor's rider and he knew. Amanda would ride in the race herself.

The wind continued to whip the trees at the back of the track. The crowd was hushed.

The pistol fired and the two horses tore away from the gate, matching each other stride for stride. Then the English horse seemed to gain, bit by bit. Around the turn, into the backstretch.

Amanda lifted herself in the stirrups and leaned over, whispering to the great chestnut horse. She could feel his energy, his heart thundering as he lunged forward.

"Come on, Thor. Come on, boy. You have to win. There can be no more midnight rides for the Jasmine Bandit. Nobody suspects me, but if I'm caught Franklin will triumph."

Into the return curve they raced, one being, moving at a thundering pace. Thor's gait was smooth, but he was still a half length behind. Then she felt the great horse take a sudden lunge forward. One stride, then two strides.

The wind stopped.

She didn't hear the crowd noise. She didn't hear the other animal. There was an eerie silence that swallowed up everything but Amanda and Thor.

Down the backstretch the two horses came, hooves pounding, great strings of saliva flying from their mouths.

Thor was moving ahead. More, more. Amanda was laughing. The wind picked up again, blowing in gusts behind them, pushing them forward. They seemed to be flying. They were going to win.

Then it happened. The scarf Catherine had given Joeboy for luck came untied and swept in front of Thor's vision. He faltered, frightened by the red sliver of material that danced for a moment in the wind and was carried away. But that moment was enough.

King Arthur swept by and crossed the finish line.

Franklin had won.

Amanda reined Thor to a slow gallop, and they completed the circle around the track and back to the barn, where Rush was standing white-faced and silent. She let the reins fall into Settie's hand and after a long moment slid from the horse into Rush's outstretched arms where she rested for a moment. Then she straightened up and pushed him away. She could hear Catherine sobbing in the silence.

"Thank you, Mr. Randolph. I very much appreciate your kind effort in my behalf. I realize that you won't want to buy Thor now, but he's a fine horse, and since I am unable to make good on your loss, I would like you to have him."

"I can't take your horse, Amanda."

"Of course you can. It's the honorable thing to do. Now if you'll excuse me, I shall return to Cadenhill. I have tobacco beds to see about. Good afternoon."

Rush watched her walk up the path to the clubhouse. He understood her shock, but he understood, too, that she was saying a lot more. Last night she'd let down her guard and let him in, just for a moment. But that moment was over and he didn't know whether he'd experience it again.

Franklin, all smiles, dashed forward to meet her, beaming from ear to ear. "Amanda," he said, catching her arm and stopping her at the door, "don't worry about anything, my dear. I'll see to Cadenhill and you, just as I promised. If you need seed, I'll send it out."

"I don't need seed, Franklin, and I don't need you. Stay away from Cadenhill!"

Amanda jerked her arm from his grasp and marched to the wagon, unfastened the reins and climbed in. "I'm going home, Franklin. Mr. McLendon will see to Mother and Catherine.''

Behind Franklin, his guests were smirking at his put-down. Hearing the giggles diminished his victory, but not much. He'd regained full ownership of his warehouse, and he still held Cadenhill's debts. In addition, he'd won a considerable purse from his guests. He smiled broadly and went looking for his former partner.

But Rushton Randolph was gone.

The next day, Franklin caught Rush in his office. "Removing your things, Randolph?''

"Not yet, Franklin. I have another proposition.''

"If it's as profitable as the last one, I'll be happy to hear it.''

"Nothing like that. I'd just like to rent this office, if you don't mind. I need someplace to conduct business. After all, I still have a stage line to run.''

"Why not? It's vacant. Can you afford it?''

"I can afford it.''

"Fine, I'll enjoy seeing your expression every morning as you walk past the tobacco that doesn't belong to you. And by the way, Randolph, stay away from my fiancée.''

"I told you before, Franklin, she isn't your fianceé. Amanda Caden is going to marry me.''

"Not unless you can save her precious Cadenhill. And I can tell you now she doesn't lose lightly.''

After Franklin left, Rush stood on the balcony overlooking the warehouse floor. He wasn't penniless. There was still some gold left from his inheritance. He had the stage line and there was Patrick McLendon's plan to invest in a cottonseed-removal machine. Because of Rush's dream of growing cotton, the machine was rapidly becoming more interesting than a tobacco warehouse.

"Someday,'' Rush said quietly, "this warehouse is going to hold cotton, Cadenhill cotton, and it's all going to belong to Amanda and me.''

Chapter Sixteen

Patrick McLendon was sitting in the front parlor of the Caden home having tea with Catherine and her mother. He'd never thought that he'd find himself calling on a young woman, but he had. And what was more unsettling was the anticipation with which he found his way to Cadenhill two or three afternoons a week.

"Why won't your sister see Randolph? It's been almost three months since the race. He's very hurt."

"Amanda won't even talk about him," Catherine said sadly. "She leaves before the sun is up and rarely comes to the house until we're in bed."

"Is there that much to do on a plantation?"

"My daughter has some very unusual ideas about growing tobacco," Iris said with a sigh. "And she's determined to find a way to pay off our debts."

"Yes," Catherine added. "She had frames constructed over the tobacco beds and draped muslin over them. Under the tents she kept ovens burning all day and all night. Now she's setting the plants in the field."

"What's so unusual about planting the fields in April?"

"The size of the plants," Catherine said brightly. "They're already eight inches high. Would you like to see them?"

"What I'd love to see are your sister's tent beds. I think she might be on to something." Patrick rose, turned to Mrs. Caden for permission to leave and was pleased to have her nod.

"Catherine, please tell Amanda that I want her to come inside in time to have supper at the table with us."

"I will, Mother." Catherine scooted through the door before her mother changed her mind, or decided to send Lovie or the little girls to accompany them. With Patrick at her side, she skirted the garden and walked sedately toward the barn beyond which Amanda's beds lay. Once they reached the barn, Catherine darted inside, pulling Patrick into the darkness behind her.

"Ah, Patrick McLendon. While it's very proper for you to join us for tea, I'm thinking it's time you devoted a bit more effort to teaching me about kissing."

Just as she'd planned, before Patrick knew what was happening, she looped her hands behind his neck and rose on her toes to reach him, parting her lips in breathless anticipation.

"Catherine, stop this. I'm not going to kiss you."

"Why ever not? Nobody can see us."

"It isn't that. I've told you before, darling, you're a temptation to me, but you're still a wee lass, and I'll not be putting a black spot on your reputation."

"Oh, blarney, Patrick. I want you to kiss me. My heart is thumping so loud that the horses think Lucifer is coming for them. Do you hear?"

"I don't hear anything except us. Even the horses are quiet. More's the reason for us to get out of the barn."

"You aren't listening, Patrick."

Catherine took his hand and placed it on her breast. As he touched her it seemed to swell and fill his palm. Warm, tempting, desirable she was. And God's teeth, how he responded. Even as she waited, pressing herself against him, he felt himself harden.

"Ah, Patrick." She moved her hips. "I knew that you felt it, too. But women don't show their needing like men, do they? But it's there, inside, throbbing just as strong. Do you like to touch me? I like to be touched."

"Catherine Elizabeth Caden," Patrick said throatily, "you've got to stop this."

"Not until you kiss me, Patrick, darling."

The little schemer. He couldn't seem to pull his hand away. It ranged across the little indentation between her breasts and found the other one, already puckered and demanding to be touched. She wasn't going to cooperate unless he kissed her. He might as well get done with it. If only she wouldn't cling so tightly.

Patrick lowered his head, brushing her lips lightly, then settling on them with gentle pressure. For a moment Catherine remained still. Then, almost as if he were inside her thoughts, directing her, she parted her lips, tasting, feasting, drawing him inside her mouth like a wild hungry creature experiencing its first taste of sweet honey.

She made a soft sound in her throat and Patrick was lost. The kiss changed, becoming urgent. Her hands left his neck and ranged wildly down his back, his sides, sliding across his chest and lower until she was holding the hard part of him in her hands.

"Catherine!" Patrick pulled back, gasping for breath. "What are you doing?"

"I want to touch you. I want to feel this part of you that is announcing its pleasure. Don't you like it?"

"Like it? God, yes. I like it. But you can't. Catherine, you don't understand. A man can be pushed too far. Then he might not be able to stop before—"

She'd slipped her hands down inside his breeches so that she could free him. "Before what, Patrick? Tell me. I want to know everything."

Patrick growled and swung Catherine into his arms. He marched across the barn and slammed her down on a bale of straw. "Now stop that." He adjusted his trousers and sat beside her. "We are going to talk. You're practically a child and I'm thirty years old. I do not intend to take advantage of you, no matter how much I might like to."

"Why not? Are my breasts too small?"

"Catherine, my darling. I love kissing you. I love your little breasts. They're perfect. But you mustn't let a man do this to you. Your mother must have told you to save yourself for the man you love."

"Oh, but I have, Patrick darling. Of course I understand that men are different. You've probably let many women touch you. But I shall forgive you for your past indiscretions. After all, you didn't know me then."

"Stop this, Catherine. You'll be a wife someday and you want to remain untouched for your husband."

"I have," she said solemnly. "But I don't think we'd better wait too long before we marry, Patrick. Do you?"

"I am not interested in marriage, you witch. I've nothing to offer a wife. I shall be leaving here soon, sailing a ship stocked with foodstuffs to the Spanish port of New Orleans. From there, I may sail to the Caribbean islands to buy sugar to bring back to Savannah."

"Then I'll come with you." Catherine suddenly sprang to her feet and sat across Patrick's lap, sliding her arms around his neck.

"You can't. Don't kiss me."

"Why not? It feels so good, Patrick. Why do you want me to stop? I think there must be more, else why do you keep twisting about so?"

Patrick groaned. "You're going to drive me crazy, Catherine. What am I going to do with you?"

"I'm not sure, Patrick. I've only seen animals do it. But I think it would be ever so much more pleasurable if, together, we took off our clothes."

"That does it. That's all. Get up, Catherine." Patrick stood, dumping Catherine out of his lap. "I'll not take you in a barn, spoil you, get you with child!"

Catherine's lower lip trembled. She wasn't accustomed to being shouted at. She'd pushed him as far as he was going to allow himself to be pushed for now. He wanted her, and he wanted her the way a man wanted his wife-to-be. Otherwise he'd have taken advantage of her. She smiled and brushed the straw from her dress, openly studying his body.

The man part of him was very big. He couldn't hide it in the skintight trousers he was wearing. And the way he cupped himself she was certain that it was painful.

"Will it go away?" she finally asked.

"What?"

"The swelling. Will it disappear on its own, or will you have to do something to it?"

Patrick rolled his eyes heavenward. This child was going to drive him crazy. "I'm not sure even I know the answer to that question. Now, find your sister, and stop tormenting me."

"What if someone sees us? Will they know what we've been doing?"

"They'll know. You just walk in front of me and by the time we get to the tobacco beds there will be nothing for them to see."

"Oh, what will you do?"

"Think about snowstorms and icy waters."

"If you're sure that's the only way."

"I'm sure," he said, trying unsuccessfully to think about ice when her saucy bottom was swinging about in front of him.

"You wouldn't want to kiss me again?"

"Absolutely not!"

Catherine sighed in disappointment and led him through the back of the barn into the sunlight. Patrick glanced around, grateful that none of the slaves was watching.

They didn't find Amanda at the beds—only a dirty farmhand stoking the small rock oven with small pieces of wood. Inside the tent the temperature was toasty. With the sun overhead and the oven inside, the plants were extraordinary.

"Where is Amanda?"

"Right here." The farmhand was Amanda in men's clothing.

"Miss Caden? Catherine told me about your tent. What a splendid idea."

"Yes, good afternoon, Mr. McLendon. Where have you two been?" Amanda studied them carefully before picking straw from Catherine's hair and dropping it to the ground.

"Catherine volunteered to show me around."

"By way of the barn, I see."

A flush of color stained Patrick's face. He felt as if he'd been caught without his trousers. "Ah, yes. We did make a stop in the barn."

"Just be certain that you don't hurt my sister, Mr. McLendon. I wouldn't take kindly to that."

"Amanda! I can take care of myself. Besides, Patrick is going to ask me to marry him, eventually, aren't you?"

"Now, Catherine, I won't be nagged into—"

"Oh, never fear, Patrick, I'll never nag you into doing anything you don't want to do. Now, come along and I'll show you the fields where Amanda is planting the tobacco."

Catherine took Patrick's hand and started out of the tent. "Oh, Amanda, Mother says for you to get to the house for dinner tonight."

"By the way, Miss Caden," Patrick said casually, "Mr. Randolph is doing very well with his stage line. He's rebuilding three of his stations that were burned out, and running a tight schedule now."

"That's nice. I'm glad for him."

"He misses you, you know."

"I'm sorry about that. But I'm too busy to entertain."

"He understands, but he'd like me to tell you that he's received a message from President Washington that he will visit Augusta and inspect the new stage line. Rush has arranged for the three Caden ladies to accompany Judge Taliaferro and his daughter, Charity, to Augusta to attend a special reception in honor of the President. He seemed to think that the three of you would like to attend."

"President Washington?" Catherine let out a scream of excitement. "In Augusta, and we're invited?"

"Amanda and Catherine, that's what Rush said."

"Patrick, darling, why didn't you tell me? When?"

"In a little more than two weeks. He thought that would give you time to finish your planting, Amanda, and still give you ladies time to pack your fanciest dresses. Shall I tell him to have the judge make the arrangements?"

Amanda simply stood, shock taking her words. He was doing it again, finding a way to help her achieve what she wanted—a trip to Augusta, in May, before the June deadline. In just one second he'd wiped out all the hopeless schemes she'd already rejected, and presented her with the possibility of a solution. She could go to Augusta and maybe, somehow, she could find a way to convince the men to whom Cadenhill was indebted to extend the mortgage.

Amanda looked around. She wished she could bring them here and show them what she was doing, let them know that her tobacco would come in weeks before any other crop in the valley. She knew it would work. If she could just convince them. If she could get to Augusta.

Now she had the means.

A reception and ball for the new President of the United States of America. A tear spilled over and ran down her face, making a dirty streak down her cheek.

"Please, Manda. Please, please, please."

"Yes," Amanda finally answered. "Please tell Mr. Randolph that I—*we* will be very pleased to accept the invitation to attend the President's ball with the Taliaferros. Thank you.''

Long after Catherine and Patrick had gone, Amanda stood looking at the green shoots waving in the fields. Tears ran freely down her cheeks now. Tears of joy and release.

She was going to see him again, the man who had filled her soul with guilt, the man who'd come to occupy her thoughts more completely than her family, more than Cadenhill—Rush Randolph. He was helping her again.

But this time she must be strong. This time she wouldn't give in to temptation and fall into his arms. This time she would remember that she had a mission and Mr. Thomas Rushton Randolph couldn't be allowed to interfere.

If the debt holders wouldn't agree to her pleas, there were other ways to find money. She thought about her mask and her guns—Rush's guns. She wondered how difficult it would be to get around in Augusta without her horse. Maybe she would take Roman. He knew about her second self. He might be able to help.

If Amanda couldn't find an answer, the Jasmine Bandit would.

To Amanda, traveling in the same coach where Rush had first kissed her seemed strange. She sat beside her mother, who seemed excited about attending, leaving Charity and Catherine to share the other bench. Judge Taliaferro and Patrick McLendon rode their horses alongside the stagecoach.

"Isn't this exciting?" Charity exclaimed.

"Oh, yes! Do you suppose the highwayman will stop us, Manda?"

"I doubt it, Catherine. There are three men with guns outside. Besides, I think he only strikes in the dark."

Iris peered anxiously outside the coach window. "Judge Taliaferro said we'd arrive just after lunch."

"I hope so," Charity said crossly. "I don't look forward to spending another night sleeping four to a bed."

"Quit complaining, Charity. Just think, by tomorrow we'll be meeting the President. I wish the horses had wings," Catherine said, leaning back with a smile that spoke more of anticipation than discomfort.

"We're lucky to have a bed at all," Amanda snapped. "Somebody burned the way stations Rush—Mr. Randolph constructed. Someone who didn't want the stage line to succeed."

Iris caught her breath. "Who would do such a dreadful thing?"

"Someone who wanted Rush—Mr. Randolph to fail."

Nobody answered Amanda. The three women knew that she was quietly accusing Franklin, and they weren't certain whether it was from loyalty to the man she seemed intent on ignoring, or whether she was right.

The last half hour of their journey to Augusta was completed in silence. When they entered the bustling city, Patrick McLendon tied his horse to the coach and wedged himself inside for the purpose of giving the ladies a personal tour.

"This is Broad Street, ladies, a street like few others in the country. It's 165 feet wide, housing 100 business establishments with goods from Europe, the Far East and the West Indies. In the eastern section of the town is a street that is 300 feet wide. In the middle of that street is an academy, a combined school and meeting hall that is said to be the most elegant building of its kind in the Southern states. That is where the festivities for the President will take place."

"Oh, my, isn't it festive?" Iris was watching the sidewalks filled with people, wagons tied to the posts outside the businesses. There was an air of excitement that was contagious. Charity and Catherine couldn't be still.

"Papa has arranged for accommodations at the Planters' Hotel," Charity said.

"Tell us about the hotel, Mr. McLendon," Iris said.

Patrick smiled at the woman of whom he was becoming so fond. "No little people or creatures at the Planters'. It's a very fine establishment with a dining room to rival its namesake in Savannah. And it's within walking distance of the academy."

Charity had been chattering merrily, but now continued with a pouty sigh, "I don't see why we can't attend tonight's dinner, Papa."

Judge Taliaferro leaned his head inside the window. "Because, daughter, tonight's dinner is a political occasion, where the leaders of the state can meet with the President on an informal basis. You'll be able to attend the official welcome tomorrow night, the Presidential ball, hosted by the Governor and his wife at the academy."

Amanda didn't enter the conversation, but she, too, wished she could attend the dinner this evening. She was certain that the men she hoped to consult would be there. But perhaps she'd do better to call on them during business hours. "Who else will be staying at the hotel?" she inquired.

Patrick answered that, and also the unspoken question she had wanted to ask. "A number of local political leaders, members of the general assembly and other members of Mr. Washington's party—and, of course, Rush. He and the President are running the President's dogs this afternoon."

"Dogs?" Amanda couldn't conceal her surprise.

"Yes, President Washington brought Cornwallis and Kate, his favorite dogs, hoping to get in a little hunting."

"Hunting dogs with the President?" Iris couldn't keep the disbelief from her voice.

"Since the inauguration he's been so occupied with government and politics that he's had little time for sport. He's been looking forward to having some time away from the business of state."

Charity let out a sigh of pleasure. "Well, he can spend all the time in the woods he wants. As for me? I'm going to explore every shop on the street."

"And you, Miss Catherine?" Patrick asked softly. "What do you plan to do this afternoon?"

"Why, my mother will say I ought to rest, but I'm far too excited. I think I'd like to walk about a bit, too."

"Perhaps you'll accompany the girls, Mr. McLendon?" Iris asked, adjusting her position. Because of a broken axle on the coach, the trip from Petersburg had been very long, and she was ready to rest, even if the girls weren't.

"Of course, Mrs. Caden. It will be my pleasure to escort the ladies on a walking tour of the town. And you, Miss Amanda, will you be joining us?"

"Me? Oh, I don't know." Amanda hadn't been following the conversation. She'd been caught up in the thought of Rush and the President. He'd told her that he was acquainted with the President, but she'd pretended to discount his claim, just as she'd discounted his claim of knowing her father. Though she'd never believed Franklin's charge that Rush was a spy during the revolution, she'd never fully allowed herself to accept Rush's contention that he'd been her father's friend, either. She swallowed back a sigh. It seemed she'd been wrong about so many things.

The stage driver stopped directly in front of the hotel and discharged his passengers.

The Planters' Hotel was a two-story, whitewashed frame structure with large floor-to-ceiling windows and a porch wrapped around three sides of the building. Because the hotel was overcrowded, even the maids' quarters had been turned into guest rooms. A small single room at the end of the upstairs corridor had been offered to Iris Caden, who had taken one look at the rapt expression on Catherine's face and decided that she should share a room with her younger daughter. Amanda, therefore, was settled into the single room alone, a situation that Iris would ordinarily not have allowed.

But Iris had observed that Amanda's search for a husband seemed to have been put aside, and Rushton Randolph had made no further appearances at Cadenhill. Iris decided that Catherine's interest in Patrick McLendon was much more to be monitored than Amanda's activities, a decision she might live to regret.

After unloading their trunks and sending out their gowns for pressing, the women, wearing only their petticoats and corsets, closed the shutters and lay in the darkness resting. But with Charity and Catherine, there was to be no rest. By the time the walking dresses were freshened and returned, they'd whispered and giggled to the point that Iris was more than happy to entrust them to Patrick McLendon's care, on the condition that Amanda be included. With the three girls together, Iris decided that Catherine could be trusted. Besides, it was midafternoon and the day was bright and sunny.

The four young people strolled down the green, kept manicured by goats staked out at intervals along the sprawling expanse between the rutted areas for carriages and horses. At the first office displaying the name of one of the men holding Cadenhill notes, Amanda excused herself, sending the others on ahead on the pretense that she needed to return to the hotel for her handkerchief. Once they'd left her she scurried inside the lawyer's office, catching the clerk by surprise.

"Yes, ma'am? May I be of service?"

"Yes, I'd like to see Mr. Wainwright."

"Dear me, I'm very sorry, but he's not in his office. All the businessmen in town are engaged in assembly business and preparations for entertaining our President. Could you return on Monday next?"

"All of the other men?"

"I'm afraid so. Was he expecting you to call?"

"No, no, he wasn't. Thank you."

Amanda left the office. Her plan to contact the Caden-hill's debt holders privately wasn't going to work. They were with the President. Today was May 17. She had only two weeks until June first, when Franklin would sell a part of Cadenhill. Heart-weary, she walked toward the river, not seeing the town or its inhabitants, not enjoying the sights of a city that, like the new nation, was beginning to find its direction.

At the wharves she could see trading boats from Savannah, Petersburg boats being unloaded of tobacco and reloaded with supplies to be carried back to the Broad River Valley. Supplies she could buy here for half the price charged by Franklin in his stores. It seemed so unfair. But Franklin's monopoly would end now that people were able to travel with greater speed and comfort. They'd buy their goods here. Perhaps Franklin knew that. Perhaps that was why he was becoming desperate.

She was feeling desperate, too, the next evening as she dressed for the dinner at the academy. Last night she'd managed to avoid having dinner with the others in the hotel dining room by pleading a headache. Today a second foray into the town in an attempt to find the men she needed to see had come to a frustrating end. She was no better off than she'd been in Petersburg. On her return she had found a note informing her that the judge had arranged for someone to call for her and be her escort for the dinner and the ball afterward.

At shortly before eight there was a knock. Amanda adjusted the skirt of her green ball gown and opened the door. She didn't know why she hadn't suspected what would happen, who'd be sent to escort her, but she hadn't.

"Good evening, my Jasmine Bandit."

Chapter Seventeen

Rush stood in the doorway and looked at Amanda as if he'd never before seen her. His black eyes drank in the sight of her, filling his mind with the vision of copper-colored hair tumbling across her shoulders, reliving the memory of lying on the forest floor, touching, kissing...

"What are you doing here?"

"The judge asked me—no, that's a lie. I asked the judge if I might be your escort for the evening."

"You can't, Rush. You'll spoil everything."

"You mean spoil your search for a husband?"

"That, and other things."

A clatter down the corridor announced the approach of others. "Amanda, how lovely you look." Judge Taliaferro, resplendent in a black velvet cutaway coat with silver embroidery, stood beside Rush in the doorway and greeted Amanda cordially, then added, "Evening, Rush." He turned his head back to the corridor and asked, "Are you ready, ladies?"

Iris, Charity and Catherine joined the judge, followed by Patrick McLendon, who was quickly claimed by Catherine.

Rush lifted one eyebrow and smiled at Amanda. "Well?"

"You devil! You planned this." Amanda took his arm and they brought up the rear of the procession.

"Of course I did. Did you think that I arranged all this for you to be with someone else? If you won't allow me on Cadenhill, I had to find a way to bring you to me."

She heard the pain in his voice and acknowledged that she was responsible. "Rush, I'm sorry. I couldn't face you. I felt so bad about what happened."

"Do you realize that is the first time you've ever called me Rush? I like it. I'd like it better if you'd come closer."

For a moment she swayed, drawn by the magic of his presence. In another minute, if she didn't do something to erase the enchantment, she'd be in his arms and all her careful plans would be spoiled. "Stop flirting with me, you devil," she snapped peevishly. "You must know the reason I accepted your invitation was so that I could come to Augusta, not so that I could be with you. Please don't stop me from doing what I have to do."

Amanda felt him stiffen and wished she could take back the hateful words. She hadn't even thanked him for arranging the invitation. She knew she was behaving badly. But she had to put distance between her emotions and the turbulent feelings that crashed through her every time this man came close. She didn't want to admit that she was unnerved, that her emotions were churning inside her like storm clouds gathering over the Broad River.

"I won't interfere, Amanda. I just don't want you to be disappointed," Rush said quietly. He'd known what Amanda would try to do, but he'd hoped that she might be as glad to see him as he was to see her. He'd allowed himself to believe that the evening would be special.

The judge's party chose to walk through the twilight of the spring evening to the academy, where the dinner was being held. Blossoms filled the air with fragrance, and music spilled from pubs and private homes where festivities were taking place. Amanda and Rush didn't talk, allowing Charity and Catherine to carry the conversation.

"What kind of man is the President, Papa?" Charity asked.

"He's a large man, very plain. He attended the evening's entertainment yesterday in a brown worsted coat and breeches. He believes that it's better if he appears as a man of the people, rather than display his wealth."

"Does he powder his hair?"

"No, it's dressed in a roll over his ears and tied with a simple black ribbon at the back of his neck."

"Well, he doesn't sound very exciting to me," Catherine exclaimed. She swept her eyes down Patrick's clothing, letting him know how attractive she found his pale blue waistcoat with dark lapels and the crisp white ruffle of his shirt.

Patrick swallowed hard and tried to focus on the buildings they were passing. It was becoming harder and harder to keep a distance between himself and the adventurous Miss Catherine Caden. If it hadn't been for the upcoming meeting Rush had arranged with Joseph Watkins, he'd have taken the next boat for Savannah. She was much too appealing at a time when he needed to concentrate his attention on other things. Then Catherine slipped her arm beneath his and cast her hazel eyes upward, smiling that teasing, secret smile, and he forgot all about leaving.

At the academy, diners were already being seated. The tables were covered with crisp white cloths, and silver candlesticks provided glowing flames of light. Seated on a platform at one end of the dining hall were the President, the Governor and his wife, and other members of the assembly and the academy. The room was quickly filling with guests, who found their seats as the black waiters began to serve.

The meal had scarcely begun when the first toast was offered to the President. It was followed by a toast to the uniting of the Colonies, to the new government of the state of Georgia, to the Governor. By the time the first course was

complete, Iris motioned to both Catherine and Amanda that
their wineglasses should not be refilled.

Amanda felt Rush's eyes studying her, though he said
little. Every bite she ate became harder to chew until she finally laid down her two-pronged fork and made no further
attempt to eat. Instead she allowed her eyes to sweep the
dining hall. Every table was laid with mismatched china and
eating utensils, evidence of the combined efforts of the
women of the town.

Amanda caught sight of one of the men to whom Cadenhill was in debt. He was sitting at a table in deep conversation with two other businessmen and their wives and—
Franklin.

Amanda gasped. She hadn't counted on Franklin being
involved in the evening. Even as she watched, he turned toward her and smiled, bowing his head slightly as he seemed
to be pointing her out to the man with whom he was in deep
conversation. A ripple of fear ran down her spine. She instinctively understood that Franklin was up to something.

"Easy, Amanda," Rush said. "Don't let the man know
he's getting to you."

Amanda cut her eyes back toward her unwanted companion. Rush was a mind reader. He seemed to know what
she was thinking, even as she was thinking it.

"Smile, darling. You aren't going to attract bidders
looking like you've just lost your tobacco crop—if you still
insist on searching for a husband, that is."

"I've long forgotten about husbands," she admitted. "I
only want to talk to the men to whom Cadenhill owes
money, and offer them a business deal."

"Oh, and what kind of business deal do you think will
interest them?"

"The first tobacco crop of the year."

"What makes you think your tobacco will be first?"

"Because it's already eight inches high in the fields."

Rush couldn't hold back his surprise. The ground was only just now warm enough for the seed to sprout and grow without danger of being killed by frost. "How?"

"I have my methods," she said, warmed by his apparent interest. "I'm a planter."

Rush thought he'd never seen a woman so beautiful as Amanda Caden tonight. But now, with her mind on her tobacco, her eyes glittered like precious stones. Her hair caught the light of the hundreds of candles and turned into shimmering fire.

At that moment their host stood, and after a final toast, signified that the long meal was finally over.

"Please, do join us in the assembly hall for dancing," the Governor said, and led the procession into the ballroom where the President was expected to lead the Governor's wife in the first dance.

The President didn't seem to be enjoying himself, Amanda decided. There was a strain about his eyes and his lips remained firmly closed. "He looks as if he's been sucking on a persimmon that wasn't ripe," she whispered.

"No," Rush explained with a chuckle. "The man has false teeth. He doesn't want them to fall out."

The thought of the President's teeth falling out brought an unbidden smile from Amanda, and from that moment, the course of the evening seemed to change. Rush claimed the first dance, then stepped back and allowed all the other gentlemen attending the ball to dance with Amanda.

Rush had been watching Franklin, still in deep conversation with the merchants to whom Cadenhill was indebted. Something was going on, Rush thought, otherwise Franklin would have been pursuing Amanda. The fact that he wasn't proved he was planning to thwart her intentions.

Under the guise of sharing a cigar with the gentlemen, Rush adjourned to the small game room in the rear of the building where Franklin and his followers were busy emptying a bottle of French brandy.

"Evening, Franklin."

"Ah, Mr. Randolph. And how is the rebuilding of your way stations progressing?"

"Very well. How is the warehouse doing?"

"Very well. We've had no more threats by the highwayman and his gang of cutthroats."

Rush bit back a smile. It was hard to see the Amanda he'd danced with as a cutthroat, though he understood her temper well enough to know that Franklin might be more accurate than he thought. At least she'd stopped her midnight marauding. The Jasmine Bandit had been severely limited by her decision to rob only Franklin and his associates who'd refused to renew her loans.

"I'm glad. Otherwise citizens might avoid Petersburg and cost the Broad River Valley a prosperous future."

"Indeed," one of Franklin's friends agreed, "if all goes well, I intend to become a member of the Petersburg community—very soon."

"Oh? Do you plan to grow tobacco?"

"Oh, yes. In fact, I understand that part of the land I'm considering repossessing is already planted."

"Eh, Wainwright, I wouldn't talk about our plans just yet," Franklin interrupted. "We wouldn't want anyone else to outbid you, would we?"

Franklin's companions became suddenly silent, as Franklin turned the conversation to horse racing.

Rush stood for a few minutes longer but he'd learned as much as he was going to. Franklin was up to something. If Rush was any good at second-guessing he'd guess that Franklin had made arrangements to sell part of Amanda's land to these gentlemen, the part she was planning to use to guarantee an extension on her loan. In spite of Franklin's threats Rush was surprised that Franklin was desperate enough to allow the land to be claimed. If he was.

For the better part of the evening he studied the situation, keeping an eye on Amanda. Her attempt to meet with her creditors was thwarted at every turn. Each time she worked her way close to one of them, the object of her stalking would suddenly disappear. It was as if Franklin had given them instructions to avoid her. Rush decided the only choice he had was to tell her the truth.

In a rare moment, the President had asked Amanda to be his partner in the minuet. When the dance came to an end they strolled toward the refreshment table.

"I see your escort for the evening is my old comrade, Rush Randolph," the President was saying. "A fine afternoon of hunting we had, except for poor Cornwallis. My favorite hunting dog was taken ill this afternoon as he ran through the woods. He died in my arms. Rush buried him. He's a fine man, Rushton Randolph, with as good a heart as Cornwallis's."

"I knew the stories about Mr. Randolph weren't true."

The President frowned at Amanda. "Are those old tales about his being a traitor still being circulated?"

"Yes, I'd heard something to that effect."

"Well, there was a traitor in the Broad River Valley all right, but it wasn't Rushton Randolph. I thought your father and I put the charge about Randolph to rest for good."

"Mr. Randolph said he knew my father, but I never heard Father mention his name. I was told by someone that Mr. Randolph went north to British territory with Benedict Arnold, that Mr. Randolph was a traitor to the patriot cause."

"True. Under your father's instructions Rush followed Arnold. Your father agonized over sending the young man, but it was necessary."

Amanda took a sip of punch. Her father had sent Rush to the British. The President had confirmed it. Now nobody could doubt Rush anymore.

"During the time Rush took orders from Houston, I think Houston came to look on Rush as his own son. The two of them were always talking about land and growing cotton. Your father is the one responsible for bringing Rush here. I'm glad to learn that Rush—"

The kind thoughts the President was building in Amanda's mind about Rush were shattered as she heard his final words "—plans to marry you. That's a sensible move for both of you. Cadenhill will grow fine cotton."

A sensible move? Rush planned to marry her? How dare he discuss her future with the President as if she were some piece of farmland. Her father couldn't have intended that. But from the first Rush had told her he'd come to Petersburg because he wanted land to raise cotton. What Rush hadn't said was that he'd come here with the intention of marrying her to get the land to do it.

The hypocritical devil! He'd kissed her until he turned her mind to mush. Well, she wouldn't have that kind of man as a husband. Rush was no different from Franklin. They both wanted the same thing, Cadenhill. And they'd both found the way to get it—marriage. Except, she admitted, Rush approached her from a different perspective. He was trying to blindside her. The truth smarted.

Well, she'd refused Franklin and she'd refuse Rush. Cadenhill grew tobacco and would continue to grow tobacco as long as Amanda could run her fingers through the soil. Amanda managed to smile and excuse herself from the President, glancing around the room until her eye caught that of Patrick McLendon, who was watching Catherine dance with the Governor.

Patrick McLendon wasn't a planter. He was a gambler. He ought to know someone, somewhere who would appreciate the kind of chance she could offer him. If she'd taken time to think through her plan she might have considered how her action would look. But Patrick was the only man she saw at that moment. And she was so filled with fury that she struck out blindly.

"Patrick, you haven't danced with me." Amanda swept past Rush, who was directly in her path, and pressed herself into the startled Patrick's arms.

"Eh, no, I haven't, have I?" Patrick took one look at the surprise in Rush's eyes and swept Amanda out onto the floor. The waltz lent itself nicely to whatever game his partner was playing. She smiled and flung back her head, using the crowded ballroom as an excuse to lean against him. Patrick caught sight of Catherine and realized that dancing with Amanda was having a dual reaction. Amanda had done it now. The battle was about to commence, and there was nothing he could do except hope that he wasn't caught in the cross fire.

"What are you doing, Amanda Caden?" Patrick asked.

"Why nothing, except enjoying the dance, Mr. Mc-Lendon. By the way, you do understand that Mother will never allow Catherine to marry until I've chosen a husband."

"You do realize that I have no intention of marrying at all, Miss Caden."

"My thoughts exactly, Mr. McLendon. But I'm forced to change my mind. I believe that you'll agree that Cadenhill is a worthwhile prize, don't you?"

"Indeed, but not at the cost of my life, and I'm satisfied that's what it would be if we were to wed."

"Your life?" She laughed. She hadn't meant Patrick to think that she was proposing, but he had. "Would marriage to me demand such a price?"

"I believe it would. Now in order to prolong both our lives, I'm going to arrange a change of partners."

Just then Rush appeared on one side and Catherine on the other, effectively containing the dancers until Patrick deftly stepped aside and transferred Amanda to Rush, while at the same time he claimed Catherine.

"Thank you, Catherine darling. I do believe that Rush would have murdered me if you'd waited one moment longer."

"You think you were in danger from Rush? Wait until you find out what kind of killing weapons I have hidden beneath my dress, Irishman."

Slipping her hand away for a moment to adjust her belt, Catherine slid it between them and caught a part of Patrick's body that instantly responded.

"What are you doing, Catherine?"

"Just checking, Patrick, just checking." Catherine leaned back and smiled. "I wanted to make certain that I'm still the object of your affections. After all, Amanda is in love with Mr. Randolph."

"Oh, how can you be sure?"

"Because he's already stolen her away and I suspect that she's being passionately kissed right now. Well, that's all right, she's the oldest. She's entitled. Just so long as I don't have to wait too long for my turn."

Patrick gulped. The witch had a way of taking away all his reservations. Before he knew it he was waltzing through the French doors and onto the patio. He didn't see Rush and Amanda. He no longer cared about anything except kissing Catherine.

"Rushton Randolph, unhand me this instant!"

"Shut up, Amanda Caden, before I do more than stroll down the promenade!"

"What could you possibly do to me that you haven't already done?"

The answer to that question was so staggering that Rush couldn't answer for a long moment. Finally, he took a deep breath and slowed their pace. "I could turn you over my knee and give you a spanking. And believe me, I'm tempted."

Amanda jerked her arm away. "You wouldn't dare!"

"God knows, Amanda, I've tried to be patient with you. But I see that you aren't going to cooperate. Too bad, you'll have to suffer the consequences of your stubbornness." With a sudden move that caught Amanda by surprise, he reached down and lifted her over his shoulder, carrying her down the street like a sack of flour.

Amanda beat on his back. She kicked. She swore. She threatened.

Rush simply walked on, speaking to everyone he met as if he were simply out for a Sunday stroll.

Finally Amanda grew quiet. "Why are you doing this?"

Rush came to a stop beneath the limbs of a mulberry tree. He let Amanda slide to the ground. "I think you will agree that the most important thing either one of us can do is prevent Franklin from selling your tobacco fields. And that's just what he's doing."

"What?" Everything went black for a moment. Amanda felt her knees turn to tallow. "How do you know this?"

"I heard enough of a conversation between him and the creditors to know that he's already made a deal with them to sell your tobacco fields to satisfy your debts. He has to be stopped."

Amanda started to argue, then she remembered watching Franklin during dinner. She realized, too, that every time she attempted to talk to one of the debt holders he'd turned away. With certainty Amanda knew that Franklin had never had any intention of settling the Cadenhill debt. That would involve using his own money. He didn't care about the land itself. It was the idea of usurping Houston's place that drove him. He wanted everything that Houston had had, including Amanda, and he'd found a way to claim it. She'd run out of time. There were no more options. Franklin had won. Unless...

Amanda felt a strange coldness settle over her. There was a way. Her father had given it to her. She'd have to do the one thing she'd refused to consider. She'd have to marry Rushton Randolph.

She straightened her shoulders and raised her eyes. She couldn't see him in the dark, but she could feel his eyes watching her. "You're right. Franklin must be stopped. If you still want to marry me, Mr. Randolph, I accept. The marriage must take place at once. I'll do whatever I have to do to keep Franklin from claiming Cadenhill. But if we marry, you must agree that the marriage will be a business arrangement only. You want land to grow cotton, and I need a husband. I don't have to look any further."

Rush and Amanda were as close as they could be, without touching. He could feel her determination, and share her courage. But if he'd expected her to fling herself into his arms and say that she loved him, he knew that would never happen. He was in love with this woman, as he had been since that night in the carriage, but she had no idea of his feelings. Not yet, but that could be changed in time.

"Are you asking me to be your husband, Amanda Caden?"

"My husband?" She hadn't thought of it quite that way. "I'm agreeing to marry you, that's all."

"And why should I?"

"Because you want to grow cotton."

"But I can grow cotton anywhere."

"You can grow better cotton on Cadenhill."

"That isn't enough, Amanda."

"That's all I can promise."

The air was charged. She raised her eyes, searching his face, imploring him to accept what she could offer and not ask for more.

"Please, Rush."

This time she lifted her arms and pulled his head down to meet her lips. She didn't love this man, she told herself. She had no knowledge of love and wanted none. She was simply saving Cadenhill.

As their lips touched, the resistance went out of Rush and the kiss became a pledge of commitment. She thought that she didn't love him, but he believed her wrong. In time that would change. In time she'd come to him openly and willingly. He believed that as he pulled her into his arms and returned her kiss.

Judge Taliaferro performed the ceremony at midnight, in the parlor of the Planters' Hotel. He might have resisted, but the thought of history recording his part in a marriage witnessed by the President of the United States swayed his judgment.

Iris Caden seemed bewildered by her daughter's sudden decision until she saw the look pass between the couple when Rush was allowed to kiss the bride. She'd wished that Amanda would have a marriage based on love, and she knew at that moment that her wish had been granted. Houston would be pleased. The feeling was so strong that she could almost feel him standing there beside her, nodding in pleasure.

Catherine Caden was overjoyed. Now that Amanda was wed, she could begin in earnest to plan for her own wedding. Having Rush at Cadenhill would make it easier for her to leave. For Catherine was wise enough to understand that she'd chosen a forward-seeing, wandering man, a man who welcomed the challenge of the unknown. He wouldn't stay in Augusta or Petersburg, or Savannah. She'd go with him. Somehow.

As the ceremony ended, a loud voice interrupted the congratulations of the well-wishers. "What do you think you're doing, Randolph? I'll not allow you to marry my niece."

Franklin Caden, his face red, the veins in his temples bulging with barely contained fury, tore into the room, followed by his business associates.

"You're too late, Franklin!" The triumphant Amanda faced her uncle. "I'm married. And my marriage nullifies any further control you have on Cadenhill—now and forever!''

"What about our deal, Franklin?" one of the men asked.

"Yes, not two hours ago you took more of our money and promised us we could take possession of the land."

The creditors studied Franklin, then turned angrily to Rush. "The tobacco fields are ours, Randolph. We've paid for them in good faith."

"Then you've been taken in by a crook," Rush said quietly. "The land isn't Franklin's to sell, and you can't legally claim it until June first."

"No!" Franklin protested. "The land isn't yours, Randolph. You can't do this. For years, I made certain that Cadenhill was always in debt. Cadenhill is mine."

"No, Franklin," Rush said. "Cadenhill belongs to Iris Caden. Amanda's marriage to me voided your control of the land. Explain it to these men."

"Is that true, Franklin?"

"No—I mean yes, but..."

"Then we want our money back, Franklin."

"But I don't have it on me now."

"Fine, tomorrow morning. And Randolph, no more extensions, the debts must be paid in full," the man called Wainwright said. "And if they aren't, we don't need Franklin to claim the land. You have two weeks, Randolph!"

Suddenly the glow disappeared from the evening. Amanda stood, staring at her uncle, proved finally to be the thief she'd always known he was. But was she any better off than she'd been in the beginning? Instead of being able to pay the interest and persuade the creditors to give her more time, she would have to pay the full amount due. And she could never meet the debt. Her marriage had bought only two weeks.

"We'll meet the loans. Now, gentlemen, if you'll excuse us." Rush took Amanda's arm and made a great show of offering his. "We have a honeymoon to get to. Will you join me, Mrs. Randolph?"

Amanda felt herself being swept across the red carpet and up the stairs. "Mrs. Randolph?" she whispered through lips as cold as ice. "You don't expect me to call myself Mrs. Randolph, do you?"

"Of course I do, darling. You're my wife now."

Amanda Randolph. His wife. Suddenly Amanda couldn't breathe. How could this man think about a honeymoon, about being married, when Cadenhill was in danger of being torn apart? Franklin had lost control. Technically the plantation belonged to Iris. If the lien holders refused to deal with Rush, Cadenhill was no better off. And her husband didn't seem concerned!

She felt her fury begin to mount. There was no time to waste. Where could she find the money? Then she remembered the mask and guns hidden at the bottom of her bag.

Franklin!

The men said they'd already paid Franklin, two hours ago. If she could get that money from Franklin tonight maybe she could—Her mind whirled with possibilities, none of which included Rush's lifting her in his arms, taking her into his room and locking the door behind them.

"What are you doing, you black-eyed devil?"

"I'm about to make love to my wife."

"You are not. I told you that this was a business arrangement—nothing more."

"You said it. I never agreed, Amanda. I'm your husband now and I intend to be, in every sense of the word." He started removing his clothing. First his shoes, his breeches, then his hose and finally his shirt—until he was standing in the candlelight wearing only his undergarment.

He was serious. Amanda gasped. She didn't have time to—to do whatever he had in mind. She had to get to Franklin before those men reclaimed their money. Frantically she thought. She had to distract Rush. Then she knew.

"All right, Rush," she said in a low hesitant voice. "But I'm afraid. If this were a normal wedding you'd wait downstairs until I'm ready. I need my things."

"They're already here. I had the proprietor move them during the ceremony."

"Couldn't you just go outside?"

"Oh, no. I'm not leaving you alone. You'd probably disappear."

"But I—I need a few minutes alone, to compose myself for what is to come." She even managed a convincing sniffle as she glanced helplessly around. There it was, her valise. The mask and her highwayman's costume and guns were here. If she could just distract Rush long enough to claim them....

"All right, darling, I'll wait on the balcony for a moment. But if you so much as touch that door I'll turn you over my knee and give you that spanking I didn't give you earlier."

Rush opened the balcony door and stepped into the darkness outside. Amanda walked over to the door, casually making a big show of removing her shoes and stockings, keeping an eye on Rush as she moved about the room. Good, there was a lock on the balcony door. She'd thought there would be, a protection for the hotel guests from thieves. Pausing, so that she was standing between the light of the candle and the glass-curtained door, she unbuttoned her dress and slid it and her undergarments to the floor.

Satisfied that her silhouette had caught Rush's attention she slammed the bolt into place and pushed a chair beneath the knob. With a prayer that her barrier would hold him until she could get away, Amanda opened her valise and pulled on her trousers and boots, threading her arms inside her frock coat as she dashed toward the outer door amid pounding and curses from Rush.

"Hell's doorknobs!" Her mother and the judge were coming down the corridor. They'd hear Rush beating on the door to the balcony. "Hurry, hurry," she pleaded, willing her mother to enter her room quickly. But it wasn't to be. Her mother and the judge had come to a stop outside. She couldn't tell what was being said, but the whispers suggested a happy moment.

Then she realized that Rush's curses had hushed. There were no more attempts to break down the balcony door. Where was he? She blew out the candle and tiptoed to the glass door. Peeking out from behind the curtain, she could tell that the balcony was empty. Anxiously she moved the chair, slid back the bolt and opened the door. Perhaps she could escape that way. Time was running out.

Then it happened. The door to the hallway burst open and Rush stood, outlined by the candles of the hallway beyond, thundering with fury, daring her to move. Beyond Rush, Amanda could hear the whispers and giggles of other guests. Wearing only his underwear, he had climbed down from the balcony and marched through the lobby and up the stairs.

Amanda felt her face flame with embarrassment. What would he do?

"Mr. Randolph!"

"No, madam—not 'Mr. Randolph.' Your husband. Close the door and remove your trousers."

"No, Rush, you can't. I have to go. Don't you understand?"

"I understand more than you think, Amanda. And I also know that Franklin has guards following him twenty-four hours a day. I have no intention of spending my wedding night in a jail cell. Not even for you."

"Oh—"

"Not 'oh,' my Jasmine Bandit. The answer I expect is 'yes, Rush darling,' and I expect it now! For once in your life, Cadenhill is not the master you have to please."

Amanda slowly closed the patio door. It was all over. She'd lost her last chance. Rushton Randolph was not a man to be run over. He was strong and determined. Fine. If she had to allow him in her bed, she'd do it. There'd still be time, later. The Jasmine Bandit had to find a way.

"All right, Mr. Randolph," she said softly, and closed her eyes in resignation. "You're my husband. You've accomplished what you set out to do. Now, do what you will to me. Quickly, please. There are things to be taken care of."

Rush felt his anger drain away. He'd won. But in winning he'd lost. He wanted Amanda, wanted her so badly that he could hardly breathe from the tight wanting of her. But she had to want him in return. And she didn't. She was surrendering, giving up, and he couldn't stand to see her vulnerable—defeated.

"No, you're wrong about me, Amanda. I didn't come here to marry you, and I'll never force you to be my wife. When you love me, it will be because you want me. I only hope you will. And, Amanda, don't try to leave this room. With the President in town, there are guards on every corner."

When Amanda opened her eyes he was gone.

The room was empty, so very empty, and she was cold. The spring air had lost its warmth. The scent of flowers was masked by the scent of the man who'd walked away.

She hadn't fooled Rush. He'd known what she planned to do, and he'd let her know that the Jasmine Bandit wouldn't be allowed to ride.

Later, as she lay in the big bed alone, she realized that this was her wedding night. She'd never thought about a wedding night, but if she had, she never would have imagined that she'd spend it alone.

Moisture welled up in her eyes. A single tear spilled over and rolled down her cheek. She wouldn't cry. Cadenhill was hers—for now. There was still a chance. She didn't know how, but she'd find a way.

And she'd find a way to live with this black-eyed man, as well. Like Cornwallis, he was strong and of good heart. It was her own heart that she wasn't sure of. It hurt.

Chapter Eighteen

Iris was hardly dressed when Rush knocked on her hotel room door the next morning and asked her to walk with him. She might have questioned him more thoroughly about his purpose this time, but one look at his tortured expression and tired eyes and she'd agreed. Her concern over the hasty marriage performed the night before was lessened when Rush explained the reason for the ceremony.

They walked on the wide promenade around the fountain in the middle of the green that stretched from one side of Broad Street to the other. Already merchants were displaying their goods on makeshift carts outside their establishments. A black woman, wearing a piece of yard goods twisted into a turban on her head, was standing in an alley between two buildings, frying sweet dough in a black iron pot of boiling fat. She was doing a brisk business with early risers.

Rush plodded woodenly for some time before he began to look at the activity taking place around him. He wished he could share this scene with Amanda. She was probably still in bed. The thought of her sleeping in the big four-poster with the canopy hit him in the stomach like the kick of a mule. He'd slept in her small room at the end of the corridor—or he'd tried. If he'd closed his eyes he didn't know it. In the darkest hour of the night, the need to creep down the

balcony and slip into Amanda's bed became so strong that
he'd had to move, and his pacing became so measured that
someone in the room below finally pounded on the ceiling
in protest. At dawn he decided to pose his problem to Iris.
Now he didn't know where to begin. He didn't have to.

"Rush, may I assume that you have not enjoyed your—a
normal wedding night?"

"No, I have not. I slept in Amanda's room. She occupies
mine."

"I see. And what do you want from me?"

"I don't know. For you to listen, I suppose. I came to
Petersburg because Houston thought I might find a future
here. What you don't know is that I made him a promise
that I'd look after Amanda if anything happened to him. I
never expected that I'd care for her so much."

Iris smiled. "I suspected so. You do care for her?"

"I do, very much, though she doesn't believe that yet. She
thinks I arranged the marriage to save Cadenhill only because I want her land."

"And you didn't?"

"No. I mean yes, of course I did. But that wasn't the only
reason." Rush knew that he was stuttering. He felt as if he
were working out his emotions even as he tried to explain
them to Amanda's mother. "I think," he finally said, "that
Amanda and I are right for each other and I believe that we
can make a good marriage."

"A good marriage would have been my goal for Amanda,
Rush, but my daughter has never considered marriage to be
a part of her future. I never understood her commitment to
land and growing, but it's been the driving force in her life."

"As is mine, but of late I've begun to see that a commitment shared is all the stronger. I think that, except for your
husband, the people I've cared about in my life have never
been able to care in return. I no longer put my faith in people and promises. Like Amanda, I always believed the land
is forever. Turning seeds into crops that can be harvested

puts a man in opposition only to nature. I can deal with that. If I fail, it isn't because I depended on people. If I succeed it's between me and a higher power."

Iris smiled. "That's very sad. Like Amanda, I think you have a great capacity for love. I loved Houston first and shared his life because of that love. You and Amanda have reversed the process. But the end result can be the same."

"I—I'd like to think that Amanda will learn to love me, but if she doesn't, I'll still be a good husband."

"Perhaps you're very wise, Rushton Randolph. Perhaps you and Amanda do belong together. My marriage to Houston was the sustaining joy in my life, that and my children. Now Houston is gone. Amanda is committed to you now, and Catherine is only a step away from giving herself to a husband. I'm thinking that I'll marry again."

"Oh?"

"Not now, maybe not next year. But my life is a life apart from my children. Cadenhill was Houston, and though he is still in my heart, without Houston that part of my life is over. I shall leave Cadenhill to you and Amanda."

"Not if Amanda keeps locking me on the balcony."

Iris's smile turned into a muted chuckle. "That was an interesting development. Ten years from now it won't be the President's visit that people will talk about, it will be your trek through the lobby of the Planters' Hotel in the altogether."

"I was wearing undergarments!" Rush snapped sheepishly.

"That you were," Iris agreed meekly. "I confess that I'm as curious as everyone else as to why you were outside in the first place."

"Amanda seemed to be of the opinion that our marriage was a business arrangement only. She didn't expect—I mean when—"

"I don't wish to seem indelicate, but what you're saying is that she didn't welcome you to her bed?"

"That is putting it mildly. The woman lured me onto the balcony and locked the door. I ask you, what did she expect any self-respecting man to do?"

Iris swallowed her laughter. "Rush, under normal circumstances I would have explained your expectations to Amanda. I'm sure Amanda never considered that you'd be so bold. But knowing her feelings for you, I suspect that she wasn't as shocked as she might have led you to believe."

"Perhaps I was too bold. And I should have been prepared for her reaction." Rush allowed himself a grin at his own expense. "I guess I was a sight to see. I hope that I didn't embarrass you."

"I don't embarrass easily, Rush. I may have the reputation of being a mere woman, but I've fulfilled the role I was expected to play. Which I'll continue, once I find out what you want me to do."

"I guess what I'm asking you, as my mother-in-law, is to give me counsel."

"Am I to assume that you expect this marriage to be a real marriage in every sense of the word?"

"You're damned right, I do! Forgive me, Mrs. Caden. That was inexcusable of me."

"Don't worry, Rush. Houston was inclined to use a choice word, too, if he was emotional about an issue. He never put me on any kind of pedestal, not in private. We were very frank."

"Then tell me what to do."

"All right, Rush. I'll be blunt. I believe that Amanda finds you—appealing."

It was Rush's time to blush. He remembered Amanda's abandon by the river, when he kissed her, when her blood pulsed hot and free. "Yes, I think so."

"Then perhaps what you want to do is use that. Amanda always patterned herself after Houston, and one thing Houston could never tolerate was being refused. If he was ever rejected that simply made him more determined to succeed.''

"But I haven't rejected Amanda. In fact, I find it difficult to maintain a proper distance from her when we're in mixed company. When we are alone, it's damned impossible.''

"Apparently, from your expression and what you haven't said, Amanda reacts the same way."

"I think so. Yes, definitely so."

"Then all you have to do is reject her. If she's anything like Houston she'll stop at nothing to have the thing being withheld—you."

"Providing I can find a way to put off those creditors," Rush said, wondering how best to broach the second subject he wanted to talk about.

"Yes, I agree. Though I don't know how you'll do it."

"I have an idea, but I don't know if you'll be willing to go along."

Iris listened and concurred. By the time they'd made the full circle and were back in front of the hotel where people were beginning to gather to watch the departure of President Washington and his party, the practical control over Cadenhill had been transferred to Rush. His plan might not work, but it was the only thing he could come up with. At least he could buy some extra time.

As for Amanda, Houston himself had suggested that Amanda was as stubborn as he was. And Rush's change of heart in deciding to join Benedict Arnold's staff as a spy for the Colonies was proof enough of how determined a Caden could be when he was turned down.

Rush began to smile. The first thing he would do in his new position was to have a little talk with Cadenhill's creditors to arrange an extension on the loans. His stage line ought to be collateral enough for the debts. But he wouldn't tell Amanda.

Then, following Mrs. Caden's suggestion, he'd start his
grand rejection by giving a few unwelcome orders to his
wife, just to let her know who was in charge at the plantation. That ought to start a fire. She'd hate his taking over.
But there was a fine line between love and hate. Rush began to smile.

"Mrs. Caden, will you awaken my wife? Tell her that I
want to get home and see to the tobacco. Oh, and start
planning a wedding reception, two weeks from now, at
Cadenhill."

"Two weeks? That's very short notice for the guests."

"Don't worry, Mrs. Caden. All you have to do is issue
invitations. Folks will come."

Rush began to whistle. He leaned over, gave his new
mother-in-law a kiss on the cheek. "But don't tell Amanda
about the party just yet. We'll keep that as a surprise."

As he disappeared into the crowd, Iris glanced up. There
was a rippling movement of the curtain at the bedroom
window—Rush's bedroom window.

Good. They'd had an audience. More certain than ever
that she'd been right in talking to Rush, Iris Caden marched
inside and up the stairs and knocked on Amanda's door.

"Good morning, Amanda," she said as the door opened.
"Your husband asked me to tell you that we'll be returning
to Cadenhill as soon as you can get ready. He's worried that
the planting isn't being seen to while we're away," Iris added
on her own. She might as well give Rush a little help.

"He's what?" Amanda couldn't conceal her astonishment. The nerve of the man. Sending her own mother to tell
her that she was being derelict in her duties. What did he
think he was going to do, march in and set her workers
straight?

"He's concerned. I'm very pleased about that. As your
husband, he will be responsible for Cadenhill now. I need to
start teaching you about running the household." Iris let her
gaze slide around the room. Only one pillow was mussed.

Poor Rush. Poor Amanda. She was wrapped in the sheet looking more like a teepee than a new bride.

"He's responsible? Over my dead body! Cadenhill is mine and I'll look after it."

"No, Amanda. Houston's will very clearly spelled out that Franklin was to oversee Cadenhill until one of us married. Then control was to go to the husband. I'll admit I was shocked at your hasty marriage. But now that I've had time to reflect on your decision, I am in full agreement."

Amanda bit back a scathing retort, came to her feet and began to gather her things. "Mother, see that Catherine is ready to depart in fifteen minutes. I shall secure a private coach for the three of us, and we'll go home."

"But your husband?"

"He isn't my husband! The marriage wasn't consummated, Mother. We—we didn't—ours is a marriage in name only. When the problem of Cadenhill is settled, I—I'll get an annulment."

"Then you'd rather sell part of our land and let Franklin continue his management? If that's what you want, Amanda, I'll ask Lewis to handle the arrangements for you. I'm quite weary of the responsibility."

Amanda dropped her valise on the bed and sank down beside it, her anger turning into defeat. Iris felt her daughter's pain and shared it. Before Amanda could fling herself off in another direction, Iris sat beside her and folded Amanda into her arms. She hadn't held and comforted her eldest daughter since she was a little girl.

Amanda gave in to the sobs that were threatening to choke off all the air in her chest. "Oh, Mother, what am I going to do?"

"What do you want to do?"

"I want things to be like they were."

"I know." Iris stroked Amanda's back, threading her fingers through the riot of red color that covered her daughter's shoulders. "But we can't go back. Life changes and we have to change with it. Rush Randolph is a fine, honest man, Amanda. I think you know that or you wouldn't have married him.''

''Yes. But he's only doing this because he wants Cadenhill.''

''Perhaps he did promise your father that he'd look after you. Houston must have thought he could do it.''

''But I don't want a man to look after me.'' Amanda pulled away, wiped her face and stood up. ''I can look after myself. I just want him to...to...be.''

''I don't think a man would be much of a man who just was. You know that a slave has to have a job that is his, one that gives him responsibility and respect or he's no good to himself or the plantation.''

''Yes, but Rush isn't a slave. He isn't going to let me give him a job.''

''You've already given him one, Amanda, when you married him—being your husband.''

''But I don't want a husband. I don't know how to be a wife.''

''It's a little late for you to think about that now, Amanda. Could it be that you're afraid of—of being a wife? I know I never prepared you for your marriage night.''

''Hell's doorknobs, Mother! I know what happens on a woman's wedding night. I've bred too many horses and cattle not to. It's Rush Randolph. He just makes me angry. I want to reach out and hit him, to scream. I—oh, Mother, you're right. I am scared. He makes me want to fly apart, and I don't like it.''

''Amanda, my dear, that isn't always a bad thing. People aren't horses. They have feelings and those feelings direct our lives. Your feelings for your father, for your family, are very special. But nothing can compare with the kinds of feelings you will experience when you fall in love.''

''I don't intend to fall in love, Mother. That isn't one of my goals.''

"But we weren't talking about goals for you, were we? We're talking about your husband, the man to whom you promised honor and obedience. What did you think he would expect from you?"

Amanda slumped to the bed, chaos storming across her face. "I didn't think about anything except keeping Franklin from selling Cadenhill."

"And you did, Amanda, at least for now."

"But what else have I done?"

Over and over again for the next few days, Amanda asked herself the same question. Thor was returned to the barn. Amanda didn't ride him. She wouldn't. He was no longer hers.

From the time they'd reached Cadenhill, Rush seemed to settle in with remarkable ease. He was pleasant, even reasonable, consulting Amanda each morning in her father's office before setting out to deal with his own work and those projects on the plantation she'd entrusted to him. Over supper, Rush was entertaining, sharing with her his stories about his adventures as if their relationship were as normal as that of any other husband and wife. He was amusing and well informed, and Amanda might have liked him—if they hadn't been married.

So caught up in repairing the damage left by the fire, and by Rush's presence, Amanda never noticed the housecleaning and the extra cooking that was taking place in readiness for the wedding reception.

Rush took a room adjoining Amanda's, without making an issue of their separate sleeping arrangements, for which Amanda was grateful. She avoided the questions in Catherine's eyes by leaving even earlier each morning and returning later each evening. But she'd known that sooner or later her sister's questions would have to be answered. She hadn't expected Catherine to ride out to the field in person with the dinner wagon. But she did. And from her attitude

Amanda knew that she had no intention of leaving until she was satisfied.

Amanda accepted cool water and a piece of the same corn bread and fried meat that the hands were issued. She found a shady spot beneath a pine tree away from the workers and sat, leaning wearily against the trunk of the tree as she ate. She had refused to acknowledge her lack of sleep, or her weariness, but Catherine wasn't fooled.

"I don't know why you're running from him, Manda. If Patrick was devouring me with his eyes like Rush is you, I'd positively melt."

"Then you'd be making a mistake!" Amanda snapped.

"Why? Rush Randolph is a real man, Manda, and he wants you. And you're just as interested in him. I know how you feel and I've watched you trying to pretend it isn't so."

"I don't think you should be talking about what goes on between me and my—Mr. Randolph."

"That's just the problem, nothing's going on. You're a fool, sister dear. You may be older than me, but I'm telling you that the first time Patrick McLendon offers to take me to bed, I'll accept, and I'll be loving every minute of it."

"Catherine!"

"And if you and Rush don't work things out, you're going to lose him to some woman who appreciates what he has to offer. Is that what you want?"

Amanda was dumbstruck for a moment. Would Rush go to another woman? Sharing the marriage bed had never been her intention. She didn't care if he did find his pleasure elsewhere. She didn't!

But she did.

From the night of the wedding Amanda and Rush operated under an unarmed truce, each unfailingly polite, each avoiding the other. From the beginning the slaves took their problems to Rush, though never openly flouting Amanda's authority. Even Iris catered to Rush. When he mentioned a special dish he liked, it appeared at the next meal. He was appreciative and seemed to feel affection for his new family.

Amanda, on the other hand, was increasingly irritable. When communication was necessary, Rush was calm and reasonable with his suggestions, overlooking Amanda's bad temper as if it weren't being evidenced. Did everybody know what was happening?

At night she lay awake, listening until Rush mounted the stairs and closed the door to his bedroom. She heard him pace back and forth endlessly before the room finally quieted and she managed to snatch a few hours of badly needed sleep. She awoke with an ache that she couldn't identify. She only knew that she carried it around with her all the time now.

Catherine was right about one thing. Something had to be done—not about her marriage, but about Cadenhill. She wouldn't be put off any longer. She had to talk to Rush about the loans and what they were going to do.

From Iris, not Rush, she'd learned that Rush and Judge Taliaferro had met with Franklin. He had fumed and argued, but in the end, Franklin had no other choice but to follow the very terms he'd intended to take advantage of when he'd drawn up Houston's will. Rush, not Franklin, now had legal control of Cadenhill.

Franklin had been circumvented. But Amanda couldn't pretend that Cadenhill's problems would just vanish, and she refused to depend on Rush to solve them. They were running out of time. Avoiding Rush was only making the tension worse. She told herself that she was glad Rush had accepted their marriage as a business arrangement only, though she'd never expected him to give up so easily. Every night she rehearsed what she'd say to him if he entered her chambers. Every night she lay awake until he retired. He never came. She should have been overjoyed, but some secret part of her felt shame, shame that she'd married a man who obviously wasn't interested in her.

His absence only reinforced her belief that Cadenhill had been his target from the start. If Rush truly wanted to be her husband he wouldn't have let a closed door stop him.

Amanda's feeling vacillated between unacknowledged dismay over being rejected and anger at Rush's failure to address the debt deadline, less than a week away. There were decisions to be made, she told herself, decisions in which she intended to have a say. Whatever their private arrangements were, they needed to talk. Privately. But for the past two days she'd only seen him at the evening meal, then he'd retire to his room, leaving her restless and wide-awake. Amanda made up her mind that she'd talk to Rush tonight, after everyone was in bed.

She took her usual evening bath, adding a small amount of the special bath oil that her father had sent from Savannah for her twentieth birthday, the oil that smelled of sweet jasmine. She glanced at the dwindling amount with regret. Few things appealed to the feminine side of her, but this gift from her father had and she'd hoarded it. Now, it was almost gone. The thought was somehow symbolic of the other changes in her life.

The dressing gown she was wearing had never been worn before. Its pale creamy color seemed to shimmer like moonlight. Amanda folded her arms across her breasts and slid her hands up and down the silky fabric with unconscious sensuality. Without admitting what she was doing, she had dressed herself to put Rush at a disadvantage, to show him that she made her own choices, whatever they might be.

The veranda wrapped around the second floor of the house like a snowy apron, each room opening out to it with both large windows and doors that could be opened in summer to cool the still, hot air inside. Tonight Amanda stepped outside, drawing in the scent of the climbing roses that clung to the trellis beneath her window.

There was a fat, butter-colored moon rising over the stand of trees that ribboned the river in the distance. Hugging herself, she leaned out, across the rail, drinking in the smells and sounds of the night. This was her place, where she belonged. No matter what had changed in her life, this was the same.

"If only..." she whispered.

"If only I'd go away and stop tormenting your dreams? If only I'd kiss you and take you to bed? If only you'd relax your guard, Amanda Randolph, you wouldn't be standing out here fantasizing about something that is so much better than anything you could ever dream."

Rush was standing on the balcony in the shadows and she hadn't known he was there.

"No!" she answered, almost as a protest.

"No? You don't feel the heat in the air that touches you?"

"No, I don't know how to relax."

"Yes, you do, darling. And sooner or later you're going to beg me to make you mine in every sense of the word."

"No," she whispered, damning his devil-black eyes and his soft, confident voice. The moonlight cast his face in shadows on the beard he hadn't shaved from his face. She could see droplets of water from his bath caught in his hair like diamonds on velvet.

With a frustrated motion she tilted back her head, trying to release the tension gathering in her neck. She turned her back to the banister rail, the tight grip of her arms the only physical restraint on the overwhelming urge she had to move closer to him.

She could feel the dew on the floor, wet against her bare feet. The cool May air caught at her tousled hair, whipping it into an unruly mass across her shoulders. She didn't have to look to know that Rush was smiling at her discomfort, understanding and enjoying every skittish breath she managed to draw. She could feel the heat of his gaze and she shivered, not from the night, but from the restrained anticipation of his touch.

And then it wasn't restrained anymore. For he was beside her, pulling her into his embrace, his hands catching her strong and hard beneath her bottom. He was so close that their lips almost touched, almost, but not quite. Everything disappeared from her vision and her thoughts, everything except this man who'd so completely caught her in his spell.

Amanda's lips parted. She waited, her heart pounding wildly, her body engulfed in such a mass of conflicting emotions as she'd never known.

"Are you asking me to make love to you, Amanda?"

"Of course not. What do you mean?"

"Your invitation to me—is it a conscious decision, or are you just drunk on moonlight?"

The cold came crashing over Amanda, the cold that brought sudden understanding, the cold that brought such bewilderment that she could neither move away, nor answer.

Rush's gaze never wavered. He didn't know what her game was, but he didn't intend to pretend. Either she wanted him and all that making love represented, or they'd continue to sleep in separate beds. It took every ounce of willpower he possessed to keep himself from lifting her into his arms and taking her to bed.

"I don't understand."

"Amanda, you're asking for something that I don't give lightly. You want my body, but that isn't enough, my darling wife. I won't let you use me and reject me in the morning."

"You think I'm asking you to my bed? You're a devil, Thomas Rushton Randolph!"

"No, I'm your husband. When you're ready to tell that to the world, you know where to find me."

And then he was gone, taking the moon and its light with him. The veranda turned as black as Amanda's mood and the breeze turned even cooler.

She shivered and knew she'd lost something that she never had. She was wrong about Rush. He wasn't a devil. Devils lived in hell, and where she was standing was much too cold for that.

Chapter Nineteen

The morning after their encounter on the balcony Amanda took her coffee and fled to the office, hoping to avoid sharing the breakfast table with Rush. She was studying the ledger that listed her schedule and the progress she'd made. It also listed the plantation's mounting debts, along with her shrinking supplies of coins.

In the twelve days since she'd confidently departed for Augusta, intent on confronting the men who held the loans on Cadenhill, she'd searched unsuccessfully for another answer. There was none. Even a foray by the Jasmine Bandit wouldn't help. Nobody in Petersburg had the kind of funds she needed now that Franklin had been forced to return the money for the sale of Cadenhill land. Even if a possible victim should appear, Amanda knew that Rush would prevent any further midnight rides.

She sighed. As if the mere mention of her husband brought him to life, he appeared in the doorway.

"Amanda, I want to speak with you."

"I don't think we have anything to discuss, unless you're offering me the funds we need to meet the June deadline on our debts."

"I can't. We need what money I have to operate the plantation. Try to be patient, Amanda. I promise that I'm working on repaying the loans. But that's not what I came to talk with you about.''

"What then?''

"The land beside the river. I want to plant it. For the past few days I've had Roman moving mud from along the riverbank to the field to replace the top soil washed away by the flood. In another day or so I'll be ready to plant.''

"Rush, this is the third week of May. It's too late to plant anything. Besides, all tobacco plants have already been set out.'' The man was more concerned with planting than saving the land. Amanda felt a flood of frustration welling up. All her life she'd been in charge. She didn't know how to give up control without losing part of herself.

"Not tobacco, Amanda, cotton. This is an experiment. If it works, Cadenhill will never have to borrow money again.''

"Rush, even I know that Sea Island cotton won't grow here, and planting green cotton isn't practical. It takes all winter and every hand on the place to remove the seed. I have neither the hands nor the time to plant cotton.''

"I'm making arrangements so you won't have to.''

Arrangements? Taking care of the loans? He was taking over without any pretense of consulting her wishes. A cold fury swept over her. ''And do you have arrangements with your British friends to remove the seeds themselves?'' Amanda wished she could call back the words. Her emotions were strung onto such a tight thread that she lost all restraint, flinging the one accusation that would wound Rush the most. She was confused and tired, and that weariness had loosened her tongue, allowing her to strike out against her husband.

Rush winced. He didn't miss the implication of her words, *British friends*. ''Patrick and I have an answer—at least we're working on one.''

"Patrick? Somehow he doesn't seem to be the cotton planter type. I thought all his business here involved Catherine. It seems that every time I look up he's calling on my sister.''

"Catherine isn't the only business he has here. But you're right. Patrick isn't a planter. He's a gambler, an investor. He finds people with ideas and goods, and finds a way to make a profit from them.''

Amanda couldn't keep the jeer from her voice. "He's going to lend us money? Is he planning to marry Catherine and become your partner?''

Rush forced himself to speak slowly. He knew how on edge Amanda was. He'd wanted to tell her what he was arranging, but he couldn't, not until it was done. She couldn't take more disappointment.

"Not exactly, Amanda, there is a man right here in Petersburg who is working on a machine that will remove the seeds from the cotton.''

"And he's going to share it with you?''

"Patrick and I are providing the funds and the facilities to manufacture the machine when it's ready.''

Amanda gasped. "You're investing in a seed-removal machine when we need the money for Cadenhill?'' She couldn't keep the disbelief from her voice. "No wonder you're here in Petersburg instead of back in Virginia growing tobacco. You'd rather take a chance on some wild scheme than to do what's sensible!''

"Amanda, if what we're doing works, Cadenhill will be more than you ever imagined. Can't you trust me?''

"Why should I? Your own family didn't.''

"I see.'' His face was as stiff as his voice. "Fine. I shall be away for the next two days. While I'm gone your mother will be preparing for the wedding reception we're holding here at Cadenhill on Saturday evening. I'll see you when I return.''

Rush turned and was halfway out the door when Amanda's voice stopped him.

"Rush?" she called out, searching for a way to apologize, to delay him, to force him to include her in his plans. "Why river mud?"

He expected her to issue a protest about his leaving, or about the party, but she didn't. Not Amanda. Amanda was more interested in planting the bottom land.

"Why not bring in loam from the woods instead of river mud?"

"We're using that, too. But the river mud makes for rich topsoil when mixed with regular soil."

"Something else you learned from President Washington?"

"No, something I learned from an Indian tribe I wintered with several years ago.

"Trust me, Amanda," he said softly. Then he was gone.

Long afterward she studied his answer. Who was this man she'd married? Not just a soldier, he was a man who had dreams and was willing to invest in them. He'd been to school in England, lived with Indians in the west—she'd heard about his adventures at the dinner table for the past week—and now he was investing in a machine that removed seed from cotton. Maybe it wasn't a wild scheme. She cringed when she remembered her hateful words.

He wanted land to grow cotton. She understood that. What she hadn't understood was his wagering part of his inheritance with Franklin to satisfy her debt. She felt as if he'd gambled on her, and he'd lost. Now, in some way she didn't understand, he was taking a chance on some machine that would make Cadenhill more than it had ever been. Everything about him sent conflicting emotions through her. One minute she was railing out at him, the next minute she felt regret. What was happening to her?

She didn't understand her feelings or the man who set them off. Now he was planning a wedding reception in celebration of a marriage that was only a sham. What was he up to? She wished her father were here so that she could talk

to him. She'd been so sure she knew where her life was going, but now she wasn't certain about anything, except that
from the moment he'd come, Rushton Randolph had done
nothing but confuse her.

But he'd helped her, too. When a man comes to help you,
Amanda, marry him, her father had said. If only her father
were here to counsel her.

What should I do, Father? Did you really send Rush here
to marry me? Why? I hate him. I hate the way he makes me
feel. Why?

But there was no answer. Houston Caden was gone. She
could almost hear her father explaining, when he left Petersburg to help set up the new government. ''A man has to
think, not just with his mind, Amanda, but with his heart.
The heart knows, Amanda. Listen to it.''

Amanda paced the small office. She'd stop trying to understand and listen to her heart. It hurt. Rushton Randolph was her husband. She might not have wanted it, but
like Cadenhill, she had made a commitment to him now.
And, she realized with surprise, she wanted him by her side.
By her side, but hell would freeze over before she'd let him
turn her into some simpering wife. They were partners. She
might not be able to stop part of Cadenhill being sold, but
she'd not give up one ounce of her authority. He wanted to
raise cotton, they'd raise cotton. But they'd raise tobacco,
too. He wanted to have a reception, fine. They'd have one.
Rushton Randolph would soon find out that his wife could
be a partner. Then he'd have to do the same.

Iris had already issued invitations to the party. Fortu-
nately Cadenhill was close enough to Petersburg for most of
the guests to attend the reception and return to their homes
on the same evening. But Iris was making space available for
any who chose to spend the night. Catherine and the two
little girls would be moved into Iris's room, leaving Catherine's room as a common room where the women could
sleep, rest or just ready themselves for the ball. Rush's room

would be designated for use by the men. Jamie and Cecilia's room would house the ladies' maids.

For the next two days the house was a flurry of activity. Everybody avoided Amanda's short temper. Only Lovie was allowed in Amanda's bedroom. Trips to the storage attic were not explained, and neither were the long hours the two women spent behind locked doors.

On the day of the reception Rush returned. While Amanda was in the field he bathed and dressed for the evening. He was gone before Amanda returned and found his clothing hanging on a nail behind the Chinese screen that normally hid her bathtub and toilet area. The bathtub was wet. It had been recently used.

"Lovie!" Amanda's voice rang down the upstairs.

Finally Lovie appeared. "What's wrong, Miss Amanda?"

"Why are Mr. Randolph's clothes in my room?"

"Miz Caden had them moved. His room is being used for the gentlemen staying over after the party."

"She did what? Go downstairs and find Mr. Randolph. Tell him I want to see him immediately."

"But Miss Amanda, he's entertaining your guests."

"But I want—" What did she want? Other than using her tub and hanging his clothes in her room, Rush had certainly not come near her. Surely he didn't intend to stay here tonight. She felt an unexplainable shiver of excitement.

"Come and help me dress, Lovie. I intend to show my husband that his wife is just as much a prize as Cadenhill. He's going to be sorry that he didn't consult me about going wherever he's been. This is a partnership. What's good for the gander is good for the goose. He's going to worry that I just might decide to—to leave."

"Miss Amanda, you ain't going nowhere, except into that man's bed. You're standing here getting all hot and bothered just looking at his clothes. You ain't fooling me. And it's time you quit fooling yourself. Trust me, once you lie with him, ain't neither one of you going want to leave."

* * *

The reception Iris had planned was the kind of gala affair that she'd always dreamed of for her daughter. Everyone attended. There was no possibility that all the guests could be housed overnight, but that hadn't stopped carriage after carriage from making the trip from Petersburg. They'd sleep on the drive home, or simply stay up all night.

The chandeliers were studded with white candles made of myrtle wax, which gave the air a pleasant scent and cast the guests in silver and gold reflections. The wall tapestries had been removed to give the room a feeling of light and openness. All the windows were uncovered, doors opened, and a gentle spring night seemed to go on forever.

Elegant chairs lined the walls. Benches had been placed on the veranda so that those who chose not to dance could watch from a cool place. There was a fruity punch for the women, and one with a fiery jolt for the men. In the middle of the refreshment table was a wedding cake, iced with spun white frosting and decorated with real roses from Iris's garden.

A harpsichord, sandwiched between the music stands of two violinists, had been set in one corner. The musicians were tuning up, ready to play, but they had not yet begun. Jamie and Cecilia were dressed and standing beside their mother, enthralled with the splendor of the occasion and the people milling around. Everyone was waiting. But nobody was more on edge than Rush. Would Amanda accept what he was offering? Would she allow him to be a real part of Cadenhill and her life? Would she even come downstairs?

Upstairs, Amanda's stomach was fluttering about like Charity Taliaferro's fan at the President's ball. She stood up, walked toward the window where she could see evidence of the party goers walking in her mother's garden, then strode back to the mirror and glared at the woman she saw looking back, her face white and filled with panic.

"Miss Amanda, you're going to have to go down, sooner or later. It'll just get harder the longer you wait."

"I still don't understand. Why on earth hold a wedding reception? It's silly. We aren't even truly married."

"Maybe it's because he wants the world to know that you have a husband."

"Why?"

"Why don't you go down and find out?"

Amanda glared at her reflection again. "Are you sure I look all right?"

She was wearing a blue satin dress. It had been originally designed to be worn over a full petticoat with what she called false hips, before Lovie had recut the fabric into a softer style that flowed and rustled as she walked. The extra cloth making a winglike appendage meant to be stuffed down her bosom had been discarded, leaving the neckline scandalously low in front. She wore no jewels except her mother's pearls, which had been woven into the ringlets that Lovie had fashioned in her hair.

She looked plain, and cold, she thought. Good, that was what she intended to be, aloof and untouchable. Why Rush thought that he could conjure up a bright and happy affair in the midst of disaster was a mystery to her. He hadn't bothered to consult her about his purpose; therefore, she wouldn't cooperate with him. He'd learn soon enough that she dictated the activities on Cadenhill.

Thus resolved she decided that the time had come for her to make her entrance. Bidding Lovie to remain in her room, Amanda pulled on her long gloves, slid the loop of her lace fan around her wrist and stepped into the hallway at the top of the stairs.

As if on cue, Rush looked up and saw her—saw her and caught his breath. Cool, icy blue...and crimson. Fire and ice. Amanda was a vision. He smiled and walked to the bottom of the stairs holding out his hand. At the nod of his head, one of the violinists played a quick trill and the guests turned toward the foyer.

"Ladies and gentlemen," Rush said proudly, "my wife."

Amanda took a quick gulp of air. The man was out of his mind. He was treating her as if she were royalty, announcing her, waiting at the bottom of the stairs to escort her like a consort. And she had to get down those steps without falling on her face, wearing shoes that felt like stilts. Tightening her expression, she caught the banister and started down. One step. Two steps. Finally she reached the bottom and took her husband's arm, grateful for the support.

"You are beautiful, Amanda. This is your evening. You're the queen of the valley."

"The queen who's about to lose her throne!"

"Not if my plans work."

They were walking into the mass of smiling people who greeted Amanda as if she were one of them—people Amanda didn't even know. Her lips automatically smiled as she managed to murmur a thank-you for their congratulations. But it was Rush who remembered their names, and commented on their children and their businesses. He knew everybody there, he who had been in the valley only five months.

"Your plans?" she said under her breath.

"Yes, this party says to the world that Cadenhill is taking a new direction."

"You'd better find the direction quick. Those notes are due tomorrow."

She was smiling and talking between clenched teeth. The guests might think she was merely nervous, a bit rattled, but she had to find out what Rush intended to do.

"I've already arranged an extension on the notes."

Amanda stopped and turned to face him. "You did what?"

"I did that before we left Augusta."

"How? Why didn't you tell me?"

"Because you've been so busy trying to show me that you're in charge that you haven't been interested in giving me any part in our future."

"Our future?" He was doing it again, taking away her resolve and forcing her to change directions. "Explain!"

"We have guests, Amanda. I'll explain later."

"You'll explain now!"

"Play," Rush said to the musicians as he caught Amanda in his arms. "The first waltz is for us."

Before she could protest he'd swept her away, dipping and swaying with the music as if he hadn't just said the most important words she'd ever heard.

"Smile, darling. This is our first dance as husband and wife."

"You're my husband in name only, and I won't smile!"

"Fine, then frown like a fishwife on the docks. I'd think by now you'd recognize the soundness of my advice. Look what happened the last time we danced."

"I didn't find a husband, darling."

"Yes, you did, darling. You married the only man who'd have you."

"Oh! You're not only a dictator. You're a—a—"

"Black-eyed devil," he finished with a smile that caught at her innards and made her giddy. "I know, Mrs. Randolph, and I'm sure you've heard the expression, 'water finds its own level.'"

The waltz ended, and Amanda was descended upon by a host of men who suddenly vied for her attention. She might have been more shocked when Franklin stepped into the circle of dancers, but Amanda was still seething with Rush's observation that he was the only man who'd have her. He was wrong. Franklin had offered for her hand.

But Franklin had only wanted Cadenhill.

Franklin's voice broke into her train of thought as he claimed her hand for the next step in the dance that she hadn't even been aware had begun. "Good evening,

Amanda. You are lovely this evening. But then you always are."

"What are you doing here, Franklin?"

"I'm here because I was invited. It would be expected of me. Your husband may think he has won, but he hasn't. I don't know yet how I'll do it, but Cadenhill will still belong to me, and so will you."

The next movement in the dance was a change of partners and Amanda was more than ready to step forward into Shaler Hillyer's clasp. Franklin's claim that he wasn't done yet, coming on top of Rush's statement that, without consulting her, he'd arranged a loan extension, was the crowning blow to her self-esteem.

Amanda felt like a rag being tugged on by two dogs. She ought to show them both. She didn't know what Rush was intending to prove by holding this reception, but she wouldn't be kept in the dark. Not knowing made her very nervous. She'd already learned about not knowing in her dealings with Franklin.

With more ease than she'd expected, Amanda forced herself to respond to her partners. Between dances she managed to speak to every man there. Secretly she kept an eye on Rush and his dances with Charity, Catherine and the other ladies present. He never danced with the same partner twice, nor did he seem to be paying much attention to her newfound success as the belle of the ball, except for the narrowing of his lips and the frown creased in his forehead.

But across the ballroom Amanda's success was being noticed by both Franklin and Judge Taliaferro. The judge was pleased. It was much too soon to mention his plans, but when he was certain that the proper amount of time had lapsed he intended to ask Iris Caden to marry him. Charity would soon take a husband, as would Catherine. Though Iris and Houston had been very much in love, the judge had reason to believe that Iris would entertain the thought of marrying a second time. With Rush firmly in charge of Cadenhill, Iris would be more likely to leave.

"Well, Franklin, what do you think of Amanda's husband?"

"I think that he isn't as smart as he thinks."

"Oh? Why? Because of his bet on the horse race? I've been known to make a foolish wager a time or two. Somehow I don't think his heart was in the warehouse anyway. From what I can tell he's as much into planting as Amanda. Fine match, I'd say."

"It won't last, Judge. There is something wrong. I just don't know what. But I'll find out. Houston intended me to see to his family, and I shall, in spite of Mr. Randolph."

Franklin didn't elaborate on his thwarted financial goals for which Rush had been responsible. He'd had to refund the advance he'd gotten from Cadenhill's creditors, though a refund was temporary at best. He'd been furious to learn the deadline for debt repayment had been extended for Rush, when the same creditors had refused that courtesy to him. But that, too, was temporary. He'd see to it. There had to be an answer. Franklin headed for the punch bowl, sliding a flask from his pocket. He needed more than punch and cider to get through this evening.

By midnight Amanda was tired, tired of smiling, tired of being gay and happy. Her feet hurt, her hair had long ago slipped from the carefully arranged ringlets and now hung in a fine mist of flame about her face and shoulders. She was hungry, yet she knew that if she ate anything her protesting stomach would revolt. When the music stopped, she was grateful, until she saw Rush heading toward her. He'd seemed to avoid her since the first dance. Now he was smiling and holding out his hand.

"Come, darling, we're going to cut the cake."

She stared at him, confused by the proceedings. "Cut the cake?"

"Yes, so that our guests may have a piece to put under their pillows."

"Yes," Catherine spoke up, "if you sleep with wedding cake under your pillow you'll dream of the man you're going to marry. I, of course, shall dream of Patrick."

And then Amanda and Rush were standing behind the table, cutting the cake and smiling at each other through eyes bright with controlled emotion. "You've been quite the femme fatale this evening, darling," Rush said.

"Oh? I think I'm beginning to like flirting."

"I've noticed. I don't suppose it would do me any good to ask you to limit those sultry looks to your husband?"

"Why, are you worried? You and Franklin think that you're the only men who want me. You're both wrong. I understand," she said recklessly, giving in to that constant overriding need to wound the man who was slowly overcoming all her resistance, "that men take mistresses. What is it called when a woman finds—a friend?"

"A lover?"

"Yes, a proper word, I think."

"There will be no lover for you, Amanda Randolph!"

"Why not? Thomas Rushton Randolph, darling, now that you've tricked me into marriage, you'll take your pleasure elsewhere." The shocked look on his face goaded her on. "I understand that. And I say that can work both ways."

The black eyes staring at her suddenly lost all their false merriment. His expression went from teasing to thunder, and Amanda suddenly knew she'd gone too far.

"I don't think you have any idea what I want, my darling wife. But I think it's time you did."

Rush took the knife from Amanda's hand and handed it to Iris. He lifted the stunned Amanda into his arms, gave a bright smile to his guests and came around the table, the crowd parting into a corridor through which he marched, across the room, and up the stairs, stopping at the top.

"Dear friends, do enjoy the party. Don't let our departure spoil the evening."

Rush didn't hear the gasps of amazement. He didn't stop to open the bedroom door; he kicked it open.

Lovie, waiting inside, came to her feet and stood in silent amazement at the spectacle of her mistress, pummeling her husband's back and kicking like a wild mare as he held her in his arms. Lovie turned down the lamp to a pale glow and with a smile of approval closed the now swinging door, secured it on the inside with a sash and slipped into the adjoining room. She'd wondered how long it would take Rush and Amanda to be together. This was the night.

"Put me down, you rogue, you bully, you black-eyed devil!"

"Stop it, Amanda."

Rush stood, making no effort to release her, allowing her blows to his body to rain harmlessly.

"Why, why are you doing this?" She wanted to wound him, force him to go away and stop making her hurt inside.

"Because I want you, Amanda. God knows why anybody would want a wild hellion like you, but I do. I've tried to earn your trust but you won't let me. Nothing I try to do is going to change that. I know that now. There's only one way to make you see. I shall take what's mine."

"Well, I don't want you. And if you don't let me down I'll scream for Roman. I'll call my mother. I'll—"

But her words were swallowed by Rush's lips as they captured hers with an intensity that swept all thought of protest from her mind. A loud pounding filled her ears while her blood seemed to quicken and rush through her body. She was drowning. She was being wrapped in a blanket of fire. And then he wasn't taking anymore. She was returning his kisses with total abandon, encircling his neck with her hands, scorching her breasts against the heat of his body.

Hands touched, pulling at fasteners, ripping cloth that refused to give. But none of this registered as Amanda and Rush gave way to long-pent-up feelings. Her dress was gone, then her underthings. The chest that was pressed against hers was bare as well. An agonizing pain cut through her as Rush pulled himself away. Through a haze of desire she watched him remove his breeches, unbuttoning the front flap, freeing that part of him that sprang erect and pulsated against her as he again lifted her. He carried her to the bed and placed her on the coverlet, all the time kissing her and touching her so that she was wild with want.

Rush's mouth left a trail of hot wet kisses down her body, capturing her nipple with a moan that bespoke the intensity of his feelings. Her body changed, turning into some fluid wave of heat that swelled and rippled from every spot that Rush touched. She knew she was losing the last shred of her composure, knew it but felt compelled to welcome the sweet mystery that loving promised.

Perhaps she was dying. Perhaps she was crazed with some dreadful sickness that had taken her reason and left her with a raging fever. She couldn't think. All she knew was that Rush Randolph was creating feelings that she'd never dreamed of in all her wildest longings.

When it was right between a man and a woman, the woman would know. Her mother had said that, and Lovie. At last Amanda understood.

"It's right," she whispered, her breath mingling with his, the taste and smell of him surrounding her like a fog of sensation. "It's really right."

"Yes, my darling, this is very right."

He slid his leg across her upper thighs, moving half over her. She could feel his trembling, his man-part throbbing rhythmically against her. Every inch of her was melting like frost meeting the heat of the sun.

She was simmering, her body twitching now in growing urgency. She wanted—she needed—she felt his hands moving down, caressing the inside of her legs, brushing the hair, seeking the moisture that was bubbling to the surface. Then one finger gently parted her legs, moving beyond the lips that curved over the core of her discomfort. Amanda gasped.

"What are you doing? Don't—" But her voice was so ragged that even she knew that the "don't" was a lie.

Then she began to arch against him. Gently now, his finger moved in and out, gathering intensity as her body responded until she thought surely she'd die.

Rush let out a deep breath. "I'm afraid that I shall hurt you, just for a moment, my darling, but then…then we shall fly together."

He pushed himself to his elbows and moved over her, laying his hardness against her, smiling at the automatic response of her body. Holding her face with one hand, Rush kissed her, running his tongue in and out of her mouth as he lifted himself enough to put his manhood where his fingers had been. He intended to move slowly, to enter her gently, to protect her. But Amanda didn't give him the chance. In a frenzy of movement she raised her hips and took him inside her, moaning as she met him plunge for plunge.

For Amanda, deep inside, her body seemed to be giving way to some rumbling wave of heat. She let out a low whimper then tried to draw it back, tried to stop the shattering sensation that grew and grew. Then it was too late. Her body was flying, trembling, whirling into a reverberation that echoed through every part of her being.

But it wasn't just her. She felt the same rolling, trembling, in Rush, followed by a hot wetness that felt like soothing honey deep inside her body.

For a long time he held still, as she seemed to float back to earth, to the bed, beneath his body, which was still joined to hers.

"Amanda, open your eyes and look at me."

She couldn't. She didn't want to see, to let him see what she was hiding. "Why?"

"Must you always ask why? Tonight I want you to feel and see and want. We've just been together in the most perfect way a man can be with a woman, and I need to know that you are—all right."

Amanda drew her mind together and looked at him, taking in the glazed look of desire in his eyes. Desire, yes, and more. There was tenderness, vulnerability, uncertainty.

"I'm all right."

"Did I hurt you?"

She shook her head, unable to respond.

"Am I too heavy?"

"No, you just feel very... large. And I seem to be quite small. Am I hurting *you?*"

He chuckled and bent to kiss her. "No, being held tightly inside you doesn't hurt. It makes me want to stay right where I am. It makes me want to do this again." He moved slightly, inserting himself deeper.

"Oh."

"I'm sorry. I know you must be tender. We'll wait."

"No!" She arched herself against him. "I only meant I didn't know it would go deeper. I think you've touched the core."

"Core?" Rush knew that he was smiling broadly. He'd expected a fight from Amanda. He'd expected her to be outspoken and perhaps even a bit bossy, but he'd never expected such honest discussion of lovemaking.

"I don't suppose that's what it's called. But it feels, of late, as if there is something there that is constantly... active. Just being touched by your..." she faltered, blushing. "It makes me feel as if I'm burning inside. Does my heat pain you? If so, I'll try to quench the flame."

"Ah, Amanda darling. Your heat fires my heat. Can't you tell?"

She wiggled. "Oh, it's like before."

"Yes, like I've been every time we've kissed."

"Like Thor."

"Well, not really."

"Have you . . . I mean before me—"

"No-not like this. Never like this."

"But before, I mean the other women, did they feel like I do, as if a thousand moths were fluttering inside?"

"I don't know. I can't say they ever talked about it."

"Oh," she said, allowing her uncertainty to show for a moment. "I'm sorry. I won't talk about it either."

"It's all right if you're drowsy," he said, "it's part of the good feeling afterward."

She kept quiet for at least a minute before moving her hips and taking in a quick breath of air.

"But I'm not, Rush. In fact, I feel much like a pot of hot pudding, shimmering and bubbling on the stove." Amanda gave a slight upward arch and tightened herself around him. She sighed. "I never suspected. Oh, Rush, please . . ."

This time her response was lightning-fast as was his own. He didn't speak. He couldn't. Afterward he slid to her side and drew her into his arms, watching her long after her eyes closed in satisfied sleep. Tomorrow she'd be sore. Tomorrow she'd be his fighting wildcat again. But tonight they'd loved each other in sweet surrender.

She was fully his wife now.

And he loved her, perhaps too much. Loving meant giving a person the means to wound and hurt. Loving also meant such tender closeness as he was experiencing now. Rush touched his lips to her hair and caught her breast in his hand. She smiled and adjusted her body so that her leg reached intimately across him, pressing the hot, wet part of her against his thigh.

He felt his manhood stir to life again, felt it and smiled. They suited each other well. She'd fight him every inch of the way until she learned to trust his love. He'd wait until she waked and perhaps later they'd talk out their misunderstandings, until she was ready to admit that they belonged together.

Loving Amanda would never be easy. She'd spent her life with no thought of ever sharing it. Giving up one inch of her freedom would be tantamount to giving up it all. Change would not come easily, but it would be all the sweeter in its coming.

Rush drifted into sleep, feeling the subtle motions of Amanda's body, intimately pressing his, exploring, asking, waiting until they awakened.

Chapter Twenty

Franklin left his horse at the livery stable and walked across the street to the warehouse. He'd drunk too much punch, laced first with brandy, then later with whatever Jed Willis had added to the men's punch bowl. Now his head ached and his stomach rumbled.

Nothing about the evening had provided any illumination about where Randolph and McLendon had been for two days before the reception. But Franklin was convinced they were up to something.

Inside the warehouse he moved through the darkness, feeling his way to the foot of the stairs and up. Tonight, for the first time, he felt no pleasure at surveying the warehouse and his other business establishments that could be seen from his window. No matter how much wealth he amassed, it would never be enough. No one would ever understand the need of a young boy, taken into a wealthy home and allowed to see, but never really be a part of it.

From the first time he'd seen Houston, in his clean clothing, eating at a table lit by candles and served by slaves, he'd felt something twist inside. From that day on he'd sworn that he'd sit at the head of that table someday. Now, just when he was finally about to reach his goal, an outsider had usurped his place. At least the only part of Franklin's warehouse that Rush shared was an office, which he still paid rent on.

Franklin was struck by a thought. Rush's office. Why would he pay rent on an office when he didn't even use it? Unless he was hiding something from Amanda. Franklin could understand secrets.

He lit a lamp and using a spare key he let himself inside Rush's office. There were no drapes to conceal the light of his lamp, but he was certain there would be no eyes watching this night. He could probably carry off the town and nobody would be the wiser.

The top of Randolph's desk was bare. One drawer held ledgers that dealt with the stage line, which didn't interest Franklin. But the drawer below held a valise. Franklin licked his lips and opened the satchel. What he found didn't make sense. There was a black silk mask, smelling faintly of flowers—jasmine, he thought. Beneath the mask was a pistol, a pistol that Franklin recognized.

The weapon was one of a matched pair that once belonged to Houston Caden. It hadn't been fired. But it was the mask that held his attention, the mask that held a strand of red hair tied in its knot.

A bandit's mask.

Red hair.

Houston's pistol.

And then he knew. With sudden clarity it all came clear, the slim body, the muffled, youthful voice. The odd telling of the story of the robbery of the stagecoach by his guests from Augusta. Randolph's thwarted apprehension of the thief.

The thief had red hair.

The thief was a woman, a woman who needed funds for new dresses to search for a husband. A woman who needed seed and supplies to plant a new crop. A woman who'd robbed him, not only of his gold, but of the thing he'd spent his life plotting to steal—Cadenhill.

Franklin held in his hand the proof that the highwayman of the Broad River Valley was Amanda Caden Randolph.

He licked his lips as he considered the ramifications of his discovery. The answer to all his problems had been found. Even Randolph wouldn't be able to protect Amanda—not when they were obviously partners. There would be no disagreement about that. The robberies hadn't started until Randolph came. And he'd been involved in each occurrence except the holdup of the barge. That time the thief had taken seed and fertilizer—to plant a new crop for Cadenhill.

He hadn't been able to use the information he had about Rush's having been a spy. Amanda and Iris either didn't believe him or didn't care, and President Washington had publicly put an end to any lingering gossip. But President Washington was gone, and with this damning proof coupled with that old charge, Rushton Randolph was a ruined man. After all, the valley was dependent on Franklin Caden.

Franklin fastened the valise and locked it inside his safe. He didn't need to hurry. He'd give himself time to consider his options before he made his move. Maybe he'd have them arrested. Maybe he'd simply be generous and let them leave Petersburg. He had the means to demand it.

Rush was caressing Amanda when she opened her eyes. The sun was streaming through the window, casting a glow over the man who'd spent the night in her bed. She wanted to say something, anything, but for once words escaped her. Perhaps it was because of what had happened last night, and perhaps it was because what he was doing felt so good.

Amanda shifted her position and groaned.

Rush pulled back, a look of concern on his face. "Are your breasts sore, my love?"

"No, not my breasts." She moved again. "It's my..."

"Don't worry, darling. When I entered you last night, I took your maidenhead before I filled you with my seed. But I'm afraid we might have overdone it."

"Is that why there's some blood on the bed linens?"

"Yes." Rush had replaced his lips with his fingertips and was drawing little circles around her nipple.

Amanda groaned. Everyone would know.

"In some cultures, the linens are examined the next morning as proof of the bride's previous virginity."

"Why would anyone care?"

"There you go again, asking why. Every man wants to be his wife's first and only lover, just as I was for you. As I shall continue to be from now on," he said in a husky voice. "You're finally mine, all mine."

All mine. Amanda moaned, as he kissed her. Then it came to her. He was branding her, controlling her with his lips and hands. He'd already taken Cadenhill, usurping her authority completely. Now she knew that with only a touch he could take away all her resistance and turn her into a willing slave. She bolted upright.

"No. I don't want you to do this. I can't. I just want you to leave, go, get out of here. I simply had too much punch last night. That's why I lost my willpower. Well, you can't do this to me whenever you feel like it. It won't happen again."

Rush refrained from smiling. She hadn't had too much punch. He knew it and she knew that he knew. "No, Amanda. I shall share this bed with you every night for the remainder of our lives. I'll love you when I want and you'll enjoy every minute of it. No more pretending, Amanda Caden Randolph. You're no lily-livered, fainting maiden. You loved me and you loved what we did. Now let that be enough!"

Amanda's eyes were sparkling with green fire. Her hair a tousled riot of color that practically shimmered as she visibly tightened her resolve and readied herself for the fight she was set to wage. Rush wanted to sweep her back into his arms and turn her rage into desire.

"Lovie!" she called out.

"It won't do you any good to shout. Nobody will come."

"How do you know?"

"I gave explicit orders to Lovie earlier this morning when she brought up a breakfast tray."

Amanda gasped. "Lovie came in here? She saw me—us?"

"Yes, and she said that I should tell you that she hopes there will soon be a little Amanda for her to care for. She wishes you great joy."

"Oh. Oh, no! That can't happen. I won't have a baby!"

This time it was Rush's turn to blanch. Then his look of shock turned into a broad smile. "Well," he said with exaggerated indifference, "I suppose you could already be with child, but then maybe not. To be sure, I think we'd better work on it a bit more."

Amanda simply stared at him, her eyes wide and comprehending. "That can't be. Not me. I don't . . . I mean . . . I never thought to have a child, Rushton Randolph. I expected that we'd have the marriage annulled."

"On what grounds, darling?"

She couldn't answer. The consequences of her actions crashed over her with cold reality. Her last hope to end the marriage had been eliminated.

"You did that on purpose, you brute. You deliberately forced yourself on me, you wretched, wicked, hot-blooded man." Amanda looked around for something to throw. Her hand closed on a vase on the table beside their bed.

"I wouldn't do that, darling."

"I'll do what I like."

"So will I, my love, and this is what I like." He jerked her into his arms and kissed her with all the passion that he'd stored up for the past hour since he'd wakened. She was confused and fighting back, but that was understandable.

Amanda would always be volatile, and he wouldn't change her if he could.

The vase fell harmlessly to the floor.

The next time Amanda awoke, Rush was gone. Lovie was entering the room, tiptoeing across the floor.

"I'm awake. You don't have to slink. Where is he?"

"You mean Mr. Randolph?"

"Who else would I mean?" Amanda drew herself to a sitting position, gingerly moving her lower body, trying to disguise the soreness that she didn't want to acknowledge.

"He's seeing the last of the visitors off. He sent me up here with hot water for your bath. I'll bring it in now."

"Hot water?" Amanda wanted to rail out at him for being bossy, but she couldn't. He'd understood how she would feel, and ordering a bath was evidence of that concern. She didn't want concern from him. She didn't want anything from him except for him to go away and leave her alone.

"A hot bath will make you feel better."

"Bring it in." Amanda wrapped herself in the spread, trying not to see the stains on the sheet. Her face blushed hot with color as she walked slowly to the tub and stepped inside, embarrassed as she'd never been in her entire life. First Lovie had seen her in Rush's arms, now this. She leaned back and closed her eyes, acutely aware of Lovie's movements as she pulled the soiled linen from the bed.

"Miss Amanda, why do you feel bad about what happened? It's natural, and it's good."

"I can't have a baby, Lovie. I wouldn't know how to have a man's child."

"If Mr. Rush gave you a child, it will be fine. If not—" Lovie gave a little chuckle "—just think how much fun you're going to have trying to get one."

"I won't. I shan't enjoy—"

"From the looks of you and this bed, and what I heard last night while I was guarding your door, I'd say that you already have, and you will again."

Amanda's eyes flew open. "We—I—it could be heard?"

"Just by me."

"Well, it won't happen again, so there's no point in you losing any sleep over it."

"If you say so." Lovie wadded the linen and stuck it under her arm as she started to leave the room. "I've made your bed and I'll be back to help you dress in a bit. You just soak."

"Oh, Lovie, what am I going to do?"

Lovie paused at the door. "Do? About what?"

"I've lost all my bargaining power. I have no authority left, no way to control him. He's won."

"Miss Amanda, you're wrong. Don't you see? You have the only means you'll ever need to control a man. You have you and what you just shared back there in that bed, if you really think you need it."

Long after Lovie left, Amanda sat in the tub and considered what she'd said. Was it true? Was making love a way to control a man? Certainly Rush had used it to force her to be quiet and accept his kisses.

The water began to cool before she took her cloth and began to bathe away the aftermath of their lovemaking. She was beginning to understand what Lovie meant. She had welcomed Rush into her bed and she would again. What she needed to know was how he felt. She needed to talk to the man who'd made her his wife in every way. She needed to know that she hadn't lost all control.

Talk to Rush. It was already happening. After one night in his bed she was ready to concede the solving of problems to him. No. Cadenhill was still her responsibility and she wouldn't let herself start relying on Rushton Randolph. She stood, draping the bath sheet around her as the door opened.

"A door is to be knocked on," Amanda said sharply, fully expecting to see Catherine standing there ready to demand that she share everything that had happened.

But it wasn't Catherine. It was Rush, carrying a breakfast tray. He closed the door and pushed a chair in front of it.

"They've all gone. The judge and Charity were the last to leave. Your mother took Orphe and the girls and went with them for a short visit. Lovie is here, but she's with some sick child in the slave quarters. And Catherine and Patrick are on a picnic. Scandalous, I suppose, as they have no chaperon," he went on. His voice had become lower and lower as he talked.

"You mean we're alone in this house?" She should have been concerned about Catherine, but all she could focus on was the man who was standing over her.

"Except for Lovie."

"Good. I want to—to—talk to you."

Amanda stepped out of the tub, pulling the cloth tighter around her.

This morning he was wearing butter-colored breeches, an indigo-blue vest with stockings to match and a crisp starched lawn shirt. His hair, always unruly, fell across his forehead in a dashing way that made her want to reach out and push it back in place.

Amanda still remembered the love words he'd uttered during his passion of last night. But that didn't mean he loved her. She also remembered her mother's words that once she fell in love, love would produce feelings she'd never known before. Her mother was a wise woman and Amanda finally believed her.

She'd thought that her father's death was the worst thing that could ever happen to her. It wasn't. She was in love with Rushton Randolph, the man who'd married her for Cadenhill. He'd been right. She wanted him to make love to her, to spend every night in her bed, in her arms.

But she knew that could never be. She'd already lost control of her land; now she was losing herself. She was beginning to understand that a man was different. He could separate loving from belonging.

Amanda was afraid as she'd never been before. Loving a man was too great a risk. She couldn't let him know what he'd done to her. So long as he wasn't sure of her feelings she still had some means of controlling him. She had to do something, say something to recover her position.

Taking a deep breath, Amanda stepped forward to meet her husband.

"What do you want to talk about?" His voice was so husky that Amanda could barely understand him.

About me, about us, about this, she wanted to say. But suddenly she couldn't talk about what they'd shared. Simply giving voice to the loving made her body quiver in expectation.

"Is that tray for me?" Amanda asked, drying herself with the bath cloth. He was watching her, his breath coming shallow and fast. At that moment Amanda began to gain a glimmer of understanding about the new power she wielded.

She didn't know what he was feeling, but she knew that all her resistance had evaporated the moment he entered the room. She could no longer pretend that she felt nothing for this man who was her husband. Even now she wanted to drop the cloth and take him inside her body once more. She recognized the power he held over her. Could such power work in reverse?

"It was for us, if you were interested in sharing breakfast with me."

"I might be."

Rush's mouth felt dry and he was having difficulty marshaling his thoughts. "Lovie says there's enough for two. She said you'd need help in dressing."

"Or—undressing." Amanda gulped in a breath of air, dropped the bath sheet and stood before Rush, openly, trying not to tremble as she waited to see if she'd judged her power correctly.

She had. Rush put the tray on the floor and covered the remaining steps between them.

"You're offering yourself to me?"

"Loving you gave me great pleasure. You are a man who believes in equal exchange of services. I'd like to bargain further with you, if you're agreeable," she said stiffly.

Rush reached for her, then stayed his hand as his mind replayed her actions. She seemed to be offering herself, but not willingly.

Iris's advice that he reject her had worked well enough. But did it mean that she was beginning to care for him? No. By withholding himself he'd made her want him, but that wasn't love. He'd been told that he was a skillful lover, so perhaps Amanda's response was no surprise.

But this was different. Men could become so carried away with passion that they found themselves agreeing to actions that under normal circumstances they would never agree to. But he'd never expected that Amanda would deliberately make use of that passion, until she spoke.

"And afterward we'll talk ... about the future operation of the plantation? I think I'm offering a fair exchange."

"Why would you think you had to bargain?"

"Don't I? What chance do I have, otherwise?" She hadn't meant to be so cold. But she didn't know how to bargain with her body. The power of what they'd shared was still too new, too overwhelming. She blundered on, trying to recapture the special feeling that had suddenly disappeared.

"You've claimed Cadenhill. You talk to me about crops and land but I no longer make the decisions. Our marriage was to be a business arrangement, not a marriage based on love. I can't say that you took advantage of me last night, for I was a willing participant—at least my body welcomed you. But my mind knows that making love with you doesn't change anything.

"Tell me I'm wrong, Rush, that last night meant something to you, that I don't have to use my body to bargain. Tell me, please."

"I don't think I did anything that you didn't welcome," he finally said.

"No. You're a very good lover and I'm woefully inexperienced. I suspect that I never had a chance. You understood well enough that you were taking away the grounds for an annulment. So now we're married, in every sense of the word, and if pleasing you in the marriage bed will earn the money to satisfy our creditors, I'll do whatever you want. I did please you, didn't I?"

Amanda heard her words and flinched. They were talking about her paying for Rush's help with her body, when all she wanted to hear from her husband was that he loved her. That was all she'd wanted—needed—to stop the flow of incriminations she was hurling.

But he didn't say the words. Neither did his facial expression. He didn't love her. Lovie was right. All he wanted was her body and her land.

Rush heard the underlying resignation in her voice and felt his heart twist. He'd defeated her proud nature and turned her into a wanton in bed. But he hadn't earned her respect, and by loving her, he'd crushed her defiant spirit.

Finally he answered, his words uttering the final blow of division. "If not love, Amanda, there must be honesty and mutual trust between us. If you want something from me, I'll try to provide it. But never, never offer yourself again as payment for fulfillment of a request."

"Why not? What else do I have to bargain with?"

For Rush what they'd shared was tarnished. What had made him think that Amanda would want his love when he'd told her from the first that he wanted her land? He'd waited for her to see that they were suited, for her to accept that he cared. Yet, even after last night she still didn't want him. He'd fooled himself long enough. There was only one thing left to do and it must be done now. Rush stepped back, fastened his breeches and left the room.

Amanda heard the slam of the door and shivered. She watched the door swing back and forth on its broken hinges. A broken door, a broken marriage, a heart that was shattering with the knowledge that in her pain she'd lost something that she was only just now beginning to understand.

She picked up her bath sheet and wrapped it around her. So be it. She didn't need Rushton Randolph to be her husband. So long as he stood between her and the men who would take her land, that was enough. She'd gotten along very well without a man up to now, and she'd do it again. Cadenhill's debts had to be paid. If Rush wouldn't discuss their payment with her, she'd find a way to solve the problem herself.

If not, there was always the Jasmine Bandit.

Chapter Twenty-One

Patrick McLendon glanced over at his companion and wondered what on earth he was doing going on a picnic, alone, with the woman who was making it more and more evident that she intended to ask for more than he was prepared to give. Every time he saw Catherine Caden he swore that it would be the last. And then he found himself back at her door on some flimsy pretext or other.

She flirted with him, touched him, kissed him. She was slowly driving him crazy, and no matter how good his intentions were, it was only a matter of time until he'd forget she was a lady and take her to his bed. He'd already moved up his departure date. He and Rush had drawn up the agreement to advance funds to Joseph Watkins for the completion and manufacture of his cottonseed machine. It would take time, but like his other investments, the profits would eventually begin to mount. More, he'd made a rare friend in Rushton Randolph, and friends were something that Patrick found more difficult to keep than money.

"The sky looks like blue muslin," Catherine said, leaning back against the seat of the buggy as she untied and peeled off her hat. "Don't you love blue skies? Do they make you feel all warm and happy inside?"

Patrick's thoughts were running more along the lines of innocent smiles, and small firm breasts that were threatening to spill out over the top of her dress. But the question of feeling warm and happy and the answering picture that presented itself hit him in the stomach and slammed downward from there.

"I guess I never thought much about blue skies," he finally admitted, desperately pulling his attention to the horses, who'd practically slowed to a stop.

"Is the sky this blue in Ireland?"

"Aye, bluer even, and the grass is greener and the hills seem to go on forever."

Catherine sat up and slid closer to this man who continually erected fences between them. "Do you have a family back in Ireland?"

"No, not anymore. At least not that I'd claim."

"I think you're lying to me, Patrick. Tell me about your family."

Patrick drove the horses beneath the live oak tree by the river and dropped the reins. He sat staring at the gray-green water rushing past and wondered for the first time in a long time whether his father was still living. He couldn't say he cared; a leather strap had finished off that concern when Patrick was twelve.

He'd never had a mother. After bringing him into the world, she'd given up and died, leaving a house as cold as the hearth where no fire burned and no laughter was ever heard. He'd never even been able to imagine her.

"Aye, two older brothers, and if drinking hasn't killed him, the man who was paid to claim me as a son."

Not a father, but a man who was paid to call himself such. Catherine sat quietly beside Patrick, wishing that she hadn't brought up the subject of his family. The pain on his face spoke well enough of memories he'd wished to leave behind. Well, she was about to become his family. She'd make him forget all those unpleasant things.

"And is there a girl?"

"A hundred of them, darlin'. I'm a friend of the leprechauns and they give Irishmen special powers."

"I don't believe you. I know about Irishmen and how they spread their blarney."

"Oh, you do? And just what do you think blarney is?"

"I don't know. But I surely intend to find out. You know here in Georgia we have African magic, and according to Roman, it's much stronger. I've already put a spell on you."

"That you have, darling. That you have."

"Help me down, Patrick. I'm hungry."

She held out her arms and waited until he lifted her. Then she leaned against him for a maddening moment before gathering up the quilt. Patrick swallowed hard and lifted the picnic basket from the buggy.

"Looks like a nice place to swim."

"Could we? I mean, not here, but there's a small inlet upriver that I'll show you after lunch. We can swim there, hidden from the world."

Patrick looked around. They couldn't be more hidden from the world than they were in this spot.

"Swimming is the one thing I can do as well as Amanda," Catherine chattered as she spread the quilt beneath the tree on the riverbank and collapsed on it. "Well, do you intend to enjoy our picnic standing up?"

The view of Patrick McLendon standing was truly breathtaking. She let her gaze move up the green breeches that hugged Patrick's muscular thighs until she reached that part of him that made itself known more and more often of late. Even now as she watched, it began to grow larger. She couldn't pull her eyes away.

"Oh, Patrick, you are quite magnificent. At least I think you are. I'd like to see you without clothes. Would you like to see me?"

Patrick groaned and dropped to the quilt beside her. "Hasn't your mother explained that it isn't proper to talk that way to a man until you're married?"

Jasmine and Silk

"Oh yes. But since we're going to marry one day, I can't see why I shouldn't be honest with you. Does that not please you?"

"You please me, more than you'll ever know. And you're much too tempting. How did you manage to convince your mother that you would be safe out here alone with me?"

"My mother wasn't the one I convinced. She's away."

"Then who?"

"Rush. I simply told him that if I went with you, he and Amanda would be completely alone in the house—all day. I rather think that idea appealed to him, particularly when I explained that I wanted to be alone with you."

Catherine leaned back on the quilt, her head on one arm as she held out her hand to him. "Come here, Patrick."

"Catherine, up to now I have managed to treat you with proper respect, in spite of your efforts to tempt me. But when you look at me like this, you make it very hard."

Catherine gave him an impish smile and began to unfasten the front of her dress. "So I see, though I wasn't certain that it wasn't hard all the time. I asked Amanda, but she told me I was too young to know. Of course I think that when I asked her, she was not certain. By now she knows."

"Oh? How can you be sure?"

"There is a glow about her that gave her away. It wasn't there before."

Patrick couldn't speak. He watched spellbound as Catherine peeled back the top of her dress and began to unfasten the ties of her chemise, freeing the breasts that had tortured him for weeks.

"What are you doing, Catherine?"

"Asking you, Patrick McLendon. I love you to distraction. I don't see the need to wait any longer to—be with you. I'm asking you, my darling Irishman, to make me glow."

"But Catherine, Amanda is Rush's wife."

"And I will be yours."

"No," he protested, even as he leaned across her. "This cannot be. I haven't told you, but I'm leaving in a few days." He could have said that he was running for his life out of fear that, if he didn't leave now, he'd never be able to walk away from this woman who'd put a need to belong in his heart.

"Where are you going?"

"I'm taking a ship around the tip of Spanish Florida to New Orleans. This country is ready to grow and there's a fortune to be made by buying land in the wilderness beyond the mighty river in the west."

Catherine took his hand and placed it on her breast, feeling her body tremble beneath his touch. "I'll go with you, Patrick, anywhere you want."

"Ah, Catherine, I'm a man who'll never be able to stand still. Where I'm going is too rough for someone like you. I couldn't ask a woman to share the dangers."

"You don't have to, I'm asking you."

And then she drew him to her and Patrick felt the fire of all his pent-up longings sweep over him. In that moment of giving, Catherine erased the loneliness and desperation that had driven him for most of his life. She was the sunshine that dried up the rain. She was his, for the taking, just as was this country, and its future. He took her nipple in his mouth and felt her press against him.

Catherine responded with unembarrassed openness. Moments later his hands provided the answers to all her questions about Patrick, about his body, and hers. She soared through the blue skies overhead, and was then catapulted beyond the clouds before floating languidly back to earth. He hadn't taken his pleasure with her, but he'd given her something she had never dreamed of.

She'd wanted him to make her glow. He'd done so much more. She was melted and reformed, her body forever changed by the magic of their love. He'd touched every part of her and let her touch him in return, but no more. In the next hour she found the promise of lifetime love in the arms of her traveling man.

"All right, sunshine," Patrick finally said, as she snuggled in his arms and nibbled hungrily at a spot behind his ear. "You've won. We'll get married. I'll head for New Orleans and buy a house. As soon as I've made a place for you, I'll return and make you Mrs. Patrick McLendon."

"That will be wonderful, Patrick. You are wonderful. Loving you is wonderful. You go ahead and make all the arrangements you like." She cuddled closer. "Tell me about New Orleans. How will you travel?"

"I have a ship, the *Savannah Lady*." But Catherine could quickly see that Patrick had temporarily lost interest in planning ahead. In fact, as she boldly reached out and touched him, she recognized a need much closer to home.

They never waded in the cove. Later, as they drove back to Cadenhill, Patrick, filled with guilt, began to discuss his plans for their future. Catherine didn't disagree. After all, she already knew what it would be. As soon as Rush had told her of Patrick's plans to leave Petersburg, she'd planned this picnic. Now Patrick knew what she'd known from the start. They belonged to each other. Patrick would return for her.

Cadenhill was Amanda's. It always had been. Her mother and the judge would make a splendid match. There was nothing for Catherine here. She'd never understood Amanda's single-mindedness about home and the land—until now. But it wasn't land that interested Catherine; it was the light brown-haired man beside her. And she intended to have him. He never had a chance.

Amanda awoke to an empty house. It was midafternoon as she paced her father's study. Even Lovie had disappeared. And Catherine was who knew where. Once again Amanda reached for the Cadenhill ledger, determined to find something in her figures that would provide some answers.

She sighed, dragging the heavy records from the shelf, catching the book beside it, sending both volumes to the floor. Carelessness wasn't one of her characteristics. But almost from the night she'd first opened the valise filled with Rush's dirty linens, she'd been slightly out of kilter.

Now she went down on one knee, picking up the books and scattered papers. As she placed them on the desk she noticed one sheet of paper that was different. It was letter paper, with her father's writing, the spidery scrawl he'd been reduced to in the end. It was an unfinished letter to Rush.

My dear Rush,
I write to say that I hope you will arrive soon. I appreciate your intention of looking out for my family without taking one of my daughters to wife, and I understand that you want to buy your own land, but I continue to hope that you will change your mind once you are here. Amanda is a woman who needs a strong man like you. Please hurry, Rush. I worry that Franklin will interfere. See that—

The letter ended abruptly, as though he'd planned to finish it at some later time. Amanda read her father's words over and over, her heart pounding, her mind trying to comprehend her father's wishes.

She couldn't believe it. Rush had refused her father's request. He hadn't set out to marry her in order to claim the plantation. He'd been prepared to buy his own land—at least he had until he'd tried to help her and lost it.

What had she done? She'd fought Rush every time he'd tried to help her, fought her own feelings, fought falling in love. He'd lost his warehouse in a foolish bet on a horse race. How he'd managed to stave off the creditors and

Franklin was something she didn't want to think about. He couldn't have done it without using his money.

Then, instead of saying thank-you to him and being enthusiastic about his plans for the cottonseed machine, she'd accused him of wasting his money when he should give it to her. But more than that, she'd reduced what they'd shared to a bargaining tool. Herself for power.

Rush wasn't like Franklin. He never had been. Franklin took and Rush gave. And she'd driven him away.

Her mind whirled with the ramifications of what she'd done. But this time no answer came. Not even the Jasmine Bandit could make this right.

For the past four days Franklin had closed himself in his office to await the news that the creditors were demanding payment in full of the new master at Cadenhill. That hadn't happened. He finally learned that they'd given Rush an extension. Nothing had worked out as he'd planned when he'd altered Houston's will, naming himself as executor and placing Cadenhill under his control.

Thomas Rushton Randolph had married Amanda and claimed Cadenhill for himself.

Franklin had to move cautiously. There was still a possibility that Rush knew more about Franklin's past than he let on, and Franklin didn't want to make a false move.

But he couldn't wait any longer. He'd have to use the information he had to reclaim his control. His proof that Amanda was the Jasmine Bandit would be enough to return command of Cadenhill to him. He was Franklin Caden, and it was time he called on the judge.

But the judge wasn't in his office. He wasn't at home, either. Franklin finally tracked him down having his midday meal at Cadenhill.

Even better, Franklin decided. He'd confront Amanda at the same time. Delighted to find that Rush was away, Franklin agreed to join the adults for coffee and dessert.

"And where is Rush?" he inquired.

"Taking care of Cadenhill business," Iris said. "He's very dedicated, Franklin. Did you know that he's planted cotton?"

"No, but I'm not surprised. Everybody knows that cotton is a poor choice. It's obvious, my dear Amanda, that your husband is no better planter than he was a soldier."

"Oh?" Judge Taliaferro allowed Lovie to fill his coffee cup. "I understood that Rush was one of Houston's best soldiers, his special protégé."

"Maybe Houston didn't know the truth about Rush," Franklin answered glibly. "We all know that Houston was overly concerned about loyalty because he felt so strongly about the future of this country."

"That's true enough," Judge Taliaferro said. "There were those of us who had reservations against severing our ties with the mother country, but we banded together, some at great expense. It was only later that Houston became convinced that we had a serious traitor in the valley."

Amanda cut her eyes toward the judge. "Nonsense! Rush wasn't here then, and he was never a traitor."

"But Houston was right."

A familiar voice came from the doorway, a voice that Amanda had listened for in vain for the past four days. Rush stepped inside. "A man who used the code name Powderman. He supplied the British with gunpowder that was to have gone to the patriots, gunpowder used to kill friends and neighbors in Augusta."

The expression on Franklin's face didn't change. Only Iris noticed the clenching of his fists. She noted, but didn't recognize his consternation, for it was Amanda's face that could be read like an open book. Amanda made no attempt to conceal the flash of light in her eyes, the vulnerability that changed from joy to uncertainty and finally to pain as she stared at her husband.

"And how would you know, Mr. Randolph?" Franklin asked.

"I have my sources."

Franklin stared for a long tense minute at Rush, then began to smile. "Well, isn't that interesting, Judge Taliaferro? A newcomer to our area manages to find out about a traitor that even the most knowledgeable residents of the valley never discovered. I'm not surprised, considering what I've learned about you, Rush Randolph."

Iris, picking up the undercurrents in the room, didn't like what was happening. "What do you mean, Franklin?" she asked.

"That's what I came to talk to the judge about," Franklin said derisively. "It's time to bring what I've learned out into the open. I understand that you've taken up night riding, Amanda, and that you have a partner."

For a moment, Amanda started. For a moment only, then she walked slowly toward Rush. "I don't know what you're talking about, Franklin. I have no partner and anybody who says otherwise is wrong." She paused, then offered her face for a kiss as any other wife would when her husband had been away. Only her mouth betrayed her uncertainty. "Hello, Rush, I'm glad you're back."

Rush kissed her cheek, hearing the greeting in her voice, but seeing nothing but questions in her eyes. Surely she didn't think he'd betrayed her by telling Franklin that she was the Jasmine Bandit.

Four days ago when he left Amanda's bed, he'd ridden straight through to Augusta, then on to Savannah before he'd found someone willing to pay enough for the stage line. He'd finally taken less than it was worth, but enough to pay off the Augusta businessmen who held the liens on Cadenhill, and to have a small nest egg left over.

On his return, under the pretext of cleaning out his office, he'd studied Franklin's books until he determined the amount of funds needed to satisfy Amanda's debts to her uncle. What he hadn't expected to find was a letter of commendation to Franklin for his loyalty to the crown. The letter was dated 1781 and signed by King George. Inside the document was a more damning note from President Washington to Houston Caden, which confirmed Houston's suspicion that the long-sought-after Powderman was a merchant in Petersburg. Only someone like Rush, someone involved in espionage, would understand the reference to Powderman. Now everything was clear.

Houston had never received the note, but he must have learned or suspected that his stepbrother was the Petersburg merchant who supplied the loyalists with gunpowder during the Battle of Augusta. For it was soon after the date on the letter when Houston started to press Rush to come to Cadenhill. There'd been no more suggestions that Rush come and meet Houston's girls—no more promises about the land. He had sent an urgent plea. *I need you, Rush. Amanda will need you, too. If anything happens to me, promise me that you'll help Amanda.*

"I know what you've been up to, Amanda," Franklin went on smugly. "And I blame your new husband. None of this started until he came to the valley. Don't worry, Iris. Because you are family and because Houston would have wished it, I'm prepared to drop all charges against Amanda, provided she cooperates."

There was a sudden silence. Rush felt a great anger sweep over him. He'd just spent the past four days seeing that Franklin would never be able to interfere in Amanda's life again. Now this petty little man had come here with the intention of threatening Amanda. He would never have become so bold unless he thought that he had the means. Rush bit back a retort. Better to find out what Franklin knew.

Judge Taliaferro cleared his throat uneasily. "Franklin, according to Houston's will, so long as Rush and Amanda are married, Rush has legal command of Cadenhill."

"Unless there are criminal charges that would render that document unenforceable," Franklin said smoothly. "Or unless Amanda divorces her husband."

"Hell's doorknobs, Franklin!" Amanda finally exploded. "You'll never get our land, no matter what. I wouldn't give you the effort it takes to sweat!"

"Careful, my dear niece. Not even to avoid a jail sentence?"

"Are you threatening me, Uncle Franklin?"

"Now see here—" Judge Taliaferro began.

"That's why I'm here instead of talking with the law," Franklin cut him off with obvious enjoyment. "I have proof that the highwayman who robbed me was not an outsider as we'd thought, but someone with an inside contact who planned the crimes. Someone who desperately needed money. Someone who deliberately set out to rob—only me."

"Now just a minute." Rush stepped in front of Amanda, and stood glaring at Franklin. Then Rush saw it, the valise, the valise from his desk, the valise containing the gun and the mask he'd held on to so foolishly.

He'd been so concerned about Amanda's debts when he'd been in his office that he hadn't checked his own desk. It was clear that Franklin had found the valise containing the mask and gun that Rush had locked in his lower drawer. But what Rush knew about Franklin was enough to stop any attempt to harass Amanda.

"Yes?" Franklin glared triumphantly, daring him to protest. "Not only do I know the identity, but I can prove that the bandit had a partner."

"I think you ought to know, Franklin," Rush went on smoothly, "that Cadenhill is free and clear. All loans were paid in full, yesterday, by me. Amanda's husband."

"Really? Well, no matter. Marriage was only one of Amanda's sins, one of the more minor ones. I have other proof that will give me everything you've taken."

Rush searched his mind desperately for a way to stop Franklin's disclosure of Amanda's banditry, finally settling on the truth, couched in oblique terms that only Franklin would understand. "Franklin, you're a fair man, why don't you and I talk about this a bit before either of us does anything rash?"

Franklin eyed Rush suspiciously.

Amanda swallowed hard. Rush had done it again, taken care of her and her land. Now Franklin would be furious. He'd punish Rush. She couldn't allow him to do that.

"But Randolph," Franklin said, "there are still very large unpaid bills owed to me. And I doubt that you have enough funds left to buy me off."

"Oh, but I have something better. If you make any accusations that might tarnish the reputation of those I care about, I'll be forced to make public certain information I have. I don't think you want to do that, Franklin."

"Don't threaten me, Randolph. I have proof of the identity of the highwayman. The people in the Broad River Valley won't tolerate a thief, or the thief's partner."

"I'm certain you're right, Franklin, but you should know that certain documents have also come into my possession, documents that will reveal the identity of the mysterious traitor called Powderman. Personally, I see no reason to reveal his identity. But I will unless he agrees to my demands. I'm willing to put the past behind all of us."

Franklin's lips tightened. "I see. Is that where you intend to get the funds to pay your debts—through blackmail?"

"Well, I hadn't thought about it quite that way, but that's an idea. Frankly, I'm more into standoffs and mutual respect. If you understand what I mean?"

Amanda felt as if she were watching a melodrama performed on a stage by a traveling troupe of actors. She knew the players, but the scene was a jumbled reenactment of veiled threats and secret information. Obviously Franklin

had come there with what he considered proof that she was
the bandit, and Rush had counteracted his charge before it
was made. She didn't understand the veiled references to
Powderman, but she understood that Rush had paid off
Cadenhill's debts.

How? What did all this mean? Why hadn't he talked to
her about his plans? Her debt was to Rush now, not the
outside world. Franklin hadn't won, but until she'd made
things right between her and Rush, neither had she. Her
marriage would die before it began if she didn't make Rush
understand that this marriage must be an equal partnership. First she had to crush Franklin.

Amanda moved around the desk, coming to a stop behind it. "I don't know what either of you think you're doing, but Cadenhill doesn't belong to either one of you unless
the Caden women decide to allow it."

She slowly opened the desk drawer and closed her fingers around her father's remaining pistol. She drew it slowly
out of the drawer and pointed it at her old adversary. Rush
had done so much for her. It was her turn to pay him back,
starting with Franklin.

"I may have to tolerate a husband, but I don't have to
tolerate you, Franklin. Get off Caden land, or I'll have you
thrown off. And don't tell me that it's my husband who has
the legal rights here, Judge Taliaferro, because it isn't legal
rights I'm enforcing here, it's moral. And I'll shoot Franklin if I have to."

Iris gasped.

The judge slipped his arm around Iris and held her pro-
tectively.

Rush simply stared at Amanda, partly in admiration and
partly in regret. Iris had been wrong. Rejecting Amanda had
brought her to his bed, not joined her to his heart. She'd
used him to get rid of Franklin, and her body to bargain for
control, but she wasn't happy about it. She'd put Cadenhill
first, doing what was necessary to protect her land. He'd

given her everything he owned, but she would never acknowledge that she needed him. He doubted she even cared where he'd been or what he'd been doing for the past four days. She cared only about Cadenhill.

So be it. The last hope he'd held dried up and blew away in the air of distrust and struggle for power. Nothing had changed. The woman he loved, loved something else more. He'd been a fool to let his heart believe when his mind knew better.

"I think you'd better go, Franklin," Rush said in a tight voice. "Amanda, these papers are for you. Please see that they're properly filed. Iris, being your son-in-law has been a pleasure."

Amanda watched in astonishment as Rush kissed her mother and shook hands with the judge. He took a long sad look at her and left the room.

He was leaving. Amanda gestured helplessly toward her mother, then, still holding the gun, followed her husband up the stairs and into their bedroom.

"You're leaving, aren't you? I won't let you go!"

"Put the gun away," he said. "You won't need it anymore. Cadenhill is and always will be yours. The judge will file the papers to your name."

"My name?" She glanced down at the legal documents in confusion. They were marked, paid in full by Thomas Rushton Randolph, owner of Cadenhill plantation. "But this says that you're the owner? How is that possible?"

"Because your mother arranged to sign Cadenhill over to me before we left Augusta."

"Then I guess you got what you came for. Cadenhill belongs to you."

"No, Cadenhill belongs to you." He turned to leave.

She'd been ready to forget about equal exchange of services, ready to give herself to Rush, to stand side by side with him to make their marriage real. And all the time in spite of what he'd said, he'd been scheming to get her land.

No! She didn't believe that. It made no sense. No matter how it looked, Rush was her heart. If she'd only told him she loved him earlier, he wouldn't be leaving. Amanda had to stop him. "Rush, where are you going?"

"I don't know yet. Patrick and I are going to sail his ship to New Orleans. New Orleans first, then—who knows?"

"Why are you doing this?"

"Because I had a dream, but I understand now that a dream was all it could ever be."

"No, Rush, you can't leave. I won't let you."

"Are you going to shoot me?"

Amanda glanced down at the gun and dropped it to the floor. "It isn't loaded."

The bedroom door had been repaired. There was even a lock on the inside of the door. Amanda moved behind him, slid the bolt across and leaned back against the door. "But it can be loaded if you don't tell me why you're leaving."

"I've done what I came here for. I've repaid a debt in the only way that I could."

"You mean fulfilling my father's wish, his wish that you marry me in exchange for Cadenhill."

Rush was stunned. He'd never intended Amanda to know what her father had in mind. "How—who told you something like that?"

"Surprised? My father told me, indirectly, of course. He didn't expect me to ever find out about his plan. You refused him and I know that my father never accepted rejection. You knew that. So you—you black-eyed devil, you set out to seduce me, to make me, love—want—you. I was to be your prize. Don't deny it. It's the truth, isn't it?"

"All right. I won't." But you're wrong, he wanted to say, wrong about everything. He'd promised Houston he'd look after Amanda but he'd never intended to be more than a friend. Yet, from the moment he'd laid eyes on the Jasmine Bandit, even before he'd known who she was, he'd recognized that he'd found a woman he could love.

Duty became desire. And a promise became a commitment. He'd let it happen, falling in love with her with every kiss, knowing all the time that he'd be hurt. He'd gambled on more than a horse race; he'd gambled on his heart. And he'd lost.

Losing his inheritance was only a temporary setback. Losing Amanda was an anguish from which he'd never recover.

Even now, he wanted nothing more than to hold her.

He wondered if she knew how she looked, standing there with that lush, half-glazed look that promised twisted sheets and loving sighs. She had learned quickly the power she had over him. And he'd learned, too, learned that while she might welcome him in her bed, Cadenhill would always be the center of her life and she'd do anything to protect it.

Today she was wearing her usual work clothing—a pair of men's trousers and a rough shirt tucked in at the waist. There was a crease across her brow that told him she'd been wearing a hat before she came inside. Now her hair hung free, cascading across her shoulders and wildly down her back. It was all Rush could do to keep from tangling his hands in it.

Amanda continued to lean against the door, trying desperately to still the galloping beat of her heart. Rush was simply looking at her. Gone was the amused grin, the teasing lift of his eyebrows, the challenge in his eyes.

Instead there was a steely resolve, a cold acceptance that she didn't know how to get through. He was leaving. She hadn't believed it until now. But it was true. He'd come into her life and taught her to be a woman. Now he was about to go away and leave her alone to deal with the emotions he'd freed. For the first time in her life she didn't know what to do.

She loved him. She knew that he was committed to the same things she loved—the land, home and family. Her family had become his family and they'd quickly given him their loyalty. And, the truth was, she trusted him, too.

Without making an issue of doing so, he'd offered his support, constantly coming to her aid. Without knowing it was happening she'd learned the joy of loving a man, and having that man love her in return. Could she lose that and face a lifetime of loneliness?

Was it too late?

"Rush," she finally said, "I'm sorry, and I thank you for paying the loans. As soon as there are funds, you'll be repaid."

"You're welcome. Consider it a parting gift."

"I—I think I'd prefer another gift."

"Oh?"

Amanda didn't know what else to do. She didn't have any choice. She took a deep ragged breath and spoke boldly. "We have no grounds on which to get an annulment, and I don't know that the courts would recognize a divorce, so I shall have to accept the fact that for as long as you live you will be the only husband that I'll ever have."

What was she up to? "You need not fear that I shall abandon you, Amanda. I've left the means to take care of you and Cadenhill with Judge Taliaferro."

"But you will leave. Mother will probably marry again. Catherine will certainly go."

"You must have known this from the start, Amanda. Families change and grow. At least you have your land."

"If you go, I'll be alone—unless—"

"Unless what, Amanda? Surely you're not asking me to provide you with a consort?"

"No, Rush. But there is something I want. I want—want you to give me a child."

Amanda began to remove her clothing, one piece at a time, until she stood before him completely nude. No maidenly blushes, no hesitancy, no pretense.

"Love me one last night, my black-eyed devil. Spill your seed in me over and over again. Give me a child."

She was taking the biggest gamble of her life.

If he touched her he'd be making the biggest mistake of his life.

Then he saw the vulnerability in her eyes and the need. He knew that what he was doing was killing his heart, and still he began to unfasten his shirt.

Chapter Twenty-Two

Rush knew that he should refuse. He knew that he should back away before the crack in his heart widened. But he couldn't seem to think. Thinking was long past as Amanda moved close. Only the touch of rough hands against his bare skin was real, only the taste of lips that demanded, and ignited with fire. She slid her fingers behind his neck, holding his lips against hers. Her fingertips grew bolder, dancing down his back, playing against his spine, across his stomach and downward with an urgency that couldn't be denied.

And then they were on the bed. Sunlight dappled her body with flecks of gold, caught the red of her hair and spun it into a mantle of fire that tumbled across her shoulders and breasts.

Their heartbeats merged into one pounding beat that echoed the erotic thrumming of their desire. His hands meshed with hers, touching, exploring, memorizing skin only touched before, skin now being singed with the heat of their passion. The scent of jasmine was everywhere. For the rest of his life he'd carry the touch and smell of this woman with him.

Every sigh was a new word that had never before been spoken by lovers, every breath shared, every movement copied and responded to with such completeness that neither could tell where one ended and the other began.

They branded each other with their touch, spinning a cocoon of fire in which they built the flame higher and higher until finally they exploded, catapulting into sweet release.

Suddenly the room grew lighter, the very air caressed their bodies with honeyed repose. Her head was resting against his shoulder, her tongue making little forays across his chest. Rush had never touched a woman this way, never known such completeness.

She whispered, with sudden brazen honesty. "I—I never understood, Rush. I never knew what it was to want a man. I'm sorry that I was so stubborn. Perhaps we can live together if..."

She leaned on one arm and shoulder, casting her gaze on his face with searing intensity. After what they'd shared, surely he'd tell her that he loved her.

Amanda's blue eyes were filled with some new emotion that Rush didn't recognize, some new need that he couldn't comprehend. Live together without love? Could they share what had just happened without love? He studied her as he accepted the reality of what she'd suggested. She'd never minced words or failed to take action to reach her goals. For Amanda, making love and creating a child were pleasurable—she couldn't conceal that—but clearly she was saying she didn't love him.

He'd foolishly thought that for Amanda, loving and making love were synonymous. But Amanda wasn't an ordinary woman. He felt a great sadness that the family he'd thought he'd found would never truly be his. He'd stayed one day too long. Only hours ago he would have been able to leave, knowing that what he'd done was make a sacrifice for the good of the woman he loved, just as he'd done for his family, who couldn't love him either.

Amanda saw the birth of pain in his eyes. Why? He'd seemed so happy moments ago. Now bitterness marked the softness of his face. "What's wrong, Rush? Don't you want to have children? I thought all men wanted sons to carry on their names and daughters to—"

"And daughters to love. But you're wrong. All men don't want sons, particularly when they don't live up to the father's expectations."

Amanda reached out and touched the stubble of whiskers on Rush's face. "I can't imagine a father not being proud of you. Surely he didn't believe all that nonsense about your being a spy."

"Why not? You did. I'm afraid he did, too. That and more."

"Not really," she confessed. "I just didn't want to like you and I was afraid that I was beginning to. It was a foolish attempt to push you away. Why didn't it work?"

"I'm not sure. Because of your father, maybe. I respected him, you know. He was the father I never had."

"But you saw so little of each other. I don't understand."

"Neither do I. But from the very first he accepted me and made me feel important. I would have done anything he asked me to, willingly."

"I think," she said softly, "that you did. What about your mother?"

"She loved me, I think. But she was so concerned with what others thought about me that I got lost in my reputation."

"And your brothers and sisters?"

"Only one brother, an older brother, who was just like my father. He never had a chance to be my friend. He was too busy being what my father expected him to be."

"And you were a rebel as a child, just as you are as an adult."

"A rebel? Me? Just because I have a dream, a vision of fields of cotton plants all speckled white in the summer sun. Yes, I guess I am. I want so much, so much that I'll never have."

He waited for her to disagree, to say that they'd share his dream, that the children she wanted were part of a future that included him. But she didn't. Instead she lay back and closed her eyes, letting out a little sigh that she wasn't even aware of. The words he wanted to hear wouldn't come. This was her time and her place and she'd worked as hard to fulfill her dream as he had. Her dream just didn't have room for him.

Time after time, during the rest of the afternoon and evening she had the opportunity to ask him to stay, to tell him that she loved him. But she didn't. She wanted a child; a child for Cadenhill. Perhaps he'd given her what she wanted. But he couldn't face being rejected again. He'd tried to live through that once, no more. He wouldn't stay to find out.

Being with Amanda made more bitter the understanding that the part of him that had survived all the other rejections in his life had finally died. Because he loved her, he would move on. For he couldn't stay without asking for what he would never have. He'd left his past in North Carolina. He was leaving his future on Cadenhill, along with his heart, captured by the Jasmine Bandit.

She was sleeping when he left, when he bent low and whispered, "I love you," in her ear. She didn't answer. She didn't hear. He thought that it was just as well.

It was after midnight when she awoke. The air was still warm. The growing season, Amanda thought, and gently touched her stomach with her fingertips. There would be a child. She knew it as surely as she knew that Rush loved her.

She had been wrong not to trust her father's wishes, wrong not to trust her husband. The two strongest men in her life had cared for her and provided for her well-being in the only way they knew. Their love for her in no way diminished her as a person. She'd become more than she was before Rush came into her life.

From this day on, she'd be Mrs. Thomas Rushton Randolph, openly, proudly, with no reservations.

If her husband wanted cotton, they'd plant acres of it—together.

And he'd give her black-eyed children to harvest and protect the land.

Amanda stretched. She felt like the barn cat who'd just filled herself with rich, fresh cream. She felt like a woman who'd been thoroughly loved, a woman who was once again ready to be cherished.

Throwing her feet over the edge of the bed she pattered barefoot to the window, totally unconcerned about her nakedness, welcoming the whispering caress of the night air. Rush, my darling, where are you?

Quickly she pulled on her dressing gown and ran lightly down the stairs and into the kitchen, where Lovie was banking the coals for the night.

"Where is he, Lovie?"

"Gone. Left 'bout an hour ago." Disappointment tightened Lovie's voice.

"No, he can't be!"

"Sold his stage line to pay off your debt and signed over his interest in some cotton machine, too. Heard him tell the judge and your mama yesterday."

"I don't believe it. Why would he leave me now?"

"You tell me."

"But all afternoon and night we—he—I—"

"I know. Did you tell him that you love him?"

"No, but he knew. He had to know. I would never have lain with him if I didn't love him."

"Did you tell him that you wanted him to stay?"

"But I asked him to—" What she'd done was ask him to give her a child so that she wouldn't be alone when he'd gone. Throughout the hot afternoon he'd loved her. He'd told her about his family, about how he'd wanted so badly to belong and how he'd been rejected. Then he'd loved her again, tenderly, desperately; over and over again he'd brought her to the edge of insanity, and back. More than she'd ever believed possible, she loved this man. Not just for the incredible feelings he brought her, but because he'd been there for her at every turn. He'd made things right, saving her life and her mind.

Surely he knew what she felt. She knew that beyond Cadenhill, beyond promises, Rush Randolph loved her. And there was no way that he was going anywhere without her.

"Where was he going, Lovie?"

"Didn't say. Just had Roman saddle his horse and asked if Wildcat Creek was low enough to ford."

"Wildcat Creek?"

If she hurried, she could catch him.

"Lovie, have Apollo saddle the black horse."

Ten minutes later Amanda was dressed, mask in place, hair concealed beneath her tricorne hat, both French pistols in hand. The Jasmine Bandit would ride again.

As Amanda rode her horse through the forest she felt her confidence grow. It was no longer Cadenhill that she wanted to save. It was her marriage. She wouldn't allow Rush to leave her. She'd been stubborn and she'd been wrong. It wasn't the land her father had fought for, it was home. Home wasn't a house or land. Home was, no, *is* any place where love is nurtured. She wondered why she hadn't understood that before.

And love, she'd come to understand, was Rush. Amanda had to convince Rush to come back, to share Cadenhill with her and their children. If not, she'd go west with her husband, the man she loved.

She'd convince him. And she knew how.

A whippoorwill sang in the woods close by. Rush listened to him call repeatedly. But there was no answer. Rush knew how the bird felt. Leaving Cadenhill was the most difficult thing he'd ever done. If Amanda had made even one move or gesture that showed she loved him, he'd never have gone.

With every step his horse took, Rush was assailed with memories. He could still smell the flowery scent of the bold bandit who'd stopped his coach and demanded his money. He'd applauded her quick response in paying her debt with a saucy kiss. Then later, he'd watched her hair streaming behind her in their mad race along the riverbank. From the moment he'd caught sight of her standing in the doorway at the Christmas dance, he'd known that he'd found the place he wanted to stay.

But home, to Rush, was based on trust and sharing and love. And once again he'd been rebuffed, first by his family, then by the woman he loved. For most of the night he'd waited for her to say the words he wanted to hear. She'd answered his pleas with her body as naturally and as completely as a woman could, but she'd held back the final commitment. When at last she slept he'd stood over her, his heart filled with sadness.

And finally he'd understood.

For Amanda, it was important to harvest that which had been planted. But it was the land that she treasured, not the harvest. He'd thought that he could convince her to share her dream, her future. But he was simply a part of her whole, never the center. With a heavy heart he'd dressed and left, pausing only to instruct Lovie to care for Amanda.

"Once I'm settled, I'll let you know how I can be reached. If Amanda ever needs me, I'll come."

"She needs you now," Lovie had said.

"No, she wants me, but she doesn't need me anymore."

He decided not to wait for Patrick. He'd go now, before he changed his mind, overland, through this rough country in which he intended to invest his future. The western territory wouldn't be Cadenhill, but it would be his.

He slumped in the saddle and prepared to ride through the night. By tomorrow he'd be far enough away to start leaving the hurt behind. By next month he'd be in New Orleans. By next year he'd have made a new start.

Then he heard it, a clandestine sound in the woods in front of him, or was it behind, in the darkness? Wildcat Creek was just ahead. If he could get to the creek he'd have open land to make a run for it. He touched his heel to his horse's flank.

Suddenly the scent of jasmine seemed to permeate the air he breathed. It grew stronger and stronger—as did the pounding of his heart.

Rush began to smile.

About fifteen miles out of Petersburg, beyond Wildcat Creek, the highwayman waited. As Rush forded the stream, an auburn-haired bandit stepped into the path, guns drawn, mask in place.

"Halt! The Jasmine Bandit has you in her sights."

"But I have nothing left for her to take."

"Not to take. She's come to give, the only thing she has of value. Her love—forever."

"Identify yourself, madam."

"My name, rogue, is Amanda Caden Randolph."

Rush climbed from his horse, holding out his arms in acquiescence. "I willingly surrender myself into the hands of the woman I love," he said with a wicked smile.

Beneath a pewter-colored moon that showered the creek with ribbons of silver, the highwayman dismounted and dropped her guns.

"The Jasmine Bandit has made her last run," she whispered, "straight into the arms of the man she loves."

* * * * *

HISTORY IN
THE MAKING!

Join Harlequin Historicals as we celebrate our 5th anniversary of exciting historical romance stories! Watch for our 5th anniversary promotion in July. And in addition, to mark this special occasion, we have another year full of great reading.

- A 1993 March Madness promotion with titles by promising newcomers Laurel Ames, Mary McBride, Susan Amarillas and Claire Delacroix.

- The July release of UNTAMED!—a Western Historical short story collection by award-winning authors Heather Graham Pozzessere, Joan Johnston and Patricia Potter.

- In-book series by Maura Seger, Julie Tetel, Margaret Moore and Suzanne Barclay.

- And in November, keep an eye out for next year's *Harlequin Historical Christmas Stories* collection, featuring Marianne Willman, Curtiss Ann Matlock and Victoria Pade.

Watch for details on our Anniversary events wherever Harlequin Historicals are sold.

HARLEQUIN HISTORICALS . . .
A touch of magic!

HH5TH

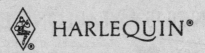

HARLEQUIN®

THE TAGGARTS OF TEXAS!

Harlequin's Ruth Jean Dale brings you
THE TAGGARTS OF TEXAS!

Those Taggart men—strong, sexy and hard to resist...

You've met Jesse James Taggart in FIREWORKS!
Harlequin Romance #3205 (July 1992)

And Trey Smith—he's THE RED-BLOODED YANKEE!
Harlequin Temptation #413 (October 1992)

Now meet Daniel Boone Taggart in SHOWDOWN!
Harlequin Romance #3242 (January 1993)

And finally the Taggarts who started it all—in LEGEND!
Harlequin Historical #168 (April 1993)

Read all the Taggart romances!
Meet all the Taggart men!

Available wherever Harlequin Books are sold.

ROMANCE IS A YEARLONG EVENT!

FEBRUARY
S M T W T F S
1 2 3 4 5 6

MARCH
S M T W T F S
1 2 3 4 5 6

APRIL
S M T W T F S
1 2 3

JULY
S M T W T F S
1 2 3

AUGUST
S M T W T F S
1

SEPTEMBER
S M T W T F S
1 2 3 4

OCTOBER
S M T W T F S
1 2

NOVEMBER
S M T W T F S
1 2 3 4 5 6
7 8 9 10 11 12 13
14 15 16 17 18 19 20
21 22 23 24 25 26 27
28 29 30

Celebrate the most romantic day of the year with MY VALENTINE! (February)

CRYSTAL CREEK
When you come for a visit Texas-style, you won't want to leave! (March)

Celebrate the joy, excitement and adjustment that comes with being JUST MARRIED! (April)

Go back in time and discover the West as it was meant to be . . . UNTAMED—Maverick Hearts! (July)

LINGERING SHADOWS
New York Times bestselling author Penny Jordan brings you her latest blockbuster. Don't miss it! (August)

BACK BY POPULAR DEMAND!!!
Calloway Corners, involving stories of four sisters coping with family, business and romance! (September)

FRIENDS, FAMILIES, LOVERS
Join us for these heartwarming love stories that evoke memories of family and friends. (October)

Capture the magic and romance of Christmas past with HARLEQUIN HISTORICAL CHRISTMAS STORIES! (November)

WATCH FOR FURTHER DETAILS IN ALL HARLEQUIN BOOKS!

CALEND